FALLEN IS BABYLON

MICHAEL WENTELA

grey gecko press

Grey Gecko Press
565 S. Mason Road, Suite 154
Katy, TX 77450
www.greygeckopress.com

Printed in the United States of America

Also available as an eBook

Library of Congress Cataloging-in-Publication Data
Wentela, Michael
Fallen is babylon / Michael Wentela
Library of Congress Control Number: 2013935825
ISBN 978-1-9388215-7-8
10 9 8 7 6 5 4 3 2 1
First Edition

To my wife, Stephanie: you have been,
and still are, my rock and my inspiration.

Without you,
this would not have been possible.

Lo! I tell you a mystery: We shall not all sleep, but we shall all be changed—in a flash, in the twinkling of an eye—at the last trumpet.

1 Corinthians 15:50

And he cried with a mighty voice, saying, "Fallen, fallen is Babylon the great, and is become a habitation of demons . . ."

Book of Revelation 18:2

The only thing more astounding than the heights mankind will ascend is the depths to which he will descend.

Alexander William Victor

PART ONE

When Darkness Cloaked the Land

ONE

The stench of death no longer permeated and fouled the air, but the city was still dead.

At one time—during a different era, before The Collapse—it had been a shining and vibrant, semi-urban jewel, a flourishing center of commerce and government, with parks and amenities and cultural offerings enjoyed by a diverse and largely affluent population. It had been a trendy university town and a historic state capital that consistently ranked as one of America's best places to live by the magazines that rated such things. It was a city that had bustled and pulsed with effervescent life, an unexpected home to both the conservative and eclectic lifestyles. The city had been a radiant beacon of contemporary American life, an example of the lifestyle that many people aspired to live.

The city was now little more than a rotted corpse.

Vann Arnett stood on the widow's walk of the once-elegant four-story Victorian mansion and surveyed the perimeter defenses from this perch nearly fifty feet above the ground. From his high vantage point, it appeared as if the triple ring of fences was undisturbed and none of the booby traps had been tripped.

He wasn't surprised. It had been more than a week since *they* had stood beyond the outer fence, taunting and tormenting him with their provocative catcalls like perverted and demented Midway hawkers. The males, with their insults and challenges to his manhood, were bad enough, but the females . . . they were worse. Much, much worse.

With the sultry temptations of an ancient siren song, they called out to him with promises to fulfill every one of his erotic fantasies and dirty desires. They danced and stripped and more, in an attempt to entice him out from behind the defenses of his fortress.

Oh sure, their provocative and unrestrained behavior had an acute but expected physiological effect on him as he stared through night-vision goggles or binoculars at the young women as they performed their unscripted pornographic routines—he was a red-blooded male, after all—but he wasn't lonely enough or horny enough to climb down from the ramparts of his citadel and surrender himself to them. He craved physical intimacy like a junkie ached for the next needle spike, but he wasn't *that* desperate. Not yet, anyway.

In a previous life, the century-old mansion had been known as Wolveshaven. It had regally sat secluded on a large, tree-shrouded lot. The eccentric multistory structure had dominated the block in a residential neighborhood a half mile northeast of the downtown square and state capitol building. Nestled in the narrow isthmus that sliced between the city's two largest lakes, it was a block and a half from the larger and northernmost body of water, which was visible from the sniper's nest in the widow's walk that rose fifteen feet above the fourth story.

The mansion, primarily charcoal gray in color, with rust, black, and white trim and accents, still retained its stately appearance, despite the defensive embellishments created by Vann, Sylvie, and Hal. A series of photovoltaic panels on the eastern and southern rooflines captured solar energy, which was then converted into electricity that was used daily, while an industrial-sized gasoline-run generator in the basement offered another source of electricity, should it be necessary.

Chimneys from four different fireplaces sprouted up from the asphalt-shingled roof, but only the fireplace on the third floor—the living quarters—was actually used for heat during the winter months. The top floor of the building was primarily the arsenal, while the first and second floors were used for storage. At one time, the basement had been furnished as a high-end living area with all the latest accessories and necessities of contemporary life, but now it served as additional storage space.

An armored, armed, and fully stocked panic room—a fallout shelter in a different era—had been constructed in one of the interior basement rooms for a last stand. The double main doors were centered in a long, wraparound porch, and the railings had been reinforced with sandbags behind them. Mimicking the architecture of the house, a three-vehicle garage was discreetly tucked away from the residence.

Wolveshaven, the onetime grand mansion with its lupine-inspired Victorian adornments and ornamentation, now possessed an apocalyptic Mad Max–fortress feel.

Arnett stared out at the blasted and desolate landscape that surrounded the mansion. It was a barren no-man's-land, void of all trees and other greenery or any signs of life at all. It was a vision of perdition. He sighed and frowned. As he often did, he fought a losing battle to stifle the ever-present urge to feel sorry for himself.

So this is what my life has become, he thought. *A day-to-day struggle to not only stay alive but to prevent myself from going insane. Some life, huh? I survived the greatest calamity to befall mankind, only to live like this, if you can call it living. I'm no secluded desert father or contemplative hermit-monk, so why me? What did I do to deserve this fate? Who did I piss off?*

He absently glanced down, and when a tiny flash of sunlight forced him to make an unexpected double take, his mouth dropped open. Vann stared at the delicately detailed gold band on the third finger of his left hand. The intricate Celtic design captured those colorless rays and glinted them back in soft amber-white flashes. He wriggled his fingers and made the light dance playfully along the surface of precious metal.

A smile creased his face, but the feeling lasted only a fleeting moment before those unexpected and unwanted memories came flooding back. They crashed down over him like murky floodwaters, threatening to suck him under the roiling torrent of emotional debris and mental flotsam, drowning him in the wreckage of his life and all of humanity. He was helpless as the memories poured into the gaping wound that was his soul.

They had been demoralized by despair and immobilized by grief. It had been two and a half weeks—eighteen days, actually—since they had buried their twelve-year-old daughter, Shelane, but it seemed like an eternity. It had consumed them and left them with nothing. They had suffered the heartbreak that no amount of time would heal and no parent should have to endure: they had outlived a child, their only child. In response, both of them had withdrawn into their own inner sanctums to confront the demons that taunted them and the ghosts that haunted them.

Arnett had been so caught up and isolated in his despondent world of anguish, just trying to somehow get through the day if only to face the burden of the next one, that he hadn't even realized that Susannah had come down with some kind of bug. The once-vibrant and trim red-haired woman appeared fatigued and gaunt as she reclined in their bed, her freckle-dusted pale skin with an unhealthy gray pallor to it.

"I'm just tired," she said, trying to smile but failing miserably. "I haven't slept well in days, since . . ."

Susannah didn't finish the sentence—*couldn't* finish it—but she didn't have to.

He, too, had not slept through the night since Shelane's condition had taken a turn for the worse and they had rushed her to the emergency room of the university's world-class medical facilities. The medical staff assured them that everything would be all right. Little did they know they would never again take their girl home.

A few days after that conversation, he realized that Susannah had the same early symptoms that their daughter had exhibited: perpetually running nose, coughing deep from the lungs, puffy joints that were stiff and sore, and no appetite to speak of. Vann feared that his wife had come down with the same virus that had taken his daughter. He dreaded it. He couldn't bear the thought of losing her, too.

He tried to get Susannah to go to the clinic to see a physician, but despite her weakened condition, she adamantly refused to even consider it. With the thought that it had done Shelane absolutely no good lingering in his mind like a fresh wound, he couldn't argue with his wife. Instead, Vann concealed his worry and fear from her. He kept it locked inside and suffered in silence.

Over the next week, Susannah's condition worsened. Her nose had turned into a spigot for stringy mucus that no amount of blowing could completely clear. Each cough seemed as though a piece of the lining of her lungs would painfully rip free. Her joints had become so swollen that the skin around them had pulled grotesquely taut. She had been able to keep some water down but nothing else: even the soup broth he fed her had induced violent vomiting.

She had slept restlessly, tossing and turning under the bedcovers while perspiring profusely, and during those moments when she was awake and lucid, Susannah whispered of bizarre nightmares with no elaboration.

Arnett had kept a constant vigil at her bedside, giving her water, trying to get her to eat something, and changing the sweat-soaked T-shirt and panties that she wore. While Susannah slept, he had halfheartedly worked on his own projects—proofing the galleys from his second novel, whose deadline was rapidly approaching, or going over a pair of manuscripts that his agent believed would be his third and fourth novels—but he found he had no energy or inspiration for it.

He slept in either the contemporary leather chair in one corner of their bedroom or on the floor beside their king-sized, four-poster bed. He had called the English Department at the university to let them know he would be taking more sick leave, and he was surprised to find out that the university had shut down. Preoccupied with his own issues, he had not watched the local news or CNN, much less read the local newspaper, in almost three weeks.

And then—as if from nowhere—Susannah's condition began to improve.

Vann thought it was a miracle. The prayers of a non-practicing Catholic had been answered. It was the only explanation he could come up with, and the only one that made any sense to him. It was a miracle, and he repeatedly thanked God for it.

Sure, she was pale and tired and weak, her appetite had not returned, and her eyes were still hypersensitive to light, but her nose had stopped running, the cough had pretty much dissipated, and the swelling in her joints had diminished to mere puffiness.

Despite the lingering grief over the death of his daughter, Vann was silently elated. He felt as though he and Susannah had dodged death this time. They had looked the Grim Reaper in the eye, smiled, and flipped him the bird. Each day she improved a bit more and got a little stronger. Arnett was confident that it was just a matter of time before Susannah was healthy again.

He couldn't have been more wrong.

Days later, Arnett took a break from his writing and tiptoed into their bedroom to check on her. He opened the door and softly called out, "Susannah."

Because her eyes were still light-sensitive, the blinds and room-darkening shades were drawn tight. Even though it was mid-afternoon, the room was shrouded in charcoal shadows, and Vann, whose eyes had not adjusted to the dimness, couldn't see very well as he stepped over the threshold.

"Susa . . ."

He never finished her name.

Small but strong hands roughly clutched his shoulders and hurled him into the room, propelling him off balance into the darkness.

"What the . . ." Arnett muttered loudly. Carrying sixty pounds too many on his six-foot frame, he stumbled into the room and tripped over the footboard of the bed. As he fell, he attempted to grasp one of the posts but missed. He tumbled onto the bed and hoped he wouldn't land too hard on top of his wife. When he sprawled onto the firm mattress, he was more than a little surprised to find that Susannah wasn't in the bed. "Fuck."

Confusion poured into his brain, filling the vacant spaces created by the fleeing of rational thought. Fear had not entered the picture—yet.

With hands moving in spastic jerks, he felt around the surface of the bed in search of his wife. He sought the familiar shape of her legs, her thighs, her hips, her arms, her shoulders—any part of her body. Nothing here. Nothing there. Again, nothing. One more time, nothing. Vann's fingers found only the textured surface of the fluffy and thick comforter for his efforts. It gave him no comfort. His heart thundered in his chest, thumping behind his ribs like a bird trying to escape its cage.

"Susannah?" he said softly in the quiet of the bedroom, uncertain of what the response would be.

Arnett's solitary word was met with a snarl, throaty and deep with the hard edge of malevolence.

"Susannah?"

"O-o-over here, Vann, my sweet."

The voice did—*but didn't*—sound like Susannah, but she had never, ever called him "my sweet" during the decade and a half of their marriage. Fear seeped into his mind and forced its way to the forefront of his thoughts as he struggled to see in the darkened room. "W . . . where's Susannah? What have you done with her?"

"I'm right here, my sweet."

She said it again!

Keeping his attention focused on the area of the bedroom where the voice had come from, Vann searched out the small lamp on the nightstand beside the bed. His fingers groped and probed the stale air for the distinctive shape of the lamp. Like an unexpected piece of shrapnel from a distant explosion landing nearby, he remembered his surprised response when his Susannah had told him that she had spent more than three hundred and fifty dollars for the matching pair of designer lights. He shook his head to clear the rogue thought.

In the dark umbra, Arnett just barely made out the indistinct shape slipping away from the doorway and gliding farther into the room. He wondered where his wife was. She couldn't be the figure creeping in the darkness. *She couldn't be.* He smiled when his fingers found the lamp and, an instant later, its switch. Fearing what he might actually see, Vann held his breath and turned on the light.

The room was flooded with unexpectedly bright light from an energy-saver sixty-watt bulb. Caught off guard, the person who had been Susannah Arnett hissed and covered her eyes with her forearm.

"What the . . ." Vann was not certain *what* he was looking at. The . . . the creature looked like his wife—thin with red hair—and it wore the same oversized, white T-shirt and white cotton panties as earlier in the day, but there was no way this was Susannah. No way. She was a ghostly white apparition, more nightmare than wet dream.

"Turn it off!" she shrieked as if in pain. "Turn it off!"

For one brief moment—an indeterminately long, agonizing instant—his fingers flexed on the plastic switch. Just another couple ounces of pressure would have done the trick, would have snapped off the light and plunged the bedroom back into darkness, but Vann hesitated.

"Turn it *off!*"

He stared openmouthed at what his wife had become. Transfixed by horror, he couldn't take his eyes off her and what she had become. Vann couldn't help but notice that her breasts were visible as one of the straps of the undershirt slipped off her shoulder. He involuntarily glanced down to points south of the border before returning to her head.

"*Turn it off!*" It was more snarl than three-word sentence.

Arnett snapped out of his daze and managed to ungracefully roll off the bed.

Susannah, with one arm locked tight across her eyes, blindly grasped out with the other. Her fingers clutched open and closed like claws as she attempted to catch something—anything—in them. She shuffled her bare feet toward the bed, moving closer and closer with each mini-step.

Was it panic? For whatever reason, Vann dashed around the foot of the bed and toward the door just as Susannah lunged onto the mattress with a growl. As he pulled open the door, Arnett glanced back at the bed, and what he saw chilled his soul like a tombstone in winter.

Susannah, with pure animal fury and litheness, scrambled to her hands and knees atop the bed. She slowly turned to face him, tilting her head in an animalistic manner. A snarling hiss revealed razor-sharp fangs in her mouth, but he only distantly noticed them. Vann could only stare at her eyes, which glared back at him with a smoldering rage and hunger. Those twinkling deep-blue Irish eyes—the ones that had helped him fall in love with Susannah Mullins on their first date many years earlier—were almost entirely devoid of color, as if they had been washed away. It gave them an eerie and almost translucent appearance.

The woman he had loved and who had loved him was nowhere to be found in those strange, savage eyes. A sharp fragment of sadness penetrated his heart. A beat later, the urge for self-preservation kicked into high gear.

"I'm sorry, Susannah," Vann whispered.

He stepped over the threshold and pulled the door shut behind him. The clicking of the catch was followed by a pissed-off snarl from deep in the bedroom. Arnett fled down the hallway toward the afternoon sunlight that flooded into the living room through huge picture windows.

A body thudded loudly into the other side of the bedroom door, and it was violently flung open. As he ran into the living room, Vann heard another animal yelp of pain, and he stifled the urge to run back and comfort his wife. *She's no longer my wife*, he thought as he sprinted out the main door of their home and into the chaos the world had become.

Without even realizing it, Vann had removed his wedding ring while absently lost in his memories, and he idly spun it on his pinky. He silently battled against a wave of sadness that swept over him and wrapped up his heart in something other than a lover's embrace.

He was lonely and depressed, but there was little he could actually do about it. All the shrinks had other activities penciled in on their calendars or PDAs, iPhones, or BlackBerrys.

Arnett clenched his wedding ring tightly in the palm of his hand, closed his eyes, and sobbed once. He sniffed back his tears and opened his hand, staring at the gold band. He had squeezed it so tightly that the metal had left indentations in his flesh. He knew he had to stay strong and vigilant, but some days it was difficult—so goddamn difficult.

With a ragged sigh, Vann slipped the ring—a love token from a past but forever-gone life—back onto the third finger of his left hand as he surveyed the horizon of a battered landscape.

Toughen up and ride this thing out, his father, the well-respected but bitter trial lawyer, would have said to him.

He frowned at how much his life had changed during the past nineteen months—*eighteen months and twenty-two days, but who's counting?*—and definitely not for the better. His daughter, one of the shining lights of his life, had died a grotesque and horrible death. His wife, the other illuminating beacon in his existence, had suffered a fate worse than death. She had changed and become . . . one of *them*.

Civilization had death-spiraled into anarchy before completely grinding to a collapse. The world was now populated by nocturnal, somewhat human creatures that hunted down the last remaining survivors of mankind for sustenance. And he was now almost totally alone—save for the ever-present Irish setter, Rusty—and he had been for the past seven months.

Sylvie and Hal had disappeared without a trace one early spring morning in late March. The two of them had left to do chores at the farm where the trio grew an assortment of fruits and vegetables west of the city, and they had never returned. They had planned to spend the day preparing manageable tracts of farmland for planting, so Vann knew they would be out of range of the two-way Motorola radios each of them carried like a talisman clipped to their belts, but he also knew Sylvie and Hal were well-armed and ready for any and all kinds of trouble.

In these desperate days, trouble came in many shapes and sizes, not just the night-wandering ghouls. He thought nothing of it when he hadn't heard from them all day, and he became only slightly concerned that they had not contacted him when the sun began its inexorable descent toward the western horizon.

Fear and worry, however, simultaneously entered Vann's consciousness after sunset, when darkness cloaked the land and *they* came out of hiding. It was dangerous—practically suicidal—to be outside after sunset.

Shortly after sunrise the next morning, Vann and Rusty searched for them, traveling to the farm ten miles from the western fringes of the city. Sylvie and Hal had obviously been there, for the evidence of their day's labor was plain to see. Several acres of farmland had been tilled in preparation of the planting that would take place in a couple of weeks. The turned topsoil, rich and black, looked like a fresh wound on the gray earth, and its heavy, loamy odor hung in the air like fecund musk. The self-armored Ford Explorer was nowhere on the farm.

Vann traded his prized Mossberg 930 autoloader 12-gauge shotgun for a smaller and more lethal M4 submachine gun, and he and the muscular male Irish setter scoured the nearby town for a sign— any kind of sign—that the two of them had taken shelter there and spent the night holed up in one of its more secure deserted buildings.

During the first few hours, it was a methodical and thorough search, Vann proceeding logically through vacant stores and empty homes with the dog never venturing too far from his side, but frustration and anxiety eventually led to haphazard and quick scans. He dismissed many of the buildings with little more than perfunctory glances because neither the thick dust that covered almost all surfaces, nor the clinging cobwebs suspended like string at the finish line of a footrace, had been disturbed.

It didn't matter how or where they searched, the results had been the same. Arnett concluded that Sylvie and Hal had not ventured into the desolate village to seek shelter or refuge or anything else. They had not been there, but that didn't answer the questions of where they had gone or what had happened to them.

Vann and Rusty spent every hour of daylight over the next week and a half searching for them. They returned to the village one more time. The man and the dog went to the safe houses that had been set up at locations throughout the city. They randomly searched buildings, and the two of them prowled streets and alleys in hopes of catching a glimpse of the Explorer.

For all their tireless efforts and risks to life and limb, they found absolutely nothing, not so much as a trace. It was as if Sylvie and Hal had simply disappeared from the face of the earth, almost as if they had never existed. Arnett didn't think they had just run off without him, not wanting a third side to a love triangle or to live out the scenes of the film classic *The World, the Flesh and the Devil*.

If the two of them had just slipped away, they wouldn't have spent the day working at the farm, and they certainly wouldn't have left the treasures and trinkets of their past lives behind at the citadel. He had initially feared that the Explorer had broken down on their return trip to the fortress, but he uncovered no evidence of that scenario. Arnett simply refused to contemplate the other circumstance. He convinced himself they had just vanished.

Vann abandoned the search after nine gut-wrenching days. It wasn't that he and Rusty had exhausted all the possible locations for exploration—literally thousands of them remained—but instead it was that his obsessive search had nearly cost them their lives in an unexpected dusk encounter that had left three Kindred sprawled dead at the curb and him trembling from an adrenaline spike and embarrassed rage in the Tahoe.

Before that memory could flicker to life like an old 8mm home movie and tug him down a troubled Yellow Brick Road, he shook the unwanted thoughts from his head. They were reminders of his foolish carelessness, his single-minded pursuit of futility. Dumb luck and blind fortune had intervened to save him and the dog from a disastrous end that day. It was a harsh lesson—one taught in the School of Hard Knocks, his father would have lectured him—but it was one he had learned and learned well.

"C'mon, Rusty, we've got work to do today," he said to the setter.

Arnett slowly wheeled the SUV down the residential street in a neighborhood a mile or so southwest of the citadel. It had been a quiet and law-abiding neighborhood, but it was now as still and peaceful as an ancient crypt.

In that past life, it had been an ordinary upper-middle-class street lined with a mishmash of houses that were between and fifty and seventy years old, but now it appeared the same as any other street in the city: dead and gone.

Grass grew in thick clumps and spiky tufts where the freezing and thawing had cracked open the pavement of surface streets and sidewalks. Spindly weeds and prickly thistles dominated once-manicured lawns that, untended, had withered and turned brown, while shrubs and bushes grew wildly out of control with the threat to take over some yards, and vines entirely encased several homes.

Homeowners, who had once paid off their mortgages and had taken pride in the upkeep of their dwellings—brick ranches, 1970s-era split levels, nondistinctive two-stories, and the odd-out Cape Cod bungalow or contemporary Victorian—would be mortified and saddened by their current state: Paint had chipped or peeled off. Aluminum siding had faded to chalky paint residue under the unrelenting summer sun and frigid temperatures of winter. Shutters hung askew or had fallen off entirely. Broken windows had exposed the interiors to all the elements, from monsoon-like rains to white-out blizzards. Birds nested under the eaves and in sagging soffits and bats roosted in brick chimneys and attics, while other wildlife made itself at home throughout the rest of the house.

The disrepair was such that collapsed porches had fallen into the yards, complete sections of roofs had been ripped away by tornado-like winds, houses here and there had burned down to the foundations while adjacent dwellings had been partially burned or merely scorched, with vinyl siding hanging like something from a Dali painting, and a number of homes had suffered the indignity of having the large tree—a once-stately ash or majestic oak that had been the centerpiece of the front yard—crash down upon the house, punching holes in the roofs in most cases but spectacularly snapping the spine of the roof joists and ripping open a chasm three-fourths of the way to the foundation in one instance.

Time and the elements had conspired together to remove most of the detritus of throwaway trash and other disposable goods and newspapers and missing-person posters that had been left behind by man, scattering them about by circumstance and chance. It had been replaced by carpets of soggy leaves, fallen branches of all shapes and sizes, and downed trees.

Chunks of pink fiberglass insulation, sections shattered two-by-fours, pieces of asphalt shingles, shards of glass and other debris had been violently ripped out of damaged homes and other structures. The occasional dead power line drooped above the roadway like an inverted arch or lay snake-like across the pavement.

All automobiles, from sleek sports car to cumbersome mini-van to monstrous SUV, rested on tires that ranged from just a little soft to pancake-flat. Some were parked in driveways and others at the curb, while a few were left askew in the street, having ended their last journeys with an accident. Those vehicles unfortunate enough to have had their final parking spot under trees were now painted with mottled spots of white and gray from excessive bird droppings. Not very many—maybe one in fifty—still contained their long dead and desiccated final occupants.

No children or adolescents had played on this street—or any other in the city, for that matter—in well over a year. There had been no impromptu games of street soccer or street hockey. No bikers or skateboarders had sluiced down the pavement or concrete sidewalks. No toddlers and attentive parents had fun in the front yard in tiny wading pools to beat the heat or made snow angels in fresh powder.

There were no children's toys forgotten in the front yard, no mountain bikes awaiting their riders' return, no music thumping loudly from a teenager's pimped ride while he waited at the curb for a friend, no riding lawn mower operated by an obsessive-compulsive amateur landscaper buzzing in the distance. The neighborhood was just empty, with no energy pulsing through it or vigor driving it forward.

It was devoid of life.

Vann, as he drove down the street, scanned the houses and consulted the makeshift map spread across his lap and the center console. He was looking for a sign—literally.

Arnett had broken the city's various neighborhoods down into sections and proceeded to do a house-by-house search for anything useful. He identified those dwellings that had already been explored by spray painting a black *X* on the front door, while a red *X* indicated that he had discovered creatures in the house, summarily dispatching them to their final judgment.

He also duly noted his findings on the map with a similar, albeit, smaller symbol. As if that were not enough, in a spiral-bound notebook, Vann logged all that he recovered during his pillaging expeditions. It was a curse of his gold-colored personality and habit of his scholarly training. The likelihood that his life depended on it was merely an afterthought.

He stopped the Tahoe in the middle of the street—travel lanes were irrelevant since he seemed to be driving the only moving vehicle on the road these days—checked the map and then the houses along the street. Arnett found the last dwelling that he had searched, a black *X* prominent on the door, and dropped the gearshift into PARK.

"This is it, Rusty," he said to the dog, "the end of the known world."

The Irish setter, who sat upright in the passenger seat and had spent most of the drive with his black nose stuffed in the three-inch crack of the open window, turned to him as if to ask, why have we stopped? For all the indifference the animal showed him, Rusty was still a dog that loved to go for a ride, especially if he could stick his face into the breeze.

"I know it's fun, but we've got work to do."

If a dog could contort its facial expression into a frown, Rusty did so.

"Don't give me that shit. You knew this was a work trip, not a joyride."

The setter turned away and stuffed its muzzle in the open space at the top of the window. His actions succinctly said, *if I ignore you and pretend that you are not here, I will not have to do what you want. So there.*

"Yeah, I love you, too, flea bag."

Vann took one last glance at the map and mentally noted there were only three red *X*s in the neighborhood—the nearest one several blocks away—and no red *K*s, his notation indicating where he had found and exterminated members of the Kindred.

He didn't know much about them or how they managed to exist from day to day, preferring to eliminate rather than interrogate. Arnett knew they had some rudimentary hierarchy, but he believed it was similar to that of a wolf pack led by an alpha male. He suspected they were more organized than they appeared, knowing that they had warriors who were always armed among their ranks, but he didn't want to give them too much credit.

The few he had bothered to interrogate spoke of a charismatic leader called the Prophet who preached an apocalyptic message, quoting from the Book of Revelation, but Vann was skeptical of their life-fearing delusional ramblings. The Kindred shunned contemporary conveniences and weapons, preferring low-tech and minimally mechanical devices that functioned without electricity, along with armaments such as bows and arrows, crossbows, swords, and knives.

They spray painted their symbol—a cross that extended down into a sword blade with the hilt encircled by a serpent—in bright red or orange on structures all over the city to mark their territory, and the Kindred tattooed or branded or scarred themselves with that same ornamentation as a means to identify one another.

He also knew the Kindred were wickedly dangerous and would kill him without hesitation or regret if the opportunity ever presented itself. He had seen the phrase Their dead bodies lie in the streets of the city spray painted throughout the capital. If the unthinkable happened, he suspected that his head would end up on a spike and displayed somewhere in the city. He had come across a few of them during his travels and couldn't help but wonder what happened to the rest of the body.

Arnett folded the map and stowed it in the center console. He hopped out of the SUV, and the dog followed him out the door.

It was a beautiful fall day—the temperature had warmed up and the air smelled pure, as if untainted by the presence of man and his machines—but Vann felt little pleasure or enthusiasm as he geared up for the task ahead. It was a necessary evil, a chore that he had to perform.

Oftentimes, he felt like a grave robber as he stood in the dusty solitude of someone else's home, sorting through their private and personal possessions in search of something that he—and he alone—deemed useful. Many people had desperately hoarded canned goods, boxed meals, bottled water, liquor, and all sorts of other items as The Collapse played out its apocalyptic drama, meaning some houses were veritable treasure troves awaiting his discovery.

Decked out in full battle rattle—he rarely left the citadel in anything but his battle dress uniform—Vann headed toward a ranch with a combination of brick and wood siding that was still in remarkably good shape, suffering only minor humiliations from its perpetual state of neglect.

With the M4 slung over his right shoulder and a mesh bag similar to what divers used to haul up treasure over the other, he held the Stingray in his right hand and two high-intensity Surefire U2 Ultra Lights in his left. He strolled up the walk to the front door, which was unlocked. He twisted the knob and stepped over the threshold into another world.

Arnett entered a living room that had not seen human activity in probably a year and a half, the dog slipping past him but not venturing farther into the house. He removed his wraparound Oakley sunglasses, slid them above the bill of his black Chicago White Sox baseball cap, and surveyed the room. He snapped on the Stingray and got a better view.

The style was a mixture of contemporary and traditional furnishings. It was as though the residing family had been in the ongoing process of replacing serviceable hand-me-downs from their parents and other relatives with pieces of their own choosing. It was pretty much the same thing that he and Susannah had done during the first decade of their marriage.

A slow sweep of the flashlight revealed a large sofa and matching chair, a coffee table with magazines casually strewn across the top in front of the sofa, a non-matching recliner, end tables with matching lamps between the sofa and chair as well as next to the recliner, and an antique-appearing sitting chair with a long-stemmed reading lamp adjacent to it.

A flat-screen plasma TV was affixed to the primary wall while an entertainment center with all the latest technological accessories and toys was near it, and surround-sound components had been mounted in strategic locations throughout the room. The other walls were adorned with knickknack-covered small shelves, pieces of undistinguished artwork, small mirrors, and such. A layer of dust covered everything in the room, and delicate cobwebs had softened the harsher features.

The beam of light swept past and then returned to a pair of framed eight-by-ten photos on the wall opposite the sofa. They were school photos of the two children—a girl and a boy—who had lived here. The girl was around twelve years old with long, blond hair, blue eyes, and a shy smile, while the dark-haired boy was probably two years her junior with dark eyes and a sly smile. They were cute kids.

"Oh shit." The last thing Vann wanted to do was think about what had happened to the two children, because that would lead to thoughts about what had happened to his own daughter, inevitably taking him to a place in the dark recesses of his mind that he did not want to visit. He took a deep breath from the stale air and exhaled loudly. He repeated the process a couple more times, as if it would actually chase the thought-demons that had infiltrated his mind.

"Screw it, Rusty. Let's get this over with."

When he and the Irish setter finally walked out of the house about four hours later, it had proven to be a valuable search, a more than worthwhile afternoon of work where he had gained useful provisions.

Arnett had discovered a couple dozen cans of Campbell's soup, Chef Boyardee SpaghettiOs and ravioli, Bush's Best Baked Beans, StarKist tuna fish, and an assortment of Green Giant vegetables, along with several packets of Maruchan ramen noodles, a half dozen boxes each of Kraft macaroni and cheese, Uncle Ben's wild rice, and three different varieties of Creamette pasta in one of the kitchen cupboards.

Unfortunately, insects had found and plundered the bags of flour and sugar, rendering them useless. There were three unopened gallon jugs of bottled water and partially opened twelve packs of Coke, Diet Coke, and Mountain Dew on the floor near the refrigerator. He had snagged a half-dozen plush body towels—you could never have too many towels, Susannah had said many years earlier—from the linen closet adjacent to the main bathroom, where he had nabbed the five remaining unused bars of Dove bath soap, along with unopened boxes of Q-tips, Crest toothpaste, and EasySlide dental floss from underneath the sink. Arnett was obsessive about his dental hygiene because he knew there was no dentist down the street with whom to schedule a checkup.

Too much for the bag, he had loaded the booty in a cardboard box retrieved from the Tahoe and hauled it back out to the SUV.

In the rear of the house, the children's fashionable bedrooms and the simply adorned guest room had yielded no treasures or useful plunder. The master bedroom, tastefully and stylishly decorated, had offered an interesting search but ultimately yielded no necessities or luxuries. Despite the haul, he wasn't sure how to feel because he was always on the lookout for a cache of a more adult nature.

Disappointed, he frowned and scratched the whiskers on his chin. "C'mon, *dawg*, let's go home." Vann then pocketed his small black Stingray flashlight, gathered up the two high-powered Surefire flashlights that he had placed on the end tables, and left the bedroom, Rusty padding silently at his heels.

That night, after he had eaten supper, fed the dog, and decided the Kindred were going to ignore once him again, Arnett wandered into the high-tech entertainment room of the citadel. It had been state-of-the-art for the past year and a half. He studied the huge collection of DVDs, organized by genre and alphabetized by title, for a couple of minutes before he plucked an old favorite.

Vann slid the disc into the player, grabbed the remote, and sat down in his high-back Lane recliner. The fifty-five-inch Vizio LCD flat-screen TV flickered to life as he fingered the buttons on the remote, waiting for the familiar opening scene of a film he had watched countless times to begin.

He spent the next couple of hours laughing and shooting lines in perfect timing with Chris Knight, Mitch Taylor, and the other characters of *Real Genius*.

Two

At first, he didn't know where he was, but before Arnett could panic, it came rushing back to him like spring floodwaters over an earthen dam. He had fallen asleep in his recliner while watching a video. At least he had been coherent enough to shut off the DVD and TV. He didn't need them running all night and drawing down the power supply. He stood up from the chair, stretched, and tried to work the kinks out of his neck.

Vann didn't fall asleep in the entertainment room very often. He preferred his own bedroom suite or the sofa in the main room of the third floor. His bedroom afforded him most of the comforts he wanted right at his fingertips, while the great room, which was the largest and most open space on the level, had all the defensive perimeter-monitoring equipment, including the alarms that would sound if there had been a breach.

He was fairly certain that he would hear the alarms no matter where he was in the citadel or Rusty would alert him, but his paranoia had always served him well in the past. In this world, it was better to be paranoid and somewhat safe, rather than complacent and an unexpected turn from death—or worse.

Rusty trotted over to the hallway that led to the kitchen area, stopped, and looked back at him.

"I know, I know," Arnett said. "You're hungry and you want your breakfast."

The setter just stared at him with an unreadable expression on his canine face. Vann believed the dog tolerated him and endured the work they did because he was an easy meal ticket. The wild dogs in the city—and there were a lot of them—existed mostly in packs like wolves and fended for themselves.

During the final spasms of The Collapse and the chaos that followed, it was not uncommon to see these newly formed packs gorging themselves on human corpses, snarling and growling at one another while tearing and gnawing at the flesh of the dead. Now they survived by hunting down other animals, including the odd-out stray dog or those in smaller packs.

"Okay, okay. You eat and then we'll check the perimeter. Is that okay with you?"

Apparently it was. Rusty turned and padded toward the kitchen. He knew where his dog food was kept in a huge Rubbermaid tub, right next to his food and water bowls. The setter would be waiting ever so patiently for his provider.

Arnett smiled and shook his head. He knew who the master was in this particular man-dog relationship, and it was not him.

Arnett and Rusty had finished their ritual inspection of the perimeter defenses and found all the trip wires, booby traps, and mines to be undisturbed by any nocturnal activities, which was what he had expected. There had been no alarms or other warnings set off during the night, so, barring a system failure, he knew the defenses had not been approached, much less breached.

Strolling easily in the sunshine and cool temperature of the morning, he stopped on the inlaid brick driveway that led back to Wolveshaven and stared at the huge dwelling. He surmised the former owners—wherever they were—would hardly recognize the place in its current condition. It looked like a wartime command post during a past military campaign, say Europe during World War II or the late twentieth-century war in the Balkans. The beauty of the architecture had been compromised, but it still shone through.

The gabled windows on each side of the fourth floor of Wolveshaven had been converted into sandbagged pillboxes—complete with 50-caliber machine guns jutting out from them with plenty of ammo stored in nearby boxes—to protect each flank of the mansion, while high-intensity spotlights could illuminate the grounds around it.

Most of the mansion's elaborate, multi-paned windows had been boarded up, and those that weren't covered by wood had been reinforced with heavy, wire mesh. The main doors, complete with ornate detailing, had been reinforced with steel bands. Two secondary side doors had been sealed, and the basement bulkhead had been reinforced and chain-locked. The mansion, which had been one of just three homes on the block, was the only one left standing. The others had been reduced to ashes.

The once abundant and stately oaks and black walnut trees had been cut down and turned into firewood. The shade and isolation they had provided was surrendered to security and visibility. The original ten-foot wrought-iron fence had been topped with loops of razor wire, and two inner rings of eight-foot chain-link fence had been erected.

There was only one means into the grounds of Wolveshaven, through the main gate and those of the inner fence lines, and each one was electronically locked with a manual override, of course. The weed-grown grounds between the three rings of fences had been booby-trapped with anti-personnel mines and claymores, but there were none of these defenses between the innermost fence and the mansion building itself.

The inner fence was also electrified with five thousand volts running through it when Arnett tripped the switch. It wasn't enough to seriously hurt anything that came in contact with it, but it was sufficient to make them think twice about approaching it. Running a current through the fence was a huge drain on the power supply, so he flipped the switch only when the Kindred showed up outside his doorstep.

Arnett stared at the battlements. He thought it was an impressive array of defenses and made even more remarkable by the fact it had been constructed by only three people, none of whom had any military background. And it had been brutally effective.

In the time since the trio had taken over the abandoned Wolve-shaven, only about a half dozen of the creatures had even penetrated the outer fence ring. They had managed to endure the slicing and dicing of the razor wire only to be cut down and shredded by the 50-cals. The message had been sent loud and clear—do *not* fuck with us, unless you are willing to suffer the consequences—and it had been received.

From that point on, the Kindred had been content to taunt and torment the residents of the mansion from outside the perimeter of fences, scrambling for cover from the occasional sniper-shot from the widow's walk. Even after Sylvie and Hal disappeared, they had made no concerted effort to breach the fences, just a couple of what-the-fuck forays that ended with dead creatures littered outside the wrought-iron fence.

Arnett had no compunction against shooting the Kindred. Males or females, it didn't matter. It was merely a case of putting a target in the night vision crosshairs and squeezing the trigger. Deep breath, slow exhale, smooth and even pull—*boom!*—and a vaguely human figure dropped to the ground while the rest of the creatures scattered like cockroaches caught in an unexpected light.

He hadn't had much need to do it during the past few months. The creatures stayed warily away from the fence, and a well-placed errant shot from the 50-caliber sniper rifle was an effective means to encourage them to keep that distance. It didn't stop them from continuing with their antics, mind you, but it did make them think twice about how close they got to the perimeter.

He manually secured the innermost gate, making certain it was properly connected with a couple of tugs on the cold steel handle, and started to walk slowly toward the mansion. "C'mon, Rusty, we've got things to do today."

The Irish setter watched him take several strides and trotted after the man.

Arnett walked slowly and respectfully—but with a purpose—through the garden. The sounds of his combat boots crunching the gravel and his body armor rattling followed him like the wake of a boat.

Rusty zigzagged behind him in a random search for new scents to seek out and explore. It was one of the few times the Irish setter actually behaved like a dog. Without even glancing over a shoulder, he knew what the animal was doing, and it brought a slight smile to his lips and a tempered sense of joy to his heart. Vann could never be truly happy when he came to this solemn place, a garden where loved ones had been planted like seeds in the earth but only cold granite had grown like crops that would bear no fruit from the consecrated soil.

He had parked the Tahoe about a quarter mile from his destination. He used the easy walk to collect his thoughts and gather his courage. Strangely and unexpectedly, Vann always found comfort and solace in his irregular visits to this place. It was like going to church as a boy. He had complained and protested to his parents that he didn't want or need to go, but he always felt a sense of peace and forgiveness after the mass had concluded.

He cut across ragged brown grass that at one time had been immaculately manicured but was now left unattended to the whims of nature, weaving his way past tombstones and smaller grave markers. Arnett stopped in front of a nondescript plot of grass, distinguished only by a small, handmade cross with a laminated photograph of a pretty, red-haired adolescent girl attached to it.

"Hi, baby," Vann said softly as he sat in the grass. "It's Daddy."

Shelane Arnett had been among the very first victims in the city of this modern-day microbial scourge. She had been unsuccessfully treated at a world-class medical facility and passed to that great unknown beyond just thirty-seven days short of her thirteenth birthday.

The middle-aged priest, the same man who had baptized her and had overseen her first communion, had given the nearly unrecognizable young girl the last rites in a sterile hospital room, a visitation wake had been attended by several hundred red-eyed mourners who passed by a closed casket, a solemn Catholic funeral mass had been conducted, and Shelane's mortal body had been interred in a perpetual-care plot at a local cemetery. The green sod had been carefully replaced atop the grave and the site had been prepped for a headstone that would never be completed by the monument artisan.

Society had still dictated that it was important to respectfully and sanitarily handle the dead, but that pretense had changed quickly in the weeks after the young girl's death.

Shelane Arnett had been one of fewer than a couple hundred people in the city who had received a ritualistic funeral—hers in a Catholic church named after a long-dead saint and burial in a consecrated cemetery—but when the world spiraled out of control in the proceeding days, such ceremonial niceties became irrelevant.

As the number of the dead and dying literally piled up in hospital corridors and back rooms, an overwhelmed local emergency management system could not keep up, and the deluged federal government could provide no help. In nightmare imagery more suited for the Middle Ages than the twenty-first century, tens of thousands of corpses were tossed haphazardly in the back boxes of dump trucks or on flatbed trailers and hauled away to a deep open pit that had been carved in the earth of a county park just south of the city.

With no ceremony—much less dignity or respect—the bodies had been emptied into the mass grave and torched on a nightly basis by workers encased in biohazard suits. For many months, even after the unpleasant grim task had ground to a halt because there was no one left to perform it, the fires had smoldered on, and the distinctive odor of charred human flesh hung in the air, regardless of which way or how strong the wind blew.

"Things are pretty much the same here," Arnett said to the grave. "I'm okay, for the most part. I actually feel healthy. I haven't been in this kind of shape since I thought I was an athlete back in high school." He laughed and smiled. "I get enough to eat, so I'm not really hungry, and it is actually a fairly balanced diet. You'd be proud of me. But you know what, kiddo?" He glanced around conspiratorially. "Just between you and me, I really miss chocolate. I haven't had any for a couple of weeks, and you know me and chocolate.

"Oh, there's still some of it around, mind you, but what the bugs haven't gotten into is pretty stale right now. Of course, that doesn't stop me from looking for it. Hey, you know me, you just never know when you might stumble upon that pot of gold. Or, in this case, a hidden stash of Milky Way bars."

Vann didn't know if he had been a good father or not, but he had tried to be. He liked to think that he had learned from his own parents what not to do, but he had still found himself doing some of those things that had annoyed him as a teen. It was called being a parent, he had rationalized to himself, understanding that his parents had done the best they could to raise him. Parenting was the toughest job in the world but also the most satisfying one. He had realized that only too late, when he was no longer actually one.

"Baby, you wouldn't recognize your city," he said.

Though only an adolescent, Shelane had loved living in the city, so much so that he and Susannah had jokingly called it "your city" to her. There was so much to see and so much to do, and the young girl had eagerly wanted to do as much as possible. It was as if she wanted to breathe in everything around her, to fill her soul with it, to get as much out of life as fast as she could.

Vann and Susannah had been happy to oblige their daughter. They had taken her to museums and art exhibits, upscale stores and eclectic shops, sprawling malls and farmers markets, free concerts and high-priced symphonies, movies and the ballet, family get-togethers and neighborhood block parties, and, of course, thousands of university-affiliated events and activities.

Shelane had never been embarrassed about doing things with them, but approaching her teenaged years she had begun to test the bounds of her independence and her parents' willingness to let her go. Arnett had loved her free spirit, her open curiosity about things she didn't understand, and her positive outlook. They were all qualities identical to her mother, so how could he not love them in his daughter?

"Your city has changed so, so much," Vann said softly.

This twelve-year-old ray of sunshine had been the light of his life and the joy of his world. She had been Daddy's little girl, and he would have done anything—anything at all—for her, to protect her and keep her safe. But in the end, he had failed. He had been unable to do anything for her.

Shelane had died a horrible death, and he had been helpless to make a difference. Her life had ended, and with it went a large piece of his soul. Arnett took solace that she had gone on to a better place, that she had received her final reward of eternal life. His Catholic catechism had taught him that much, and he clutched to that piece of his conflicted faith like a shipwrecked sailor clung to a floating piece of debris in the darkness of a stormy sea.

Vann inhaled deeply and raggedly exhaled.

"Hey, baby, I'm still finding quite a bit of usable stuff during my scavenger hunts, but I have to go farther and farther away from the citadel to find it. I know, I know, I know. It's dangerous, but I am careful, and I made a decent haul from a house yesterday."

A mental image of the children's school photos on the living room wall slammed into his brain. It came out of nowhere like a distant thunderclap on a hot and humid late spring afternoon. Was the girl a friend of Shelane's? Did they know each other? Were they in the same grade? Did they even attend classes at the same school? Would they have gone to the same high school? Or would they have been athletic rivals on the basketball court and soccer field?

"I . . . I . . . I . . ." He could not finish his sentence. He could not grasp his thoughts, much less organize them into something coherent.

Arnett swayed under the weight of his burden, both mental and physical, before he steadied himself. His once full and vibrant life, one that he had cherished, was now a hollow shell, a one-dimensional and single-minded existence with nothing to add depth or provide texture to it. His life was empty . . . just empty.

"I miss you, baby." He sighed loudly and frowned. "I miss you and your mom so much. I can't help but wonder why I'm still here when everyone I love is gone. I . . . I just don't know why. I hope there is a reason, but . . . but I feel like I'm in purgatory, that I'm trapped between heaven and hell because of something I did or didn't do. Or, I don't know, maybe this is my hell. Wouldn't that be something, huh? What would your grandparents think? They'd be mortified at the thought that their good Catholic son has been condemned to hell."

He smiled sadly and shook his head. "Wouldn't that be something? Oh, I can just see them trying to explain that one to Saint Peter. Grandpa, ever the lawyer. That would be a sight to see, wouldn't it? Grandpa trying to litigate on my behalf at the Pearly Gates." He smothered a sob in his throat. "But I know you'd be cool with it. Yeah, you'd be cool with it."

Vann stared at the ground ahead of him, but tears obscured his vision. He felt her hand slip into his, just as it had thousands of times before. The sensation was so real that he turned and expected to see Shelane standing beside him. His right hand was empty and no one stood next to him, but he knew she was there. Vann knew it in his heart, even if his eyes betrayed him and suggested otherwise. He squeezed the lids shut and sobbed as tears fell down his cheeks.

"Thanks, baby." Vann opened his eyes and smiled at the thought of his daughter standing beside him, her small but strong hand cradled in his. He *needed* it to be that way. "I love you, baby. I miss you, too. I'll see you when my time here is done."

The street really wasn't much different from the last time he had driven down it.

Was it a month already? he asked himself as he absently wheeled the Tahoe toward his destination. Had a month really passed? It had to be, because the calendar in his room at Wolveshaven said so. It had been a month since the last time he had visited his own home, but it did not stop him from questioning the wisdom of what he was about to do.

Why am I doing this? Why am I tormenting myself?

'Cause suffering builds character, his father had gruffly said to him many, many years earlier when he was an angst-ridden teenager listening to the likes of Nirvana, Pearl Jam, and Soundgarden. *Character.*

Fuck character, I'm the only character left. The only one!

Do you believe that, Vann? Do you really believe that?

Haven't I suffered enough?

One can never suffer enough, Vann. You should know that.

He sighed as he slowed the SUV and pulled it into the driveway of the split-level house. The architectural style with an exterior a combination of wood and brick had been popular when it was built. He slipped the gearshift into PARK and switched off the engine but didn't get out of the vehicle. Vann stared at the front of the house and sighed, emotion catching in his throat.

Why do I do this to myself? Why? Hell, I don't even know if it's . . . I just don't know, damn it. So why do I keep doing it?

You know why, boy. You know why.

"Yeah, yeah, yeah," Vann muttered as he opened the door and yanked the keys out of the ignition. "Shit." He got out of the Tahoe, and the setter followed him. As the dog stretched in the yard and cautiously sniffed at the air, he grabbed a backpack from the backseat and slung it over his left shoulder. Next came the assault rifle, followed by the Stingray, which he tested even though he knew the batteries were good.

"What do you smell, Rusty?"

The dog turned and stared at Arnett for a brief moment, as if pondering a profound answer, but without saying anything, the setter returned to his sniffing.

"Sometimes, I swear, you are a fucking cat wearing an Irish setter costume."

Rusty ignored the insult and trotted toward the front door.

"Okay, okay, I get the message."

He flicked off the safety of the M4 and followed the dog up the sidewalk. Thirty seconds and a couple of deep breaths later, Vann stood in the entryway of his home, living room on the right and dining room off to the left, while Rusty performed a quick reconnoiter of the premises. He knew the routine. The dog returned in less than three minutes, cobwebs and dust clinging to his fur, and Rusty gave the silent all-clear.

Vann clicked on the flashlight and hesitantly stepped into the living room. The beam illuminated nearly bare and empty walls, dark ten-penny nail heads poking out of cream-painted drywall like proverbial sore thumbs. He had long ago removed the photographs and other keepsakes from the house, taking them to Wolve-shaven, where he kept them in plain sight and within easy reach of his fingertips, like sacred talismans.

These treasures—several dozen precious remnants from his past life that he could look upon and touch, that he could clutch to his heart and shed remorseful tears over—kept him grounded in the dual reality of what he had been and what he had become. These everyday mementos, keepsakes, and photos that would have been taken for granted before the end of the world, enabled him to maintain his humanity in an inhumane world.

Removing these prized possessions from his own home was a no-brainer, but Vann could hardly look at similar objects in the houses he plundered. Instead, he stole glances with downcast eyes at family photographs hung on the walls of these dead dwellings, and he avoided photo albums and collections of VHS tapes that captured vacations and family milestones as if those items carried the very plague that brought about the apocalypse.

He preferred to be a voyeur, to glimpse their lives from a safe distance with only the illusion of a shared history. It was the only way Arnett could perform this necessary task and retain what was left of his sanity.

His heart rate unconsciously quickened and his breathing slowed as he moved the flashlight's beam to the dusty coffee table in front of an equally dust-covered, high-back sofa. The light illuminated only an empty tabletop, the surface marred by several subtle disruptions in the layer of dust.

It was gone.

Vann had expected it to be gone, but he was still flooded with a wave of emotion, a mixture of joy and relief, when he saw that it was not there. It had always disappeared in the past, but he secretly dreaded a time when it would not be gone, that it would still be on the tabletop where he had placed it. It was not this time, however. The top of the eight-hundred-dollar dark oak and wrought-iron table with claw-foot legs was empty. There was nothing there. It was as barren as a windswept desert plateau.

On suddenly weak and unsteady legs, he half-walked, half-staggered to the table and practically fell to the floor in front of it. He managed to place the Stingray on the floor with the beam pointed straight up. Arnett, breathing raggedly, stared at the spot where it had been.

The markings in the dust were short and unhurried, unlike the first couple of times when it was obvious that it had been grasped by palsied and feverish hands. Over time—about a half year—a routine had been established, and it had played out in a familiar manner every time. He didn't dare deviate from the steps of this particular dance for fear of what the unplanned consequences would be.

Vann took a deep breath and exhaled slowly, repeating the procedure several times as he willed himself to settle down. He stared at the scuff marks in the dust. The marks had obviously been made by someone who had come into the house, someone who had entered the house for a specific purpose. He resisted the temptation to touch the table, the want to finger the marks in the dust, the desire to place his hands on the same spot where someone else had placed theirs, the need to share contact with whoever it was.

Was it . . . ?

Arnett did not know if it was her or not—in his purely emotional mind, he fantasized and held out hope against all hope that it was—but he had no way of knowing for sure. He didn't care. It was all hopes and dreams—wishful thinking, if you will—but that was why he kept doing what he did, why he carried on. If you didn't have hopes and dreams, you truly didn't have anything.

Vann slid the backpack off his shoulder and placed it on the floor beside him, unzipped a front pocket, and reached inside. It was still cold, but he had known that it would be. In fact, he would have been surprised and disappointed and maybe even a bit concerned if it had not been. He stifled a smile as he wrapped his hand around it but could not hide the feeling of contentment and satisfaction that had blossomed warmly in his heart and spread throughout his chest. He slowly took it out of the bag and held it up in front of his face, examining it in the diffused light of the flashlight.

He moved it over the bright beam of artificial light, and it practically glowed in the din of his living room. The nearly translucent color cast an eerie, haunted-house glow about the room. Arnett sighed and carefully placed it on the table, putting it in a spot where the dust was thick and undisturbed. He stared at it—out of the direct light its color was dark and rich—and whispered a solemn prayer as if he were making an offering to an ancient pagan deity.

When he finished, Vann made the sign of the cross, plucked the light from the floor, and quickly stood up, battle gear and body armor rattling noisily in the church-like quiet.

"Let's go, Rusty."

Without hesitation, Arnett turned and purposefully walked to the door. He paused in front of the threshold as the Irish setter scooted past him and out of the house. Cursing himself under his breath, he looked back and shone the light on the coffee table. The beam illuminated it, red and ripe.

One unit of his own blood shone brightly in the transparent plastic medical storage bag and then disappeared into a gray oblivion as he swept the light away and walked out of the house.

The sprawling and multi-story mall complex, one of several once-shining monuments to corporate greed and entrepreneurial excess throughout the city, continued to lure him with a seductive commercial siren song, calling to him with a promise of fulfilled got-to-have-it consumerism.

Of course, the latest and greatest and newest and most improved products were more than a year and a half old. The name-brand stores within the massive steel and concrete and glass building had been unsystematically pillaged of their glitz and bling, but, in a society that prized style over substance and flash over significance, the opportunistic but injudicious looters had left behind most of the goods and items that would be truly useful and practical in this brave new world.

Only a handful of never-to-be-used-again vehicles were scattered throughout the parking lot, and most of them had been abandoned between faded white lines. Despite the abundant availability of front-row parking, Arnett drove the SUV to the curb and stopped there.

Walking through a parking lot, his skin tingled unpleasantly when he moved past long unoccupied vehicles. In all honesty, he knew there was nothing to fear in those rusting heaps, but it still made him uneasy. He couldn't explain the irrational feeling of anxiety to himself and would not even begin to consider the implication to his long-term mental sanity. It just wasn't worth it. So, rather than fight it or test himself, he parked as close as possible to wherever his destination was. He thought it was a small price to pay for one less trouble on his mind.

Having secured the Tahoe and geared up for battle, Vann and Rusty walked to the main entrance of the mall. Some hyped-up looter, during the final death throes of civilization, had thrown cinder blocks through the large panes of safety glass that had been the doors and adjacent walls of the entryway. Vann could visualize the young man raising his arms and screaming in triumph as he surveyed what he had done.

Shattered glass was littered all over the floor, but, during a prior visit, Arnett had cleared a path for him and the dog to safely navigate into the building. He had also tossed the cement blocks safely out of the way. There were enough unforeseen and unknown dangers lurking in the city, so whenever possible you minimized the seen and known dangers.

That lesson again: he had learned not to take high-risk gambles or unnecessary risks. Nothing like a lot of caution and a little dose of paranoia to keep you on your toes.

The two of them stood in what had been the mall's food court, which was lit only by open entryway and dirty skylights above. Past sights and sounds and scents rushed back to him: People of all ethnicities and ages hustled from store to store or queued up at food vendors. The blunted hush of hundreds of simultaneous conversations and tinny mall music from overhead speakers served as smothering white noise. The enticing aromas of several dozen types of food in various stages of preparation and consumption wafted through the open air.

He slipped back to reality and saw scenes of chaos from the end days: tables and chairs and other accessories overturned while some were broken beyond repair. Franchised restaurant neon signs hung darkly askew while some had fallen to the floor and shattered. Litter, plastic serving trays, and other debris were scattered about the floor. Unprepared food of all kinds had spoiled and deteriorated to dust. Wind-borne dirt and leaves covered the floor and many other surfaces, especially near the open entryway. An unnatural, tomb-like silence hung in the air like high humidity on a blistering hot summer afternoon.

It was hardly the first time he had journeyed to the mall since The Collapse, but he was always wary. The complete stillness and utter solitude of a place that at one time had throbbed with commercial energy and youthful vigor seemed out of place, seemed wrong, and those sensations kept him on edge. It was that paranoia thing again.

Arnett snapped on the flashlight and shined the beam around the food court as he and the dog wandered farther into the massive building. Nothing had really changed since his last visit a month or so earlier, except the interior had continued to deteriorate a little further along its path of neglected disrepair and the spiders had been working extra hours in preparation for the coming winter.

"You know, Rusty, I think I'm gonna have to call mall management or send them a tersely worded e-mail," he said to the dog. "This place has really gone down in the dumps since the new owners took over. Lights don't work, no water in the bathrooms, trash all over the place." Vann chuckled. "Hell, Rusty, it's not fit for man or dog."

The muscular setter ignored his attempted humor, but that did not deter him from pushing forward.

"So, are we looking for something in particular on this little journey, or are we just browsing for something that catches our eye?"

Thirty minutes later and moving like phantoms in the darkness, Arnett and Rusty trolled aimlessly down the wide corridor of one of the wings of the mall. They had stopped at several different stores and browsed without purpose, but he did not need any more pots and pans from Williams-Sonoma nor did he want diamond jewelry from Zales. FYE held no allure because he already possessed all the newest-released DVDs, while shops like the Gap, the Buckle, and American Eagle had previously been plundered by him. Besides, a person can only have so much stuff that he really needed, the rest was just overkill.

Vann absently wandered toward the glass-encased storefront of Victoria's Secret, practically gawking at the less-than-lifelike mannequins attired in sexy lingerie, while the Irish setter trotted on a few yards ahead of him, enamored with his own canine pursuits. In the nearly nonexistent light, Arnett could almost imagine the mannequins were real women, especially if he let his mind amble down that particular pathway. If he had spent another moment or two lost in the lurid pull of that silent siren song, he wouldn't have even heard it.

Arnett stopped dead in his tracks, an abbreviated breath catching in his throat. He stood stone-like and strained to hear this distinctive and unmistakable sound again. He willed his ears to pick it up, to capture once more the sound he had heard. He needed to hear it, needed to know it was not just his own desperate imagination toying with him. Afraid to so much as move even a little one way or another, Vann snuck a quick peek in the dog's direction.

Rusty stood at alert attention in the middle of the corridor, head held high and ears cocked. The setter stared in the direction of a darkened PacSun three stores down and on the other side of the hallway. The security gate was down and locked in the recessed doorway, but the storefront windows had been busted out long ago.

"Shit!" a voice snarled from the direction of the PacSun. "You little . . ."

Two heartbeats later, a small and dark shape streaked out of the storefront, bolting into the corridor. The shape skidded to a clawing stop when it realized there was a dog standing in the open hallway, and once it secured its footing, scrambled in the opposite direction as fast as it could.

"Come back here, you little shit!" from the PacSun.

It took Arnett a couple of seconds to realize the shape had been a feral cat, but the setter had known almost instantaneously. "No, Rusty," he growled in a voice hardly above a whisper.

Too late. The Irish setter, a bird dog trained to act on command and hold point while awaiting his master, did what his entire species had done for eons: the dog bolted down the corridor after the cat, disappearing into the darkness.

"Goddamn it!" from the PacSun. A moment later, a much larger and vaguely human shape emerged from the broken windows of the storefront and jumped into the corridor, stumbling to its hands and knees. "Get back here, you little . . ." The voice stopped with an audible gasp. It was tinged with surprise and fear. A terrified whimper followed.

Vann, startled into action, shone the flashlight beam on the dark shape and fumbled with his assault rifle. "Don't move!"

He glanced down the corridor—but Rusty was long gone in hot pursuit—and turned back to the figure captured in the light. "Don't fuckin' move!" He managed to get the M4 pointed in the general direction of the form in the hallway and cautiously walked toward it.

The shape collapsed to the floor and put its arms protectively over its head. "Don't . . . don't . . . don't . . ." it whimpered. It was obviously a female.

Vann hesitated in mid-step. There was something distantly familiar about the voice. "Sylvie?"

"Don't . . . don't hurt me."

He shook his head to clear those thoughts. It was not Sylvie. "Don't move," he commanded, but his voice had lost most of its intensity. "Stay right where you are." Arnett stepped toward the figure but stopped about ten feet away.

"Don't hurt me. I . . . I . . . Don't hurt me."

"Look at me."

"I . . . I can't," she said. "The light . . . it . . . it hurts my eyes."

He moved the flashlight beam off the dark shape but kept it close enough so he could see just what he was dealing with. Although he had a pretty good idea. "Sit up and look at me."

"The light . . ."

"It's not on you."

"But . . ."

"Do it!"

The figure rose to its hands and knees and shifted to a sitting position on the floor.

In the reflected light of the flashlight beam, Arnett saw that it was, indeed, a female. She wore Columbia hiking boots, Levi's blue jeans, with a dark Nike hoodie, all of which was under a black Wilson's leather trench coat. One dark bandana and mirror-lens black Speedo swimmer's goggles hung at her neck, while another bandana was tied snugly around her throat. Long, dark hair billowed out from under a third bandana that was tied tight just above her eyebrows and topped by a charcoal Linkin Park knit beanie. Her entire ensemble probably came from this very mall, he thought.

The little facial skin that he saw was alabaster white, and, even though he could not actually see them, Vann knew that her eyes were pale remnants of whatever color they had been. He was also aware that they would reflect red like an animal's if he shined the light directly at them.

He had encountered hundreds of them before, and his past practice had usually been to shoot first and not even bother with the questions. It had not mattered—males, females, or children, the only good creature was a dead one. Oh sure, he had interrogated some, but he eventually killed them once he gleaned whatever useful information they had possessed. But this encounter was somehow different.

"Look at me."

She turned to him and stared directly into his eyes. She wanted to be defiant and strong, but her lower lip quivered in fear.

Arnett examined her face, complete with several dirt smudges. She had a pointy chin and a narrow but straight nose, with high cheekbones. He still could not tell what color her eyes were. She had been a pretty young woman before The Collapse and still was. He guessed she was maybe in her late teens or early twenties at most.

"What are you doing here?"

"Food."

"Food?"

She nodded, starting to relax just a little. "Yes, food."

"There's no food left here. It's all spoiled."

"We catch it."

"Catch it?"

"Yes." She nodded at him. "We catch squirrels, rabbits . . ." She shrugged. "Rats. Anything we can catch in a live trap."

"But you're . . . you're one of . . ." He couldn't finish the sentence.

"Yes, I am." She started to smile but suppressed it. "We still need to eat."

"But I thought you needed . . . blood?"

"We do. Animals have blood and fresh meat has blood in it."

"Don't you need human blood?"

"It's best." She looked down and then turned her gaze back at him. "But any blood will do, any kind of animal blood. Humans are just another kind of animal."

"That's comforting."

She shrugged and said softly, "That's the way it is."

"You said *we*. How many of you are there?" Arnett felt strangely at ease with this conversation. It was not really an interrogation, and this didn't trouble him.

"I don't know." She shrugged again. "A lot, I guess. I don't have a number. But we're not with . . . with them."

"The Kindred?"

"Yes." This time she couldn't hide the smile. "You know of them?"

"Oh yeah." Arnett nodded and returned her grin. "I know of them."

The cat having eluded him, Rusty trotted back down the corridor and began to growl and snarl when he realized what was sitting on the floor. The hair along his spine stood up like a mahogany Mohawk.

The woman's pale eyes went wide with fear as she scrambled into a defensive posture, reaching for something inside the long coat.

"Don't do it," Arnett warned and wiggled the assault rifle, and she withdrew her gloved hand with nothing in its grasp. "Rusty, come. Come!"

The Irish setter skirted wide of the young woman and came alongside Arnett. The dog growled deep in its throat.

"Easy, Rusty." The setter settled just a bit but still growled. "He won't hurt you, unless I tell him to."

Her skeptical eyes went from Arnett to the dog and back to Arnett. She knew she had no choice but to trust him. "O-okay."

"I didn't think you came out during the day. Doesn't the sun . . . hurt you?"

"Yes, it does. It burns our skin and blinds our eyes. But if we cover ourselves and protect our eyes, we can go out in the daylight."

"But why?"

"Many of the animals we trap come out at night. They won't go to the traps if we're nearby. We leave them alone at night, and a few of us check them by day. It's hard, and we have to be very careful."

"I've never seen any of you out in the daylight before," Vann said, shaking his head. "I've heard stories, but I thought they were just bullshitting me."

"Now you know."

"Yup." He nodded. "Now I know." Arnett turned to the dog. "What do you say, Rusty, should we call it a day and head home?"

The setter growled a little louder but did not move.

"I agree. Let's go home."

The female's mouth dropped open, revealing her fangs for the first time. "You're not . . . not going to . . . to kill me?"

Vann shook his head. "No. I'm not going to kill you, or even hurt you."

"But . . ."

He knew she had trusted him with Rusty, and he was going to return the favor. "Give me a few minutes to get out of here, and then you can check the rest of your traps. I assume you have more in here."

"Yeah." It was practically a whisper.

"Don't follow me or try anything, okay? I really don't want to hurt you, but I will if I have to. Understand?"

"Yeah."

"C'mon, Rusty, let's go home." Trusting—not to mention praying—she did not have a pistol stashed inside her coat, Arnett turned his back to her and began to walk down the corridor, moving away from the woman. The dog cautiously matched his pace but still warily watched over his shoulder.

"Wait."

Vann stopped and looked at her. The setter circled ahead of him and stopped.

"You're . . . you're him, aren't you?"

"Who?"

"*Him.*"

"Who?"

"The Su . . . the man from the wolf house. The . . ."

Arnett smiled and let out a quiet laugh. "Yeah, I suppose I am."

She could only stare at him in wide-eyed disbelief as he turned once again.

"Good luck," he said over his shoulder. "Maybe I'll see you again sometime, and we can talk some more."

Three

Several hours later, as the darkness of night embraced Wolve-shaven and the creatures of the Kindred flooded the streets in the faraway center city, Arnett sat at an antique, blond oak rolltop desk and stared at the monitor of his Dell Latitude Notebook laptop, the desktop image on the flat screen displaying a photograph of a family vacation to Mexico.

With a couple of deft movements from the fingers of his right hand, Vann opened the Word document file that had become his journal. Several more movements brought him to the end of his last entry. He read the last few paragraphs of the words he had written several days earlier, inserted a page break at the end of the final paragraph, and the blank sheet of page four hundred and seventy-three appeared.

Arnett took a deep breath, chased that down with a sip of vodka, and began to type.

I had a very strange encounter today.

This morning I visited Shelane, and we had a good talk. After our visit, I stopped by the house to drop off . . . the package. It was difficult to be inside the house—harder than usual, for some reason—but I knew I had to go there; I had to take care of business. In that respect, my life now really isn't all that much different from before The Collapse. I still have to take care of the business, but now it's just a different kind of business.

I was feeling kind of down, I don't know, maybe even a little depressed, so Rusty and I went to the mall, the one on the West Side that Shelane always liked so much. We didn't really need anything, so we just kind of wandered about the place. I guess being there, in a familiar place where my daughter loved to shop, made me feel better. I certainly wasn't paying attention when it happened. Rusty and I were just strolling about the shops, as The Moody Blues used to sing, and—boom—there she was, crashing out of PacSun.

I know, I know, I wrote she and not it, quite a departure for me. At first, when she came tumbling out of the store, I didn't know if it was a survivor or one of them. For some dumb reason, I thought it was Sylvie. I don't know if I actually thought it was her, or if it was just wishful thinking. The voice I heard didn't really sound like Sylvie, but it kind of did, if that makes any sense. Maybe it was just the fact that it was a female's voice, and Sylvie was the last woman whom I conversed with. Crazy, I know, but I can still remember how she sounded, the way she said some words. I guess I wanted it to be her. I miss her.

Don't worry, Suze, I still remember how your voice sounds, how you said certain phrases, the way you used that sexy little Irish brogue when you were trying to be cute or funny or seductive. God, I miss you. But I also know that the woman I remember as my wife no longer exists. She no longer exists in any way, shape, or form. If you are still alive out there somewhere in the city, you are one of them, one of the creatures. Heaven forbid, you may even be among the Kindred.

The creature—the young woman—I encountered this afternoon wasn't Kindred. She was just one of them, struggling to survive, to stay alive. Pretty much just like me. She didn't ask for what fate had dealt her, but she just took the cards and was trying to play the hand as best she could. Again, pretty much just like me.

How's that for an eye-opening thought? A couple of days earlier, that thought would have never occurred to me. Hell, a couple hours earlier and it wouldn't have slipped into my brain. I'm not sure where it came from, but I could hazard a guess, even though I might not like the implications of such a notion.

I suspect, if I had shot first and not bothered with any questions at all, I wouldn't be writing this right now. However, I did ask questions first and never did actually shoot, and now I have to deal with that on my own terms.

I'm not sure if what I did today was right or wrong, but, by the same token, I'm not sure if what I've done in the past was right or wrong. That's the dilemma I face each and every day I try to survive in this purgatory on earth. I also know that the rules of the old world don't apply in this new one.

The bottom line—funny how it still comes down to that, even now—is that I didn't kill her because I chose not to kill her; because I didn't want to kill her. Instead, I chose to talk with her, to communicate even for just a few minutes. We were two . . . two people talking. I guess I just needed to have some social contact with another individual capable of communicating back with me. No offense, Rusty. I had hoped she was another survivor like me, but the fact that she wasn't doesn't diminish the fact that it felt good to talk with her. I needed to talk with her; it made me feel almost real again.

I don't think my actions or inactions make me weak; I think they make me human . . .

In a world gone insane with mindless chaos and savage disorder, he sat with a full belly in a warm home and a glass of Grey Goose vodka on ice. Vann was safe and secure and comfortable inside Wolveshaven, but he was also alone and isolated. Wolveshaven was his fortress, his sanctuary. His prison. Arnett longed for the simplest and most mundane pleasure of living: social interaction with another human being.

Four

He knew exactly why he was driving to where he was, but not that he would admit it to himself. No, to do that would have been to confess a weakness and display it in public. In this world and this age of man, however, such an exhibition of weakness was a luxury he could not afford. The price was just way too steep.

So, instead of acknowledging the previous day's encounter with the female had caught him off guard and left him craving social companionship more than usual, Arnett convinced himself he was headed to the fortified town house on the city's Far West Side to do a little friendly bartering, some end-of-the-world horse-trading. It was a rationalization that enabled him to keep his hard-edged, take-no-prisoners survivor persona, even if it was bullshit.

Vann had loaded four bottles of whiskey—three of them were Phillips brand and the other a quart of Maker's Mark that he would hold back and use as leverage to seal whatever deal he made—into a cardboard box, placed four frozen venison steaks and a half-dozen bags of frozen vegetables that he had harvested from the garden into a small Igloo cooler, and hauled the small cache of extravagant and desirable treats to the Tahoe. He had checked and then double-checked his battle gear along with the never-leave-home-without-them supplies he kept in the SUV before hitting the open road.

The trip halfway across the city from Wolveshaven to Trig and Aaron's town house took less than twenty minutes. Before The Collapse such a journey would have taken at least a traffic-dodging thirty minutes, but probably more like a blood-pressure-raising forty-five. Streets and boulevards platted through neighborhoods in the middle of the nineteenth century were incapable of accommodating contemporary traffic from unfettered urban sprawl. Thoughtless and careless drivers only exacerbated problems that none of the original city planners had ever contemplated.

The result had been a daily bumper-to-bumper miasma of fiberglass, sheet metal, plastic, chrome, rubber, glass, and exhaust fumes, not to mention short-fused tempers, which less often than one would have imagined came together like comets whose orbits crossed paths at a most inopportune time. The plague, however, had addressed all those problems that had been discussed at length during countless city council meetings and made them irrelevant. Now, travel in the city was a just a matter of avoiding the odd-out rusting husks of dead vehicles that littered the roadways, as well as slaloming around potholes that dotted the pavement like exploded land mines.

The cautious optimism that had filled Arnett when he and Rusty left the citadel in the cool morning sunlight seeped slowly but inexorably away as he wheeled the Tahoe down the gently curved street lined with condominiums and town houses that were nearly identical to one another, save for paint color and exterior accoutrements. Something just wasn't right. He could feel it in both his head and his gut. Arnett couldn't put his finger on what it was, but he couldn't and wouldn't deny the uneasy physiological sensation that had permeated his body. He had learned to trust his own intuition: if it didn't feel right, it probably wasn't right.

"I got a bad feeling about this, Rusty," Vann said, glancing at the dog that sat in the passenger seat. "A bad feeling."

The Irish setter stared back at him with dark chocolate eyes, but no emotion or mannerisms betrayed the dog's thoughts. If Rusty possessed uneasy feelings about this venture, he kept that opinion exclusively to himself.

Arnett's trepidation only grew as the SUV rounded the bend that led to the cul-de-sac where the fortified, two-story town house sat atop a low, tree-speckled ridge. The dwellings on either side of it had been razed to the ground, and razor-sharp concertina wire had been strung atop the eight-foot-high chain-link fence surrounding the residence.

From a distance, the dwelling looked as it had the last time he had been there. The appearance of the dwelling didn't change as he drove the SUV closer. Still, he couldn't shake his feeling that something was not right.

Perched atop a bent light post, a large crow stared at him as if he were an intruder.

He stopped the Tahoe in front of the chain-like gate at the end of the twenty-five-foot driveway and stared past the metal mesh and wire at the town house. It looked okay. Vann beeped the horn twice, holding it down for a couple of seconds the second time. He opened the door and climbed halfway out of the SUV, blowing the horn again.

Vann listened intently but only heard the crow raucously scolding him. He stepped completely out of the vehicle and stood in the middle of the cul-de-sac.

"Hey, Trig," he called out. "Aaron. It's me, Vann. Hey, guys." Stifling an inappropriate grin, Arnett resisted the temptation to yell out, "*Hey, you guys,*" a classic line from one of his daughter's all-time favorite movies, *The Goonies.* Vann looked up at the big black bird as it restlessly fluttered its wings but didn't take flight.

He stepped over to the gate and put his hand on it.

"Hey, Tr—"

Vann stopped in mid-word as the steel gate swung slightly inward when he leaned some weight against it.

"Uh-oh," he said, quickly backing away and removing his hand from the steel as if he had been burned. "Oh, shit. This can't be a good sign."

Less than five minutes later, with the M4 casually leveled for business, Vann and Rusty entered the ground floor of the town house that Trig and Aaron had fortified and survived in. Entry, which should have been difficult and fraught with life-threatening danger, had been as simple as pushing open the gate at the end of the driveway, walking up the seal-coated blacktop, going to the main door, and opening it.

Definitely not a good sign, Arnett thought as he stepped over the threshold and into the lower level. Nope, not a good sign at all.

"Aaron. Trig."

He held his breath as he listened for a response, but there was nothing. His call was greeted by silence. Stillness like death. Vann frowned as he scanned his surroundings in the tight beam of the Stingray. There were distinct and unmistakable indications that a firefight had taken place.

Like at Wolveshaven, the lower level of the town house was used almost exclusively for storage. The various rooms had been packed with a wide array of supplies, everything from dry goods to munitions, nonperishable foodstuffs to automotive replacement parts, medicine to booze, building materials to clothes, and much more. Just like the upper levels of his own citadel, the second floor of the building was the primary living area and had been much more heavily fortified and reinforced with protective measures.

"Aw, shit," Vann muttered under his breath as he surveyed the damage.

Dozens of bullet holes pockmarked the walls near the doorway, but, surprisingly, the back of the heavily reinforced door itself was pretty much unscathed from the gunfire.

That's because the shooting didn't start until the door was already open, he thought as he examined it closer in a combination of artificial light and sunlight. *They* had already breached the external security before Trig and Aaron even realized it, and by that time it was too late. Once they were inside the town house, trying to stop them would have been like trying to stop rapidly rising floodwaters with a tin bucket. The creatures would have literally poured through the doorway in numbers far too great to be halted.

Vann shuddered at the terrifying thought of the Kindred rushing through the door, hatred and rage and bloodlust fueling the maddening thirst that relentlessly drove them forward into a storm of automatic weapon fire.

He lowered the flashlight beam to the floor and saw smears and streaks and pools of darkened crimson covering the gray and white Italian marble tile. The stains were thick near the doorway, almost entirely covering the floor, but dissipated slowly to just here and there the farther Arnett moved the light away from the entryway. The blood splatters had dried like paint. Even the puddles had coagulated and hardened into blobs like chocolate that had been melted and tossed about to cool. It appeared the Kindred had paid a heavy price to get into the condo, but it was one they had been quite obviously willing to pay.

Arnett hoped Trig and Aaron had fled to the safety of a panic room or some other secure area in the town house to hold out until morning light, but he didn't even know if they had made such preparations. If the two of them had not planned that far ahead, it really didn't matter at crunch time.

"What the hell happened here, Rusty?" he asked the Irish setter, which had not strayed more than a step or two from his side since crossing the threshold. "How did this happen? How did they get in?"

He shined the flashlight around the wide foyer: open archways fronted hallways that led to other rooms on the first floor of the residence, while an open iron-railed spiral staircase stretched to the second-story veranda that overlooked and wrapped completely around the top of the open vestibule. Surprisingly, aside from the doorway, there were few—if any—indications on the ground level of the struggle that had occurred. It was as if the Kindred had arrived at the town house, swiftly gained entry and took control of the situation, grabbed what they wanted, and left without pillaging or plundering. It appeared to have been brutally quick and efficient.

Against his better judgment, Vann climbed the spiral staircase and, with each step, dreaded what he expected to find on the second floor. The destruction and chaos wasn't as bad as he had anticipated, but the finality of it was much worse. Armor-piercing bullets had punctured Sheetrock and masonry without pattern or form. Hundreds of brass shell casings littered the floor like dry leaves in fall. Bloodstains were splattered around as if Jackson Pollock had entered a monochromatic phase.

Three arrowheads—crossbow bolts, most likely—were snapped off near the base of the shaft and embedded in drywall like pieces of primitive art. Both large and small pieces of furniture had been undisturbed while others had been broken and shattered with the randomness of a tornado's violent destruction. A black New York Yankees baseball hat, the brim molded into the shape of an inverted *U*, lay upright on the floor near the door to one of the bedrooms. A single bullet hole marred the flat-screen surface of a sixty-five-inch Toshiba high-definition DLP plasma television in a nearly undamaged living room. A novel, Cormac McCarthy's *No Country for Old Men*, had been set down open-faced to mark the reader's place on the coffee table in front of a leather Natuzzi sofa.

But Trig and Aaron were nowhere to be found.

Vann stood on the balcony at the back of the town house and stared out over the gently sloping valley covered with upscale, one- and two-family housing units. There were hundreds of them within his sight and thousands more throughout the city. He couldn't grasp the magnitude that all of them were lifeless and empty, nothing more than dead husks and soulless reminders of a civilization that had flourished—and died. The city had been home to more than two hundred thousand souls at the onset of the plague. He wondered how many were left unchanged, unaffected physically by the plague. Was there anyone else? Or was he the only one?

They—Arnett, Sylvie, and Hal—had been aware of seven other tiny enclaves of survivors in the city. The largest one had five people and two had only one person. One of the solos, a middle-aged man named Garwood, had mentally gone around the bend, deteriorating into raving paranoia, and was avoided because he was heavily armed and dangerous. The other solo, a thirty-something woman named Bethany, kept pretty much to herself, only rarely contacting any of the others.

There was a couple, Hector and Melinda, who looked upon The Collapse as a means to live out some kind of post-apocalyptic sex fantasy and always tried to entice others to join them for a day or two or even longer of Lord knew what. Another couple, Nathan and Laura, who were in their twenties, kept to themselves and had only rudimentary contact with anyone else.

There was a trio—Bennie, who was in his mid-forties, Annie, who was in her early thirties, and Josie, who was in her late teens—that had isolated itself from the others because Bennie feared someone would try to "steal" the women from him. A fivesome comprised of Irena, who was in her late forties, Kurt, who was in his early forties, Daryl and Kelly, who were both in their mid-thirties, and Jared, who was in his mid-teens, had caravanned out of the city many months ago and not been heard from again.

And, of course, there was Trig and Aaron. There could have been others in the city, but Vann and his partners had not encountered them. There were also subtle signs in some of the suburbs along with the smaller towns of the region that there were more survivors, but none of them had chosen to reveal their presence when anyone from the city had been there exploring and pillaging.

It was early afternoon, and the sun had passed its zenith and begun its trek toward the western horizon. The dog lay quietly just inside the open sliding glass patio doors that led out to the balcony, but the Irish setter kept its keen eyes on the man.

Arnett was hardly conscious of the fact the diurnal dance was more than half over. He was lost in his own troubling thoughts. He had contemplated grabbing the bottle of Maker's Mark from the Tahoe but decided against it, knowing that it would have neither been prudent nor wise to start drinking in the afternoon—on the other side of the city, no less. Without the aid of hard-liquor lubrication, he racked his brain trying to remember the last time he had actually visited or seen Trig and Aaron, but nothing came to him.

He couldn't accurately recall the last time he had spoken with any of the other survivors, having virtually made himself a hermit after Sylvie and Hal disappeared. He had wished Irena and her crew good luck and Godspeed several days before they ventured out on their journey into the unknown, but that had been in early June, if not late May.

Beyond that, he couldn't remember the last time he'd spoken to any of the more sociable holdovers. Of course, he had avoided the city's ragtag survivors who desired no contact with any of the others, leaving them to do battle with their own demons, both real and imagined.

He surmised that the battle at Trig and Aaron's had taken place at least several weeks, if not months, earlier. It was his best guess, based entirely on factless speculation. Vann was no criminalist trained in the methods and voodoo of forensic science. He couldn't examine the scene, collect evidence, and construct a more-than-plausible theory. He knew the blood spilled throughout the town house had dried, even in those places where it had poured out like syrup. Arnett didn't know for sure how long it would take for that to happen, but he thought it would surely be a couple of weeks.

The potent copper-penny smell of blood and the stench of burned gunpowder no longer lingered like wood smoke in the stale air of the condo. Those smells had been replaced by the gentle and earthy musk of early fall, subtle and natural scents that pledged decay in winter but promised rebirth in spring. Again, such a transformation and recirculation of air didn't happen overnight, but took weeks.

How had he missed it? The interior of the condo was a battle zone, the site of a brutal but futile firefight. How had he not heard all this gunfire? Hundreds—if not thousands—of rounds had been fired from automatic weapons. It had been a cacophony of chaos and death. And he had missed it all, oblivious to the life-and-death struggle that had played out on the other side of the city, away from his sanctuary at Wolveshaven.

Vann knew he had been lost in his own pathetic world of self-pity and self-doubt and self-imposed isolation, embracing his own despair and loneliness like the familiar contours of a lover's body. He had been all too happy and willing to play the end-of-the-world martyr.

That's how I missed it, he chastised himself. *That's how.*

That's right, you dumb shit! The disapproving voice in his head sounded just like his long-dead father's. *Too busy feeling sorry for yourself! Useless piece of ...*

In the distance, a low and throaty growl pierced the afternoon silence.

Rusty snapped his head up from his large paws. His bright eyes were quickly alert and his ears suddenly at attention. The heavy muscles in his torso tensed for quick action.

Arnett turned to the dog. "Easy, Rusty."

Another growl, this one more a roar, cut like a knife. It came from a distant part of the city but still struck a primal nerve.

"Sounds like Tony is on the prowl, hunting for something to eat. I hope he's not too hungry, but we'll have to be careful driving home. What do you think, Rusty?"

The Irish setter rose to its feet and, just for a brief moment, the dog looked like it was going to wag its tail and walk to the man's side. Instead, Rusty hesitated for a moment or two before he turned his head toward the interior of the town house.

"Okay, okay, you're right. It's time to go home." He snorted derisively at his own comment. "Home."

Vann took one last look past the wrought-iron railing of the balcony, staring at the valley of empty condos and town houses as far as the eye could see in the distance below. He couldn't help himself—really, he couldn't. He stared in dumbstruck awe and disbelief at the utter desolation and barrenness of the panoramic residential cityscape. No matter how many times he saw this or similar vistas—and there were thousands of them throughout the city—his heart always sank and a sickly knot dropped into the pit of his stomach. It was the unnerving finality of it all, of everything that had happened. It was the finality of death.

They had made it safely back to Wolveshaven without encountering Tony—as in Tony the Tiger—and at least ninety minutes before sunset, putting all their gear away and securing the perimeter defenses as sunlight faded, shadows lengthened, and temperatures slipped downward.

It had been a long and difficult day. Arnett was emotionally drained and mentally worn out. He had ventured out into the city with the noble intent to have some human social interaction, but instead, the trip had only reinforced his sense of isolation and loneliness. His small spark of guarded optimism had been replaced with claustrophobic depression that smothered him like an overprotective mother. He was caught in its web but helpless to get out of it.

Vann attempted to assuage his troubled feelings by delving into everyday routine. He fed the dog, generously mixing dry Pro Plan with half a can of Eukanuba beef and rice, and he couldn't help but smile when Rusty greedily downed the combination like his distant and wild lupine cousins. It eased his heart just a bit to pretend that the dog actually needed him for its survival, but he also knew that if push ultimately came to shove, the Irish setter would turn more red wolf than dog and be able to make it on his own. Strangely, that knowledge was a source of satisfaction for him, rather than fuel for the smoldering embers of his despair.

"That's a good boy, Rusty," he said as he watched the dog nose the metal bowl around the floor to capture the final morsels of kibble. "You must have been hungry, even though we didn't really do anything today."

Feeding himself, however, was an entirely different matter.

Arnett stared blankly at the cluttered pantry shelves stacked with hundreds of cans and jars and boxes of dry goods. Nothing captured his attention and spurred his taste buds on toward salivation. Numerous times he plucked a can or a box from a shelf, studied it, only to return it to the spot from where he had removed it. From the pantry he wandered over to the stainless steel–faced Sub-Zero upright. He pretty much came up with the same results but kept the hands-on attention to a minimum. Unable to decide on what to eat, he reached the conclusion that he would have a liquid supper and pulled an open bottle of Grey Goose vodka from its spot on the freezer door.

"Hey, I'm more thirsty than hungry anyway," Vann said to the dog as he headed toward the third floor with the distinctive tall and thin bottle, a balanced Mikasa crystal tumbler and bucket of ice cubes in his hands.

Placing the simple elements of his so-called supper on the desktop, he sat in front of a half-dozen television monitors that were connected to exterior security cameras and operated from a single computer system. The screens revealed no movement or activity in the growing darkness as twilight surrendered to night. Arnett absently studied each monitor while at the same time he dropped ice cubes in the glass, twisted the cork stopper from the bottle, and poured the clear alcohol into the crystal. Multitasking, that's what it was called. Without a second thought, he brought the glass to his lips and drank.

The first swig was iced fire as the frigid French vodka hit his tongue, swirled over it, and smoothly slid down the back of his throat. He closed his eyes, smiled to himself, and savored the sensation: a liquid arctic blast that left behind a diminishing trail of flames to mark its descending passage.

There was nothing quite like that first drink, Vann thought as he leaned deep into the high-back leather chair. The effects were as much psychological as physiological. Your mouth went from dry anticipation to liquid reward. Your body instantly responded to the introduction of hard liquor with its phantom warmth and fluid wrench that would ultimately loosen the nuts and bolts that secured your inhibitions. Was it the craving or the satisfaction of that desire? He didn't really care.

Arnett took another drink and then a third deep swallow. Refilling the glass, he stared at the monitors and got lost in their unflinching and monochromatic images. He could have manipulated the cameras to pan left or right, tilt up or down, zoom in or out, but he kept his hands away from the mouse and keyboard, preferring instead the half-dozen views that were already displayed.

Vann found himself standing out in the courtyard of the citadel, holding the bottle in his hand and drunkenly shouting curses into the darkness.

"Fuckin' cowards," he slurred. "Where the fuck are ya now?"

He was bare-ass naked, except for a gold cross on a fine-link chain around his neck and a beat-up pair of Nike Shox running shoes on his feet, and spoiling for a fight—or at least a verbal confrontation.

"I'm right here, ya fuckin' leeches! Right fuckin' here!"

He took a drink from the bottle and held his arms out away from his sides.

"I got nothin' to hide, ya fuckin' cowards! Nothin' to hide!"

Arnett stumbled but caught his balance as he almost tumbled unceremoniously to the ground.

"Here I am! Come and get me, if ya want me!"

He tripped again, but this time dropped to one knee and one hand, looking almost like a football player in a three-point stance waiting for the snap of the ball. Arnett managed not to drop the bottle nor spill any of its contents.

"Whoa, shit," he slurred. "Gotta be careful, don't wanna break the bottle." He laughed. "Would be a tragedy, a fuckin' tragedy."

He began to get up, but his equilibrium staggered away from him. He thought better of standing up and sat down in the dirt and grass. Arnett took another deep pull from the bottle, dribbling some of the liquor down his unshaven chin.

"Aw, mother's milk," he slurred in an Irish brogue and laughed at his own words. "As sweet and fine as any that comes from Mum's tit." He took another drink as he gazed drunkenly at the triple-fenced perimeter. It was ringed in darkness and murky shadows.

"Where the fuck are ya tonight?" Arnett called out. "Got somethin' better to do? Ha! Your loss, fuckers! YOUR LOSS!"

Vann took a deep breath and exhaled noisily. His torso swayed as if pushed by a strong wind, and, a moment later, he slumped to the ground, curling up in the brittle grass like an exhausted child after a long and hard day of playing. He had passed out and slid drunkenly into unconsciousness in a matter of minutes.

Arnett bolted upright in startled surprise.

Where the hell *am I?* was the single question that ripped through his mind. An instant later he realized that he was slumped in the chair in front of the security monitors, which showed the same six scenes as before, less night's tight hold on the landscape.

He was still inside Wolveshaven and hadn't stumbled drunkenly out into the night.

"What the . . ." He did not finish the question.

It had seemed so *real*. He had felt the chill on his bare skin and the breeze tug at his hair, he had tasted the booze in his mouth, he had smelled the untainted air, he had seen the darkness beyond the perimeter fences, and he had felt the coarseness of the grass on his face. It has all been so lifelike, so real, but it had not happened. He was still safe and sound inside the citadel. Vann had imagined or—more accurately—relived all of it.

The scene he had flashed back to had played out last spring, a couple of days after Sylvie and Hal had gone missing and about the time he had stopped searching for them. Arnett had been in quite a mental state: despondent, frustrated, and angry. It was not exactly the trifecta you wanted to put a lot of cash down on, much less your life.

Vann had passed out in the courtyard and surfaced from that drunken stupor the next morning, a couple of hours after sunrise. He had sat up in the yard, the imprint of the grass and ground pressed into his flesh like tribal tattoos, and winced under the crushing weight of a hangover and sunshine. He knew he had been damn lucky and would be luckier still if a hangover was the only penance for his foolish hubris.

Arnett had stood up, swayed like a sapling as he waited for his alcohol-damaged brain to catch up with his head, brushed the grass and dirt from his body, and staggered back toward the citadel. With right hand held high and left hand clutching his bare testicles, he had made the pledge that from that point on he would only drink in moderation.

He laughed nervously and, smiling, shook his head at his folly from months ago as well as the previous evening. A heavy sigh and a quick glance at the desktop revealed the reason for his unexpected journey down that particular block of memory lane.

There were about three fingers of vodka left in the bottom of the bottle, and the little bit of remaining Goose in the tumbler had been diluted by melted ice cubes. He had effortlessly pounded down three-quarters of the bottle of vodka, and the booze had run roughshod over his proper inhibitions and good intentions like barbarians pillaging a convent.

"Shit," he muttered under his boozy breath. "Another promise I couldn't keep."

Five

The hangover was not as bad as he thought it would be.

Oh sure, the dull pain in his head throbbed to a rhythm different from his own heartbeat, the sinus pressure behind his eyes threatened to pop the orbs out of his skull, his mouth was desert dry and tasted like he had eaten roadkill marinated in piss and shit for supper last night, and the muscles in his neck and back were stiff and sore from spending several hours comatose in a chair, but Arnett endured it all stoically and without complaint. Plus, the Aleve he had washed down with the last of the Goose had blunted the sharp edges and made all the aches tolerable.

He knew the hangover was a small price to pay for his lapse in judgment because the cost could have been much, much higher. Vann reluctantly admitted to himself that he recognized and understood what might have happened to Trig and Aaron. They might have taken a momentary break from their austere, ever-vigilant Cold War–like mentality and let their guard down, and it may very well have been a fatal blunder that the Kindred had been able to exploit.

That stark realization pushed him down the path to another series of troubling and disconcerting questions: *How did the Kindred know? Had they been watching Trig and Aaron?* And more troubling yet: *Are they watching me?*

"Shit," he said to Rusty, paranoia trickling icily along his spine and forcing him to fight the urge to rush to a window. "Shit, shit. Shit."

He had not thought the Kindred capable of anything as remotely sophisticated as surveillance, but a couple of days ago he also had not thought that any of the creatures were capable of having an actual, interactive conversation with him. Vann had been wrong about that one. Was he also wrong with the other part of that line of thinking? What else about them had he misjudged? Were they more intelligent and complex than he had given them credit for? Was their existence more than hand-to-mouth survival? Did they have some kind of society? What was their military capability?

"How deep is the shit I am standing in?" Arnett asked the dog. "*We're* standing in?"

The Irish setter only cocked his head to the side and stared at him with dark eyes.

"Rusty, we know next to nothing about them. Hell, we don't really *know* anything about them, the Kindred or . . . or the others. That's not good, Rusty, not good at all."

Arnett rose from the kitchen table where he had been drinking coffee made from stale grounds. It seemed, once he cracked open the vacuum seal on the cans, the coffee just did not hold its freshness. It did not stop him from drinking it, of course; the coffee just lacked potency and flavor.

"Rusty, what do we know about them?" he turned and asked the dog. "What do we really know about them?

"We know they need blood to survive, not necessarily human blood—although they prefer it—but they will dri . . . ingest animal blood, as well," Vann continued, making a face of distaste at the thought. "Whatever they can get their hands on, I assume. Yeah, I know, I know, given the chance, they would make a tasty meal out of me and you. We also know that sunlight, especially direct sunlight, burns their skin and blinds their eyes, but we also know that at least some of them aren't afraid to venture out during daylight hours, as long as they wear protective clothing. I don't know how we managed to miss that one for all this time, but we did.

"Based on what the female in the mall told us, her group isn't part of the Kindred and don't particularly like them," he said to the dog. "The Kindred seem to have the numbers advantage, but we really don't know that for sure, do we? We don't know if all the Kindred show up here when they pay us a visit or if there are others elsewhere out there in the city, doing Lord knows what. We don't know how many Kindred there are. Hell, we don't have a clue how many non-Kindred there are in the city, either.

"Neither one of these facts is a good thing, Rusty. We might be outnumbered a couple hundred to one, or it might be several thousand to one. Hell, it might even be fifty thousand to one. We don't know, Rusty. We just don't know."

Vann took a drink from his well-nicked insulated travel mug with the university logo on it and wrinkled his face. "Eww. Cold coffee." He dumped the mug's contents down the sink drain and poured the last of the coffee from the Bunn coffeemaker into the mug. He sipped the hot coffee and smacked his lips in something other than pleasure. "Well, it's hot anyway."

He took another sip and sighed noisily. "God, I would kill for a cup of Starbucks right now. Rusty, it wouldn't even have to be a specialty brand, nothing fancy like that. Just a strong cup of coffee, hot and fresh. Where the fuck is Juan Valdez when I need him?"

The setter stared at him with a face that might have been canine disgust. Or it might have been understanding on some kind of level of primal longing. Those dark eyes were so expressive but so damn hard to read, and the dog sometimes had the disposition of a disingenuous feline.

"I know, Rusty, I know," Vann said. "If we don't know something, what should we do?" He smiled at the dog. "We should learn all we can about that something. We need to learn more about the"—he frowned and mentally sighed as he struggled to actually spit out the words—"the creatures that live in this city with us. And, starting today, that's what we're going to do. Know thy enemy, Rusty. Know thy enemy."

In another lifetime, Arnett had been a professor of English and creative writing as well as a published author. He knew how to methodically and systematically conduct research to write his academic papers and commercial fiction, and it was not a big stretch to put those investigative skills to use in a slightly different capacity. Instead of taking copious notes from library books and websites on the Internet, Vann put his boots on the ground and performed a physical, house-to-house search of all the buildings, about two dozen or so, on the blocks immediately ringing the citadel. He did, however, jot his findings down in a spiral steno notebook for reference in the future—like the leopard's inability to change his spots, some things never change—but what he and Rusty found troubled him.

Some—most, in fact—of the structures had been left alone since they had been abandoned many months earlier. Arnett wouldn't have been surprised if these buildings had not been entered by a human—or a reasonable facsimile thereof—since he, Sylvie, and Hal conducted similar searches shortly after they had staked their claim and taken over Wolveshaven. It had been one of the very first things the trio had done as they went about securing the defensive perimeter around and near their fortress, and the sun had faded the spray painted *X*s on the main doors.

The dust and cobwebs and fallen debris and other detritus of abandonment were undisturbed by any animal that walked upright on two legs. However, five other buildings, each with limited but different views of Wolveshaven, showed the telltale signs of visitation and short-term occupation. There were single-file pathways, clearly visible in a year and a half's worth of dirt and rubbish, which led to the uppermost floor of the structures.

Partially obscured spider lairs provided some cover and minimal comfort for two people had been established at one window in each of the buildings. Each nest had a small stash of supplies— stale energy and granola bars, unopened cans of soda pop and bottles of water, couch or seat cushions and blankets, rudimentary first-aid kits, a *Penthouse* magazine in one and a dog-eared copy of a romance paperback novel—the latest and probably last effort from Jennifer Donnelly—complete with a bookmark about two-thirds of the way through in another. The recon teams had been very careful not to leave trash behind in or near the buildings, but

Vann still found a couple of 3 Musketeers candy bar wrappers on the floor near one of the stakeout hideaways.

Arnett exited the last structure—a three-story office building with a minimal view of Wolveshaven—and stopped on the side-walk. Rusty halted after a couple of strides farther down and peered back at the man. He sighed out loud and an unexpected chill sent a spasm through his core as though a ghost had passed through him. The implications of what he had uncovered terrified him, but it also pissed him off.

The cold, hard, stark reality was that he was under surveillance from five different vantage points around the citadel. Vann didn't know if the surveillance was regularly conducted or randomly undertaken. He didn't know if it took place during the nighttime or in daylight, or both. He didn't even know who conducted the surveillance but suspected it was the Kindred, although the unex-pected stash of food kind of threw him off. He also didn't know why they watched him or what their motives were, but he could fathom a guess and those paranoid-tainted ruminations were not good ones.

Standing in the early afternoon sunshine, with the silence broken only by the noisy chirping of nearby chickadees flittering about, Arnett smiled as he realized that he did have one advantage and it was a big one: he now knew that he was being watched while those doing the surveillance were unaware that he possessed this knowledge. As far as he surmised, his watchers had failed to take advantage of their insight on him. He wouldn't make the same mistake with them.

"Come on, Rusty, we've got things to do"—he winked conspir-atorially and smiled at the red dog—"and plots to scheme."

During the next five hours, as the sun climbed to its zenith and began its descent, the two of them made four trips to Trig and Aar-on's town house and back to Wolveshaven. They scavenged and salvaged pretty anything and everything of value, picking it al-most clean to the bone like turkey vultures with a piece of roadkill.

It was a difficult task, more from an emotional standpoint than a physical one. In these peculiar and dangerous times, Trig and Aaron were his friends—more than casual acquaintances, but less than constant buddies—and they were missing, presumed dead, victims of a very bad and nasty encounter with the Kindred. But what if they weren't? What if they were still alive and in hiding? Was he stealing their supplies and dooming them to the fate he thought they had already encountered? If they were dead at the hands—or, more appropriately, the teeth and claws—of the Kindred, should he rob them? Should their misfortune be his good fortune?

Vann had always felt a twinge or two of discomfort—as if he was immorally and disrespectfully treading on consecrated ground—when he plundered abandoned homes like a pirate in search of ill-gotten treasure and provisions, but he rationalized and justified his actions as the means of his survival. Sure, it was easy to take the moral high ground and be harshly judgmental when you had nothing on the line. Those were luxuries he didn't possess nor could he afford.

So, despite his moral misgivings and ethical awkwardness, he and Rusty made the trip to the town house four times, hauling away strictly utilitarian products: all manner of food (both cans and boxes, not to mention nutritional supplements and vitamins) and beverages (water, soda pop, and alcohol), all the medical supplies (everything from Band-Aids to Vicodin) and dry goods he could find, a couple of small household appliances (an Osterizer blender and a GE toaster) and an assortment of building supplies, all the gasoline he could carry in a half-dozen five-gallon gas cans and spare vehicle parts (two complete sets of Goodyear SUV tires, three heavy-duty Interstate batteries, a couple dozen halogen replacement bulbs, all the Pennzoil motor oil and various Fram filters he uncovered, and gallons of Prestone coolant and generic windshield wash).

Vann avoided all of their personal items and belongings. He just could not bring himself to enter the bedroom they had shared and only passed through the upstairs living room when necessary.

With the back of the Tahoe filled to capacity for the final trip back to his citadel, Arnett nailed the note, written in forty-eight-point Arial type and printed on a piece of heavyweight copy paper, to the front door. He knew it wouldn't survive the elements very long, especially with the arrival of fall and winter chasing it, but he had left an identical one under a paperweight on the antique oak hall tree in the main foyer, just in case. The note was simple and to the point. In the subtly receding sunlight, he read it to himself one last time:

Trig and Aaron—

I don't know where you're at or what happened to you. If either of you reads this, I've removed some of your stuff but you can have it back. You know where I'm at, stop by and see me.

Vann

He had used a black Sharpie—ironically, one he had previously used at his own book signings in another lifetime—to write his first-name signature with its distinctive flourish.

Arnett frowned and turned away, walking slowly toward his heavily laden SUV. Deep inside the dark recesses of his heart, where brutal honesty always prevailed in the constant struggle between unflinching truth and idealistic hope, he didn't believe either Trig or Aaron would ever see the note.

It had been a long and troubling day.

Vann had come to with a hangover and the aftereffects of a vivid flashback burned fresh into the consciousness of his mind like a raw wound. On the bright side, he had been inside the citadel and had not passed out in the front courtyard. He had pondered what had possibly happened to Trig and Aaron, and no matter how he tried to spin it in a positive manner, every scenario he ran through his mind ultimately turned out bad.

He had discovered that someone—probably the Kindred—had been covertly keeping watch on him from several different locations near Wolveshaven for an unknown period of time. They knew far more about him and his habits than he did about them, and that prospect gnawed at him and only served to heighten his sense of paranoia and isolation. It was one thing to be a voyeur, but it was an entirely different thing to be the voyeur's unknown target.

He had spent the afternoon callously picking through and reluctantly szalvaging the useful items that had been left behind at his friends' town house, naïvely hoping that they had gone into hiding or had fled the city but realistically knowing that they were dead. He had felt more like a grave robber looting a pharaoh's tomb than an end-of-the-world survivalist laboring to ensure another day's existence, but he still managed to plod his way through it, despite his heavy heart and weary body.

He had fed Rusty his usual supper, taking a small measure of satisfaction in watching the dog devour it as though he wouldn't get another one. His own meal had been less inspiring but strictly functional: a box of Uncle Ben's long grain and wild rice heated in the microwave and a frozen venison steak, slowly fried in an antique cast-iron skillet with onions, powdered garlic, dried basil, and a healthy blast or two of burgundy. The food had been flavorful, even though his enthusiasm to consume it had been lacking.

With his body nourished and fortified for another day but his soul without salvation or contentment, Arnett sat down with his laptop and opened the Word document that was his journal. After a couple of minutes of thought, he began to write.

Six

I got drunk last night.

I got drunk as a skunk on some fine French vodka—hell, I pounded down almost three quarters of a bottle of Grey Goose while just staring the security monitors—and passed out. Passed out tombstone-cold. Gone. Do not disturb. See ya later, alligator. After a while, crocodile. Adios. Sayonara. Completely out of it. Mentally tabula rasa. The slate wiped clean with an alcohol-soaked sponge. Fortunately for me, I came to inside Wolveshaven and not out in the courtyard like last time. It was really a pretty stupid thing for me to do, and I am just lucky that nothing exorbitantly bad happened while I was off spending time in Drunken Foolsville.

The Kindred didn't show up. The other creatures didn't show up, either. I didn't burn the place down and leave myself homeless—or worse. I didn't break or damage anything. I didn't stumble down any stairs and hurt myself. I didn't choke and die on my own vomit. Hell, I didn't even puke. I didn't go up to the widow's walk and taunt God. I didn't curse him, either. I didn't really even hurt myself, other than a self-inflicted headache and sore body. I guess I had that one coming, but I didn't do anything truly foolish or stupid.

Again, damn lucky.

Little did I know when I woke up suffering from the effects of a hangover—not even a particularly brutal one at that—

that my day was only going to get worse. Didn't seem like it possibly could, but it did. I had been silly for thinking along those lines, and I know better. But it hadn't stopped me, and somehow, some way, the cruel fates that govern my existence had conspired to make things even worse. Yeah, I know, it doesn't quite seem fair, but there isn't much I can do about it. Sometimes the best you can do is be thankful that things didn't turn out worse.

While still pondering what had happened to Trig and Aaron, I had thoughts that were more than a little unsettling. How did the Kindred—if it was indeed them—do what they had done? How did they do it? How did they know when the opportunity presented itself? Was it just dumb luck? Or was it careful planning?

Neither prospect provided any comfort, because I couldn't decide which was worse. Well, in my mind, the only real answer to those questions was that they had been spying on Trig and Aaron, keeping them under surveillance. Which led me to the truly troubling question: if they were watching them, are they watching me?

As much as I hate to admit it, the answer is yes.

To prove it, Rusty and I did our own little recon mission and found not one, not two, but five—for lack of a better term—observation nests in five different buildings around Wolveshaven. None of the nests afforded them a real good view, but they were sufficient to keep a discreet eye on the mansion and what I was doing.

I have to admit, it's damn unsettling to think that I've been under observation for Lord knows how long. My skin crawls just thinking about it. Hey, I'm no prude; in fact, it was a big turn-on when Susannah watched me, but this . . . this is something entirely different. This isn't some kinky little peep show between lovers; this is nothing less than a life-and-death matter.

If I consider it anything less than that, then I'm underestimating the severity of the threat, and those consequences could be fatal, which is what I suspect happened to Trig and Aaron. I doubt they even knew they were being watched. I believe it's the Kindred that have kept an irregular watch on me. Who else could it be? And for some reason, I just don't think they have my best interest in mind. Call me crazy, but I think they mean to do me harm. They are biding their time, waiting for just the right moment to execute their nefarious plan.

Well, fortunately for me, they had their chance, but they blew it.

I scoped out their surveillance windows from the widow's walk, and I've got fairly clear views of all of them. With my night-vision goggles, I will be able to see if they're spying on me, and with the low-light telescopic scope, I will be able to punch somebody's ticket or really give them something to think about with a deliberate near-miss. I now have the drop on them, and I want to keep it that way. If you don't use it, having the advantage really doesn't mean anything.

The rest of the day was difficult. Very difficult.

Rusty and I returned to Trig and Aaron's town house and scavenged everything we needed or could possibly use. It took us four trips in all. It just didn't feel right in my heart and my head, but that didn't stop me. I knew it had to be done; there really wasn't a choice. I'm not so callous as to take satisfaction that their fate is a bonanza for me. I found no fulfillment in it. It's simple: They were my friends, but they're gone now. I can't bring them back, and their supplies and provisions would go to waste if I didn't take them. I guess I felt like a surgeon harvesting organs from the body of a recently deceased donor; even though some good comes from the tragedy, it doesn't lessen the impact of that tragedy on those on the wrong end of it, those who must endure it and carry on with their fractured lives.

Knowing that didn't make me feel any better, it didn't ease my troubled mind or comfort my weary soul, but I am determined to soldier on. It's all I can do . . .

Seven

The view from the widow's walk was spectacular, even if the canvas laid out before him was less than inspiring. It gave him a bird's-eye, three-sixty view of the barren grounds around Wolveshaven and the desolate area beyond the perimeter of the fence lines that led to the dilapidated structures in the distance. Stars, like tiny diamond studs in the ears of an ebony-skinned woman, winked brightly in the black velvet panorama of the night sky.

Darkness enveloped the citadel—there were no working streetlights or any other exterior building lights in the city—and held it close. Sometimes its presence felt like a lover's longing hug while other times it was a rapist's controlling grasp. The air, no longer tainted by vehicle exhaust or smokestack refuse or other parts-per-billion contaminants, was as pure and crisp and refreshing as any found around a mountaintop ski resort, and a deep breath was almost therapeutic, if not downright tantric.

Daytime was quiet, but at night it was utter silence. There was no buzzing traffic noise, no distant blaring sirens, no man-made urban discourse, no soothing New Age earth sounds, no covert sounds of a stalking predatory animal nor panicked screams of its startled prey, no lover's voice that you cherished hearing as she breathlessly whispered your name. There was only stillness.

No longer affected by man's scourge, the earth had begun the process to cleanse itself, purging from its systems all the impurities and blights brought on by him. During the course of the next several years, maybe as much as a decade, it would return to the pristine, arboreal state it had been eons ago, perhaps the way God had intended it to be. As George R. Stewart had written decades earlier, earth abides.

Vann had gotten used to the lack of secondary light during the hours the sun had retreated from the sky, night-vision optics had helped compensate for that, but the lack of sound was all too often unnerving. Having grown up in the high-tech and industrial age of man—a world of never-fast-enough telecommunication and scurrying soccer moms, of unrestrained scientific advancement and uncomplicated global travel, of sound-bite celebrities and self-righteous moralists—he had been surrounded by a cacophony of noise. Whether made by man or nature, direct or indirect, deliberate or unintentional, there had been a blaring soundtrack to his existence, and it had always been there.

Now that it was gone—or replaced by one that was subtler and considerably less intrusive—there seemed to be an unnatural void. Life was supposed to be noisy and loud, but his was not.

And he missed it.

Arnett sighed and gazed up at the stars. The lack of urban light afforded him an unfettered and unimpeded view of the overhead vista, a dark and deep bowl dotted with sharp jewels. His knowledge of constellations was nonexistent—yeah, pretty much like any typical five-year-old, he could locate the Big Dipper and the Little Dipper but not much else—although that didn't stop him from admiring and appreciating their simple beauty from light-years away. He had a half-dozen books on stars and constellations in Wolveshaven's library, but he had never actually gotten around to more than thumbing through any of them. It was one of those things that Vann always meant to do but never seemed to have the chance to actually do. In that respect, his life had not changed at all, just his priorities.

He returned his attention to a less infinite view and sighed. *This is some life I lead*, he thought. *Some life, indeed.*

His earlier surreptitious survey of the five spotters' nests had yielded nothing. All of them were unoccupied—at least they had been at that time, but he doubted the status had changed much in the past hour or so—and there were no signs of anyone or anything moving into position. Vann was actually kind of disappointed about that. He had been hoping to see someone or *something* in one of the outposts. Yeah, it was petty, but what was the point of having an advantage if he was unable to actually use it? What good was it if he couldn't lord it over somebody else?

He sighed loudly and pursed his lips, contemplating going back inside the citadel for a little while. The temperature had been slowly dropping since the sun dipped below the western horizon, and he considered putting on a field jacket over his body armor or maybe grabbing a blanket to wrap around him like a cloak. At his feet, Rusty, who had been lounging comfortably and quietly cleaning his forepaws, perked to attention.

"Uh-oh," Arnett said, glancing down at the dog and then back at the courtyard and beyond. "What is it, Rusty? What's got your attention?"

The dog sprang to its feet and a moment later put its front paws atop the sandbags behind the wrought-iron railing. His canine eyes searched and scoured the darkness for visual confirmation, while his hypersensitive nose sniffed and probed the gentle breeze to draw a more focused bead on the scents it had already picked up.

"What is it, Rusty?" Vann repeated the question but pretty much already knew the answer. This was not the first time this scene had played out. His heart rate accelerated just a bit as he slipped the military-issue night-vision goggles over his head, placing them on his eyes, activated the device, and adjusted the dials to sharpen the focus. With one hand atop the sandbags to guide him along and careful not to trip over the dog, he slowly circled the widow's walk after taking a moment or two to allow his eyes to adjust. The luminous, green landscape that panned out before him did not reveal what he searched for, displaying only an eerie and ethereal view of a nightmarish still-life world that no artist's imagination could conjure, much less accurately capture.

Vann heard them before he actually saw them.

"*ARRRR–netttt!*"

It was the singsong siren call of a female member of the Kindred. It was always the same female who announced their arrival, part Midway hawker and part Tokyo Rose but one hundred percent alabaster-skinned seductress. Vann even recognized her from her previous life. Shari Landry had been a rising-star television reporter with one of the local stations, a long and tall and curvy brunette in her late twenties with runway model looks and a smoky voice more suited for one-nine-hundred work than TV news. She had been an excellent reporter, but that wasn't really why local viewers had tuned in to watch her. He had to reluctantly acknowledge and tip his hat to their strategy. The Kindred knew which buttons to push and attempted to exploit what they thought was his biggest weakness. They were right about his major fault, of course, but he was also much stronger than they actually gave him credit for. And, besides, much to his dismay, the siren never took her clothes off and cavorted naked for him.

"*ARRRR–nnnnett!*"

A group of about twenty of them came into view from the southwest, approaching from the area of the capitol square. They hooted and hollered like drunken college students celebrating after their team had won the big football game. This was a smaller gathering than usual, although he suspected that it would probably double in size as the night wore on.

As Rusty softly growled at the creatures, he watched them draw closer for a couple of heartbeats and then felt and scurried his way to the other side of the widow's walk. Arnett searched the open terrain beyond the fence line, seeking out any movement in the luminous landscape. Just like most every other time, there was none. There was no attempt to sneak up behind him while the others distracted him with their provocative catcalls and lewd striptease acts. The couple of times that they had actually tried, that maneuver had resulted badly for them, as in Little Bighorn badly.

"*ARRRR–nnnnett!*"

Vann scrambled back to the other side of the walk and scanned the group as they moved closer. He counted only four warriors among their number, all of them armed with either bows or crossbows, while one also carried a sheathed long-bladed sword. If the shit hit the fan, he was the one going down first, Arnett thought. Shari was in charge, but he was the lead warrior in this motley crew.

"Hold down the fort, Rusty, I'm gonna turn on the fence."

He pushed the night-vision goggles atop his head and disappeared through the door that led back into the mansion and the stairwell that went down. A couple of minutes later, the hum of the rooftop solar batteries, which had been as inaudible as a bumblebee passing in the distance, picked up in intensity as an electric current was sent through the innermost fence ring, increasing the output more than twofold. The defensive perimeters had never been breached to that point, but he was not about to take a chance. Deviation from practiced and tested routines was never advisable in life-or-death situations. A moment or two passed, and Vann emerged through the doorway, not even out of breath.

"Hey, Rusty, did you miss me?"

The dog ignored him and kept his eyes on the slowly approaching group of the Kindred. They had almost reached the point where they usually stopped to gather and taunt him. He was not the only slave to a routine.

"*ARRRR*–nnnnett!"

"Ah, Shari's in fine voice tonight, Rusty. Fine, fine voice. Do you think she'll take her clothes off for us?"

The setter cast him a quick, indecipherable glance and then returned to his vigil along the sandbags. He, apparently, did not have time to deal with that particular carnal element of human nature.

"No, I don't think she will, either." Arnett stared out into the darkness, knowing where the creatures were but not really seeing them in the murky din of charcoal-colored shadows. "Shame, though. Damn shame."

"Arnett! Come out and play!"

He sighed, removed the goggles from his head, and hung them up on a hook near the door. Vann was fastidious about putting things in their place—especially those items he had deemed as vital to his survival—and had screwed in four hooks around the exterior of the widow's walk so he always knew where the night-vision optics were.

A 50-caliber military-issue sniper rifle, with a sleek PVS29 night-vision sight attached to it, was kept from April through October in a gun rack just inside the door to the widow's walk, always within quick and easy reach. You just never knew when you might want or need to get your hands on it in short order, especially if it was not already slung over your shoulder.

He stepped back to the doorway, plucked the heavy but perfectly balanced rifle from its post, and returned to his spot along the sandbags. He uncovered the lenses of the scope and raised the weapon to his shoulder, resting the long barrel atop a sandbag. A moment later he had several of them centered in the gun sight.

They appeared almost larger than life in the enhanced field of vision, raucously milling about like rioters in search of an ignition spark. Arnett knew they would get rowdy and insulting—and then obscene—but that would be pretty much it. The Kindred knew their limitations and normally never went past them. Still, you just never knew.

"*Arrrr*–nnnnett!" Shari called out to him. "Come out, come out, wherever you are!"

He smiled and seconds later sighted the rifle on her. The former TV reporter wore a long and dark leather duster over an equally dark turtleneck sweater, blue jeans, and low-heeled boots. It was the rage among the fashion-conscious Kindred elite. Even with no makeup on her face and her long hair finger-combed, she was a very attractive woman. He felt an unwanted tickle of lust stirring in his balls and an unexpected flutter of emotion in his heart.

"Fuck," Arnett grumbled more than spoke.

Almost as if she knew he was watching her, Shari brazenly flipped him the bird and sneered in contempt. He chuckled and grinned. Hell, he had been a professor in another lifetime and had dealt with more irate college students who thought they deserved a better grade for substandard work than he cared to admit. Vann inhaled deeply of the cold night air, held and warmed it in his lungs to steady himself, and slowly pulled the trigger.

CLICK!

Arnett had known the safety was on but he squeezed the firing lever anyway, partly just to see if he could actually do it while the crosshairs were centered on her heart. He also knew, however, it was easier than it would have been if the safety had not been engaged because there were be no life-and-death consequences for either of them. Deep in his heart of hearts, with the safety off, he didn't know if he could actually pull the trigger on her or not. He told himself that he could, but he just did not know. And it was that little uncertainty, that nagging little doubt that bothered him like a tiny pebble inside his shoe during a long walk.

"Luckiest Kindred bitch in the city," Vann muttered under his breath as he watched her turn and say something to the lead warrior and scrawny goth teenaged girl who stood nearby. "She just doesn't know it." He lowered the rifle and winked at her. "I own you now, Shari. I had your life in my hands and spared you. I spared you, and now I *own* you. You owe me, bitch. Your life is mine."

He slung the rifle over his shoulder, plucked the NOGs from their hook, and placed them back over his eyes. Arnett blinked several times as his eyes adjusted to the new, optically enhanced view.

"I think it's gonna be a long night, Rusty."

And it was.

A dozen or so non-warrior male Kindred and several females had spent the first couple of hours of their evening visit verbally taunting him. They called him out for a fight, questioning his manhood. They challenged his machismo, screaming out that he was a gutless coward. They loudly pondered the sanity of his decision to take refuge in the fortress, urging him to give up his hopeless struggle. And they occasionally launched the odd-out rock or chunk of brick in the direction of the mansion, but each fell woefully short of Wolveshaven, landing harmlessly in the courtyard. All in all, it was a pretty juvenile and futile attempt to provoke a response from him.

As the evening relentlessly wore on like a bad movie you just could not seem to force yourself to walk out on, the tenor of their taunts changed from empty bravado to risqué innuendo to blatant sexual pandering. The transformation was inevitable—maybe even anticipated, although he would be reluctant to admit that one—but that didn't make their striptease acts that ultimately deteriorated into vignettes of provocative solo sex or unrestrained animalistic couplings any less bothersome or arousing for him.

The Kindred knew he was safely stashed behind the walls of his fortress, keeping a watchful eye on them, so they performed exclusively for him. They had long ago realized they couldn't strike at him physically, so they attacked and punished him in a different capacity.

Arnett couldn't help but stare as many of the women and a handful of men took turns exposing their unnaturally pale bodies to him with wanton lust and unashamed disregard for modesty. He could only gawk at their brazen displays and gape at their salacious performances, wrestling with his own longing desire for emotional closeness and aching need for physical intimacy.

He could *not* help but watch them.

It wasn't that the women were hard-bodied and plastic-surgery-enhanced beauties who worked the poles and lap-danced in gentlemen's clubs or the buff and clean-shaven studs who hip-swayed and stripped down to their white-toothed smiles in taverns during deer-hunter-widows' weekends. Nor did they radiate a potent sexual energy or ignite illicit thoughts of erotic fantasies.

No, they appeared malnourished and unkempt, pallid—regardless of ethnicity—and almost sickly. Their looks—whether pretty or homely, handsome or ugly—had been altered by the plague, facial features becoming gaunt and subtly more pronounced as angles and curves sharpened. They moved with an uncanny, animal-like fluidity as if some viral parasite controlled their motor skills.

In his mind, the Kindred were just not *quite* human, but that didn't stop Vann from watching them through night-vision optics as the creatures unabashedly performed in open view on the street below. More often than he cared to admit, he found himself lost in their uncontrolled and reckless sexual behavior, drifting away as his blood flooded to points south of the border with a predictable effect. He was human, after all.

The Kindred males were bad, but the females were far worse. They touched a dark and secret spot in him that he didn't like to confess that he possessed. The women brazenly exposed themselves to him and satisfied their primal urges with single-minded vigor and a greedy, frenetic urgency that would have made a porn star blush. Arnett was a captive audience, so they went out of their way to show him what they could give him—would give him—if only he walked away from the barricades of Wolveshaven.

Part of him—just a tiny sliver, like a fragment of mental shrapnel in a tormented recess of his psyche—ached to abandon the protection and isolation of the citadel, to join the Kindred and lose himself in their perverse and deviant carnival of sexual lust. Those thoughts slipped unwanted and unannounced into his consciousness, hesitated for just a moment or two in the forefront of his brain, and flittered away like butterflies in a summer breeze. It was just enough to force him to shake his head and turn away from the wicked orgiastic spectacle that Caligula would have been proud of.

Arnett endured their sexual antics and taunts for several hours, wrestling with his own demons and struggling to stay awake and working hard to stay warm. An hour or so before the eastern sky showed the first hints of dawn, the Kindred began to slip away in the still unrelenting darkness, while the others gathered up their discarded clothes, many of them wandering away without bothering to put them back on.

Much to his annoying disappointment, Shari Landry, the goth teen, the lead warrior, and another Kindred soldier had silently disappeared in the din without his notice, but two warriors remained until the last of the creatures began to slink away like burglars who had encountered an impenetrable home security system.

The sun had crested the horizon less than an hour earlier, initially blossoming pink like the inside of a woman's rose before offering up rays of muted sunlight that would illuminate but not warm the day. Vann wearily stumbled into the main room on the third floor.

The Irish setter slowly trotted beside him. Like a soldier returning from patrol, he dropped his rattling and clattering battle gear on the hardwood floor beside the sofa, peeled off his body armor and deposited that atop the rest of it, then stretched in a futile attempt to work the kinks out of neck, shoulders, and back.

He was dog tired—in fact, he was more fatigued than Rusty—having spent the entire night up in the widow's walk spying on the Kindred. He had become accustomed to functioning on little sleep, sneaking a two- to four-hour power nap when the opportunity presented itself during the day, but never going without any sleep at all. Arnett slumped down to the sofa with a groan.

"Oh, oh, Rusty, I don't think this was a good idea."

The dog merely stared at him with unreadable dark eyes. The setter might as well have been a statue or the excellent work of a taxidermist.

"Not a good idea."

He sighed loudly and swung his legs up onto the seat cushions. A moment later he slowly slid back and lay flat with his head resting on the arm, precipitating another sigh.

"Nope," he mumbled, already half-asleep but fighting it, "not a good idea at all."

Despite a valiant struggle, gravity won out and inexorably pulled his eyelids down over his eyes. And kept them down. A comforting darkness embraced his field of vision and blotted out the world. Less than two minutes later, Vann was sound asleep.

Rusty padded over to the side of the sofa and lay down. After a moment's hesitation, he placed his mahogany muzzle on his fore-paws. The dog moaned softly as if to assure Arnett that he wouldn't fall asleep but remain vigilant.

It had been a canine display of domesticity that had been re-played countless times throughout the eons of the interdependent relationship between the two, a nearly silent oath of loyalty and de-votion from dog to man. It was, however, an extremely rare show of attachment and affection from this setter to the man who had taken him in.

And Vann missed it entirely.

EIGHT

Arnett gathered up his belongings—a spiral-bound notebook, manila folders with papers stuffed haphazardly in them, and a grading book—and placed them inside a black canvas Lands' End attaché case. He carefully stacked them atop the Dell laptop that occupied its own padded compartment within the bag.

"Professor Arnett, do you have a minute?" a female voice asked him.

Vann looked up from his task and saw a pretty, fair-skinned coed in her early twenties standing next to him in front of the desk. Shoulder-length dark hair cascaded around her heart-shaped face, brown eyes were set atop high cheekbones, while a narrow and straight nose complemented seductively full lips and a more-than-kissable pointy chin.

She was tall and thin, and her fashionable attire—an un-zippered blue Aeropostale hoodie with layered crop-topped T-shirts of white and light blue along with hip-hugger khaki capri pants—only accentuated the shapely curves of her body. She wore white flip-flops on her feet, and a hot pink and black book bag was slung casually over her shoulder.

He had to force his eyes to meet her gaze and not let them wander down to the swell of her breasts pushing against the thin cotton of the layered tops or the tiny, silver dolphin in her pierced belly button below the hem of her T-shirts.

"Sure, Alicia, I've got some time," Van said. "What can I do for you?"

"I've talked with my friend Colin—Colin Parkhurst, he's a graphic design major and a really talented artist—and he is willing to do the drawings for my story."

"Okay, that sounds good. I think it will add even more depth and texture to your story. How many drawings are you looking to have included, and what kind of timeline did he give you?"

"I'm looking to have three or four full-page, color drawings and about a half-dozen to ten smaller black-and-white ones included in the body of the story. We met last week to discuss some of my ideas for the drawings, and he's already started on about half of the smaller ones and has done some initial sketches for the full-page drawings."

"Wow, I'm impressed."

Alicia smiled shyly at him, flashing her cosmetically whitened and orthodontically straightened teeth. "Colin likes me and"—she shrugged and almost blushed—"and I guess by doing this project for me he thinks he stands a better chance of . . . oh, I don't know . . . of landing me as a girlfriend." The young woman unconsciously moved back a half step but then covertly swayed forward about a foot.

She stood less than a yard away from him, and Vann could smell the shampoo scent that lingered in her hair and the body lotion she had rubbed on her skin. Neither was unpleasant. He made a conscious effort to casually sit down on the desk, acutely aware of Alicia's presence in front of him.

Interacting with attractive coeds on a regular basis was an occupational hazard, but Arnett was a tenured professional educator at a major university. Plus he was happily married to a red-hot redhead. He always made it a point to meet with the women and men he mentored either in a classroom, a lecture hall, or his office when there were secretaries and other staff members around.

Still, he was grateful for the fact he was not a professor in one of the schools in the Art Department. He and Susannah never missed an on-campus exhibit, so he was aware of what went on in those studios. Some of the work was provocative, while other pieces were simply erotically enticing, and many of the artists used models who attended class on campus. He always felt awkward when he encountered one of those students whose nude image he had seen in an exhibit.

Against his better judgment, he asked, "And you don't want that, do you?"

She hesitated, organizing her thoughts so her answer did not sound too shallow or superficial. "Colin is a nice guy, but . . . but he's not the guy for me. He . . ."

Before Alicia could continue, Arnett interrupted, "That won't cause any problems with the two of you working together on your project?"

"No," she answered, shaking her head. "He knows how I feel, but . . . he still likes to hang around with me and my friends."

"You sure?"

"Yeah."

"Okay."

"Don't get me wrong, he is a nice guy and all, but—"

"I understand." Vann wanted to divert the course of the conversation quickly. "I just don't want this to adversely affect your project. I'd hate for you to have it nearly finished and then have some problems with the 'artist.'"

Alicia smiled again and shook her head. "It won't be a problem. He's getting the artwork done faster than I could have imagined and . . . well, if he does become a prick about it, I can always turn it in to you without the drawings."

"Yes, that's always an option. How is your writing coming along?"

She was enrolled in an upper-level fiction-writing class where every student's final project was a minimum twenty-page short story. Genre did not matter, but the structure and quality of the writing did. Alicia had chosen to write a vampiric horror story in the vein of Steve Niles's *30 Days of Night* and have it illustrated in a style similar to Ben Templesmith, whose artwork had enhanced the graphic novel series. It was an ambitious plan and one that she had hopes for beyond the scope of his course.

Alicia smiled and edged forward closer to him. Her upper right thigh was less than six inches from his left knee and leg, which dangled over the edge of the desk and fell just short of reaching the floor.

"I've got the outline completed and I'm adding just a little depth to it," she said, "but I can turn that in any time you want it. I'm also fleshing out my characters a little more, developing and writing some of their backstories."

"Very good." Arnett was uncomfortably aware of how close the young woman was to him. It was unsettling. "I'd like to see what you've got . . . what you've written so far."

"I can do that," Alicia said. She closed the small distance between them, her hip brushing against his knee as she pressed her torso against his. Sexual heat radiated off her as her breasts touched his chest and her hips made provocative contact with him.

"A-A-Alicia . . ." Vann muttered as he attempted to slide back on the desktop.

She wrapped her left arm around his shoulders and pulled him tight, bending her head down toward his face and licking her lips with the tip of her bubblegum-pink tongue. She pushed her pelvis against his groin, and he involuntarily flinched.

Arnett snapped awake on the sofa in the main room on the third floor of Wolveshaven, amber light spilling into the room from high angles through the western windows.

"What the . . ."

He shook his head to clear the cobwebs of dream-sleep and struggled to sit up, fighting against the large and soft cushions of the couch. As he moved, his lower back screamed with the ache from having spent too much time sleeping in an unusual position.

Rusty, who had been prone on the floor near the sofa, effortlessly rose to his feet and enthusiastically stretched the way only animals can.

"Where in the hell did that come from?" Vann asked and rubbed the long whiskers on his chin. He could have made the comment to the dog, but he was hardly even aware the canine was in the room.

He had more pressing matters on his mind. Vann wanted to ponder and analyze his somnambulistic wanderings before this new and wholly unexpected tale faded into the backwater nothingness of his mind. He searched his brain for shreds and tidbits of the dream, trying to remember the details, to scrutinize them, to distinguish fancy from reality.

Arnett had had plenty of female students—more than half of those who took the writing courses he taught, actually—but he could not recall anyone named Alicia nor could he bring to mind one who looked like the young woman in his dream. He had had female students flirt with him, some of them pretty outrageously, but none ever took their harmless advances to less than innocent physical contact.

Only one student had ever approached him about having illustrations accompany the final short story, and that had been a young man who was writing a story and creating artwork from the Japanese anime, *Ghost in the Shell*, and he had done everything himself. He remembered the young man's work. It had been a so-so story with okay writing but his illustrations had been top-notch, so Vann had rewarded his effort with an A-minus. Nothing from his teaching career served as the impetus for this dream.

He sighed and slumped back into the couch with a groan. *Who was she?*

And then it hit him: the young woman in his dream was the female from the mall. It had to be her. Arnett was certain of it—she could be no one else.

Because of the protective clothing she had worn, he had not gotten an unobstructed look at her face in the din of the mall, but he had seen enough to know or at least think that she was pretty, and the features and details he did not know, his mind had been more than willing to fill in and embellish. He knew the two women were about the same height and, despite the layers of baggy clothing the young woman in the mall had worn, he presumed they had the same body build. He surmised—based on nothing more than his gut feeling or maybe a sensation a smidge further south—that they were roughly the same age.

It had to be her, his mind told him. It just *had* to be.

Satisfied with his deductions about the identity of his mystery dream woman, Vann was left to ponder the significance or irrelevance of the dream. Why did he dream about her? Who was she? Was there a message in the dream? A warning? A prediction? What did it *really* mean? Did it mean anything? Or was it just a dream?

Questions. Questions. And more questions.

It seemed that his life had become little more than an ongoing series of troubling questions to which he had no logical or meaningful answers. Something as innocuous as a dream—not even an erotic wet dream, mind you—should not generate this many unanswered questions. During these dangerous times, if one was not careful or wary, unanswered questions were only a couple of heartbeats away from becoming unexpected problems, and the last thing Arnett wanted to have to deal with was unforeseen problems. Such problems were . . . well . . . problems. They created disruptions that interfered with the structure and regiment of his life, and these unexpected disruptions could be fatal.

He believed in his heart and head that such a disruption had proven to be fatal to Trig and Aaron, and Vann had vowed to learn from their mistake. He could not shake the tickling sensation that this was the vanguard of a monumental change. He prayed it was something positive and not the calm before the storm.

All of this because of a troubling dream? Crazy.

Arnett needed to clear his mind. He need to get his head in order, or at least less out of order. He had too many thoughts beyond his control cluttering his mind and clouding his judgment. That was an invitation to disaster. He needed to simplify and streamline what was transpiring in his head. Vann wanted to sort it out and get a better handle on it. He didn't like puzzle pieces that did not fit. He had a difficult time accepting random coincidence as the reason for anything, much less everything. And during the past few days, there had just been way too much weird shit taking place in the city for all of it to be random coincidence.

Vann did a double take as he passed the floor-length mirror in the open foyer of the main entrance to the mansion. He didn't recognize the soldier-image reflecting back at him. The man wore a rag-gedly trimmed full beard under long, sandy brown hair that had been the victim of a self-inflicted haircut. The visible skin of his face was taut and tanned and weathered, while the blue eyes were as weary and troubled as a restless ghost's. As he moved nearer to the glass, well-defined muscles rippled like serpents beneath a black Under Armour shirt that led to a tapered waist, while ur-ban-camouflaged combat pants, cinched tight by a military belt, led down to scuffed and battered combat boots that had once been highly polished black leather. A fully loaded, dark backpack was slung over one shoulder, body armor was carried in one hand and an assault rifle in the other.

Arnett stared at the man, who appeared to be part of some ragtag militia unit in Eastern Europe at the tail end of the last cen-tury. He stepped even closer to the mirror, never taking his eyes off the image.

"Who the hell are you?" he asked in a hoarse whisper but got no response.

He couldn't recall the last time he had actually looked at him-self, *really* studied his physique. He was surprised. Vann knew he had lost weight—courtesy of the End-of-the-World Diet Plan, he had joked to himself on more than one occasion—but not as much as he would have if he had not bulked up from regular year-round workouts on the Bowflex Xtreme, summer rides through the city on a Trek hybrid, and winter cruises around the neighborhood on Fischer cross-country skis.

Not having stepped on a scale in more than two years, he es-timated that he had lost upward of fifty pounds during the past eighteen months. He had not been in this kind of physical condi-tion and aerobic form in the past twenty years—if ever.

As impressive as his physical transformation was from over-weight college English professor to hard-body apocalyptic survivor, his gaze was inexorably drawn to his own face and eyes. He couldn't help but stare at the azure orbs, at them but not into their depth. There was a war-weary fatigue to his eyes. They weren't completely empty and lifeless, mind you, but they were sufficiently drained of energy and vitality. His eyes were pained. They had witnessed too much death, too much senseless violence, too much suffering. They had seen *too* much. If the eyes were, indeed, the windows to the soul, then Arnett's soul was a tortured and tormented one haunted by, as Poe had written, ill angels only.

"What have I become?"

He received no answer from the ghost in the mirror and sighed loudly. It was a weary and pessimistic sound.

"Who the fuck am I?"

Vann easily slipped the contoured shift lever into the next gear, while at the same time his right foot eased the accelerator down and his left popped the clutch up. The high-end German precision sports car responded as if it were an extension of his body and mind. The change in speed was hardly noticeable as the increased G-force guided him back into the leather seat. Even though he had not performed these maneuvers for several months, the practiced routine came back to him, without the jerks and jolts of badly timed shifting and clutching. Once learned, the hand and foot-work were *never* forgotten.

A breathless heartbeat later, he shifted the Porsche Cayman S into fourth gear as he sluiced the smooth-as-silk sports car around a forever-dead and rusting SUV that had taken up permanent residence on the inside lane of the four-lane highway that traversed the south side of the city. It seemed as though the silver car operated on rails. He drove like a madman desperately trying to escape the pallid-faced ghouls of his waking nightmares. They were an ever-present and unyielding anchor around his neck that continually threatened to drag him down under the dark water and drown him.

Vann counted on German automotive engineering at its finest to distract his fragmented brain from the numbing problems at hand, and he was not disappointed. The sports car accomplished that mission in spades.

He downshifted and slipped the Porsche off the main arterial that in another age would have been clogged with bumper-to-bumper traffic throughout much of the day. He power-slid the sports car through a left turn onto the U.S. highway that led out of the city, ignoring the non-functioning stoplights that were suspended above the roadway. Vann speed-shifted the car up two gears and raced westbound on the multi-lane highway. He ran every stoplight as he blew out of the city and bypassed its western suburbs, never hesitating for an instant as he flew through the regulated intersections.

A moment later, the typical commercial cityscape adjacent to the highway was transformed into the ever-expanding urban residential sprawl. Near-identical single-family, two-story homes dominated the large tracts of one-time prime farmland that had been converted into housing developments. He hardly noticed as the subdivisions gave way to neglected farm fields still awaiting spring planting from eighteen months earlier and untended pastures, where only the heartiest of livestock that had survived last winter and predators grazed on diminishing alfalfa and increasing wild grasses.

The speedometer's needle danced around one hundred miles per hour—far below the Cayman's top speed of about one-seventy—as Arnett piloted the sports car effortlessly past the exits that had led to small but onetime thriving towns west of the city. He itched to slip the car into sixth gear and push it closer to its top-end capabilities, but he knew such a move would be a risky gambit. The highway's concrete surface, with no Department of Transportation or county highway department maintenance, had cracked and pot-holed from the elements, and Lord knew what else had fallen across it since he had last been out this far out of the city. He had to be content inching the needle a little further into triple digits while roadside scenery blurred past him.

What a rush! he thought and then screamed the words out loud.

His heart thumped rapidly in his chest like a caged bird, and he could hear his blood pulsing through his ears above the wind rushing past the open windows. Pure, uncut adrenaline surged through his veins. What a rush, indeed. Vann felt alive as he tempted death.

His soul was invigorated as he danced on a high wire suspended above oblivion of the greatest mystery.

Dodging the occasional pothole and weaving around the odd-out obstacle on the pavement, the Cayman zoomed westward. It streaked past the small towns that the four-lane had bypassed in the name of progress and transportation efficiency. With his eyes virtually glued to the highway, Arnett did not pay attention to, much less acknowledge, the weathered and fading reflective green road signs that announced the exits to the empty husks of these dead communities. He didn't notice the different-colored strata of rock in the limestone walls as the sports car plunged into the valley west of the small city that had been home to a different campus in the state's university system.

Moments later the sleek Porsche rocketed nearly silently out of the valley. Only when he realized that the large metal and concrete bridge looming over the big river was rapidly approaching in the distance did Vann consider slowing the car down, but he did so reluctantly. He eased off the gas pedal and downshifted, eventually stopping the Cayman in the middle of the expanse of the divided four-lane bridge. He was literally and figuratively between states.

Arnett got out of the car and with shaky legs walked over to the bridge railing. Rusty followed him out of the Porsche but shied away from the edge of the bridge, preferring to keep a safe distance from the open space beyond it.

Vann took a deep breath, held it for a handful of seconds, and let it out slowly. He repeated the process a couple of times, extending the duration a little bit with each one, before the quivering in his legs began to ease up. It was as if the blood had begun to replace the adrenaline in his limbs. He pushed his Oakley sunglasses up on top of his head and stared down at the muddy water a hundred feet below him.

The river was unchanged but always different as its waters inexorably flowed south.

Golden sunlight winked and shimmered like Fourth of July sparklers across the top of millions of ripples in the murky water, which was cleaner than it had been for decades. Buoys still marked the navigation channel for barge use, although no barge had operated in these waters for a year and a half. The surface of the river was void of trolling pleasure crafts, cruising speedboats, and racing Jet Skis. No anglers patiently tested their skills and tackle gear from the riverbank in hopes of landing a trophy catch. The small arboreal park and campground on the western shoreline was barren and empty of visible life except for five white-tailed deer that had been grazing on the long grass but stared guardedly at the man and dog. The eastern outskirts of the onetime river port city—a conglomeration of commercial, industrial, and recreational endeavors—were devoid of all signs of human activity and inhabitation as far as the eye could see.

Arnett frowned and sighed in bewilderment at his own folly. He did not know what he had hoped to accomplish with his reckless hundred-plus-mile mad dash—much less if he had actually achieved that unknown objective—but it had given him a pulse-raising thrill, one that had gotten his blood throbbing and made him feel alive. It also crashed down on his brain that this insane sprint across half the state had been a fool's errand, something incredibly dangerous and potentially life-threatening. It could have been fatal.

It had been dumb. Irresponsible. Stupid. Careless. Unthinking. Idiotic. He knew, unfortunately, the list could go on and on and on.

Standing on that steel-and-concrete structure near the edge of a city that was dead and gone, Vann stared down at the water of the big river gently flowing far beneath the bridge, and one startling thought came to mind from nowhere: *I am alive.* A grin creased the lower quarter of his face. *I am alive.* Three simple words, but they meant everything to him.

I am alive.

In the late afternoon sunlight, he silently vowed to do whatever it took to remain that way, to stay alive, to keep on living. For the first time in many, many months, Arnett felt that he actually had something to live for, something more than just a day-to-day and hand-to-mouth survival. It was a feeling of hope. He had decided to live his life, not just exist.

Nine

Arnett's next seven days passed in a blur of cautious optimism and broken routine.

Even though the Kindred failed to show up at any time during the ensuing week, he and Rusty vigilantly stood guard atop the widow's walk every night, armed and ready for action, and then religiously checked the fortifications each morning. As expected, the defenses were undisturbed. During daylight hours, however, Vann and the Irish setter prowled the city's West Side commercial region for hours on end, wandering through the mall and reconnoitering in the adjacent multi-level buildings that at one time housed service businesses, restaurants, and strip malls over a several block radius.

It was no big secret what he was doing. He could finally admit it to himself. His desire and curiosity had gotten the better of him, and he had given in to them. Vann was searching, fretfully scouring the area for some kind of sign, any indication of where the young woman—he couldn't bring himself to refer to her as a *creature*—and her people had settled.

He hoped for another chance encounter with her, one that relied less on happenstance and more on planning. He craved social contact with the young woman. The opportunity to talk with her, to converse and interact like two normal people, despite the Book of Revelation's apocalyptic panorama.

It was that simple.

He was not overly discouraged—mildly disappointed, yes— when he could find no significant trace of them in the stores of the mall or the adjacent buildings. He had located some of their traps but had been careful not to examine the snares or baited live traps too closely for fear of disturbing them and rendering them useless.

Arnett had contemplated leaving a note near the mall's Pac-Sun outlet but dismissed the idea without much of a mental argument. He just didn't know who or what would find the message and what its reaction to it would be. Hell, for that matter, he wasn't even certain what the young woman's reaction would be to such a gesture, so he did nothing.

Undaunted, Vann continued his quixotic quest with a sense of optimism and hope, rather than desperation and fear.

He stood in the street as the late afternoon sun stretched and elongated shadows across the concrete sidewalk and on to the paved roadway in a mixed commercial-residential area on the city's near west side, head cocked and ears strained to hear the noise, if there were any sounds to actually hear.

Was his imagination playing tricks on him? Wouldn't be the first time that had ever happened. Or was it just wishful thinking? Not that that scenario had never played out before, either. Or had he actually heard something that he had not heard for many, many months? He could no longer distinguish between reality and pipe dream.

Arnett frowned as he concentrated and refocused his attention to his ears, struggling to hear it, willing himself to locate the sound—if, indeed, it actually existed—and even going so far as to hold his breath. In the receding sunlight, he stood stone-quiet and statue-still. He thought he could just make out faint echoes in the distant cityscape, a dying sonic mirage moving away from where he stood. But could he really hear it or was his mind playing cruel tricks on him?

He and Rusty had been on the top floor of a three-story building that had an eclectic pottery gallery on the ground floor and overpriced apartments that had been rented by college students on the upper two levels. It had not been a systematic and thorough search, but, instead, an unfocused and meandering one. Vann still approached each of these explorations with extreme caution. He had no desire to stumble into a makeshift booby trap left behind by the Kindred or tumble through a floor weakened by the elements and neglect.

He had been surveying the ruins of an unkempt kitchen when he thought he heard it, a sound he had not heard for many long months and one he was not sure he would ever hear again. Arnett, mouth open and eyes wide with surprise, had stopped dead in his tracks, his right arm holding the flashlight out in mid-sweep. He stood deathly still as seconds noiselessly ticked past amid the domestic ruins, listening for the steady drone like rolling thunder on the distant horizon.

His mind raced on far ahead of his common sense. As his heart rate quickened, he willed himself to slow down, but he was confident he could identify its source. Vann was certain he had heard the sounds of an automotive engine, one that powered the likes of a motorcycle, or an all-terrain vehicle or even a tiny compact car. He just knew it.

"Rusty," he called out tentatively, acutely aware that his voice had shattered the fragile silence.

A moment or two later the dog padded into the kitchen doorway.

"Did you hear it?" he asked.

The Irish setter stoically declined to answer the question and stared blankly at him.

"Goddamn it," Arnett said, muttering mostly under his breath, and quickly headed out of the kitchen.

He had exited the building less than two minutes later and jogged down the street a block and a half. Rusty followed a couple of steps behind him, not sure what to make out of all this commotion. Arnett halted to listen briefly and took off at a faster clip, covering another two blocks before he trotted to a stop in the middle of the street.

"Goddamn it, Rusty," Vann grumbled in annoyed frustration but not vindictively at the dog after several silent and agonizing minutes of trying to snag a blip of unexpected sound. He no longer heard the dull but distant hum of an engine—*if* he actually had heard it in the first place—and wondered if his wishful and imaginative subconscious had deceived his ears like a cat toying with a mouse.

The Irish setter trotted past him, nose down to the pavement in search of something. Rusty was no criminal-chasing bloodhound—hell, Arnett did not know if the setter had been a field-trial champion or merely someone's cherished pet in his past life—but he was a bird dog with a canine's acute sense of smell. And the animal had picked up the scent of something.

Mahogany-colored head swaying back and forth while its tail stood at attention, the setter drifted along the street for a few seconds in a lazy zigzag before hesitating as if to take a moment to process new data. Unexpectedly, the dog raised its head and looked over its shoulder at Arnett. The meaning of the gesture was unmistakable: *Come here.*

"What did you find, Rusty?" Vann asked as he walked toward the dog. "What'd you find?"

The Irish setter returned his attention to something on the ground near the street's curb and gutter, instinctively holding point.

A smile creased Arnett's face as he stopped alongside the dog. "That's it? That's what you found?" He crouched down beside the animal and quickly patted its head before the dog could move away. "Good boy, Rusty. Good boy." The setter hesitated an instant, as if some distant memory had kicked in, reminding him that this was how it had been many months earlier, before trotting a couple steps away.

Vann picked up the small, white object and examined it. He would have never seen it, if it had been left up to his senses. Only the dog's keen olfactory capacity had detected it. He sniffed it and smelled a distinct aroma that mingled with fading heat. It was a scent he had not smelled for almost a year and a half. He had been a snob about it in another lifetime, but he was silently pleased, especially at the implication of what it meant. Arnett chuckled to himself and shook his head at the irony.

"Do you know what this means, Rusty?"

The setter stared at him but did not answer.

"Do you *know* what this means?"

Still no response from the dog.

Arnett laughed out loud and shook his head as he examined the object he had literally and figuratively plucked like trash from the gutter.

About twenty minutes later, with sunset still more than an hour away, he drove back toward Wolveshaven, his mood visibly upbeat and his fingers tapping the steering wheel to the sounds of Lostprophets' most recent—and ultimately last—CD coming from the Pioneer speakers of the Tahoe's Alpine stereo system. Vann could only look at it, shake his head, and grin.

On the dashboard of the SUV, prominently displayed like a serial killer's coveted trophy, were the remains of a recently extinguished cigarette, a subtle hint of charred tobacco permeating the air of the driving compartment.

Ten

I am having a little difficulty grasping the implications of Rusty's and my discovery. I am trying to keep it all in perspective, but it's tough. How do you keep your giddiness under control? You really can't, not really. You just have to ride it like a surfer sluices along the trough of a wave, with the appearance of mastery because that wall of water will do what it wants. And emotions are the same way. All this obsessive enthusiasm because of a stupid cigarette butt, the unwanted and discarded remains of a Marlboro Light.

A goddamn cigarette butt.

Our government had gotten millions of men and women hooked on them during World War II and the years following the conflict, and then it spent billions of dollars generations later to counter the health complications they had helped create. For decades, it had subsidized thousands of tobacco farmers to grow something that literally killed and maimed people and then, reacting to public health outcry, reversed that course and paid them countless millions of dollars not to grow the crop.

Institutionalized idiocy, but I'm not going to complain.

It was a dirty and addicting vice, but one that I had somehow managed to avoid, not even picking it up socially or casually during my rebellious teenaged days or my binge drinking years in college or my Starbucks-swilling faculty tenure. Susannah had been even worse than me—not quite fanatical, but close. It wasn't one of my numerous bad habits—Lord knows, I have enough of them—but I was delighted that someone else had this one and had not been able to kick this disgusting dependency even through the end of the world.

What does it mean? I can only ponder the possibilities, but I know where those possibilities lead. Someone had smoked that cigarette and tossed it. Just like that, they had discarded it like the useless trash the butt was. It had been a billion-times-a-day occurrence, but it hadn't happened for more than eighteen months in this city. Now it had.

What else did it mean? I am fairly confident I know what it means. I am certain there was a stranger, at least one, in town this afternoon. I don't smoke, and I have never seen a creature with a cigarette dangling out of its mouth. Not a single one. So, if I didn't smoke it and none of the creatures smoked it, who did? And that is the million-dollar question. Someone who isn't a resident of the city, someone who had just been here earlier today in the daylight is responsible for leaving that Marlboro Light behind.

A stranger had, indeed, come to town.

Now I have a more defined mission, a more distinct purpose. No, I won't abandon my search to find the young woman whom I had spoken with in the mall; I still need to find her and . . . I don't know why I need to find her. Well, maybe I do know why, but I can't really admit it to myself. Not yet, anyway. I am now also determined to discover who smoked that Marlboro Light and left behind the butt for Rusty's nose to find.

I have to answer the question: Who was the stranger who smoked that cigarette?

I feel almost a little foolish, bubbling on like a schoolgirl who has been spoken to by the boy she has a crush on. All of this unexpected anxiety because of a cigarette—a nail-in-the-coffin, a smoke, a fag for those from the British Isles, death on a stick—that an unknown person had smoked down nearly to the filter and casually flicked away to the gutter. Absurd. It has given me another blossom of hope to pursue, or maybe, another windmill to joust with.

For me, it doesn't matter which one, because either way I have a new purpose, a new meaningful pursuit. To misquote Springsteen, I have a reason to believe.

PART TWO

The Valley of Nightmares

Eleven

They could, at best, be described as a militia with a chain of command and a modicum of discipline, and, at worst, as a band of thugs with automatic weapons and a penchant for violence. During the past nine months, the ragtag group of men and women had opportunity to be both as they traveled the wasteland of what had been the Midwest. Three-quarters of a year outside the wire with little contact from the sprawling Burton Army Base, known simply as The Base to them, and the constant threat to life and limb, the group behaved more like a street gang than soldiers, surviving by superior firepower and over-the-top brutality.

Two all-terrain vehicles, each rigged with lightweight protective metal plating, paced three military-issue, desert-camouflaged four-door Humvees down the street in the center of the city. It was an advance party of troopers, moving in to secure a location where the command post would be established. It was something the militia had done more than a dozen times in more than a dozen other lifeless cities. It was a matter of procedure: scout it out, move in, search for survivors—destroy, if necessary—and leave with anyone who wanted to join them. For nine arduous months, it had been the routine, but this was the last stop before the long trek back to The Base.

The ATVs stopped at an intersection, nonworking traffic lights suspended above them, and one of the drivers dismounted and walked back toward the slowing train of Humvees. In full military battle rattle from head to toe, including three chevrons on each sleeve, the man ambled to the lead vehicle and leaned against the driver's side door.

"So, whadda ya think, Lieutenant?" he said with a grin cutting through his dark beard. "Will it do?"

The female officer, also in combat gear but with long, brown hair tied off in a ponytail under a black do-rag, removed her Oakleys and scrutinized the structure up and down with dark eyes. It was an open-sided, high-rise parking garage. "Why this one?"

"It's on the southeast corner of the downtown square, so it will catch the morning sun early," Sergeant Briggs said. "No basement, six levels high, we can pick anyone of them we want to park on and build a campfire for our sing-along. The top floor will be ideal to set up communications, while the ground floor should be tall enough for us to bring in the deuce-and-a-halves and maybe the RV. There are only two vehicle access points and two more for pedestrians. We can secure those easy enough with claymores and trip wires. It has a number of other attributes, but, in short, it's a defendable high-ground position right smack-dab in the middle of the city."

The lieutenant, silver bars on the collar of her military tunic glinting in the morning sun, turned her attention to the sergeant, whose eyes were hidden behind dark safety glasses. The expression under her dirt-streaked cheeks didn't betray what her thoughts were, and she kept her mouth shut.

"Ya know, Lieutenant, if you give Major Deacon the thumbs-up," he said, "we can get things rolling here right now. Everybody else can roll in here within a couple of hours, and we can be as snug as bugs in a rug by sundown tonight."

She turned her eyes back to the multistory structure, giving it another up-and-down glance. "Any signs of activity?"

The sergeant shrugged noncommittally. "Some graffiti in all parts of the city that we've scouted and some other shit."

"Fresh?" the lieutenant asked as she turned back to the noncom.

He made a face as he pondered his answer. "A lot of it's old, probably from last summer, but some of it looks fresh, I don't know, maybe . . . probably this past summer. There's some pretty weird shit . . ." The sergeant let the statement hang unfinished.

"All over the city?"

"Yeah, pretty much, all that we've seen anyway. Funny how the end of the world brought out the artist in people."

"What other shit?"

Briggs frowned and adjusted his Kevlar helmet. "Just the usual shit you'd expect to see from them. You know . . ." He left the sentence dangling. They had all seen it before. The tattered remnants of an old world being replaced by the brutal and savage birth throes of a new one.

The lieutenant studied his face, looking past the dark whiskers. She wished she could read his blue eyes behind the Smith & Wesson wraparounds but only saw her own reflection in the dark lenses. "They're here, aren't they? In this city?"

"Yeah, I think so."

She smiled at him. "Think so?"

He gave her a look that said, *you know better.*

"A lot of them?"

The sergeant shrugged again. "Can't really tell."

"Any survivors?"

The sergeant made a face that said, *don't ask me this shit.* "Hagstrom and I didn't see any signs, no battlements on buildings or fenced-off and boarded-up houses with gun slits, but we've only scouted a small part around the downtown area—a really small part of it—and we've done absolutely nothing in the residential areas." He shrugged. "We'll get a much better look at everything in the next week or so."

"I know, Sarge, I know. What does your . . . spidey sense say?

He shook his head and stifled a chuckle. "Doesn't work that way, Lieutenant." The sergeant changed the topic with a nod in the direction of the parking structure. "So . . ."

The lieutenant turned her attention to the building. "I do believe it will suit our needs, Sergeant Briggs," she said without looking at him.

"You sure, Lieutenant Rossington?"

She turned back to him. "I just said so, didn't I?"

"Yes, ma'am."

"I will contact the major."

"Excellent."

The sergeant stepped away from the Humvee and, without saluting, slowly walked back to the ATVs, where the other driver, also splashed with road dirt and highway grime, relaxed with a cigarette dangling from his mouth.

"The lady says it will do." Briggs rearranged the M16 slung over one shoulder and leaned on the handlebars of his ride.

"I'm so thrilled I can hardly fuckin' contain myself." He took a last drag on the cigarette and flicked the butt away.

Briggs scowled at him. "Ya know, Hags, those things will be the death of you."

"Yeah, well, better them than the fangs."

He leaned against the front of the Humvee and watched the last deuce-and-a-half head toward the highway, black smoke belching from its exhaust pipe as the driver shifted into the next gear. It was the last—well, next to last—vehicle in the westbound column that was making the short hop into the city.

They had spent the last three nights encamped at a large farmstead, establishing a defensive perimeter with motion sensors and claymores set to trip wires and hidden snipers with night-vision scopes. It had been a peaceful and quiet three nights, just the way he liked it.

Boring and uneventful were good things in Major Deacon's mind. Really good things. Bad things resulted from exciting and eventful. Bad things usually meant that somebody died. He had seen enough exciting and eventful things since The Collapse, and he preferred boring and uneventful any day of the week.

Deacon had seriously thought about pulling the plug on the operation without venturing into the city on the horizon. His unit was almost at the time threshold and no one back at The Base would have known—or cared, for that matter—if he had called an end to this mission a month or so ahead of schedule. He had already sent two small caravans down south, and barring unforeseen or fatal circumstances along the journey, those groups had added seventeen bodies to the census of The Base. He had come very close to doing it after five weeks in the city on the lakeshore. That experience had just been . . . unnerving.

The city had been dead, completely and utterly. No recent indications of survivors—no evidence of *them*. The troopers had found nothing, absolutely nothing. More than sixty excursions in thirty days had turned up zip. It had been a ghost town, inhabited only by the faint specters of the long-ago departed. The cityscape had been eerie and unsettling during the daylight hours, but much, much worse after sunset. Night winds had echoed down its concrete canyons like lost souls crying out for salvation. The moon had hung like the ferryman's lantern, illuminating the asphalt bed of the Styx. None of the troopers had slept well during those five weeks along the lakeshore, bad dreams shifting into nightmares as the hours slipped past, and all of them had been relieved to put its urban skyline in their rearview mirrors. In a tormented landscape, blighted with a lost past and a forsaken future, this onetime blue-collar city had a tainted air, as if cursed by God and rejected by Satan.

Deacon had been close to calling it off and heading for home, but for some reason he had chosen to continue west. He silently questioned his own wisdom and sanity in making that decision, but they pressed on. The troopers, fueled by the desire to put the city on the lake miles and miles behind them, had crept warily through deserted metropolitan suburbs and made only precursory journeys into the small cities along the interstate. If there were survivors present, the troopers had undoubtedly missed them, but nobody really cared.

He watched the big, dark green truck turn off the farm drive and onto the access road that would take it to the interstate and, for one of the few times in the past five years, he wished he had a cigarette in his mouth. The major longed for the familiarity and comfort of its mindless routine as much as the calming effects of the nicotine addiction, but he was also troubled with self-questions of his own judgment. More than anything, Deacon hoped he had made the right decision for his troopers and the survivors under his charge. His mind told him that it was a prudent and proper choice, but deep down in the bottom of his heart, he wondered most of all if it was the right one.

Doubt was an unrelenting and unforgiving bitch of a mistress.

The first vehicles of the convoy, led to the location by Hagstrom and his ATV like rats in a maze following the Piper from Hamelin, arrived at the parking garage roughly forty-five minutes after Deacon waged an internal battle with his own personal misgivings.

The lead Humvee pulled to a stop alongside another that had been parked at the curb. The driver's side door was wide open and Lieutenant Rossington reclined less than comfortably behind the steering wheel. She was the only person in the vehicle, and hers was the only vehicle on the street. Briggs's ATV and the other Humvees had been parked in the ground level of the garage. A small group of troopers, like all soldiers awaiting the next set of orders, milled about the dirt-streaked vehicles. The passenger side window of the lead Humvee rolled down, and a black man in his early forties leaned out.

"This it?" he asked, scanning up and down the concrete structure much as she had earlier in the day.

"Home sweet home," Rossington said as she turned to look at him.

"Well, at least for the next four weeks anyway," the black man said with a wink.

"So, what do you think of it, Traynor?"

He studied the graffiti-smeared building and absently stroked the gray-streaked whiskers of his dark goatee, staring at the words Their teeth were like the teeth of lions in red spray paint. "I've stayed in better places," Traynor said with a slight shrug. "And I've stayed in worst places."

"Like Afghanistan?" Unlike most of the troopers, she knew some of his story because she had taken the time to actually ask him.

Traynor, an infantry staff sergeant in the U.S. Army in another life, had spent ten months playing hide-and-seek with the
black-turbaned remnants of the Taliban more than seven years
after he had helped drive them from power in Kabul, but he got
caught when his squad was ambushed along a rutted road, little
more than a dusty footpath, in the foothills of the Hindu Kush
Mountains of Zabul Province. Two infantrymen had died in that
nasty little firefight and five were wounded, including Traynor,
who had taken an RPG fragment just below the knee on his left
leg. The staff sergeant had kept firing his assault rifle until he
passed out from shock and loss of blood.

When he had finally become coherent in a hospital in Ger-
many several days later, Traynor found out that he had given his
left leg from the knee down to the war effort but had received the
Bronze Star and Purple Heart in return. He thought he had gotten
shortchanged in the deal.

"Yeah, like Afghanistan," Traynor said softly as his mind
drifted away. "Fuckin' Afghanistan." Years later, he was still bitter about it, not that anyone could hold that against him because
those die-hard Islamic fundamentalists had been causing trouble
right up until the world's end. His eyes cleared and his focus returned. "Find anything in there yet?"

"Not yet."

"How much of our new home has been searched?

Rossington shrugged. "Just the ground floor," she said.
"Didn't want to get too far ahead of ourselves when we're spread
thin."

"You are always the prudent one, Rossington."

"Somebody has to be, and we all know it isn't going to be
'Quick Draw' Terazo, so that pretty much leaves it up to me."

Private Butler, a pretty red-haired woman in her early twenties, snickered from behind the wheel of the Humvee. She wore
full battle rattle, minus a Kevlar helmet, and hid her eyes behind
wraparound Oakleys.

"Deke knows who he can trust and who he . . ." Traynor, who
technically did not carry a rank within the troopers but whose

opinion was highly valued, smiled at her but said nothing more on the subject. Captain Terazo, the unit's second in command and a former sheriff's department investigator from southern Ohio, was impulsive with a hair-trigger temper and had on more than one occasion rushed headlong into a confrontation that had turned out successful only through a little luck—or maybe a lot of it—and superior firepower.

Butler looked out the side window to hide her snickering. It wasn't the first time she had heard this type of conversation about the squad's number two, and, even though she shared the same opinion, the private did not want to publicly display it.

"Yeah, well . . ." Rossington did not finish the sentence.

"Are we gonna fit everything in there?" Traynor asked, changing the subject.

"Everything but the semis, maybe the RV," the lieutenant answered. "We'll just have to secure them outside, I guess. Lock 'em up tight, set some booby traps around them, and maybe put a sniper or two inside. Should be all right."

"Hey, if we can't get them in—"

"I measured it, we won't get them in," Rossington said, interrupting him.

Traynor turned to Butler. "See what I mean about being prudent. And pushy."

The private turned away, but not before a grin creased her face.

"Then, I guess we'll just have to secure them nice and tight outside, won't we, Lieutenant?"

"Yeah, Traynor, that's what we'll have to do, but why do I suspect that you already knew that?"

"Because you are not only prudent, you are wise, Lieutenant," he said with a chuckle. "You are wise."

"And you're full of shit, Traynor."

His chuckle grew into a full-blown laugh.

Less than two hours later, the relocation was complete. The troopers had moved all of their vehicles—literally the entire operation—

to the downtown square, leaving them either parked on the ground floor inside the parking structure or along the curb of the street in front. It wasn't the first time the troopers had made such a move.

"Okay, boys and girls," Captain Terazo said to the eight troopers gathered around him, "listen up. I want a thorough—and I do mean, thorough—sweep of the top five floors of this place before we get too comfy and cozy here. Wade, your squad's got three and four. Parks, you've got two and five. All of you can take care of six. I expect at least a half an hour on each one. Check all the nooks and crannies, any place a vampire might try to hide."

"Me and Skittles are on it," Wade said, petting his SAW gun, while Park just shook his head.

The troopers looked bored and paid only partial attention to what he said. It was not the first time they had done this particular task, either.

"I don't want any chance of us getting caught with our pants down around our ankles," the captain continued. Terazo stood six-two and went a lean and mean one-eighty-five, down from his imposing pre-Collapse two-thirty. He had classic Roman good looks, dark eyes, and wavy jet-black hair that hung down around his shoulders, a neatly trimmed black beard framed his jawline. He had the air of a made man about him, but he had chosen to join the thin blue line instead. "This will be the last stop before we head back home, so don't fuck it up. I don't want any accidents or unforeseen circumstances of a vampiric nature arising, *capisce*? Don't know about you, but I intend to get back to The Base all in one piece, with my Johnson ready, willing, and able."

One of the two females among the eight troopers hid a blush. Since they had headed out many months ago, she endured his advances—not to mention his Johnson—at least twice a week.

"All right, boys and girls," Terazo said as he scanned the group, "get rolling."

He hated this job most of all. Small squad sweeps into uncharted territory—it was a recipe for disaster or worse.

Corporal Wade led his three troopers, who fanned out on either side of him, into the fading afternoon light and deepening shadows of the parking garage's fourth floor. They had found nothing but handful of long-ago abandoned and useless vehicles, covered with a heavy dust and untouched for about a year and a half, on the third level. He expected the same results on this one, as well. As he moved forward, the corporal imagined he could smell the faint traces of exhaust fumes, hot motor oil, and burned engine coolant. It was as if those odors had been ingrained into the cement of the structure and slowly seeped out over time.

The sounds of their shuffling footsteps and softly rattling battle gear echoed quietly among the concrete pillars and in the low ceiling before escaping over the short walls and out into the open air beyond them. The beams of high-powered Surefire flashlights—some attached to the muzzles of their assault rifles, others hand-held—danced in the darkness of the garage in movements with no rhythm or rhyme.

"Man, I hate this job," said Wilcox, a male private off to the corporal's left.

"Yeah, but it beats the hell out of going down into a basement," said Osterman, the blushing female trooper who walked on Wade's immediate right. "I just fuckin' hate going down into basements."

"No shit," said Davis, who was on the young woman's right. "Worst fuckin' job there is. You just never know what's going to jump out and grab you in the dark."

"Hey, Osty, I'd like to jump out and grab you in the dark," Wilcox said.

"Fuck you, Wilcox," she shot back at him.

"You name the time and the place, and I'll be there with a hard-on and a smile. Might even give you a kiss when I'm done."

"That ought to take about thirty seconds," Davis cracked.

"Never and nowhere, dickhead," Osterman said. "I'm just a fantasy that you'll have to jack off to."

"Hey, you guys remember that time—where the fuck were we, somewhere in western Indiana?—when we went down in the basement of that old schoolhouse?" Davis asked.

"It was somewhere in eastern Illinois, but I don't remember the name of the town," Wilcox said. "Hell, they all look pretty much the same, right now."

"Yeah, that's right, we had crossed the state line a couple of days earlier," Davis said. "You remember, though, everything going according to plan, six of us in a nice, easy sweep with no muss and fuss and no surprises, thought we were gonna strike out and not even get anything worth scavenging, and then we walked right into that fuckin' nest of them. What was there, a hundred of them down there?"

"Fifty to sixty," Wilcox answered. "Seventy-five, tops."

"Seemed like more than that to me," Osterman said. "A helluva lot more."

"I don't think so," Wilcox said. "Seventy-five at most."

"Man, they were all just sleeping there in the dark, all snug and cozy," Davis said, which a chuckle. "We're just standin' there, shinin' 'em and starin' at 'em like we've never seen fuckin' fangs before. How fuckin' stupid were we? And then that huge, baldheaded motherfucker opened his eyes and screamed at us. And then the rest of 'em on the floor opened their goddamn eyes and started screamin'. They were fuckin' everywhere, vampires comin' out of the gaddamn woodwork, and we're fuckin' surrounded. I just about damn near pissed myself."

"Givin' me the creeps just talking about it," Osterman said, fighting off an icy shiver brought on by images of those memories.

"Then stop talking about it," Wade said quietly but with just a touch of a growl in his voice. He was the squad leader, after all. However, he, too, remembered the incident in high definition. Only superior firepower and dumb luck got them out of that one with one KIA and one wounded. "You know, we are on patrol here, so let's at least pretend that we have some discipline."

The three troopers muttered responses, but they knew the squad leader was right and pushed forward in silence.

In a dust-covered Lexus LX570 SUV, Wade found the desiccated remains of a middle-aged man in a two-thousand-dollar Italian-made three-piece suit propped up behind the wheel with an expensive security briefcase on the leather passenger seat beside him.

The corporal stared at the near-mummified dead man and pondered the scenario. As the world ended, was he still going to the office as if nothing had changed? Was he protecting corporate secrets or fleeing with ill-gotten gains? Where was he going? What were his plans? What the fuck was he thinking as he sat in the seat of the luxury SUV, too sick to drive? There were just too many unanswered questions. Too many questions that would *never* be answered.

Wade shook his head to clear his own mind of those nagging questions, then he adjusted the strap of the assault rifle slung over his shoulder and moved on.

Twelve

Deacon never slept well during the first night in a new encampment. He knew there were too many things that could go wrong, things that were beyond his control but, nonetheless, still factors in the equation. There were far too many minor details that could get overlooked in the chaos of moving from one location and setting up in another. There were way too many unknown and potentially risky variables in that unfamiliar location. There were just too many things—literally hundreds of them—that could go wrong, and any one could lead to a huge problem with dire consequences. And he made it a point to worry about all of them.

The major awoke from his restless and dreamless slumber with the first gray tendrils of dawn slipping into the parking garage from the east. Without shifting in the passenger seat of the Humvee, he scanned around the level with slight movements of his head.

He saw nothing that gave him cause for alarm. Some of the troopers had slept in goose-down sleeping bags in the front seats of their vehicles, others were sprawled across the hoods or roofs of trucks, a few had zonked out atop foam rubber yoga mats underneath high-clearance Humvees, a handful had pitched nylon pop-up tents and spent the night inside them, but only a hearty trio had been brave enough to sleep on the unforgiving concrete of the garage floor with nothing over their heads or elevating them off that surface. Without fail, they all had at least one weapon within quick reach, and many of them went to sleep cradling their assault rifles like children with stuffed animals.

Deacon rolled his skull from side to side, making the bones in his neck pop loudly in the still morning air. He shifted in the seat, and his stiff body rebelled with a series of aches and pains that caused him to wince and groan.

I'm too old for this shit, he thought. *I should be waking up back at The Base in a comfy and cozy bed with a hard-on and my arms around a nice, warm woman. Instead, I got this shit.*

He quietly opened the door and climbed out of the Humvee but did not shut the door. The major stretched and felt several vertebrae along his spine pop, initiating another grimace and a near-silent moan.

The subtle scents of wood smoke and last night's supper mingled with the sour odor of many bodies in need of bathing and lingering hints of automotive exhaust to create a distinct tang that Deacon had smelled numerous times before and would recognize anywhere. It was familiar and almost comforting, but not as comforting as the sight of the still awake—but yawning widely—sentries who had kept the nighttime vigil.

He walked to the vehicle entryway of the garage, nodding at the sentry who manned this post. "How'd it go?" he asked the black woman in her early twenties named Harper.

"Pretty bor . . . uneventful, Major."

"Are you complaining?"

"No, sir."

"I didn't think so. I think you can call it a night, private. Go tell the others to knock off, as well. You can grab something to eat and then get some rest."

"Yes, sir." Harper stood up, stretched, wrapped her sleeping bag around her shoulders, and headed toward the nearest sentry post, cradling her M16.

Deacon watched her for a couple of seconds before he turned his attention to the buildings in front of him, staring at the nearby cityscape features that became more distinct as the morning brightened with each passing moment. In his previous life, he had never been to this city—none of the troopers under his command had— so this was new and uncharted territory for all of them, making it even more dangerous. Experience had taught him the harsh lesson that no matter how much you prepare for any and all contingencies, there were always things that you had not thought about and, thus, had not prepared for. The simple reality was: things went wrong and troopers sometimes died. He couldn't change that. He didn't like it, but he could only accept that undeniable reality and try to minimize the negative effects as much as possible. Trying to account for all those possible consequences—good, bad, and otherwise—the major longed for a mug of strong coffee and a Marlboro, but maybe not in that order.

"What are you thinking about?" a female voice asked from behind.

Deacon sighed mostly to himself and turned to see Rossington stop beside him. Lost in his own thoughts, he hadn't even heard her approach.

"Nothing." He paused. "Everything."

The lieutenant chuckled softly. "Well, that pretty much covers it all, doesn't it?"

"Hey, you asked."

"That I did."

The major studied their surroundings for a moment and asked, "So tell me, Rossy, what are your thoughts about this place?"

Rossington shrugged and frowned. "Just another mostly dead —if not completely dead—city, like so many others we've been in before. Why?"

Deacon did not answer, looking at the nearby buildings for a moment before returning her gaze.

"Why?" the lieutenant repeated.

"Don't know." It was his turn to frown. "Just . . . feels different."

"They're all *different*, but they're all the same."

"I don't know. There's just something about this one."

"Is that a 'good something' or a 'bad something'?"

"Don't know," he said. "It's just . . . just different."

"Well, Major," she said and smiled at him, "all we can do is keep everything wired up tight and be ready for anything and everything."

Deacon returned her grin. "Pretty much covers it all, doesn't it?"

"Yeah, that it does," Rossington answered with a laugh. "That it does. Deke, don't ponder on it too long, it will just drive you crazy." She slapped him on the shoulder and turned back to the interior of the parking garage, which was slowly coming to life. "And not a good kind of crazy."

For the better part of the next two days, the troopers labored to turn the parking garage into their headquarters, the place that would be sarcastically called home—complete with a handcrafted *Home Sweet Home* sign hung above the main entryway—for the next four or five weeks. It was well-rehearsed routine, and only a handful of minor miscues delayed the work.

Security was the single most important element of their preparations, and the establishment of the defensive perimeter at the parking garage dominated the first day of work. The perimeter consisted of claymore mines connected to tripwires strung up in usual and unusual places, booby traps hidden in locations that appeared unprotected to the untrained eye, laser-sighted motion detectors rigged to claxons and portable halogen floodlights. Claymores were also covertly rigged around the handful of vehicles that were too big to fit into the parking garage. Sentry posts near the vehicle doorways were reinforced with sandbags, providing the troopers who drew the assignments with some protection from the outside without limiting their visibility. The battlements were put in place for nighttime protection because that's when the troopers were most vulnerable to attack. Safety—or at least the illusion of it—provided them with a small measure of peace of mind.

If security was the most important element for the troopers, then communication was number two behind it. Several dishes were set up on the upper level garage with a twofold purpose: first, to facilitate local two-way radio communication between the troopers who would be conducting the searches on the ground and the mobile command post that was set up on the open-air top floor of the garage, and, second, in an effort to link their sat phone to a still-functioning satellite so they could try to reestablish contact with The Base.

The mobile command post was the nerve center of the operation. The onetime emergency response command vehicle had been retrofitted to house all the computerized communication and monitoring equipment. A pair of two-man outlook posts were set up on opposite corners of the upper level, giving the observers a clear view of the streets below and the nearby buildings. The posts would be occupied at all hours.

Corporal Tran heaved the last sandbag atop the sentry post, positioning it just right as the other three troopers grumbled about the task they just completed, and studied the tall building with a distinct domed top across the street. Squinting into the afternoon sun, he studied a bank of windows about one floor above the level where he stood. Earlier he thought he had seen something—but what?—and sneaked peeks in that direction during the past hour.

"What you looking at, Tran?" Rossington asked as she stopped alongside him.

"Nice building."

"Sure is." After a couple of seconds of silence, she asked, "So what, you're admiring the architecture?"

"Naw." But he continued to stare at it.

"What is it?"

"Dunno," Tran answered, shaking his head.

The lieutenant turned to face the building. "Something bothering you?"

"Naw. It's just . . ." He did not finish his thought.

"Just what?"

"It's probably nothing, but . . . but I thought I saw something in one of those windows."

"Which window?"

"See the floor . . . oh . . . about our level, actually the one higher?"

"Yeah." Rossington nodded, hitching her assault rifle higher on her shoulder.

"It was in one of those, second from the left."

The lieutenant studied it for a moment or two. There were still two additional floors above the one the corporal had indicated. "What do you think you saw?

"Dunno. Shadow, maybe."

"A shadow? That's it?"

"Maybe . . . probably nothing."

She continued to squint at the building. "All the windows appear to be dirty, or at least one of them isn't less dirty than any of the others."

"I know." He pursed his lips together and frowned "It was probably nothing. Just a shadow or a trick of the light."

"You're probably right. And, besides, the vampires don't come out during the day." The lieutenant turned to the sentry post. "Good job, Tran. You and your squad know how to build these things."

The corporal hesitated for a moment before he looked away from the building across the street. "Thank you, ma'am."

"Now let's see if this stuff actually works the way it's supposed to." She plucked a two-way Motorola radio from her utility belt, bringing it up to her mouth while thumbing the Talk button. "This is Rossington, come in, Deacon."

"Deacon here," the major said into a similar radio, standing with Terazo and Traynor on the ground floor of the garage. "Good to hear from you, Lieutenant."

"It appears communications are now operational," said Rossington's voice with hardly any static breakup. "We're going to run some tests to see what our capabilities are, and I will report back to you later."

"Excellent, Lieutenant Rossington." He returned the radio to his utility belt.

"Major, I think we should send out an exploratory patrol this afternoon," Terazo said. "At least to get a look into the buildings immediately around the CP. We haven't done that yet, and . . . and I'm concerned about it."

"I know, Zo," Deacon said. "It is something we should have done two days ago, but we didn't. Too many things to do and not enough people or time to get them all done. You got somebody in mind for this job?"

"Yup."

"You know," Traynor said, joining the conversation, "we could give them some radios, and it would give Rossington an opportunity to get a real live field test this afternoon. And we can do it without much risk to our men, should there be any glitches in the system."

"Good idea, Dave," the major said. "I like it."

Terazo hid a frown at Deacon's compliment. He wasn't someone who needed the praise of his superior officer, but it was a good idea, and he was annoyed that he hadn't thought of it first. He hated when that happened.

"Zo, get your squad briefed so we can get them out there and working on it," Deacon said to the captain. "I don't want any shortcuts. If we're going to do this, then it needs to be a thorough patrol, done by the numbers. It's late in the game, and I don't want any mistakes."

"Yes, sir," Terazo said with just a bit too much false enthusiasm.

"I'll talk to Rossington and get the radios," Traynor said. "Four man patrol, Zo?"

The captain nodded in response. "Yeah."

"Sounds good. Zo, I want you to man the communication center during the sweep. It's your people out there. Debrief them and report back to me before supper, if possible, during it, if not."

"Can do, Major. Can do."

"Let's make it happen, gentlemen."

As the two men turned away from Deacon, a pretty Latina in her early thirties and wearing civilian attire—well-worn Wolverine work boots, Levi's blue jeans, and a nondescript black T-shirt—walked up to him. Her long, dark hair was pulled back and tied off in a thick ponytail.

"Good news for me, Sandra?"

"That's a relative term in this day and age, Major Deacon." In another life, Sandra Valesquez had been a physician's assistant and endured a front-row seat to the horrors of the plague that brought civilization to its knees. She often wondered how she had kept her sanity, or if she had even kept it at all.

"I know, so humor me, Sandra."

"Doc says that Medical is operational and ready for business that we hope we don't get."

"Good. Any pressing supply needs?"

"No. We are stocked up fairly well, although we never turn down anything useful, you should know that."

"I do. Should we be looking for anything in particular?"

She paused for a second or two. "You know, this is . . . was a university city, one with world-class medical facilities, right?"

"Yeah, I read something about it in the brochure, and let me guess, Doc wants to go on a little field trip to check out some of these facilities?"

Valesquez smiled at him, dimples in her cheeks popping out and her dark eyes beaming. "How did you guess?"

"Doc is nothing if not predictable. I suppose he wants to get started right away?"

"Sooner the better."

"Okay. We are in the process of getting some exploratory patrols for the next couple of days set up, so I will see what we can do. I will talk to Traynor and the officers about taking Doc along to one of those world-class medical facilities."

"I will let him know."

"Thank you, Sandra."

"You're welcome, Major."

From the uppermost story of what had been the state capitol building, Arnett watched them through the German-made Steiner military-style binoculars, desperately wishing he could read lips as the pretty dark-haired woman spoke with the uniformed man who appeared to be in charge of the group. The woman had come from an improvised-armored monster of a recreational vehicle that was parked on the street alongside the parking garage. She had spent the better part of the past two days inside the vehicle with a tall, thin African American male.

He could see the two of them plain as day. They were so close through the optics that he could almost reach out and touch them. *Almost.* Instead, Vann could only watch them as their silent conversation played out like a video with the sound turned off. He could only imagine what they were saying, but he didn't let his mind wander too far down that particular path.

Still, they were real live human beings unaffected by the plague. *Real live people.* It had been far too long since he had seen anyone like them.

A voyeur without remorse or shame, he continued to stare at them, unable to avert his eyes even if he had wanted to. It had been that way for the past two days as he watched the militia establish its command post. The officer, gold oak leaves on his tunic, and the woman seemed to speak easily and smiled at one another, but it still appeared to be more of a professional interaction than a social call.

"Jealous, Vann?" he asked himself. "No, it's just . . ."

He stopped the two-way conversation with himself—just a sliver of foolishness penetrating his consciousness—before he could finish answering the question. Talking to oneself was just one of the drawbacks of a solitary existence, but far from the worst one, he knew. Still, he didn't like to ponder the long-term implications of it.

Don't go crazy on me, boy, came an unwanted voice in his head. *And you need to keep it in your pants.*

Arnett frowned at the intrusion as he watched the pretty dark-haired woman walk away from the man, heading in the direction of the Mad Max–inspired RV. He couldn't help but stare at the feminine sway of her hips and the easy manner in which she carried herself. The binoculars digitally informed him how far she was from him, but the actual distance was irrelevant to him. She might as well have been on the other side of the moon. He wanted to reach out to her, to touch her, to stop her, to talk to her, to . . . He shook his head to clear those thoughts from the forefront. She climbed into the RV and shut the door, never knowing that she was being ogled from a distance.

"What do you think, Rusty?" he asked, lowering the binocs and turning to the setter that sat near the doorway of the room. "Should we go and talk to them?"

The dog ignored his query, as usual.

"Cat got your tongue, huh." Vann returned his gaze to the window and shook his head slowly. "Man, they sure know what they're doing, setting up a defensive perimeter like this in less than two days. They've obviously done this before a time or twenty. I am impressed, thoroughly impressed. How about you, Rusty?"

The setter kept its stoic silence.

"Yeah, that's what I thought." He looked back at the dog. "Nothin' impresses you, I guess."

He had watched them go about their duties with near-military precision and a strong sense of discipline. Sure, there were a couple of people who didn't seem to put their full effort into their tasks, but most of them worked hard and dutifully. They were effective and efficient. Each of them knew what duties had to be done and essentially did them without the NCOs' or officers' constant verbal attention. It had been a sight to see.

Still, there was something in the back of his mind that troubled him. He just couldn't put his finger on it and nudge it to the forefront of his thoughts, but it was there rattling around on the periphery. Even more troubling to him was that he couldn't truly discount the notion that it was his own sense of paranoia manifested onto what this apparent militia was doing. A couple of times he had thought to himself and then commented out loud to the dog that he would have done this or that just a little different. Vann knew he was no military tactician or defensive strategist, but he must have done something right because, after all, he was still alive. It couldn't have all been dumb luck and good fortune, some of it certainly was but not *all* of it.

Arnett turned back to the filth-covered window and raised the binoculars. Through the mid-afternoon sun, he watched as several pockets of activity percolated to life on two different levels of the parking garage.

Decked out in full battle rattle, complete with Kevlar helmets, clear or amber lens safety glasses, tactical gloves, body armor strapped up tight, and ammo-filled pockets of ripstop pants tucked into combat boots, not to mention assault rifles and one squad automatic weapon machine gun drawn and at the ready, Sergeant Briggs led Hagstrom, Stroud, and Petrovic into the building immediately across from the parking garage, the medical center RV parked on the street between the two structures. In a different time, it had been a glass and chrome multi-story office building with top-dollar lobbyists and high-profile law firms as its exclusive residents. Now it was home to roosting birds and bats as well as scavenging rodents and other small critters, which many would have said represented an upgrade in the original occupants.

Briggs was the first through the shattered safety glass front door, sliding to his right as he stepped into the lobby. The other troopers fanned out behind him in the gray gloom of the foyer lit from behind only by ambient sunlight. Almost simultaneously, they all switched on flashlights, narrow beams dancing in the darkness.

"You copy this, Captain?" the sergeant said into the radio's nearly invisible headset mic that wrapped around in front of his mouth.

"Loud and clear, Briggs," came the reply from the small speaker of the radio that was clipped to the front of his body armor and much more quietly in the tiny earpiece in his right ear. "Loud and clear. Everybody else?"

The other troopers sounded off into their mics, and Terazo informed them all that he had copied what they said.

"Okay, boys, what do you see?" Briggs asked his squad as they all shone Surefire flashlights around the lobby and carefully moved forward, daylight fading from behind and darkness enveloping from up front.

"Nothin', not a goddamn thing," Petrovic answered, a subtle Southern twang in his words. He panned the SAW gun left and right.

"Come on now, boys, don't be shortchangin' me. This is not the first time we have done this little dance step. What do you see?"

"A lot of dust and spiderwebs, dirt and other shit on the floor," Stroud said. "I bet there's bird shit and bat shit and Lord knows what other kinds of shit in here."

A little farther down the open but darkening lobby, several recessed canister lights hung from the ceiling like distended hernias.

"What's that all mean?" the sergeant asked.

"The cleanin' service sucks," Petrovic shot in with a grin.

There were three elevator doors on either side of the lobby. Five of six were closed tight, while the farthest down on the right was open about a foot or so. The opening was a leering and dark vertical grin, like that of a drunken Midway hawker.

"Besides that?"

Stroud thumbed the Up button nearest the closed elevator door on the right, but nothing happened.

"You were expectin' it to work?" Petrovic asked sarcastically.

"No, but . . ." Stroud didn't bother to finish his answer, which would have been: *You just never know.*

"Come on, boys," Briggs said. "There's dust and dirt and debris all over the floor. Cobwebs hanging undisturbed all over the place. What else do you see?"

"Nothing," Stroud said.

"C'mon. What else?"

"There's no fuckin' footprints in the dust and dirt," said Hagstrom, an unlit cigarette dangling from his mouth. Annoyance prickled in his voice.

"And what's that mean?"

"That it's been a fuckin' long time since somebody walkin' upright on two feet has been in this fuckin' building," Hagstrom answered again. He didn't care for this little game, in part, because the answers never changed, but, if they did, it was usually not a good thing. "No humans, no fangs, no nothing."

Petrovic and Stroud shined their lights on the floor around them and the corridor ahead.

"Not a single, solitary footprint . . . anywhere," Petrovic said. "Hell, it doesn't even look like the critters are using the main doors."

"Ya know, we could be the first people setting foot in this building in, like, a year and a half," Stroud said. He was seventeen years old, and the troopers had found him and two other teenaged boys in the ruins of Scottsburg, Indiana. The other two had decided to head south when the troopers sent their first caravan back toward The Base, but Stroud had opted to join the mission and continue on north.

"Fuckin' dweeb," Hagstrom muttered mostly under his breath.

"Shit, Stroud, most every place we go we're the first people in more than a year to set foot in it," Petrovic said.

"I know . . ."

Petrovic continued, "So this shouldn't be a goddamn big deal?"

"I know . . ."

"Give it a rest, boys," Briggs said, not wanting this familiar line of conversation to continue on. "Some people never get used to it."

"I know, Sarge, but . . ."

"Petrovic," the sergeant said a little more sternly and in *that* tone.

"I hear ya, Sarge."

"Where are you, Briggs?" Terazo's voice crackled over the radio.

"About halfway down the main corridor," the sergeant replied. "Well, it's really more like an open lobby than a corridor."

"What's there?"

"Three elevators on either side of the . . . whatever you want to call it. Straight ahead, at the far end is . . . I don't know . . . a common reception area or something like that. Don't think it's an office, but you never know. We're proceeding toward it."

"What's the status to this point?" Terazo asked, even though he was listening to the conversation among them.

"No signs of recent activity," the sergeant responded.

Petrovic placed his hand over his mic and said, "But a whole lotta shit—bird, bat, and *bullshit*."

Stroud chuckled, but Hagstrom just shook his head and muttered something under his breath about needing a cigarette. Briggs gave him a look.

"This place is a tomb, Captain," the sergeant said. "There ain't nobody or nothing in here."

"You will continue with your ground floor sweep of the building, Sergeant."

"Yes, sir, Captain." He tried to hide his sarcasm but wasn't sure he pulled it off. "We will continue the sweep in accordance with our rules of engagement. If we don't find any signs of recent activity on the ground floor of this building, we will move on to the next building."

"I know how it's done, Sergeant," Terazo's voice crackled over the radio. "Don't forget, I wrote the rules."

Briggs rolled his eyes and shook his head. He knew that Terazo had attended the meetings at The Base where these particular rules had been drafted by the powers that be, but the captain had failed to clarify anything beyond that point. Whether the officer had actually contributed to the process or merely sat with a thumb up his ass, who knew?

"You know the drill, boys, let's keep movin' forward."

The troopers crept down the wide corridor, tight beams of light cutting through the increasing darkness like Klieg lights over Hollywood.

"This place is dead, Sarge," Petrovic said, hand over his mic. "There ain't no vampires in here and there ain't anything of any use to us, either."

Briggs covered his mic. "I know it and you know it, but we gotta job to do. And we're gonna do it." He uncovered his mic. "Let's keep it tight, boys. I don't want any surprises."

Two slow and careful steps later, muffled sounds exploded in front of them and several indistinct projectiles raced overhead.

"Fuck!" growled Hagstrom, cigarette flying from his mouth and spiraling off into the murk.

"Ah, shit!" yelled Petrovic, just a trace of fear in his voice.

Stroud screamed girlishly and in panic squeezed the trigger of his M16. A stream of bullets ripped into the wall ahead in a jagged trail and shattered the glass of the enclosed reception area.

"What's going on, Briggs?" Terazo's voice snapped on the radio before static won out.

"Fuck!" Hagstrom snarled again.

"Briggs, report!"

The sergeant grabbed Stroud before he could swing the assault rifle around in the direction the objects had gone overhead, which would have also brought the men into the line of fire. The trooper's blue eyes were wide with terror as he released his death grip on the trigger, silencing the smoking weapon.

"Easy, Private," Briggs said calmly. "Easy."

"*Briggs! Report!*"

The sergeant released his grip on the private, whose body armor hung off his skinny frame like old clothes on a scarecrow. "Relax, Stroud. Relax."

The teenager let out a ragged sigh.

"You okay?" Briggs asked.

Stroud nodded.

The pungent smell of cordite hung in the stale air, and gun smoke wafted about in the near dark on aimless currents. Echoes of gunfire rang in the ears of the troopers, drowning out the silence of the office building.

"*Briggs!*" the radios blasted out. "*Report! What the fuck is going on down there?*"

"What the fuck was that?" Petrovic asked.

"Birds," Hagstrom said.

"What?"

"Birds. Pigeons, I think"

"*Briggs! Report!*"

"You're shittin' me?"

Hagstrom shook his head, while Petrovic laughed.

"Briggs, what the fuck happened?" came Terazo's voice, anger coming through the tiny Motorola speakers loud and clear. "Was that gunfire? Briggs, report, damn it."

"It was gunfire, Captain," the sergeant said.

"What the fuck happened?"

Briggs turned to Stroud, who sheepishly looked away.

"We got buzzed by some birds, Captain."

"Birds?"

"Yes, Captain, birds. And Private Stroud thought we needed pigeon for supper tonight, so he . . . well."

"Is everything all right?"

"Yes, Captain, and every*one* is all right."

"Good." A burst of static obscured what Terazo said next.

"Oh, and Captain . . ."

"Yes, Sergeant?"

"We won't be having pigeon for supper."

The troopers, even Hagstrom, covered their mics and attempted to stifle chuckles but without much success.

"Continue with your sweep, Sergeant," the captain growled, his anger having turned to irritation in no time at all.

"Yes, sir, Captain, sir." Briggs looked at the troopers. "You heard the man, let's go. We got a job to do."

The scent of cooking fires and grilled meat hung in the still air, while smoke from the dying embers of several portable, wrought-iron fire pits clung to the concrete ceiling of the parking garage like disconnected spiderwebs. An unrelenting darkness shrouded the outer areas of concrete structure and seeped into the unoccupied floors. Even the top-floor lookout posts were enveloped in it like a blanket.

Midnight was little more than an hour away as the full weight of night bore down upon the troopers nestled in the concrete structure. Most of them were sacked out in their now usual places and awaited sleep's arrival. A handful had already crashed due to a day full of physical labor, a belly full of warm food, and a couple of cold beers after supper in recognition of their hard work. One, however, stirred restlessly, unable to find a comfortable position and too many uneasy thoughts troubling his weary mind.

Major Deacon shrugged off his blanket and gracelessly slipped out of the armored Humvee, leaving the door open enough to kill the interior lights. He stood alongside the vehicle and surveyed the scene before him. In just a matter of two days, they had turned a parking garage into an operations base. It was an impressive feat—one they had done before—and the troopers had earned their rewards: alcohol and extra sack time. Tomorrow would be a day of planning for the officers and non-coms, and one of gear prep for the troopers. A day later, they would be in full search and—if necessary—destroy mode.

He slowed his breathing and strained to listen to the night sounds. All he heard were varying degrees of snoring from a handful of troopers and muttered complaints of restless sleepers trying to get more comfortable, even though that was a losing proposition.

The major was silently pleased that he didn't hear the grunts and groans of couples engaged in a lustful tryst. He knew it happened regularly enough, but sex created a different and not necessarily positive dynamic in the group, especially when the men outnumbered the women by about three-to-one. Jealousy could be an ugly thing. Deacon knew there was nothing he could do to stop his troopers from fucking one another, but he had made it clear that he would tolerate no sex-related problems. If the parties couldn't work things out, he would work the issues out for them and his solutions would be final and harsh.

Good, he thought, *most of them seem to be out cold, or at least getting some rest. We're going to get real busy, and I need them ready to rock 'n' roll.*

Deacon walked over to the sentry post near the main door, and the private manning it stood up from the folding chair he had been sitting on.

"At ease, Drake. How's it going?"

"It's going, Major," the private, a tall male in his mid-twenties, answered. His long, blond hair was tied off in a ponytail while his scruffy beard was nearly invisible in the gloom.

"Are you warm enough?"

"Yeah," Drake said with a nod. "I've got a nice down sleeping bag to put around me if I get cold later."

"Good. Did you get enough food tonight?"

"I sure did, Major." The private smiled. He had actually gotten seconds and for the first time that he could remember, his belly was actually full. "Thanks for the beers, too."

"Well, you all earned them, Drake." The major looked off into the darkness that surrounded the structure and back at the young man. "I need you to stay sharp and wide awake, Private. You all earned those beers, but if I find any one of my sentries nodding off tonight, those will be the last beers anyone gets until we arrive back at The Base. Understand?"

"Yes, Major." He knew Deacon was a fair man and a competent commander, but sometimes he seemed a little too gung-ho, a little too military for his tastes.

"I'm not singling you out, Drake, I'm gonna talk to everyone, even those topside. I don't want any problems, and we can't afford to let our guard down even for a minute."

"I understand, Major."

"Good. Stay sharp, Drake, and keep up the good work."

"Yes, Major."

The private watched Deacon walk toward the sentry post on the other side of the garage and sat down when the captain faded into an indistinct shape in the charcoal shadows.

"Fuck that noise," he said, putting down his M16 while picking up the sleeping bag and wrapping it around his shoulders. "Fuck, I'll be snoozing inside of thirty minutes and there ain't a damn thing you can do about it." Drake wriggled about on the metal chair, trying to get comfortable. "What you gonna do, court-martial me? Big fuckin' deal if that happens. If I get caught napping, all you're gonna do is take away my beer. So fuckin' what? The shit I've seen and done, fuck, not giving me a beer for the next month is nothin'. Abso-fuckin'-lutely nothing." The private tugged the sleeping bag tighter around his shoulders and closed his eyes.

Rusty intently watched Arnett rise up from the big comfy leather chair and pace about the main room of Wolveshaven. Sometimes, he just didn't understand the man and what he did. This was one of those times.

"We've got to make contact with them, Rusty," he said. "But how do we go about it? I mean, we can't just waltz over to them and say, 'Hi there, my name is Vann, and this is Rusty.' Can we? Of course we can't do that. Hell, we'd probably get shot. They do kind of seem like they could be a trigger-happy bunch.

"Wouldn't that be about the size of it? Survive the fall of human civilization—the greatest catastrophe known to man—only to get shot and killed walking up to someone to say hi." He looked down at the dog that lay on the floor with its head up. "Now that would be ironic, Rusty. Eye-ronic."

Vann sat down for an instant and then popped back, resuming his pacing about the room. He was anxious and undecided, apprehensive and excited. He was unaccustomed to experiencing these emotions and didn't know how to react. He didn't like it.

"We watched them for two days, Rusty, and they don't seem like an *overly* trigger-happy bunch, but you just never know. They seem to know what they're doing, and, you know, Rusty, they have managed to stay alive this long. That says a lot about how they operate. Obviously they're armed to the teeth and not afraid to drop the hammer on someone or something. It has become dog-eat-dog out there in the big, bad world, my furry, red-haired friend."

Arnett stopped his pacing and looked out a window. His own ghostly reflection stared back at him, but he saw only the darkness of night beyond the glass. He turned back into the room and resumed his mindless walking.

"Still, there is something that's bothering me, and I can't put my finger on it," Vann said, orating to the muscular Irish setter. "I don't know what it is. I just don't know, but it is bugging the crap out of me."

He hesitated in mid-stride as he racked his brain trying to come up with what he had missed or thought he had missed. His mind rewound through the events of the past two days, but nothing in that mental slideshow came front and center. Vann added frustration and annoyance to the list of unwanted emotions.

"Shit," he muttered mostly under his breath and started pacing again.

Rusty continued to watch the man, still without any canine insight as to what the hell he was doing. He dropped his muzzle down to his forepaws but still kept his dark eyes focused on the man as he wandered about the room.

Drake jerked awake with a start, eyes scanning the darkness outside the structure. He saw nothing in the gloom that hadn't been there in the light. Had he heard something, or had he been dreaming?

"Fuck," he muttered to himself, pulling the edges of the sleeping bag tighter around his shoulders. "It's getting colder out."

He turned in his folding chair and looked back at the interior of the garage. The smoldering embers in the portable fire pits glowed weakly and cast pale light that didn't venture very far from their metal confines. Other than that, there was no movement among the sleeping troopers. They were all sleeping like babies in their comfy and cozy cribs, wrapped up tight and warm in their blankies.

"What the fuck am I doing out here?" the private asked himself. "I should be in there sleeping or maybe trying to get some." He chuckled softly. "Fuck."

Drake unsuccessfully attempted to move deeper in the aluminum folding chair, pulling the sleeping bag tighter under his chin as he returned his gaze to the street outside the structure. He saw next to nothing in the unrelenting blackness.

This has got to be the *single most fuckin' boring job there is*, he thought. *Nothing is gonna fuckin' happen and I'm sitting out here looking at* nothin' *with my thumb up my ass. Nothin' is gonna fuckin' happen!*

He leaned back and found a position that wasn't too uncomfortable. In a matter of minutes his eyelids were heavy, and he struggled to keep them up, but his eyes were dry and tired as he pulled on them. It was a losing battle. His lids fluttered up and down a couple of times before they finally stayed down for the count. He wasn't even aware that he had been ambushed by the sandman—then Drake was asleep, softly snoring.

Thirteen

Like the first tentative wisps of smoke rising from numerous chimneys, the vanguards rose to full height on the cold concrete and stepped away from the iron-grated storm drains. They were immediately followed by more and more of their kind, spilling out of those narrow holes with only the soft clatter of weaponry more suited for the Middle Ages than the twenty-first century. They moved in the darkness of the predawn morning with the fluid stealth and uncanny silence of pale serpents slipping from their multiple nests, emerging from those holes with effortless alacrity that appeared more reptilian than human. In a matter of moments the number of Kindred warriors and pawns had swelled beyond one hundred. They nearly doubled their ranks before the final figure slithered out of the dark tunnel and stood upright.

With abrupt and concise hand gestures, the tall Kindred warrior commanding the group signaled his lieutenants, who, in turn, relayed those messages on to their subordinates, silently organizing the assembly into smaller, preestablished units. The raid had been thoroughly planned. It had been designed to use overwhelming numbers of a nearly single-minded organism to achieve the objective.

The warriors had specific assignments, some individually and others in groups, while the remainder would be little more than cannon fodder to occupy the troopers' superior firepower once the shooting started. Success was contingent upon the Kindred's ability to catch them unaware and a willingness to endure heavy losses, for others to blindly make sacrifices.

The leader, a tall and thin African American male whose transformation had turned his skin an almost silvery gray, surveyed the Kindred before him and liked what he saw. They were eager and they were ready, like wolves before the hunt. His name was Robert Holmes, and he had been the co-owner of a thriving company that before The Collapse had offered a wide array of security services, everything from high-tech alarm systems to steroid-enhanced bodyguards, but he had also served as a sergeant in the Army National Guard. Now he was known as General Abaddon, the angel of the abyss, the destroyer.

He thought the Prophet had christened him appropriately. His skull was shaved clean and a pointed black goatee stood out in stark contrast to his pale skin. Multiple earrings adorned both lobes, a heavy gold herringbone chain hung around his neck, and a silver star shone on each epaulette of his unbuttoned black leather duster. A skintight, black T-shirt did little to conceal his ripped torso, while equally snug Levi's accentuated, among other things, his well-defined leg muscles. A sheathed Marine Corps officer's Mameluke sword rested against his left hip, while an eight-inch combat knife was strapped outside of his right thigh. The end-of-the-world incarnation of Robert Holmes cut a menacing figure.

Abaddon pointed a long finger at one of his lieutenants and then directed it upward toward the concrete ceiling. The fierce-looking female warrior nodded and, with a wave of her right arm, took off at a jog up the incline that led to the upper levels with about twenty-five Kindred trotting after her. He looked at the other seven officers in front of him, nodded, then smiled, giving them a brief glimpse of his fangs. He silently mouthed a single word: *now*.

As their commander strode purposefully down the incline, two lieutenants led their scurrying charges past him on either side, while the remainder spread out around him. The swirling mass of Kindred moved swiftly and inexorably down the ramp like a pale tidal wave rising in the distance, building momentum and driving toward an unsuspecting seaside town. Less than a minute later, this wave slammed into the beach.

The first group of two dozen Kindred sprinted through the sleeping compound of troopers on the way to the sentry posts on the far side of the parking garage, while the second swept toward the other lookout post. The sleeping sentry in the distant sandbagged nook never knew what hit him when clubbed unconscious by the first blow from the hilt of a sword.

In the other fortified position, Private Drake snapped his eyes open in confusion as the sleeping bag fell from his shoulders. *What the fuck?* he thought as a pallid-faced female in dirty and ragged clothes jumped before his eyes. His brain kicked into gear as she drew her arm back and a single word rammed into his thought process: *fangs!* He opened his mouth to scream the word when the club—an aluminum Little League–sized baseball bat, actually—crashed down on his skull. Streaking fireworks shot through the night sky of his vision and in an instant he forgot what he was going to say. Drake didn't feel the second blow delivered by the woman nor any of the others rained down on him by the Kindred that swarmed into the post, nor did he mentally register the feral hands that clutched at him and held tight to his clothing. The creatures clambered over the wall and headed toward the vehicles in the street, dragging the unconscious private with them.

While Drake was carried away, the massive wall of more than a hundred Kindred swept into the main cluster of sleeping troopers like that unyielding and unforgiving tidal wave, knocking over the fire pits and spilling the coals to the concrete in showers of red-gold sparks. The soldiers asleep on the concrete had little chance of fighting off the attackers, those on the roofs of the vehicles had only slightly better odds but ones that only the most reckless gamblers would take, and the troopers actually inside the vehicles had the best chance but still not good.

From the top level of the garage there was a single gunshot that echoed between the buildings adjacent to the structure before dying out. And then there was only silence from above, until a high-pitched female scream shattered it.

Most of the sleeping troopers were overpowered with little effort, but some, those who slept lightly and reacted even quicker, were able to put up some resistance. Private Butler swung her assault rifle wildly while at the same time she desperately attempted to flick off the safety. Corporal Wade blindly punched and kicked at clutching pale hands as he snarled even more savagely than his attackers, actually stopping them in their tracks.

Harper groggily sat up in her sleeping bag, absently wondering what was making all the noise that had woken her up, before a dirty fist slammed into the side of her head and scattered those sleepy thoughts to the wind. Filthy hands savagely grabbed her, ripping skin and tearing clothing as they pulled her from the down cocoon. Briggs had made it to his feet and lashed out jabs and hooks with determined accuracy when a sword ran him through from behind. He stopped in mid-swing and stared down at the bloody blade extending out from his torso. Petrovic, sitting atop a Humvee in his underwear and untied combat boots, directed a heel-kick at the face of a male vampire attempting to climb up the vehicle. He ignored the snap of bone when his foot connected with the middle of the creature's face.

Stroud shook the cobwebs of sleep from his brain and deftly rolled to his knees, flinging elbows like a careless power-forward under the glass. Only through stupid luck and happenchance did he manage to snag his M16 along the way. With a Rebel yell, Wilcox burst from the passenger side of a Humvee and jumped on the back of the nearest vampire, a startled female who went down to all fours under his weight. The private hammered vicious blows down upon her. Osterman managed to draw her Ka-Bar knife and frantically slashed it out in front of her, keeping several fangs at bay. She stumbled over something—or someone—and lost her balance, enabling a creature to wrap his arms around her shoulders from behind in an effort to pin down her arms. The private hysterically struggled against his strength but screamed when he grabbed her between the legs.

Private Baumann had been enjoying a vivid and erotic dream involving a nude and shaved Asian man with a huge hard-on when the terrified scream fractured her fantasy. From her low-angle position lying flat on the concrete floor, she saw panicked chaos as a handful of her fellow troopers fought with fangs in mortal hand-to-hand combat—and not faring very well. Forgetting the loaded M16 near her side, she rolled over the weapon and scrambled to get free of her sleeping bag and under a nearby Humvee.

The young woman, breathing in panicked gasps, watched in openmouthed and wide-eyed horror at the violence before her. She flinched in startled surprise when a male trooper—she couldn't remember his name—dropped to his knees in front of her, blood running from his nose and trickling from a cut on his cheek. She stared directly into his unfocused eyes for a trembling moment before sliding deeper under the armored vehicle. He wobbled and appeared ready to fall flat on his face when two creatures grabbed him and began to drag him away. Baumann bit her hand to keep from screaming at the top of her lungs.

Deacon woke up as he felt the Hummer shake. Thinking it was some of his practical jokers, he was ready to explode with feigned indignation. Imagine his surprise when he started to growl and opened his eyes to the snarling face of a male Kindred, nose pressed against the glass of the window. The major clutched the door handle at the same instant the vampire attempted to pull it open, initiating a life-and-death tug-of-war. With his right hand, he grasped his M16 from the passenger seat. Fortunately, he kept the safety off. He swung the weapon around and released the door handle. The creature ripped it open and stepped forward as Deacon squeezed the trigger. The blast of bullets drove the staggering vampire, starkly illuminated by multiple muzzle flashes, backward into the darkness.

Chivalry had nothing to do with the reason Doc Wilkins had opened the door of the medical RV and groggily stepped out into the street. It was simple curiosity. He wanted to know what the hell was causing all the commotion in the garage and interrupting his light sleep. And he was ready to let somebody know about it. In a T-shirt, sweatpants, and untied Nike running shoes, he stared in dumb confusion at the sight of a half-dozen fangs dragging some-thing—it looked like a body—away from the parking garage.

He actually shook his head at the image that reminded him of soldiers carrying a wounded comrade. From the depths of the darkness, a small Indian woman—her caste mark prominent on her pale forehead—flung herself into his torso, body-checking him into the side of the vehicle, while a tall, blond male slammed the RV door shut as he ran up from the other side and tackled Wilkins, taking him down to the pavement.

Valesquez stared for countless seconds in uncomprehending and openmouthed terror—hands clutched over her heart—through the small window along the side of the RV at what had just trans-pired. She made the sign of the cross and turned away from the window, praying the door had locked when it had slammed shut.

In a Humvee parked away from the fringes of the wagon-train circle of other vehicles, Rossington bolted up in the driver's seat, seemingly awake in an instant as adrenaline flooded her system. In the darkness she could only make out shadows and indistinct shapes of pandemonium. Instinctively, she grabbed the M16 on the seat beside her. The lieutenant checked the weapon's safety, tapped the bellowed pockets of her combat pants to confirm that she had extra clips in them, took a deep breath, opened the door, and snapped on the lights of the Humvee. The scene of death and destruction in the harsh and unforgiving light took her breath away, and she hesitated for an instant, but just a brief one. Rossington raised the assault rifle, found a target—there were far too many of them—and squeezed the trigger in a short, controlled burst.

A little more than a mile away from the downtown parking struc-ture, Arnett sat up in his bed, awakened by something. It took him a moment or two to realize that it was the crackle of distant gunfire.

"What the fuck?" he muttered. "What the hell are they doing?"

Standing in the doorway of his darkened room, Rusty didn't answer his questions.

Vann heard the distinct *pop, pop, pop* of small arms fire. Its staccato beat was still sporadic, like a drummer sitting down behind the kit and tentatively testing the skins and sticks. Confused, he knew where it was coming from, but he was uncertain as to why. The realization dawned on him as the faraway gunshots increased in pace and intensity. It was not a good thing, Martha.

"Oh no. No! *No! Noooo!*"

He swung his legs out of the bed, stepping into a pair of Adidas trail runners without thought as he stood up. He plucked his trusty Glock from the nightstand alongside the bed and stuffed it in the back waistband of his black sweatpants. Vann didn't bother to throw on a shirt, much less turn on a light, as he grabbed the M4 from the high-back chair and slung it over his shoulder, heading toward the doorway.

"C'mon, Rusty."

Less than a minute later, Arnett stood in the widow's walk, Night Detective night-vision binoculars pressed to his eyes as he desperately scanned the area in search of something, anything. He saw only the magnified green-hued barren landscape that surrounded Wolveshaven, empty and lifeless, and was disappointed. And more than a little confused. Gooseflesh rose on the bare skin of his torso.

In the distance, from the southwest, the pace of gunfire picked up dramatically.

"Shit," he growled in the cold night air. "Shit!"

Taking his cue from whoever had hit the lights on their vehicle, Terazo flicked on the headlights of his Humvee, illuminating the battle scene in the parking garage. Ignoring the creatures scuttling around him, he cursed under his breath. He could see that it was not going well for the troopers. They were being overwhelmed by far superior numbers, but then it hit him and brought a slight smile to his lips as he heard short bursts of automatic weapon fire. They were vastly outnumbered, but not outgunned.

Almost casually, he took his M16 out of the Humvee and turned to face the battle. As a dark-haired male creature ran toward him, Terazo raised the assault rifle to his hip and let loose a short burst of a half-dozen bullets, stopping the fang in his tracks before knocking him backward.

"Fuckin' idiot vampires," he muttered as he shook his head and searched for his next target. The captain didn't have to look long and responded with another burst of hot lead.

"C'mon!" He sprayed a spurt of bullets in one direction and then a second in another. The response was screams of pain. "C'mon, motherfuckers! That the best you can do? C'mon! C'MON!"

Terazo snapped off a blast as he stepped away from the armored vehicle. Other soldiers began to follow the lead, grabbing their weapons and unleashing the firepower contained within them.

At the same time Captain Terazo started his rally, Osterman controlled her terror and panicked struggling and realized that if she didn't fight back she was dead. The private drove her head back into the nose of the vampire that held her and clutched at her groin, snapping bones in his nose, and drove her heel down on his instep at the same time. She spun away from him and backhanded the knife blade across his throat before he even realized what had hit him.

Hands clutching his belly wound, Sergeant Briggs staggered away after the sword blade had been pulled with a wet *thwook*, but he never felt the second, third, and fourth thrusts into his body. Butler finally managed to flick the safety off her assault rifle and unleashed a full auto burst at the pack of vampires in front of her. She never saw the female slip behind her and slam the sword hilt on the back of her head.

The private staggered forward, firing wildly as she fell to the concrete, and the Kindred swarmed over her. Petrovic, with his SAW gun in his right hand and an Israeli-made Desert Eagle in the left, sprayed hot lead from one and snapped off random shots with the other. A Kindred warrior slashed at him with a sword, nicking the trooper but fatally eating a half-dozen or so bullets. Baumann, with tears flowing, squeezed her eyes shut and placed her hands over her ears in a futile attempt to block out the horrible sounds around her. She even began to murmur *lalalalalalala*.

With bloodied fists, Wilcox rose from the battered remains of the female Kindred and searched for another victim to pound.

From behind, a warrior slashed her sword across his back. The private spun to face his attacker, who thrust the blade into the trooper's midsection and withdrew it with a blood-splattering flourish. Now brandishing a captured sword, Wade hacked and cut at anyone or anything that came within slicing distance, spinning in a jerky circle in absence of eyes in the back of his head.

Only dreamily aware of her surroundings, Harper's head lolled as a pair of Kindred warriors drug her across the street. She thought it was troopers hauling her off to safety. In the medical RV, Valesquez sat on the floor and sobbed quietly, desperately trying not to hear the screams from outside or the pounding on the door. She was too terrified to move, even if it was Doc at the door.

Screaming at the top of his lungs and grinning like an insane teenager, Stroud swept his M16 from left to right and then back again, firing indiscriminately at pretty much anything that came in his direction; the private, a first-person-shooter video-gamer since he had been old enough to handle the controls, appeared to be having the time of his life as a real-life game played out in front of his own wide eyes.

An explosion erupted near one of the vehicle doorways of the garage; someone or something trying to escape had tripped a Claymore, adding to the confusion and chaos and carnage. A second and then a third followed in quick succession. Halogen lights flicked on as their motion detectors were tripped but lit only the streets outside. The warning claxons added to the cacophony.

He had been a soldier in that previous life and was still a soldier, so he did what all good soldiers did: he fought back. Deacon methodically but cautiously moved through the battleground, shooting fangs when the opportunity presented itself and encouraging his troops to fight.

The major snapped off a short burst at two Kindred attempting to drag a wounded male away. With yelps of pain, they dropped the man and scurried into the shadows.

"Get to your feet and fight, soldier," he said as he stepped over to the wounded trooper. "C'mon, Powell."

The private, enough gold bling around his neck to buy a house, sat up on the dirty floor, shaking his head as if that would help clear it.

"Can you stand?"

"I . . . I think so," Powell said, trying to get his bearings and take stock of his own personal well-being.

"Good, then you can fight, Private," Deacon said, helping to the trooper to his feet.

Headlights from five vehicles now shone in the parking garage and revealed through swirling gun smoke scenes of frantic confusion and bloody death. In a world where violence was the norm, this savagery and brutality was extreme. The troopers' superior firepower was more than compensating for their inferior numbers, and it had begun to exact a heavy toll on the vampires.

In a shooter's stance, Rossington leaned against a Humvee, using the vehicle to protect her backside, and selectively picked off Kindred that passed into the beams of its headlights. It was harder than hell, like trying to shoot snakes fighting over mice without hitting the rodents. As she ejected one clip and grabbed another from her pants pocket, a tall Kindred warrior with a bloody Marine Corps sword passed in front of her. The pale-skinned black man with a pointy goatee turned to her, smiled, and subtly shook his head as if to say, *you won't get me.* She was frozen with the fresh clip halfway to her assault rifle. The lieutenant quickly glanced down, rammed the clip into the weapon, cocked the M16, and peeked up, but he had disappeared into the shadows.

"Shit," she growled. "Shit, shit, shit!"

Terazo passed into view, fired off a burst, and turned to her. "What is it?"

"Nothing," she snarled in disgust but not sure at what. "Fuckin' nothing."

The captain snapped off another blast into the darkness. "Well, then, let's go, Rossington. We're getting the upper hand, so keep pouring it on!" He moved on into the gloom, a burst from his assault rifle silhouetting him against the muzzle flashes.

General Abaddon, who had waded through the battle like Moses parting the Red Sea, stood in the street near one of the large, open doorways of the garage and surveyed the carnage. It had been a brutal and bloody surprise, but he had no idea how successful the operation had been or if it could even be considered a success. He knew, however, that the element of surprise had vanished and the tide had turned. Assault rifles were no match for swords and daggers and clubs. It was time to get the fuck out of Dodge.

Bloody sword in hand, he whistled loudly to get the attention of his officers. "Out!" he yelled at the top of his lungs. "Now!" He heard his surviving lieutenants repeat that same command. Ignoring the vicious life-or-death struggle that took place behind him, Abaddon walked away from the parking structure.

In a heartbeat, the battle was disengaged. Like a single-minded entity, the Kindred fled the garage like vermin fleeing a building in flames. One instant they were fighting and the next they were hightailing it away into the weighted darkness. A handful of troopers found themselves searching for someone to confront, while several others fired at shadows in the night before they finally realized it was just a waste of ammo.

Almost as quickly as it had started, the shooting stopped, but it wasn't replaced by silence. A dull ringing in their ears had taken the place of gunfire echoes, not to mention the moans and cries of the wounded and dying. Cordite stung their eyes and gun smoke burned their nostrils as the troopers moved like ghosts through the headlight-illuminated smoldering remains of what had been their base camp.

Arnett shivered atop the widow's walk as he stared off into the night. He sighed loudly but made no move to go back inside.

He had listened intently as the first few crackles of gunfire built into a constant disharmony of assault weapon fire—and then it petered out to nothing. Just like that, in probably less than five minutes, it had risen to a crescendo and then died. Vann didn't know what to make of it. Had the militia driven off the attackers—he was certain it had been the Kindred—or had the creatures completely overwhelmed them? Arnett had no idea which scenario had played out. He needed to know, but he also knew he couldn't leave to learn the answer at night. He was desperate but not a fool.

"Damn it, Rusty," he said to the dog. "Damn it, damn it, damn it!"

Vann was caught and he knew it. There was nothing he could do at the moment. Whatever had happened, he would have to wait until sunrise to find out.

Fourteen

"What the fuck just happened?" Rossington snarled in anger as she clutched Deacon with her left hand by the fabric of his shirt. She held her M16 in the right.

"We were attacked, Lieutenant," Deacon said calmly as he glanced down at her hand on his shoulder. They stood in the middle of the darkened and smoking ruins that had been their camp, cries and moans and sobs surrounding them.

She released her grip but didn't apologize for grabbing him. "I know that, but . . ."

"Right now, Lieutenant, we need to regroup and get organized," the major said. "We've got to get more light on the situation. We've got wounded who need to be treated, and we need to get Doc and Sandra working on them immediately."

They both flinched when a gunshot pierced the air.

"What the . . ." the lieutenant said, raising her weapon to the ready.

A second, then a third and fourth followed. They had been measured and calculated shots, not randomly popped off.

"Just me," Terazo called out from the darkness. "Doing a little housecleaning."

"Fuckin' idiot," Rossington grumbled mostly under her breath.

"Rossington, find Doc and Sandra," Deacon said to her as Traynor limped beside them. "I want them to get triage started immediately and get our wounded treated right now. We don't have time to wait."

Another gunshot echoed in the garage.

"Yes, sir, Major."

"I need you to stay sharp, Lieutenant," Deacon said to her, harshly. And in a softer tone, he added: "I need to be able to count on you, Rossy."

Two gunshots popped off.

"Sir . . ."

"He's bloodletting right now, Lieutenant."

"Is it necessary? I mean, shit, we could interrogate some of them. Maybe find out something about them."

"I know, I know." Deacon nodded. He knew she was right, but sometimes right didn't matter. Sometimes only blood mattered. "Get Doc and Sandra moving and then see what you can do about finding one or two vampires to *discuss* things with."

"Yes, Major." Rossington headed off into the gloom.

"Be careful, Lieutenant," Traynor called out. She flipped him off without looking back.

"How ya doing?" Deacon asked his trusted adviser.

"Been in worse scrapes."

"Yeah, me, too, but how are *you* doing?"

"Too old for this shit." The two of them surveyed the scene before them. Even in the headlight beams, it wasn't a pretty picture. "We just got our collective ass handed to us, Deke."

A gunshot rang out. Another followed it quickly.

"Yeah, we did."

"We've never encountered anything like this," Traynor said with a slight shake of his head. "We've seen some rudimentary organization among the vampires, hell, even some fairly complex organization, but nothing like this. None of our expeditions have reported anything like this. Nothing at all. Shit, they're organized with something like a military command structure, barking out orders. They hit us like the Chinese at the Yalu River in Korea, November of 1950." An amateur military historian, it was obvious he had a begrudging respect for them. "Shit, they hit us with overwhelming numbers in the face of superior firepower, you gotta respect that."

"Steady, Dave."

"Sorry. It's just . . ."

"I know, I know." Deacon tapped Traynor on the shoulder, causing the Iraqi War vet to wince slightly. "C'mon, let's get some lights on this cluster fuck and find out just how bad it is."

Terazo stalked through the darkness of the parking garage, smoke curling from the barrel of his assault rifle. He was in a nasty-ass foul mood and someone—or some*thing*, more appropriately—was going to pay for it.

How in the hell did this happen? he asked himself. *How in the* fuck *did this happen? How did the vampires get through? Our defenses were tight, and our perimeter was secure. Well, obviously not as secure as it should have been.* And that was another point of contention, but he didn't want to think about that now. He had other things to take care of at this particular moment.

The captain stopped when he came upon a male creature with multiple gunshot wounds trying to crawl away, leaving a significant blood trail in his wake. Without even giving it a first thought, much less a second one, Terazo lowered his M16 and fired a round into the back of the fang's head. It stopped crawling as the back of its skull erupted with a brief geyser of thick dark fluid and brain matter that landed on the cement with an audible *plop.*

"Goddamn fuckin' vampires."

Stroud, with a grin plastered on his blood-streaked face, sauntered over to him. "I've done four of 'em, Captain," he said. "How many have you got?"

More vehicle lights flicked on in the structure. It helped the lighting, but it was still piss-poor at best.

Terazo turned to the scrawny teenager, who looked even mangier in a scruffy T-shirt and dirty boxers. *I may have to settle for him because I have no idea who is even alive or left in one piece,* he thought. *Besides, I may need some of my own cannon fodder.*

"How many, Cap'n?"

"Eleven."

"Shee-it," the private said and spit on the concrete. "I don't think there's enough of 'em left for me to even think about catchin' up."

"Sorry, Private."

"Petrovic's only got five. Maybe I can catch and pass him."

As if on cue, another shot rang out on the far side of the garage.

"Ah, shee-it," Stroud grumbled.

The captain stared at Rossington as she strode purposefully in his direction. He couldn't help but notice she wasn't wearing a bra under her threadbare gray T-shirt, and he liked the way her tits jiggled and the obvious nipples pressed against the material.

"What the fuck are you doing, Terazo?"

"Takin' out the trash, *Lieutenant*. Takin' out the trash."

"Are you a fuckin' idiot or what?" She was pissed and this dip-shit wasn't helping matters at all.

"Careful, Rossington, I guarantee you won't like where this leads."

She glared at him and slowly shook her head. "You know, it's hard to believe that you were actually a cop at one time."

"Detective, as a matter of fact."

"And you're still a fuckin' idiot."

"And you were a small-town chief of police," he said sarcastically. "God's gift to law enforcement. Woo-fuckin'-hoo!"

"At least I wouldn't have killed all the suspects," she said, stepping almost nose-to-nose with him—and she would have been if she were a half foot taller. "I would have fuckin' interrogated them. I would have put their nuts in a wringer and gotten some information out of them. But that's probably too late now, because you and your merry band of dumb-fucks went and killed them all. We can't interrogate dead people."

Terazo glared at her, smoldering hatred burning inside him. *Fuckin' little bitch*, he thought, but he couldn't quite bring himself to say it out loud. He had to fight the urge to reach out and twist one of her nipples. He wanted to hurt her, to make her feel pain—and fear.

"They're animals, Rossington, animals. They're nothin' but fuckin' rodents and they should be treated like rodents. They should be fuckin' exterminated."

She wanted to say something about how those animals had just torn apart their unit, but she settled for, "Fuckin' idiot." Before he could formulate a response, Rossington stomped away and continued to mutter under her breath.

From the other side of the garage came another solitary gunshot that initiated another *shee-it* from Stroud.

Still not quite comprehending the carnage around him and how it had happened so quickly, Wade walked up to Deacon, who had just flicked on another set of headlights.

"Major," the corporal said, "I've got Hagstrom and Powell bringing Wilcox to Medical. A couple of others are still searching and taking stock of the wounded."

"Good. How's Wilcox?"

"Not good." Wade turned away, shook his head, then looked back at Deacon. "I don't think he'll make it. I'm no doctor, but . . ."

"Well, you better go to medical school, Corporal, and quick," Rossington said as she approached them. "We don't know where Doc is."

"What?" the major asked.

"Doc is missing." Rossington stopped next to them. "Valesquez said he went outside when the commotion—her word, not mine—started, he was overpowered by some vampires, and she doesn't know what happened to him after that." The lieutenant shrugged and shook her head.

"Fuck," Wade growled.

"This is not good," Deacon said. "Is Sandra ready for this?"

"She fuckin' better be," Rossington answered, a bit harsher than she had intended to. "We've got no choice now, do we?"

"Fuck," Wade repeated.

"No, we don't." The major frowned and cursed under his breath. "Okay, bring only the most seriously wounded to Valesquez. She can only treat them one at a time anyway. We'll just have to put Band-Aids on the rest of us for now." He turned to face Wade. "Corporal, do you remember any of the combat medical training?"

"A little, I guess."

"Congratulations, you just got your nursing degree."

"Fuck," he said.

"Go help Valesquez as much as you can. She's going to be pretty overwhelmed in there. See if you can find somebody to help you out on the way over."

"Yes, sir." The corporal headed off into the gloom.

"How about you, Rossy? Remember any of your training?"

She shrugged. "Some, I guess."

"Okay, you're in charge of patching up the walking wounded. Nothing fancy, just get the bleeding stopped and sew up what you have to sew up. Get some antibiotics and hand them out like Halloween candy."

"I can do that."

"Thanks, Rossy," the major said as she walked away.

Favoring his left leg, Traynor limped out of the shadows. He carried a spiral notebook and pencil in his hands.

Deacon sighed and frowned. He was not looking forward to what his adviser had to tell him. "How bad is it?"

The black man shrugged. "Bad enough but not quite FUBAR."

"Give it to me."

Traynor frowned. "Five dead."

"Who?" The major wasn't sure he really wanted to hear.

Traynor looked down at the chicken scratch he had scrawled on the lined paper and sighed wearily. He was discouraged by some of the names he'd had to jot down on the list of deaths and more dispirited to have to read them aloud. "Sergeant Briggs, Sergeant Curry, Davis, Norton, and Cooper."

"Shit."

"Wilcox and Tran are hurt pretty bad. Wilcox pretty much looks like a pincushion, stabbed at least a dozen times. Tran . . . well . . . he got hit by friendly fire, couple in the chest and another up in his neck. I'm not sure either one is going to make it. They both have lost a lot of blood. Maybe if we had a hospital or at least a decent field facility with the supplies to treat them, but . . ."

"Shit." Deacon stared off into the garage and could only see a handful of troopers moving about slowly. "Who's left?"

"Well, in addition to our I-don't-know-if-they-will-make-it pair, there's you, me, Rossington, Terazo, Wade, Hagstrom, Osterman, Valesquez, Stroud, Petrovic, Baumann, and Powell."

The major thought for a moment as he mentally tabulated it. "Shit, that's only fourteen and with five more KIA, that's a total of nineteen. Where the fuck are the rest of us? Hell, we had—what?—forty, forty-five people with us when we got here. Where'd they all go?"

Traynor shrugged again. "Missing in action."

"Missing?"

"Yup."

"What the fuck . . ."

Traynor shook his head, having a pretty good idea of what question the major had been unable to finish. "Don't know, and not really sure I want to think about it."

They had all seen some nasty, nasty things during their travels, the kind of things that made you sit up screaming in bed in the middle of the night, the kind of things that made you think that dying was the better alternative.

"How did this happen, David?"

Traynor shook his head slowly. He wished he had an answer, or even a bad excuse. "Don't know, Deke." The ex-military man shrugged again. "Shit happens."

"We gotta find our people," Terazo said, "and then hunt down the motherfuckers that did this and exterminate them. No mercy. No fuckin' mercy."

The officers and Traynor, all of whom were now decked out in full battle rattle with weapons in hand, sat around one of the fire pits that had been righted and rekindled. They all had bottles of water or energy drinks, but there had been no talk of breakfast.

Dawn was still an hour or so away, and besides, none of them felt like eating.

"And where do we find them?" Rossington asked pointedly. "Where? We don't know this city. We have no clue as to where they could be or where the fuckin' vampires are, for that matter. So what, we should go stumbling and bumbling around this whole city looking for them?"

"Should we just forget about them?" the captain shot back at her.

"No, but we need to have a plan," she answered. "We need to think this through and not go off half-cocked—"

"Fuck that!" Terazo interrupted.

"...'cause that will get us all killed. That will get us killed!"

"Fuck that!" the captain repeated. "We don't leave our people behind."

"Don't be an idiot, Terazo, we just can't stumble around blindly in a city we don't know and *hope* that we'll find them."

"And we don't have time to thoroughly recon it and formulate a strategy as to find the most likely places they could be," Terazo said.

"You're an idiot," Rossington said. "Do you know that? You're a fuckin' idiot."

"Fuck you, Rossington."

"If you hadn't gone and killed all the fuckin' vampires that were left behind, maybe, just maybe, we'd know where they were being taken," she said. "But no, that made too much sense, and now we got nothing."

"Fuck you, Rossington. It was payback."

"It was nothing! And we got nothing!"

"Fuck—"

"Enough!" Deacon yelled, shutting up both of his officers. Then much softer, "That's enough." He paused for a moment or two in hopes that the animosity between the two would dissipate a little, but it didn't. They merely glared at one another. "Right now, we have to bury our dead, get rid of the corpses of the fangs, and get this place more secure, that is, if we are going to stay here."

"Where else would we go?" Terazo asked as if there were no other options.

"We could fall back to the farmstead we were at before we moved here," the major said. "It's a relatively defensible and secure position. It's smaller, with fairly good visibility of the surrounding countryside. It's a good position, and it worked well for us once before."

"That's a viable option," Rossington said.

"Oh, of course you'd say that," the captain said, with a contemptuous sneer. "First sign of trouble, and you want to hightail it out of the area."

"Terazo, you're an . . ."

"Enough, goddamn it," Deacon said. "Enough! Fighting among ourselves is not going to solve anything. Now both of you, knock it the fuck off.

"Right now, we have no idea how the vampires got in, and, if they did it once, we have to assume that they can do it again," the major continued. "That doesn't exactly instill a lot of confidence in me about how secure this place is. On the other hand, I'm not in love with the idea of pulling up stakes and racing back to where we just came from, especially since we're a little short of manpower right now. We would have bare-bones security, at best. We'd be sleeping inside vehicles with only claymores as perimeter defenses. Not the best situation in the world."

"I say we stay here, hunt those motherfuckers down, and make them pay," Terazo said. "The sooner, the better."

"I know where you stand, Zo, and your opinion is duly noted," Deacon said. He turned to his female officer. "Rossy?"

The lieutenant was silent as she organized her thoughts. She was torn as to what she wanted to say. Part of her wanted to just get as far away from the parking garage as possible, as fast as possible, but part of her wanted to stay and fight, to exact a measure of brutal revenge. It frightened her to think that she might be more like Terazo than she wanted to admit. "We need to find our people," she said softly and slowly, "and I think we can do that best from here.

But I also think that we need to have a plan, a *real* plan, on how to go about finding them. We can't do it half-assed."

"Thank you, Rossy and Zo," the major said, with a nod to each one of them. "I will think about this and let you all know what I've decided."

"That's it?" Terazo asked, a trace of indignation in his voice. "That's fuckin' it?"

"No, that's not it," Deacon answered. "We have to get those corpses out of here, and we have to bury our dead. And then we will either prepare to get the fuck out of here or we will refortify this place as best we can. If we're going to stay here, we need to find out how the vampires got in and do something about that."

"That's not what I meant."

"Captain, make no mistake, this is not a democracy," the major said directly to the junior officer. "This is a military unit, with a chain of command. And I am at the top of that chain . . ."

For now, Terazo thought behind an expressionless face, *but maybe not for long.*

". . . and I am the one who ultimately makes the decision as to what we do and when we do it. It is my responsibility and my responsibility only. That doesn't mean I can't seek the advice and input of my officers. But the final decision is my decision to make. Do you understand me, Captain?"

After a moment or two of hesitation, the captain said, "Yes, sir."

"Good. Since you went out of your way to create them, you are in charge of getting those corpses out of here, and I expect you to get your hands dirty doing it. I don't give a shit what you do with them—move 'em and burn 'em, dump 'em in the sewer, haul 'em to a building across the street—I don't fuckin' care, but I want them out of here and right now. *Capisce?*"

"Yes, sir." Terazo stood up from his chair and walked away.

Traynor, who had sat silently throughout the impromptu command meeting but dutifully took in everything that had transpired, scrutinized the officer as he strode away. *I don't like how he's acting*, the former soldier and combat veteran thought about Terazo. *He's trouble, nothing but trouble, and he's got something up his sleeve. I know it. He's up to something, and it can't be anything good. Nope, not good at all.* He wordlessly vowed to keep a close eye on the one-time police detective who whistled to get the attention of the other troopers. A *real* close eye.

An orange-pink stain on the base of scattered pale violet clouds in the ever-lightening eastern horizon announced the coming sunrise long before the sun actually crested above the cityscape. The cold pre-dawn air was a crisp precursor to the inescapable onset of winter, but just a faint hint of the battle—the odd mixture of burnt gunpowder, distinctive wood smoke, and freshly spilled blood—lingered in the calm.

Arnett, stomach quivering in anticipation and raw nerves quaking with dread, took a deep breath and held it as he tried to steady his trembling hands. It didn't help. *Here goes nothing,* he thought as he exhaled loudly and stepped around the corner. Rusty, hackles raised just in case, trotted alongside him.

What struck him first was that nothing seemed wrong. The exterior of the parking garage was undamaged. Thin plumes of wood smoke curled out from the ground floor ceiling. Several generators inside the structure droned on tirelessly in indiscernible white noise. A group of four troopers—three officers and another man—stood with their backs to the street in the vehicle entryway, discussing something of apparent importance.

Vann was halfway to the quartet when the tall, swarthy man with long, dark hair and a beard glanced in his direction. The man's eyes went wide with surprise, and he clutched for the assault weapon that was slung over one shoulder. The other three reacted to him and spun in the direction he was looking. Arnett, his right hand on the pistol grip of his lowered M4, raised his left hand—palm open—in a nonthreatening greeting but kept moving forward.

"Hello," he called out, trying to be as natural and non-aggressive as possible. It had been a long time since he'd spoken to a real person, so he had no idea how it came off.

Terazo scrambled to cock his M16 and flick off the safety while he moved out to intercept the approaching individual, leveling the weapon at the long-haired, bearded man dressed in full battle rattle except for the black Chicago White Sox baseball cap. "Stop right there!" he yelled. "Right there, motherfucker!"

"Whoa there, buddy," Arnett called out, stopping in his tracks. Rusty halted alongside him but growled throatily.

"Don't make another move, motherfucker!" Terazo stabbed the assault rifle in Arnett's direction. "Not another move!"

"Easy, easy, easy," Vann said, lowering his left hand to a more defensive position, not that it would matter against an assault rifle. Rusty snapped off an all-business bark before returning to the growl.

"Stay right there!" the captain yelled as he confrontationally strode up to the man, glancing down at the Irish setter in a quick attempt to determine which of the two was immediately more dangerous. "Right fuckin' there!"

"Easy, easy, easy," Arnett repeated. "Don't do anything stupid."

Deacon and Rossington scurried over to where Terazo stood with the assault rifle leveled at Vann, while Traynor scuttled behind them on his bad leg.

"Drop your weapon!" Terazo demanded.

"Hey," Rossington yelled as she skidded to a stop alongside the captain. "What the fuck are you doing?"

"Easy, easy, easy." Arnett's left hand trembled in fear while his right hand quivered tightly on the grip of the M4. He turned to the dog. "No, Rusty. Stay." The setter continued to snarl menacingly but didn't move as Vann turned his attention back to the soldier with the assault weapon pointed at his chest. "Easy, man. Easy."

"Stand down, Zo," Deacon said. "Stand down."

"Drop your fuckin' weapon!"

"Easy, easy, easy," Arnett repeated again, adrenaline ratcheting up in his system.

"Stand down," the major said again. He grabbed the captain by the body armor and pulled him back. "Stand down!"

Terazo glared hard and cold at Deacon.

"You were given an order, soldier," Traynor said.

"Easy, man," Arnett said. "Easy, easy."

"Lower your weapon and stand down, now!" Deacon physically pulled the first captain back. "That's an order, Captain."

As the major pulled Terazo back, Rossington slid in between him and Arnett. She put a hand on Vann's chest and gently pushed him away, giving him a look that said, *Be cool.* She quickly looked at the dog and said, "You, too, bowser."

After a tense second or two, Terazo lowered his weapon.

"Secure it," the major ordered, and the captain begrudgingly complied.

Breathing heavily through his nostrils, Terazo scowled at Deacon.

Traynor leaned close to Terazo and softly said, "Back off, Captain."

The captain turned his scathing gaze to the black man.

"Back off," Traynor repeated.

Terazo was about to make an issue of it until he realized the hard, steel barrel of a Colt .45 automatic was tucked into his side, near his armpit and in an unprotected area just above his body armor. He let Traynor guide him a few feet away from where the others stood.

"Do what I say, Captain, and back off. Or it will be the last thing you ever do."

The captain slung his M16 over his shoulder and turned his scowl to the major.

Deacon ignored him and turned to Arnett. "Who the fuck are you and what are you doing here?"

"My name is Arnett, Vann Arnett, and I live here." He tapped his leg. "Rusty." The dog, still growling softly, sidled over to him.

"Live here?" Rossington muttered.

"In this city," he clarified.

"Well, Mr. Arnett, sorry about the rude welcome," the major said, "but we had a rather rough night, and we're not feeling very hospitable to strangers. We're just a little twitchy right now."

"I suspected as much," Vann said. "I heard all the gunfire earlier this morning, and I figured it wasn't a good thing."

"Heard it, huh?" Rossington said.

"Yeah. My . . . I live about a mile or so from here."

"Who were they?" Traynor asked. He had holstered his .45 but continued to stand behind the captain.

"Kindred."

"Kindred?" Deacon repeated but as a question.

"Yeah," Arnett said, nodding his head. "That's what they call themselves. I didn't realize it at first, but their symbol is on the parking garage."

"Symbol?" the major asked.

"Yeah. See the cross and circle?" Arnett pointed at the red symbol spray painted on the cement side of the structure. All of the troopers, even Terazo, turned and followed the angle of his finger. "It's actually a sword and a serpent."

"What's it mean?" Rossington asked. "The symbol on this building?"

"It's how they mark their territory. These symbols are painted on buildings all over the city."

"Shit," the lieutenant grumbled under her breath and turned away. She had given the initial approval to establish their base camp in the parking garage. She had led them to set up their compound in the middle of a meat grinder. "Shit."

"Who or what are the Kindred?" Deacon asked as they all turned back to Arnett.

"Creatures . . ."

"You mean, vampires?" Rossington asked, trying to regain her composure.

". . . No . . . I can't call . . ." He hesitated for a long second before he started speaking again. "Creatures with some leadership and organization. They're brutal and would like nothing more than to put my head on a stake."

"Charming," Rossington said.

"They torment me because they haven't been able to get me, but they hunt the other creatures in the city," Arnett said. "For what? I can only guess."

"So not all of the *fangs* in the city are part of the Kindred?" Traynor asked.

"No."

"You seem to know a lot about them," Terazo said through practically clenched teeth. "How is that?"

"I don't know nearly enough about them or how they manage to exist," Arnett said, turning to the captain. "But so far I have managed to stay alive despite the fact that I am outnumbered. And to the best of my knowledge, they have managed to wipe out all of the other survivors in this city, but not me. So . . . *Captain*, I am trying to learn more about them, anything I can use against them."

"Good for you," Terazo said sarcastically. "Really."

Arnett ignored him and turned back to the others. "From what I have learned, they supposedly have some kind of charismatic preacher-type leader—they call him the Prophet—and he quotes from the Book of Revelation . . ."

"Vampires who are religious whack jobs," Rossington said. "Oh, this is great."

". . . I haven't seen him, but the few creatures I have interrogated spoke of him with a mixture of awe and fear," Arnett continued. "For some reason, and I am happy as hell that they do, the Kindred shun technological weapons. They prefer swords, daggers, knives, bows and arrows, crossbows, and such. I don't know about how they live—"

"*Where* do they live?" Terazo asked, interrupting him.

"Don't know."

"This is your city, you live here, and you don't know where they live," the captain said incredulously. "You don't know where the enemy is?"

Vann turned to him. "No, I don't. I've been a little preoccupied trying to survive myself."

Terazo turned, pushed himself away from Traynor, and began to walk back toward the parking garage.

"What else do you know about them?" Deacon asked. "What can you tell us?"

At that moment, Valesquez, looking pale and weary, exited the medical RV and walked directly to the group. Blood was splashed on the front and sleeves of her surgical scrubs.

Vann studied her closely as she wordlessly passed the captain. She appeared shell-shocked. *Who can blame her?* he thought as she approached. *We're all shell-shocked, pretty much all of the time.*

The major turned to the onetime PA who was now the group's sole formally trained medical staff member. "Sandra, are you okay?"

"Wilcox is dead," she said as if she didn't hear Deacon's question. "He died a few minutes ago. There was nothing I could do to save him. He had lost too much blood. I did my best."

"I know that, Sandra," Deacon said. He reached out and squeezed her shoulder.

Arnett didn't know how to feel when she didn't react at all to the major's touch.

"I did my best."

"How is Tran?" Traynor asked.

"Alive for now, but I don't know for how much longer," Valesquez answered bluntly. "I actually thought he was worse off than Wilcox, but he's tough."

"Yeah, he is," Rossington said softly.

"Do what you can for him, Sandra," Deacon said, dropping his hand.

She frowned and nodded. "I will." It was then that she realized there was an unknown person in the group. "Who are you?"

"My name is Arnett."

"Oh, okay." She seemed distracted and unable to concentrate.

"Mr. Arnett is an uninfected survivor who lives in this city," Deacon said.

Valesquez studied him up and down, then looked him straight in the eye. "No offense, Mr. Arnett, but I don't care much for your

city." She sighed. "Major, I will keep you apprised of Tran's condition."

"Thank you, Sandra."

She nodded and walked back to the medical RV.

"How good are your defenses, Mr. Arnett?" Traynor asked.

"So far, so good."

"Do you have room for some guests?" the black man asked after a moment of hesitation.

Vann thought about it for a minute or two. In the distance, he
watched Valesquez turn and look in his direction before entering
the RV. "Yeah, I think I can squeeze all of you in."

Fifteen

Once Deacon made the decision to relocate to Wolveshaven and issued the orders, the surviving troopers poured their declining energy into preparations to make the move from the parking garage to the mansion. A couple of them did what could be done to secure the trucks and supplies that would be left behind, setting up some trip-wired booby traps, while the majority of the soldiers prepped the vehicles by packing a startling amount of necessary provisions into every available nook and cranny for the trip. It took less than five hours to accomplish both tasks.

With the early afternoon sunlight streaming down and whispers of winter in the air, they buried their fallen comrades in shallow graves that had been dug in the front lawn of the historic, white-domed capitol building, erecting small, handmade wooden crosses with personal mementos attached to or dangled over the crossbars. Before covering the corpses shrouded in their bloody BDUs and tattered blankets, the major spoke softly and somberly about each of the slain troopers, relating brief stories from better times that elicited sniffles or outright tears from the survivors. Several troopers followed those remarks with mumbled prayers for the salvation of their friends who would never witness another sunrise.

Arnett and Rusty stood discreetly off to the side during the ritual the troopers had gone through before, too many times before, it seemed. There was profound power in the simple words the major spoke and the impact they had on the others. Vann was caught off guard to find tears slipping down his own whiskered cheeks as he felt a sense of loss for people he had never met.

When Deacon finished the solemn task, Arnett kissed the gold crucifix that hung around his neck, made the sign of the cross, and hushed his own "amen" with emotion thick in his voice. He turned and walked toward the parking structure before Hagstrom and Powell began to shovel dirt into the graves. The last funeral he had attended was his own daughter's, and Vann couldn't confront those memories.

Forty-five minutes later, with the afternoon sun high in the sky, Arnett and Rusty led the small convoy of more than a half-dozen Road Warrior–inspired vehicles away from the parking garage and toward Wolveshaven.

They parked the vehicles all over the brown grass of the front yard, giving the impression that some kind of a post-end-of-the-world party was under way at the mansion, but kept the long driveway open and passable. Vann had backed the Tahoe into the garage, the troopers had shut off their vehicles wherever practical without being in the way, and the medical RV had been parked close to the front doors of Wolveshaven.

Deacon rapped on the side door of the RV and waited patiently for Valesquez to open it. When she did, he asked, "How did it go?"

"About as well as can be expected," she said.

"No change?"

She shook her head slightly. "No. On the bright side, he hasn't gotten any worse."

"Okay." The major tried to hide a frown. "We'll take our victories—no matter how small—wherever we can get them."

"Sure."

"Are you going to be okay out here with him?"

"I don't have a choice," Valesquez said. "We can't risk moving him again. Tran's probably not going to make it, but he certainly won't make it if we try to move him inside. Unless he's got a fully functional intensive care unit in there, it's just not worth the risk. I can tend him better right here."

"All right." Deacon glanced at the troopers milling about aimlessly on the lawn and then back at the woman. "Anything I can get you?"

"Yeah," she answered with a nod. "I'd feel a little better with someone who could help me out in here—somebody with a gun."

"All right." The major turned back to the militia soldiers and found who he was looking for. "Baumann, get over here."

An expression of annoyance washed over the young woman's face as she mouthed, *What?* Baumann awkwardly hitched the assault rifle on her shoulder and slowly walked over to the RV.

"Baumann, I need you to help Sandra in the RV—"

"Why me?" she interrupted with a whine.

Deacon stared at her. "Do not interrupt me when I am giving you orders. We are still a military unit, and you are still under my command and will follow the orders I give you. Do you understand?"

Baumann looked down at her scuffed combat boots. She had always been a free spirit. In high school she had worn a similar pair of boots with a flowery orange and yellow summer dress and managed to pull off the look.

"Do you understand me, Private?"

"Yes," she answered glumly, then added as an afterthought, "Major."

"Good. Sandra is going to need some help in Medical, and you're it. Tran is in rough shape and probably will not make it, but she will need another pair of hands to help. You will do what she tells you to do, when she tells you to do it. Understood?"

Head down. "Yeah."

"Good. If you give her any trouble or bullshit, I will hear about it, and you will not like the consequences. Understood?"

"Yeah." Still examining her boots and thinking she should put new laces on them.

"Look at me, Baumann."

The young woman slowly raised her head.

"Do your job, Private."

"'Kay."

"She's all yours, Sandra. You have any problems with Private Baumann, let me know immediately, and I will deal with her."

"I will," Valesquez said with a nod. "Come on, Baumann."

The private rolled her eyes but climbed into the RV.

"Very impressive, Arnett," Deacon said as he surveyed the battlements of the mansion from the front lawn. "Very impressive, indeed."

"How did *you* manage all this?" Rossington asked with a nod of her head in the direction of the residence.

"There were three of us," Vann said. "It was a lot of hard work during some very long, long days. We worked from sunup to sundown five days a week. The other two days we worked on crops or scavenged for anything we could use."

"Are you an engineer or a carpenter?" Traynor asked.

"No, but Hal worked in construction," Arnett said. "He was a high-steel welder. He wasn't even from here, he just happened to be working on a project downtown when The Collapse happened. But he knew his stuff, and we couldn't have done all this without his expertise. I guess his misfortune was my good fortune."

"You said there were three of you. Where are the other two now?" Deacon asked.

Arnett frowned and shook his head. "Don't know."

"Don't know?" the major said with an arched eyebrow.

"No, I don't." Vann wasn't sure how much of this he wanted to share. "Hal and Sylvie went out and worked a field a few miles from the city one day last spring, and they never came back."

"What happened?" Rossington asked.

"I don't know. Rusty and I searched for them—we covered everywhere from the fields they had tilled that day all the way back to Wolveshaven. We didn't find a trace, not a goddamn single trace."

"Shit," Traynor muttered mostly under his breath.

"Maybe they just took off on you," Terazo said, sarcastically. "Not everybody is into a threesome."

"I don't think so." Vann shook his head slowly.

"Why?" Rossington asked.

"Why?" he echoed.

"Yeah, why?"

"If they were just going to take off, run away, why did they spend all day working in the field? I wouldn't have done that. I would have cut out at first light and got as far away as I could before sunset. If they were going to leave, why didn't they take their things? They left all their personal stuff and mementos here. You all know as well as I do that there are certain personal things that you will not leave behind. No matter what, you will not leave them behind. It may not be the most expensive thing—maybe a photo, a necklace, or a ring, some little gift from a loved one, anything—but you don't run away without it. You *won't* leave it behind."

Every single trooper silently nodded. They all knew what he meant.

"Hal and Sylvie left all of their things here, everything," Arnett said. "They didn't just run away. I *know* they didn't."

"So what do you think happened to them?" Traynor asked, speaking out loud what they all were thinking.

Vann sighed loudly. "I don't know." He didn't even try to hide his frown this time and whispered, "I don't know."

The early evening supper had been red beans and rice with some sliced bratwurst mixed in. Arnett had gotten the half-dozen boxes of Zatarain's from his overstuffed pantry and three packages of Johnsonville sausages from the packed upright freezer. Osterman and Hagstrom had joined him in the well-furnished kitchen to prepare the meal. Even though it was something far different from what the troopers were used to eating, the majority of the men and women, who had wearily shrugged off their body armor and battle gear, only listlessly picked at the spicy but flavorful food. Their appetites, it seemed, had deserted them, and they had eaten out of necessity rather than desire.

After everyone had pitched in to bring the dishes and silverware to the kitchen, they sprawled out in the third-floor great room to take a load off and try to shove their thoughts away from what had taken place during the day.

Arnett sat in a comfortable forest-green Lane recliner, but Rusty had drifted away to sit near Rossington, who had perched herself in the khaki print armchair. Deacon and Traynor had plopped down on the maroon camelback Thomasville sofa, while Osterman had plunked herself down between them. Terazo, obviously impressed, sat in a leather office chair in front of the monitors that displayed the images from the outdoor security cameras. The other troopers found spots wherever they could, the recliner's twin or the two remaining armchairs, large throw pillows on the hardwood floor or the polished oak itself in front of the fireplace.

"How many survivors have you encountered?" Vann asked.

"More than you'd think, but not as many as we'd like," Deacon answered.

"But nowhere near as many survivors as vampires," Rossington added.

"Any . . . I don't know . . . communities, groups of survivors?"

"Yeah," the major said. "A lot of small groups of survivors, between two and five people, once in a while a dozen or so. Every now and then a single survivalist . . ."

"Who's usually crazier than a shithouse rat," Rossington piped in.

". . . who is usually crazier than a shithouse rat," Deacon repeated with a smile. "On our first run out of The Base last summer, we found one group of about sixty people in London, Kentucky. They had walled off a good part of the city, one way in and one way out. It was pretty much a military compound, but it was working well for them. We stayed there about ten days before moving on. They were still there and doing well when we passed by this time out.

"One of the other patrols sent out from The Base reported a compound of more than a hundred people near Carthage, Texas," the major continued, "but they weren't terribly hospitable. In their defense, I guess, it had been less than six months after The Collapse."

"What about . . ." Vann couldn't finish the question

"Vampires," Rossington said with a grin.

"They're not vampires," Arnett said. "They're not supernatural creatures. They don't turn into bats and fly away. They can enter your house without an invitation. They can be killed with bullets. Obviously they have no aversion to a cross . . ."

"Yes, but they drink blood, they have fangs, and they avoid the sun," the lieutenant said with an even wider smile. "That makes them vampires in my book."

Arnett sighed and began to say something but shut his mouth. He knew how to pick his battles, and he suspected this was one he would not win.

"Our experience has been that they seem to gather in packs," Deacon said, a smile disappearing from his lips, "anywhere from several dozen to several hundred. I'm sure there are smaller groups of them out there, but we just haven't encountered them. For the most part, they are unorganized and have pretty much an animalistic, hand-to-mouth existence."

Vann thought about the female he'd met in the mall. She was smart and the group she belonged to seemed to be somewhat organized. Then there was the Kindred and the Prophet. He considered bringing them up but kept his mouth shut.

"Our search patrols have encountered some groups, particularly the larger ones, that were somewhat organized with some basic structure," the major said, "but nothing like what we ran into here. Don't get me wrong, these vampires have managed to survive this long, so if they're not smart, they are at least very cunning."

"You see, Mr. Arnett," Traynor said, "there are two distinct schools of thought about them at The Base. One says that they are nothing but animals, clever and vicious, but still animals, while the other says that some of them have retained most, if not all, of their human intelligence."

"Which school of thought do you adhere to?" Vann asked.

The black man smiled at him. "Oh, you see, Mr. Arnett, I am just an old soldier and I follow orders, so it really doesn't matter *what* I think."

Deacon grinned and shook his head, while Rossington rolled her eyes.

"That's very . . . diplomatic," Arnett said, "but bullshit."

Traynor laughed. "And that, Mr. Arnett, was not very diplomatic."

"What else do you know about them?" Vann asked.

"The only good vampire is a dead vampire," Petrovic shot in from the floor.

"Besides that?"

"What do we *know*? Not much," Deacon said. "We have a lot of speculation and conjecture, but not much fact."

"You haven't attempted to capture any and study them?"

"That, too, is an ongoing debate at The Base," Traynor said. "And so far, those who favor research and examination are in the minority. So no, we haven't captured any for research purposes."

"There are concerns about security," Rossington said. "Valid ones, I might add. Nobody is too thrilled about the prospect of having even one of them inside The Base, no matter how much security is in place."

"Can't say that I would disagree with you."

"But as a consequence, we don't know jack shit about them," she added.

"Nobody does," Traynor said.

"Or at least nobody that we're aware of," Osterman said from between the two men.

Arnett gave her a look.

"Hey, it's a big country out there and an even bigger world," the private said. "I am not so naïve as to think that we are the only ones who have established a settlement on what could be loosely called a large scale. I would be surprised if there wasn't something even bigger than what we have."

"Private Osterman is right," Deacon said, "but we still know very little about the vampires"—he nodded at Arnett—"or creatures, as you call them.

"We know they need blood to survive," the major continued, "but not necessarily human blood. Animal blood will apparently work, because we've seen the corpses of animals of all sizes in and around their . . . nests, and we also know they're not above cannibalism to get that blood because we've seen evidence of that. We suspect they don't need very much blood to stay alive, but how much or how little they actually need, we don't have a clue.

"We also know they're not very active during the colder months—I'm sure you found that out last winter—but we don't know if they hibernate or what they do. We just know we didn't see very many of them—actually, we didn't see *any* vampires during the winter—and believe me, we went looking for them."

Vann thought for a moment about what the major had said. He couldn't recall seeing any of the creatures during the long winter months, but they hadn't consciously gone out looking for them, either. They had been too busy trying to stay warm. He knew the Kindred hadn't harassed the three of them during the months when snow covered the landscape.

"What else do you know?" he asked.

It took Deacon and a handful of troopers less than ten minutes to tell him.

In the fading light of early twilight, with two Tupperware containers filled with food in his hand, Arnett knocked on the door of the medical RV and opened it without waiting for a response. His heart thudded in his rib cage a little quicker than it should have, and his palms were clammy despite the chill in the air. He had no idea what to expect and only a marginal one of what he was doing.

"Anybody home?" Vann called out as he stepped into the vehicle.

The onetime recreational vehicle was packed tight with medical equipment of all sort and size. Tran, unconscious and hooked to a system monitor that beeped irregularly and cast an eerie green glow, lay on one of two retrofitted medical beds in the area that had been the sleeping section of the RV. Private Baumann lounged behind the steering wheel of the rig, while Valesquez sat on the small bench behind what had been the tiny dining nook and thumbed through a medical book. The two women turned to the door, while the sheet-covered and gravely wounded soldier remained motionless.

"I thought you might be hungry," Arnett said as he climbed up the steps into the vehicle, "so I brought you something to eat." He made a concerted effort not to trip or stumble.

"I'm starving," Baumann said, rising quickly from the captain's chair with eyes going wide.

"Easy, Private," Valesquez said abruptly and thought, *The girl has no finesse.*

"But . . ." She stopped and slumped back down into the chair.

"I'm not interrupting anything, am I?" Vann asked.

"No," the PA said. "It's just . . ." She didn't finish the sentence and shook her head slowly. "No."

"Good." Arnett placed one of the containers down on the table in front of her and handed the other to the private. "Red beans and rice with sliced bratwurst in it."

Baumann popped open the container and breathed in the aroma. "Smells great," she said, closing her eyes.

"Oh, I brought silverware, too." He plucked two forks wrapped in paper napkins from a jacket pocket and handed them out to the women. "Makes it a little easier to eat, I guess."

"Thanks," Baumann said, taking the fork and returning to her chair.

"Thank you," Valesquez said, accepting the silverware. "You didn't have to do this, but it's very nice of you."

"You're welcome." Arnett smiled at her. "We had already eaten our meal and then I remembered that you two were out here. Nobody had brought you anything."

"Par for the course, Mr. . . . Arnett," the PA said when his name returned to her. "Par for the course."

"Vann," he said. "My name is Vann, with two *ns*."

"Thanks, Vann, with two *ns*," Baumann said, smiling around a mouthful of food.

Valesquez rolled her eyes. "That charming young lady is Private Tina Baumann, and I'm Sandra Valesquez."

"Nice to meet both of you."

"This stuff is great," the private said, shoveling in rice and beans as if she hadn't eaten in a long time. A very long time.

Sandra sampled a forkful and smiled. "It is good."

"Surprised?" Arnett asked.

"No." The PA smiled at him. "Well, maybe a little."

"Hey, I know my way around a kitchen. And, I'll have you know, it takes a great deal of skill to open boxes of rice and beans and boil sausages in water. Not just anybody can do it."

"I would have fu . . . screwed it up," Baumann said.

"I was really good at ordering take-out," Valesquez said with a grin. "Had a couple of restaurants on my speed-dial and everything. And I did mortify my grandmother when I was about fifteen and told her that I actually liked Taco Bell."

Arnett smiled. "That's got to be worth something."

"Well, she just shook her head at me and muttered something in Spanish that I had never heard before—or since. I suspect it wasn't good, because it made my mother gasp. Neither of them ever told me what she said."

Vann chuckled. He couldn't help it. This was even better than the imaginary conversations he had had with her in his head.

"I actually talked to my friends about it, trying to sound it out so we could figure out what she had said." Sandra shook her head. "We tried for a week or so, but none of them had ever heard it, either. None of them dared to ask their parents. I don't know what it was, but it had to be a really good one." She smiled a little sadly as her thoughts turned to her grandmother and all that the woman had done for her. "That was a long time ago."

"Sorry," he said, not knowing what else to say after an extended silence.

"No, no. That's okay," Valesquez said, giving him another shy grin. "She was a remarkable woman, so was my mother, and I don't think about them enough. Not nearly enough."

Her expression brought a smile to Arnett's face and an unexpected tingle south of the border. "I would like to hear about them," he said.

Sandra stared at the ragtag man standing before her and couldn't help but wonder about the twists and turns of his life that had brought him to this point. Anyone still alive had already been through hell and back. After thinking about it for a moment or two, she softly said, "I'd like to tell you about them."

He stared into her brown eyes with a silly grin stuck to the lower half of his face. She had beautiful brown eyes—and he had always gone for women with beautiful eyes.

"Hey, if you guys would like some time alone, so you could . . . you know, I could go outside and finish my supper," the private said with a salacious grin plastered on her face. "And I promise I won't peek through the windows. Well, maybe I'll peek."

Arnett snorted out a laugh, while Valesquez rolled her eyes in embarrassment.

"Shut up, Baumann," the PA said, but there was no conviction or meanness in the three words.

"If we're going to have any chance at success with this, we're going to need your help, Mr. Arnett."

Vann thought about Deacon's request. The leader of the soldiers wanted him to help them find their missing comrades, to help them identify locations to search. It really wasn't much different from what he and Rusty had been doing, searching buildings for signs of their activity or the creatures themselves. There would just be more people involved with it. But did he really want that? Was he willing to do that? He had his own method to his searches, so could he give up complete control?

"What do you say, Mr. Arnett?" Traynor asked him, leaning forward on the sofa with his elbows on his knees. "We can't do this without your help."

"Yeah," he said softly, "I can do what you want."

"Good," Deacon said, nodding his head. "Very good."

"Excellent," Traynor added, sitting back into the comfy sofa and smiling.

"I know you said that you have searched the buildings near here and didn't find anything that could be used as a . . . holding area," the major said, "but the vampires had to take our people somewhere. Any ideas where that might be?"

"I doubt that it would be a one-family residence, or even a duplex," Arnett said after thinking about it for a moment or two. "I just don't see that as being practical. I don't know what you've got in mind, but if you're going to move a significant number of people—more than a dozen incapacitated people—and you want to do it fast, you've got to have the type of facility that can handle them. It's got to be a good-sized building, whether it's an office building or apartment complex or something like that. I suspect they would take them to a lower level or the basement."

He studied the faces of Deacon and Traynor, glanced at Rossington, who was expressionless, and turned back to the two men. Vann didn't like what he saw in their eyes. "What? What is it? What do you suspect happened to them?"

The major turned to his adviser, who slowly nodded his head. Deacon frowned.

"Tell him, Deke," Rossington said. "He should know."

"Yeah, he should know what he's getting into," Terazo said without looking away from the monitors.

"Tell him," Rossington repeated.

"Tell me what, Major?"

Deacon faced Vann. "The vampires use them for food."

"You don't need to be a genius to figure that one out," Arnett said with a hint of sarcasm.

"I'm not sure you understand. Our group has encountered places where the vampires have kept people like . . . like fuckin' cattle," the major said. "They kept them drugged or whatever, drained them a little at a time until they were all used up and no good to them. Then they just tossed the corpses away like trash. Every expedition that The Base has sent out has encountered some kind of setup along those lines. Every one *without* fail. We ran into them in two cities on our first journey out and three so far this time. How they do it is each a little different, but the end results are pretty much the same."

"The worst ones are where there are humans who help the vampires," Rossington said.

"Why would they . . ." Vann couldn't finish the question, the implications of it too horrific to contemplate.

"You know the vampires of legend oftentimes had human assistance," Traynor said. "Someone who protected them when they were vulnerable, someone who looked after them during those dangerous daylight hours."

"Dracula had his Renfield," Rossington said and then arched an eyebrow. "And Barlow had his Straker."

Arnett gave her a look of appreciation. "But this . . . this is . . ."

"Wrong," Terazo fired in.

"Yeah, wrong," he said, although he hated to agree with the captain. "It's just fuckin' wrong. Why would they do it?"

"A number of reasons," Traynor said.

"Worthless bastards," Osterman muttered mostly under her breath. She was half-asleep and leaning against the black man.

"Sometimes they didn't have a choice or thought they didn't," the major said, with a shrug. "The vampires held loved ones as hostages and threatened them unless the other survivors went along with what the fangs wanted. In some instances, the survivors were vastly outnumbered and thought it was their best option for survival . . ."

"Which is another way of saying at least one survivor sold them out," Rossington said, not bothering to hide the contempt in her voice.

"Shit," Vann muttered.

". . . so they made a deal with the devil," Deacon continued. "Some of them thought they could work both sides of the line, stay in the good graces of both the survivors and the vampires. Others were just opportunists, staying alive by taking steps to make certain that someone else picked up the tab."

"History is littered with people like that," Traynor said. "Traitors, carpetbaggers, quislings, whatever you want to call them, they are always there."

"And still are," Rossington added.

Traynor nodded in agreement. "And still are."

"It doesn't matter why they did it—or are still doing it—the problem is the fact that they have done it in the first place," the major said. "We put an end to it when we can, throwing a wrench in the machinery, so to speak, but other times we could only move on without doing anything.

"We had to do it once," Deacon continued, "and let me tell you, it was the single most difficult decision I ever had to make. *Ever.* Mr. Arnett, I was an inexperienced, know-nothing Army officer on the front lines during the Iraqi War. I cut my combat teeth in the dusty hellhole that was Fallujah, and men died because of the decisions I made and the actions I took." He shook his head slowly. "But none of that prepared me to make the decision to leave those people behind the way we left them. I am a soldier and my profession is death, Mr. Arnett, but that . . . that was something other than death. It was worse than death."

Traynor had spoken with Deacon at length about their similar military experiences, Rossington had heard some of it, but for the handful of troopers who remained awake, this was the first time they had heard him speak anything of his two tours in Iraq. It was common knowledge among the soldiers and at The Base that he had been an army combat officer, but, beyond a chosen few, that was it. Like many veterans, he shared only select tidbits of his service life, and usually with only those who could grasp the harsh reality and finality of such brutality.

"So you think there's such a place in this city?" Vann asked.

"No," the major said, shaking his head. "I *know* there is, and probably more than one. You've told us that you've seen at least several hundred of the . . . the Kindred and that there are other vampires in the city."

"Yeah."

"Let's just throw out a number—say, five hundred—vampires in the city, but I suspect that number is way too low. I want to know, how are they surviving?" Deacon asked. "How do they make it from one day to the next? What are they eating?"

Arnett could only stare at him with his mouth open as he tried to wrap his mind around the troubling thoughts that had escaped the Pandora's box that had just been opened. He wondered how he could have been so blind, how he could have survived all this time.

"Quite frankly, Mr. Arnett," Deacon said with a nod in his direction, "you must be the single, luckiest creative writing professor in the entire world, because that's the only reason I can come up with as to why you are still alive."

"It's not luck, it's a curse."

"A curse?" Traynor asked with a hint of a smile on his lips. "Mr. Arnett, you are alive, and, I would say, doing quite well."

Vann laughed derisively. "Quite well, huh?"

"Yes."

"You have no clue," Arnett said, a trace of anger in his words. "No fuckin' clue at all. This isn't luck, all of this . . . this is a curse."

Deacon sat back uncomfortably on the sofa, wondering just how far this discourse would go, while Rossington looked on intently to see how their host would react to a verbal onslaught. Terazo remained transfixed by the monitors.

"A curse?" the black man asked again. He had always relished playing the devil's advocate, regardless of whether it was with an officer under which he served or the soldiers he led.

"Yeah, a curse," Vann said defiantly. "My twelve-year-old daughter came down with this fuckin' plague, and I helplessly watched a beautiful and vibrant child—one of my reasons for living and breathing—die a tortured and horrible death. Did you see a loved one go through that, Mr. Traynor? A sweet and innocent child? No? Well, then, shut the fuck up, because I did, up close and personal. It was an experience I would not wish upon my worst enemy. I wouldn't even wish it upon them out there." He jerked his head in the direction of the exterior of the mansion. "And then my wife got the plague, but she didn't die."

Vann snorted out a humorless laugh. "Oh no, not my Susannah. The love of my life became one of those things . . . those goddamn *vampires* . . . and she's out there now, out there somewhere." He waved his arm in the air to indicate the city. "Actually, I don't know if she's alive or dead. I don't know if she's part of the Kindred or with the others. But here I am, still alive. So, Mr. Traynor, with all due respect to your opinion, I have to tell you that you are full of shit. I am not lucky. I am cursed."

Several hours after Arnett had verbally gotten the best of Traynor, which he had silently enjoyed, Terazo stepped out into that darkness that surrounded the widow's walk.

"Halt, who goes there?" Petrovic asked sarcastically.

"Fuck you, Petrovic," the captain responded, eliciting a chuckle from the private, who had wrapped a sleeping bag around his shoulders and battle rattle.

"Nice view, huh, Cap'n?" Petrovic asked as the officer stopped alongside him.

"Yes, yes, it is. I think this could work out for us very well." Terazo scanned the area in the darkness and smiled. "It's a good defensive position with decent battlements. They did a good job. I see a few things that we can improve, but it's set up quite well."

It was about forty minutes after midnight, and Petrovic was the second of three sentries who would keep lookout until dawn. Osterman had been the first, and Hagstrom would be the last.

"Did you see the supplies he's got?"

"Yes."

"Tons of canned goods and boxes of food, with a freezer full of meat. Hell, there are more medical supplies in this place than he could ever think about using. He's got vitamins and other pills up the yin-yang. And he's got more booze than a liquor store."

"What did you do, search the place?"

"Yeah, pretty much. When he brought the food out to the RV, I took a little look-see. Shit, this guy's got enough stuff here to last us for several years."

The officer shrugged. "Probably not that long, but there's still a lot. But you know what makes this place even better? There's good soil around here, and if we have a decent growing season, we'll be able to be able to plant some crops and have fresh vegetables at harvest and freeze the rest for later. I bet there are fruit trees around here, too. If nothing else, at least some apple trees, but who knows what else."

"Hey, I'm no farmer."

"Ah, Petrovic, but you will become one," the captain said and slapped him on the shoulder. "You will be a soldier and a farmer."

"I'd be a better hunter and gatherer," he said. "I bet there's a lot of deer around here, and I do know how to field dress and butcher a deer. There could even be some cows that survived and have gone native. We could round a couple of them up and have fresh milk and butter."

"Are you looking to pull tits, Petrovic?"

"Not on cows."

Terazo chuckled. "Somehow this guy has managed to survive, whether it's just dumb luck or some skill . . ."

"Or he's cursed," the private shot in.

". . . or a combination of both," the captain continued, ignoring the remark, "he has managed to stay alive while greatly outnumbered by some pretty fuckin' sneaky vampires. I'm sure this place has something to do with it, maybe even a lot to do with it. I know it wouldn't hold up against artillery, of course, but as long as the local fangs want to play Renaissance Fair and only use swords and arrows, it should be formidable enough to keep them out. I think we could do quite nicely here."

"Yeah, but the female population kind of took a hit."

"Our entire population kind of took a hit, but there's still Baumann, Osterman, and Valesquez."

"What, no Rossington?"

"Afraid not," Terazo said, shaking his head. "That bitch would be nothing but big trouble. Big, big trouble. It doesn't mean we can't have some fun with her first, but I'm afraid she doesn't make the cut. When we're done with her, I plan to kill her myself, slowly. Real slowly."

"So who's with us?" The private almost whispered the words.

"There's me and you, Wade and Powell. I figure Stroud won't be a problem, but I haven't told him anything. I think we'll just let him make up his own mind when the shit hits the fan and the bullets start flying. If he's with us, fine. If he's not, he's dead."

"What about Hagstrom?"

"He's the one I'm worried about," the captain said after organizing his thoughts. "We know where everyone else stands, but he's the wild card. I'm not sure which way he'll go when it all comes down." He hesitated, then asked, "You were in his squad. What do you think?"

Petrovic thought for a moment, mulling it over. "If Briggs was still here, I know he'd go with him. Whichever way he went, that's what Hags would do. But the serge is gone, so I don't know which way he'll go. He would be a good guy to have on our side but a bad one to have against us."

"That's what I'm afraid of." Terazo scratched the dark whiskers on his chin. "I'm not sure we can risk it, so I'm not going to say anything to him. I think we'll just have to play him like Stroud."

"He's a helluva lot more dangerous than Stroud."

"I know that, so that's why we'll have to watch him more closely when we make our move. If he even looks like he will fall in line with Deacon and the others, then we'll have to take him out."

"That's pretty harsh."

"We just can't risk it, and you know it," Terazo said bluntly. "You yourself said that he would not be a good guy to have on our bad side, and we can't risk it."

"I know, it just that—"

"Don't even start thinking like that." The captain pointed a finger at him. "We can*not* afford to have any doubts. We're either all-in or not at all, because when we do this, it's got to be quick and it's got to be clean. The last thing that we want is a long and bloody standoff inside this place or out there"—he nodded in the direction outside of the mansion—"wherever we make the move. That won't do any of us any good. Understand?"

"Yeah."

"Are you all-in, Petrovic?" The captain deliberately put his hand on the butt of his pistol but, in the dark, he wasn't sure the private even saw him do it. Intimidation only worked if the other person knew he was supposed to be intimidated.

"Yeah," he said softly. "I'm all-in."

"Good. I knew I could count on you, Petrovic."

Sixteen

The morning had dawned cold and damp and gray. Clouds the color of faded bruises hung low in the sky and obscured the sun, while the air was faintly perfumed with the promise of impending precipitation, yet it offered no clue as to whether it would come in the form of rain or sleet or both.

The troopers roused slowly in the relative warmth and comfort of Wolveshaven. It was something they weren't accustomed to: a roof over their heads and four walls around them. In the space of just a few hours, however, many of them had made the transition from wandering nomads who slept lightly with one eye open just in case to homebound folks who crashed hard and fast, oblivious to their surroundings. It was that sense of normalcy and safety that they desired and craved. It was also why many of them had agreed to undertake two extended missions away from the security of Burton Army Base, to receive the full rights and privileges of citizenship in a more expeditious manner.

Breakfast had consisted of coffee and energy drinks along with stale energy or granola bars. They consumed it out of a sense of necessity, the need to put fuel in the tank, but there was no satisfaction or enjoyment in the process. None of the troopers really had any appetite because they all knew what lay ahead for them. The morning meal had merely delayed the inevitable, the start of the mission.

Some forty-five minutes later, three Humvees rolled away from the mansion and headed toward the heart of the city.

Deacon halted the small convoy in the middle of a surface street where the residential neighborhood began to transition into the commercial district.

"How much of this area have you searched?" the major asked from the driver's seat of the lead vehicle.

"All of it," Arnett answered from the passenger seat.

"All of it?" Powell questioned from behind him. The private, gold chains twinkling outside of his body armor, sat uncomfortably next to Rusty, who eyed him suspiciously.

"Yeah, all of it." He pointed in the direction of a single-story brick building. "See the front door of that building?"

"Yeah," Powell said. "So?"

"See anything else?"

"It's a fuckin' building, man. Looks like nobody's been in it for years. Big fuckin' deal. I've seen thousands . . . *thousands* of them."

"Do you see anything on the building, anything . . . say . . . near the doorway?"

"Yeah, there's an *X* painted on the wall by . . ." Powell stopped as the realization dawned on him.

"Ooh, imagine that," Arnett said. "There's an *X* painted on the brick wall near the door. Will wonders never cease?"

Deacon smiled in spite of himself.

"Look at the other buildings in this area, what do you see?"

After a moment of scrutiny, Powell mumbled, "*X*s on all the buildings."

"Give the man a prize," Vann said. "A black *X* near the door means the building has been searched and I didn't find any signs of them. A red *X* means I found signs or actually found some of them in the building, while a red *K* means I found Kindred in the building. In this neighborhood, there are only black *X*s on the buildings—all of them.

"If you want to find buildings that have not been searched yet, we need to go in that direction," he continued, pointing to the left. "If you want to look in buildings I have already searched, then this is a good place to start. As good as any other, that is."

"How far?" Deacon asked.

"A dozen blocks or so," Vann answered. "We want to get west of your . . . your parking garage."

"What types of buildings are we looking at?" the major asked.

Arnett shrugged. "Factory-type buildings, warehouses and such. The odd-out office complex, not to mention apartments and such. Most, if not all of them, are brick. Some of them are multi-story, some of them are not."

"Basements?"

"If not full basements, at least some kind of lower level in most of them."

"In other words, a good possibility for what we're lookin' for, right?" Powell said.

"A lot of potential, but no guarantees we will find anything."

"Ain't no guarantee of anything in this life 'cept death," the private said. He turned his face to look into the eyes of the Irish setter. "And you can take that to the corner, dawg."

Thirty minutes later, the soldiers, all of them with radio headsets on and geared up in battle rattle, although only half wore their Kevlar helmets, parked the vehicles in the middle of the potholed street and entered the run-down brick building through the broken door. Traynor, because of his prosthetic left leg, sat in the passenger seat of the middle Hummer and monitored the radio traffic between the soldiers. He had a spiral-bound notebook and pencil to jot down notes about the progress of the search.

Ten heavy-duty flashlights—a combination of high-powered Maglites and Surefires, some attached to weapons, others hand-held—cut through the gritty darkness and illuminated the remains of a vandalized machine shop. Looters had found little of value in the building during the death throes of civilization, so they trashed it, wantonly smashing and destroying whatever they could get their hands on and scattering the unwanted debris about the floor. It was a minefield of jagged metal, broken glass, and shattered concrete.

"There's broken shit all over the place, so everybody be extremely careful where you walk," Deacon ordered. "I don't want any accidents, because now is not the time or the place."

They fanned out in two five-man teams. Arnett with Deacon, Petrovic, Osterman, and Powell at point drifted to the right, while Terazo led Rossington, Hagstrom, Wade, and Stroud to the left.

"Watch your spacing, people," Terazo said as the two groups moved in opposite directions. "Stay sharp."

It took them about a half an hour to search the building. They found nothing.

"I didn't see any steps that led down to a basement or anything that would make me believe there is even a basement in this building," Rossington said as the troopers began to assemble near the exit.

"I didn't, either," the major said, confirming the lieutenant's statement.

"I think it's a bust," Terazo said, casting a nasty look in Vann's direction. "A great big fuckin' zero."

"I would have to agree," Deacon said, attempting to defuse the captain's sarcasm by pushing forward.

"So did you find anything?" Traynor's voice crackled over the radio.

Petrovic put his hand over his mic. "Yeah, a whole lotta nothin.'"

"Zip it," Terazo warned the private without bothering to cover his mic.

"We got nothing, David," the major said. "This building is empty. No signs of any activity, much less inhabitation. We're moving out."

"Okay," the radio squawked.

It was a little more than four hours and six buildings before the troopers stumbled upon an unexpected reward for their efforts in the darkened basement of what had been an abandoned three-story factory. They had found it none too soon, for their optimistic anticipation of the morning had turned to annoyed frustration of the afternoon, but their unquenched lust for revenge had climbed toward bloodlust.

"Whoa, shit!" Osterman called out in startled surprise when her flashlight lit up three bedraggled shapes wrapped in sleeping bags sound asleep in the corner of what had been a long and narrow storage room. She had smelled them before she had seen them, but the private was still surprised when her light illuminated the dirty figures in the tight confines.

Powell shouldered his way past her, leveling his SAW machine gun with one hand and his flashlight with the other. "Well, lookee here!" He stepped forward and brutally kicked the nearest one, who appeared to be the biggest of the trio and in the middle. "Wake up, fangs!"

The male creature jumped and grunted in surprise. Fear exploded in his colorless eyes and across his dirt-streaked pale face an instant before he protectively brought an arm up to shield his eyes. His sudden movements roused the two vampires beside him: an older male and female. After a moment's hesitation came the terrifying recognition and the same panicked reaction as they attempted to scramble into defensive postures, while the tall vampire remained motionless.

"Don't fuckin' move!" Powell snarled at them. "Not one inch! Hear me? Not one fuckin' inch!"

The two creatures stopped their jerky and uncoordinated movements. They looked down and away from the lights, while the tall vampire kept his arm in front of his face.

"What have you got?" Terazo called out, his voice also crackling over the radio.

"We got three fangs," the private said over his shoulder.

"We're on our way there," Deacon said over the radio. "Everybody form up at Captain Terazo's position."

A smattering of affirmative responses came over the radio.

Terazo, with Stroud a step behind him, arrived at the scene. "Good work, Powell."

"I found 'em," Osterman said, defensively. "It was me, I found 'em."

The captain ignored the comments and elbowed his way past her.

She muttered something under her breath that sounded like *fuck you*.

Stroud turned to her, smirked, and silently chuckled.

She lowered her weapon and flipped him off.

"Stand up slowly," Terazo said to the vampires as he moved front and center of Powell. "Don't make any sudden movements or they will be the last ones you ever make."

The three creatures began to stand, rising cautiously and slowly. Their sleeping bags fell from their bodies as they did so. The tall vampire, who stood six-three but was rail thin, positioned himself in front of the other two as best he could, still shielding his eyes with his hand.

"How touching," the captain sneered. "What is this, your happy little family?"

Two at a time, the other troopers began to arrive at the storage room: Rossington and Petrovic, Wade and Hagstrom. The bright flashlight beams of the new arrivals probed the room like small searchlights until they found their targets, illuminating the frightened fangs.

"Spread out," Terazo ordered the vampires. "I want to see all of you."

They hesitated.

"Now!"

The tall vampire, who appeared to be in his late twenties, sidled to his right, while the female, who was in her late teens, moved to his left side and the forty-something male flanked her.

"What are we going to do?" the female whispered to the tall male.

"Shut the fuck up!" Powell said and took a menacing step forward.

The female and the older male cringed backward a half step, but the tall vampire defiantly held his ground.

Led by Rusty three paces ahead of them, Deacon and Arnett arrived at the storage room. The major stepped forward, with the Irish setter growling by his leg, and the troopers parted to let him through. Vann found a spot just a couple of steps to the right of Rossington. He gave her a look of concern.

"Powell found three of 'em," Terazo said as the major stopped at his side.

"I found 'em," Osterman complained but not too loudly.

"Good work." Deacon glanced in her direction, and the private smiled smugly. "Let's find out what they know."

Tossing his flashlight to Powell, the captain grinned and stepped forward, keeping his assault rifle leveled on the tall vampire. "All of you, take off your clothes."

"No," the big vampire said softly.

Terazo chuckled. "It wasn't a request. We can do this the hard way or we can do it the easy way. The choice is yours. Now take off your fuckin' clothes!"

"No." The tall vampire said the word a little louder and shook his head slowly.

The captain smiled at him. "Okay. Have it your way."

An instant later he barely turned the M16 to his right and fired a single shot. The bullet hit the older vampire in the face. He staggered backward a couple of steps before he dropped like a sack of stones as blood and tissue flowed from the exit wound. The female screamed and cowered behind the tall male.

Gun smoke curled from the barrel of the assault rifle, and the odor of burnt gunpowder filled the tight confines of the room.

Rossington turned away with a frown and in the din shook her head at Arnett. The lieutenant knew how this would play out. She didn't like it, but there wasn't anything she could do about it.

"Take off your fuckin' clothes or we will haul your fuckin' asses outside in the sunshine, and then we'll see what happens," Terazo said as he pointed the M16 at the female. *"Capisce, paisan?"*

The tall vampire glared at the captain but said nothing. Slowly he started to remove his clothing.

"No," the female pleaded to him.

"Do what he says," the male said to her.

She shook her head.

"Just do what he says," the tall vampire said, pronouncing each word slowly.

She closed her eyes and sobbed but only one time. The female opened her eyes, took a deep breath, and began to undress.

"No sudden movements now, hear me?" Terazo said to them.

Ninety seconds later the two vampires stood before them naked and barefoot, their unnaturally white bodies almost seeming to glow in the flashlight beams. They both had long, dark hair. The female's locks went well past her shoulders, while the tall male had a scruffy dark beard on his face. Their bodies were hairless except for dark patches around their genitals. Both appeared underfed—you could count the ribs in their rib cages—but not malnourished. They were thin but not emaciated. The trembling female crossed her arms over her breasts, while the tall male stood with his arms at his side, clenching and unclenching his fists.

"There, that wasn't so hard, was it?" Terazo asked. "Now we're going to have us a little talk. You see, I'm going to ask you some questions, and you're going to give me some answers. Do we understand each other?"

Neither of the vampires responded.

"Do we understand each other?"

"Yes," the tall vampire answered, while the female nodded.

"Okay, now we're getting somewhere." The captain smiled at them but there was no warmth or compassion in the gesture. "Are you part of the . . . the Kindred?"

"No," the male said, while the female shook her head.

"You wouldn't be lying to me, would you?"

The female shook her head more definitively. "No," she whispered.

"Why should I believe you?"

"We have to hide from *them*," the male said. "They hunt us . . . for food."

The female nodded her head in agreement.

"What did they do with my people?"

The male shrugged. "Took them, I suppose."

"Where?"

"For food," the female added.

"Where?"

The tall vampire shrugged again. "I don't know."

"You don't know?"

"No."

"You expect me to believe that?"

"Yes."

The female nodded. "We don't know."

"I think you're lying to me. I think you know where my soldiers are but you just don't want to tell me."

"No," the female said, shaking her head. "We don't know."

"I think you're lying to me," Terazo said, almost singing the words.

"No," the female repeated.

"Where are they?" the captain asked slowly.

"We don't know," the male said.

"Where are they?"

"We don't know," the male repeated.

"You look pretty well fed. How is that?"

"Animal blood," the male vampire answered.

"Animal blood?"

"Wild dogs, rabbits." The male shrugged. "A deer every now and then."

"Cats are too skittish," the female added. "We never catch them anymore."

"Really?" the captain asked with a slight grin slipping across his face. "You catch wild dogs, rabbits, and every now and then a deer, but you can't catch a cat. Interesting, but I don't give a fuck. Where are my soldiers?"

"We don't know," the male said.

"Bullshit!"

"We don't know where the Kindred take them," the female said. "Honest."

"The Kindred mark their territory, and we stay away from it," the male said.

"You don't go where they have marked their territory?"

"That's right," the tall vampire answered. "Where they leave their marks, we don't go. There's nothing but trouble where the Kindred are."

"So you have no idea where my soldiers are?"

"That's right," the male repeated.

"Then you are of no fuckin' use to me." As the last word came out of his mouth, Terazo pulled the trigger twice on his M16. The first bullet hit the male in the chest with a loud *thuck*, while the second hit the female in the throat.

The two vampires stumbled backward and crumpled to the floor almost in unison. The female was dead in less than a minute, blood slowly ebbing from the dark gash in her throat that she had tried to seal with her hands, while the male clutched at his wound and crawled over to her. He put his arm around her lifeless shoulders, pulled her close to his skinny body, and stared into her lifeless eyes. His breathing was labored, and he exhaled a fine mist of blood with each breath. A tear slipped from one eye as he whispered, "I am so sorry." He squeezed his eyes shut and died.

Rossington purposefully walked out of the building and stepped into the street, stopping near the sidewalk with a loud sigh and turning her face to the gray sky. She was agitated and disgusted by what had transpired in the storage room. A moment later, Vann exited the brick structure, with Rusty padding a half step behind him. They stopped beside the lieutenant.

Sitting in the front passenger seat of the middle Hummer, Traynor silently watched the two of them. He was curious to see what would transpire.

"I am afraid we have become what we abhor," she said to Arnett. "We have become the monsters that we loathe." Rossington sighed softly. "And I don't like it."

Arnett studied her face for a moment—she was pretty in a tomboy sort of way that even the smudges of grime on her face, dirty and uncombed hair, and battle rattle on her body couldn't obscure—but he said nothing.

"These missions were supposed to be about finding other survivors and giving them the choice to come with us back to The Base," she said, turning to face him. "We wanted to give them a better chance for survival, if that's what they wanted. Some did, but most didn't. Instead, they wanted to stay where they were, but that's all right. Freedom of choice, right? This whole thing began as a decent and righteous idea, *a noble and just cause*, as Senator Cameron said, but now it's become nothing more than self-righteous and self-serving bullshit. We are supposed to be doing something good, based on lofty ideals and moral principles, but now . . . now it's turned into something else, and it's certainly not good."

She frowned at him and shook her head. "That male vampire in there showed more compassion—more humanity—than we did." She snorted out a humorless laugh. "It's little more than hunting season out here, and we're not even killing for survival. We're just killing for the sake of killing. And I am as guilty as the next person."

"Our world has become kill or be killed," he said softly. "We may not like it, but that's what it is. It's not a crime or a sin. What we would have done two years ago is irrelevant in the here and now."

Rossington smiled thinly at him. "'I'm not asking for you to forgive my sins, Father. My sins are all I have.'"

Arnett gave her a surprised and somewhat startled look. She had just quoted a line from his debut novel, *Deception of Chameleons*, in which the troubled main character was a fugitive from U.S. justice who had been on the lam for more than a decade and lived a law-abiding life in a small Canadian town.

"Yes, I read your book."

"You and about two dozen other people," he said with a laugh.

"No, I know it did better than that," she said. "I enjoyed it a lot. I read it in a little more than a day, and I was really looking forward to your next one."

"Thanks," he said with a somewhat embarrassed grin. "I've got the galleys back at Wolveshaven. You can read them if you want."

"Really?"

"Yeah."

"You know, I thought I recognized your name when you said who you were, but the beard and long hair threw me off," Rossington said. "You don't really look anything like the photo on the dust jacket."

"I know." Vann shrugged but smiled. "It's not just the hair and the beard. I call it the End-of-the-World Diet. I've probably dropped fifty pounds on it. I guess it took the apocalypse for me to actually get in shape."

She smiled at him and started to say something when the other troopers raucously began to file out of the building, and she stopped in mid-word. "I'll tell you later."

"I look forward to it."

Their new plan was simple: the troopers would search those buildings where the Kindred had spray painted their symbol and ignore the other structures.

Most of the dilapidated offices and warehouses were littered with faded graffiti that ranged from intricate and artistic taggings to poorly rendered pornography, nonsensical gibberish to desperate pleas for help from unaffected survivors. The two primary themes of any words painted were sex and religion. The lower levels of some structures were so covered that the Kindred markings were difficult to find.

Outside the second building they stopped at, Rossington had tugged on the sleeve of Vann's BDU and nodded in the direction of a nearby brick structure. "I see we've got an intellectual crowd of taggers in your city," she said.

Sprayed across the bricks and mortar was: Apocalypse is here, we're just mucking in the ashes.

Arnett had smiled and chuckled. He, too, knew the paraphrased line was from Samuel R. Delany's end-of-the-world, science-fiction epic, *Dhalgren*. "Well, you know this was a university town. You pretty much had to have a Ph.D. to drive a taxi, so I shouldn't be surprised that the graffiti artists dabbled in hard-to-read classic literature."

"It's a nice change," she had said through her own grin. "I can't tell you how many times I've seen APOCALYPSE NOW spray painted on buildings and billboards."

The afternoon dragged on into early evening, and the cloud-obscured sun slipped unnoticed toward the western horizon. The troopers had found evidence that the Kindred had been inside all of the buildings they searched, some perhaps even on a routine basis, but the soldiers uncovered no indications that the vampires had actually inhabited any of the structures.

Traynor climbed out of the Hummer and stretched, reaching for the sky with both hands while favoring his prosthetic leg. He had been sitting in the damn vehicle all day, listening to chatter on the radio and taking down some notes. It was tedious and boring, but he did it anyway. His lower back throbbed with a dull ache, and the thick muscles of his neck were stiff. He closed his eyes and rolled his head slowly back and forth, listening to the bones and cartilage pop like Rice Krispies in the first splash of milk. Oh, but it felt so, so good.

When he stopped stretching and opened his eyes, he became uncomfortably aware that it appeared darker outside than it had been minutes earlier. How did that happen? The encroaching darkness of twilight seemed to descend upon the area like a malignant cloud. A sliver of concern hit him in the head and gut as he wondered what time sunset was.

The black man clicked the mic on his radio and asked, "Anybody know what time it is? Any idea what time the sun sets?"

Most of what came was over the small radio speaker was garbled, but he did clearly hear . . . *shit* . . . *probably head out* . . . *a good idea* . . . *too late I* . . .

Traynor leaned into the Humvee and picked his M16 up from where he had placed it against the front seat. He flicked off the safety and, for some reason, switched it to full auto. He felt his heart pick up the pace and a tidal surge of adrenaline hit his system as he scanned the nearby buildings. They weren't in the heart of Kindred country, but they weren't exactly in the distant suburbs, either. If the sun had already set or was about to slip below the horizon, they could be in a world of hurt in a very short period of time.

He thumbed the radio mic again. "You guys may want to pick up the pace a little bit. It is getting kind of dark out here."

Static squawked back at him, except for . . . *fuckin' scaredy* . . .

"Nice," Traynor muttered. "I'm the one standin' out here all by my lonesome as sunset approaches, if it hasn't already set, and I'm the fuckin' scaredy cat. Real nice."

". . . *our way* . . ." crackled over the radio, and he recognized the voice as Deacon's.

Traynor continued to scan the nearby buildings, looking for any signs of movement in the umbra of darkening shadows. He didn't see anything, but that didn't put his mind at ease. In another life, he had been a boots-on-the-ground infantry non-com who had served in hostile territory, and he knew that you didn't relax—didn't even think about letting your guard down—until you were safe and secure inside the wire, and then you gave yourself only a couple minutes' respite.

The first trooper—Petrovic—ambled out of the brick building and looked up at the sky. "Holy shit, you weren't lying, Traynor," he said as more soldiers followed him out into the street. "It's the fuckin' edge of night out here."

"No shit, Petrovic," Traynor growled at him. "Ain't the first time I've ever been on a mission, you shithead. I do know what I'm doing."

"Yeah, but . . ."

The private stopped in midsentence when a nearly invisible arrow sliced through the air overhead. He and the others heard it more than actually saw it.

"What the fuck was that?" Terazo snarled as every one of the soldiers, including Arnett, jumped and then ducked in startled surprise.

Another arrow whistled through the air but at a much lower trajectory, and it was followed by a head-high crossbow quarrel that glanced off the armor plating of one the Hummers.

"We got company!" Rossington yelled.

"Take cover!" Deacon ordered. "Everybody *down!*"

The troopers scrambled to the protection and relative safety of the armored vehicles, crouching down alongside them but occasionally popping their heads up in an effort to draw a bead on the location of their attackers.

More arrows and quarrels rained down on them, many of them going harmlessly over the top of the vehicles but some slamming into the sides of the Humvees with metallic-pinged *plunks*. It was not a coordinated onslaught of firing that could have had devastating effects, but a more random series of shots from a handful of unskilled and poorly trained archers and crossbowmen.

"We gotta get outta here!" Stroud screamed with panic edging his voice and his eyes wide.

"Somebody watch our backside," Deacon ordered, more pissed off than concerned. "Don't let them get behind us."

"Where the hell are they?" Terazo growled. "I can't see shit!"

Stroud stood up, screamed at the top of his lungs, and sprayed automatic weapon fire off into the darkness.

"Stroud!" Rossington screamed. "Stroud!"

"You're wasting ammo, you dumbfuck," Petrovic yelled at him.

The young private stopped firing and ducked back behind the last Hummer.

Arrows and quarrels continued to drop on their position but not with any real impact. The hidden vampires were firing from ground level and couldn't get the proper range to hit the troopers ducked behind the vehicles. However, it didn't stop the fangs from trying.

Deacon turned to Vann, who crouched beside him alongside the lead vehicle. "We gotta move. What's the best way out of here?"

Arnett flinched as a crossbow bolt slammed into the other side of the Humvee, followed by another one that shattered a passenger-side window. "I've got a safe house in an apartment complex about six, seven blocks from here," he said. "We go straight, turn left at the second intersection, and then double back the way we came."

"Safe house?" Osterman asked as she ducked even lower behind him and held tight to Rusty's body. "You got a fuckin' safe house around here? What the fuck are we doing out here?"

The major leaned away from the Hummer to get a better view of the troopers who had ducked in a row alongside the armored vehicles. "Everybody saddle up and follow me!" he called out. "Got it?"

Right down the line, all of the troopers nodded and some murmured answers.

"All right, let's go!" Deacon ordered. "Follow my lead!"

As the troopers rose from their defensive positions, a blood-curdling battle cry came from a block away. Many of them froze in terrified surprise.

"What the fuck?" the major muttered almost silently.

A motley mass of about fifty Kindred—mostly males in disheveled and dirty rags, but some females in equally tattered clothes—poured into the street from buildings on both sides and sprinted toward the Hummers. They were armed with long daggers and knives, makeshift clubs and wooden baseball bats with spikes hammered into the business end, aluminum baseball and softball bats, rakes, shovels, pitchforks, and one male even carried a hockey stick and wore a goalie mask.

The rain of arrows and quarrels slowed to a light drizzle, becoming more of a nuisance than a threat.

"*Move!*" Deacon screamed. "*Let's go!*"

Most of the troopers climbed into the Hummers from their shielded sides and then scrambled out of the way to let their comrades in, while others—Hagstrom, Powell, and Stroud—scurried around to the other sides to get in. Hagstrom and Powell fired short, controlled bursts from their M16s at the surging wave of vampires, but Stroud rounded the back of the last Hummer, squeezed the trigger on his assault rifle, and fanned it back and forth in front of him.

"C'mon, motherfuckers!" Stroud snarled. The sound of his words was lost in the roaring cacophony of assault weapon gunfire. "*C'mon!*"

Powell ducked and dove headfirst into the passenger side of the second Hummer a split second before Stroud's bullets ripped past him. Hagstrom, however, took the burst in his upper torso and it drove him forward. His body armor absorbed the impact until the final handful of slugs ripped through the back of his neck, severing his spine. The corporal dropped like a wet sack of cement, a geyser of blood spewing from the exit wounds in his neck. He was dead and gone before he hit the asphalt.

Rossington righted herself behind the steering wheel of the second Hummer and fired up the engine. From the corner of her eye, beyond Traynor in the passenger seat, she saw Hagstrom move forward and then go down. The lieutenant knew the wound was fatal and cursed out loud.

"Go, go, goddamn it!" Powell screamed as he sat up in the backseat. "*Go!*"

"C'mon, Deke, move it!" Rossington said out loud but mostly to herself.

Deacon started the lead Humvee as Arnett stuck his M4 out the broken passenger window, aimed the weapon at the Kindred, and squeezed the trigger. The major jammed the vehicle in gear and lurched away from the curb, the movement causing Osterman to lose her balance and tumble against the passenger-side back door.

The lead Hummer plowed into the swarm of vampires. The vanguard of the Kindred onslaught bounced off the vehicle, while those behind them scuttled clumsily out of the way. The other two armored vehicles, with Rossington and Terazo behind the wheels, pulled in behind.

As Vann pulled his M4 back inside the vehicle to reload, several Kindred rushed forward, clawed at the door handles, and clung to the frame of the shattered window. His hands seemed to move in slow motion as he ejected the empty clip, grabbed a fresh one from a pants pocket, and rammed it into the assault rifle. He cocked the weapon and raised it to the window as pallid hands clutched at his body armor. Arnett leaned back toward Deacon and pulled the trigger. The Kindred screamed in pain as bullets ripped into their flesh and they fell away from the Hummer.

In the middle Humvee, Rossington watched in helpless horror as several Kindred, illuminated in the headlights, managed to claw open the back door of the lead armored vehicle, reach in and grasp someone by his body armor, and yank that person out of the vehicle. The lieutenant gasped out loud as the figures tumbled away from the Hummer. She couldn't see who had just been pulled out, but she closed her eyes and muttered a silent prayer as she drove past the roiling dark shapes on the pavement. Whoever had been pulled out was dead . . . or worse.

Less than ten seconds later, the three armored vehicles cleared the ambush site and pushed forward along the darkened street.

Led by the sultry siren and former TV news reporter Shari Landry, ten Kindred literally strolled up to the main gate of Wolveshaven. Flanked by a sword-carrying male warrior in his mid-twenties— her personal bodyguard—she stared at the distant mansion and the half-dozen or so lights glowing in the windows.

A scantily goth-clad, scrawny female in her late teens and with long, unkempt, dark hair hurried to Shari's side, eager to share her information.

"Have you seen *him*?" the onetime reporter asked the teen, who had mimicked her use of excessive dark eye shadow in stark contrast to her pale skin and washed-out eye color.

"I didn't see him in the sniper's nest or in any of the windows," the teen answered, speaking very quickly. "I would know for sure if I could use night vision stuff."

"It is forbidden."

"I know, but . . ."

"It is forbidden by the Prophet, so don't even think about it."

"But why?"

"You know, my kitten, we are preparing for the time after the End Days, when such devices from the old world will be useless." Shari stroked the teen's cheek with the back of a long-nailed finger, the red polish appearing almost black, and the girl blushed with a shy smile. "The Prophet has forbidden them, so they are forbidden."

"I don't think he's here," the teen said. "He must be in the city with the rest of the soldiers."

The onetime reporter smiled. "Then perhaps General Abaddon will get him tonight, because the soldiers are still out in the city and have not come home to roost."

"We can hope," the goth teen said.

"What about the vehicle? There are lights on inside of it."

"There's at least one woman inside, I saw her through the front windshield. She was sitting behind the steering wheel."

Shari frowned. "I wish there was a way we could get in there."

"Maybe there is," the warrior beside her said. He boldly walked to the main gate, put his hand on the metal frame, and pushed it open. "Looks like somebody forgot to lock up when they went out for the night."

"No shit." A huge smile broke out on the former reporter's pale but still pretty face. "Let's go see who's in that RV. Move out, quietly."

The Kindred trotted through the open gates—one of heavy wrought iron and two steel chain-link—and hurried to the recreational vehicle. The warrior opened the side door and rushed into the vehicle, leading the other creatures inside.

Valesquez sat at the tiny dinner table and read a novel—*Duma Key* by Stephen King—while Baumann had nodded off in the captain's chair. The PA heard someone at the door and turned in hopeful anticipation that it was Vann, even though she hadn't heard the sounds of the troopers' return. That expectation instantly turned to terror when she saw the leather-clad Kindred warrior barge into the vehicle, and more vampires flowed in after him. A scream involuntarily erupted from her throat.

"What the—" Baumann mumbled as she was startled awake.

The warrior rushed past Valesquez, pushing her back into the seat, and pounced on the private as she attempted to get out of the big leather seat. His roundhouse right hook landed on the side of her jaw and knocked her out cold. Behind him the other woman continued to scream as several Kindred roughly clutched at her.

"Shut up!" Shari snarled as she stopped in front of Valesquez, whose screams subsided to uncontrolled hiccups. "Shut. Up."

Sandra, her dark eyes wide with uncut fear, complied with the order as she feebly struggled against the two male vampires holding her arms.

"That's better," the onetime reporter said, looking the Latina up and down before giving her a little smile. "Much, much better."

"You . . . you don't have . . . have to do this," Valesquez whimpered.

"Shhhhh," Shari said like a mother comforting a child awakened by a nightmare.

"You . . . you . . . you . . ."

"But I do." She caressed the woman's cheek with a fingernail and let it trail down her neck, across her clavicle, but pulled away before reaching her breast.

"No. No, you don't."

"Oh, but I do." Shari grinned at her, giving the PA a brief flash of her fangs. "I really do."

"No," Valesquez pleaded. "If you let us go, we'll leave tomorrow. I promise."

"You promise?"

"Yes." She nodded her head quickly. "We'll leave and never come back."

"And never come back?"

"Yes."

"I'm sorry, I can't do that." Shari caressed her cheek tenderly. "Welcome to one rung down on the food chain, my dear."

"No!"

"If you struggle, it will be worse."

"*No!*"

"Take them out of here."

"No," Valesquez said softly as if resigned to her fate. "No."

The two Kindred males, one of them a warrior with a crossbow slung over his shoulder, forcibly dragged a whimpering and crying Valesquez from the RV, while the sword-bearing warrior heaved

Baumann over his shoulder in a fireman's carry and headed toward the door.

Shari followed him but went to the back of the dimly lit RV where Tran was hooked up to the monitor. His vital signs were extremely weak. She grabbed the white sheet that covered him and pulled it off. He was naked except for the heavy white bandages that dressed his wounds. The former reporter resisted the temptation to reach out and touch him.

The teen appeared at her elbow and eyed the trooper up and down. "Pity."

The onetime reporter glanced at her goth companion. "Why?"

"I don't think he's going to make it."

Shari chuckled. "Then we'll just have to help him along and put him out of his misery, won't we?"

The teen licked her lips and smiled in hungry anticipation. "Yes, we will."

Vann had directed them through the unlit streets, getting them to the safe house without any additional trouble from the Kindred, but they were still several miles away from Wolveshaven. To keep the Humvees hidden from view, he had the officers park the armored vehicles in the semi-underground parking garage, on top of which the apartment building had been constructed, but lined up three across and pointed in the direction of the exit. He had unlocked the garage-level door that led into the building and secured it with double iron bars after they entered. He had repeated the process with the reinforced door of the street-side top floor apartment.

"We lost two more people in a fuckin' ambush," Terazo said as he paced what had been the living room. The remaining troopers had plopped themselves down on various pieces of furniture, ignoring the scent of stagnant air and flourishing mold. "How did that fuckin' happen? We lost Hagstrom and Osterman."

"It happened because Stroud was a reckless dumb fuck and doing his dumbass James Cagney imitation," Rossington snarled, staring directly at the private.

"Who the fuck is James Cagney?" the teenaged trooper asked.

"Fuck you." The lieutenant slapped Stroud hard across the face, the *crack* practically echoing in the dark room. "Just fuck you!"

"You hit me," he said, dumbfounded. "You fuckin' hit me."

"That's enough!" Deacon said, raising his voice. "Rossy, you need to cool your jets, and, Stroud, you shut the fuck up. You're lucky that a slap across the face is all you're going to get. If I'd had a choice in the matter, I would have dumped your ass out in the street."

"She hit me."

"Shut the fuck up!" the major said. "Your carelessness and stupidity cost us an excellent soldier, one that we need but no longer have. If you ever do something like that again, I will shoot you myself. Understood?"

"But—"

"*Understood?*"

"Yeah," the private mumbled.

"What?"

"Ye . . . yes, sir."

"What I wanna know is, how did they know where we were?" Terazo asked as he stared at Vann, who opened his mouth to respond but didn't.

"Oh, for chrissakes, we weren't exactly operating in stealth mode," Rossington said, "and we parked the vehicles in the middle of the fuckin' street. A four-year-old with half a brain would have known what we were doing and where we were doing it."

"She's right," Deacon said. "We thought that just because it was daylight out, we were safe from them. Obviously, that wasn't the case."

"Obviously," Terazo said, sarcasm dripping off each syllable.

"They must have had spotters or something to see what we were up to," the major continued, ignoring the captain's remark. He turned to Arnett. "The Kindred are damn clever. We've run into some clever bastards, but not like them."

"Well, why don't we just fuckin' give up then," the captain sneered sarcastically.

"Go fuck yourself, Terazo," Rossington said.

"Why don't we just step outside in the hallway and discuss it man-to-man?" he responded.

"Because we'd be one *man* short," she shot back.

"Enough!" Deacon yelled. "Enough!"

The two officers glared at one another in the darkness.

"We really need to get our shit together and try and salvage something out of this cluster fuck," the major said. "If we keep fighting among ourselves, we're not gonna last two more days."

Traynor limped into the living room with a radio in his hand. "I haven't been able to get ahold of the RV," he said. "Nothing but static."

"Too many obstructions between here and there?" the major asked.

He shrugged and frowned, but no one saw it in the darkness. "Possibly."

"Well, that's just fuckin' great," Terazo said.

"Zo, if you don't have something constructive to add to the conversation, why don't you just keep your mouth shut," Deacon said to him. "Sarcasm isn't going to help us out of the jam we're in."

The major rose from a kitchen chair, walked to the picture window, pulled aside the heavy curtain that covered it, and stared at the empty street. The entire mission had spun dangerously out of control in just a matter of days, and the prospects for recovery were not promising. Hell, the prospects for survival weren't promising. He knew what the prudent and practical course of action should be, but he just couldn't bring himself to say it out loud. Deacon turned back to the living room.

"Everybody get something to eat and drink and then try to get some rest," he said. "We're here for the night, but we're going to be back at it at first light. I'm fuckin' tired of being on the receiving end of all this bullshit, so let's see if we can dish out a little bit of punishment instead."

Seventeen

The morning dawned cold but sunny and clear. The brightness was a welcome respite from the previous day's overcast gloom, but a shocked sense of loss mingled with the smoldering desire for revenge, hanging over the troopers like storm clouds.

Powell walked point and led them down concrete steps into the darkness of the basement in the second building they searched. Their flashlight beams carved narrow and disjointed tunnels of light in blackness as thick as India ink. None of them noticed there were no cobwebs suspended from the slanted ceiling or clinging to the bricks.

"I hate basements," Vann whispered from the middle of the column to no one in particular. Hackles raised, Rusty kept to his side but chose not to comment. "They are the absolute worst."

"I'll second that motion," Petrovic muttered from ahead of him.

About halfway down the cinder block–lined tunnel, the dank air turned foul with a sour but unmistakable odor. The troopers knew what it was. They had encountered it before. It was never a good thing.

"Aw, man, what *is* that stench?" Arnett asked when he caught a whiff.

"You'll find out soon enough," Terazo answered from just behind Powell but there was no gloating satisfaction in his words. "And you are not gonna like it."

"Oh great," Vann said with no enthusiasm. "Can't wait."

Powell could see the wood-framed doorway where the stairs led and, with each step down toward it, the private steeled himself for what he knew he would discover when he crossed over the threshold. There was no doubt in his mind. He inhaled deeply through his mouth and exhaled slowly out of his nose, controlling the rhythm of his heartbeat and narrowing the focus of his attention. His gloved right hand, with the index finger hooked over the trigger, grasped the pistol grip of his assault rifle, while his left pointed the Surefire light down toward his boots. It was always at this point that he wished he had attached the flashlight to the barrel of the M16.

Three steps to go.

He purposefully placed one foot down on the concrete, taking great pains to be as quiet as possible. Powell moved like a phantom. From behind him came the muffled rattle of battle gear as the others followed him down. He knew it was noise that would only be heard if someone—some*thing*—was listening for it, but he was the one walking point and that put an entirely different spin on the situation.

Two steps left.

The private repeated the process on the next to last step. The inconspicuous sounds of the descending troopers behind him seemed amplified in his head. He wanted to scream at them to be fuckin' quiet, but he clenched his jaw and ground his teeth instead. Screaming would have defeated the purpose, as well.

Last step.

Powell hesitated on the landing for just a moment after his second foot touched down. He took a deep breath, held it for a couple of heartbeats, then released it slowly and soundlessly. The private knew the drill: he would go right and fan out away from the doorway, the soldier immediately behind him would go to the left and do the same thing. The troopers would keep moving in that manner until all of them were in the room. He simultaneously stepped over the threshold, squeezed even tighter on the pistol grip of his weapon, and raised the flashlight.

The beam cut through the darkness like a searchlight. A scream sliced through the silence like a razor-sharp knife.

The private found the source of the screeching an instant later. A long-haired and bearded human scarecrow dressed in filthy rags screamed in primal fear. It took Powell an instant to realize the man was actually shouting out a warning.

"They're here! Get them! Oh God! Oh God! Oh God! Get them! Get them now! They're here!"

As his fellow troopers flooded into the open room, Powell saw a sleepy vampire slowly rise up from a tattered recliner near the man. He clenched the trigger for a heartbeat or two, and, in the muzzle flash of the weapon, saw the hot lead fatally knock the vampire back into his comfy chair and unceremoniously topple it over.

"Nooooo!"

To his left, two more short bursts erupted and flared harshly.

"What are you doing? No! No! No! No! Stop! Stop! Oh God! Oh no!"

With weapons ready for business, the soldiers pushed forward into the room on search-and-destroy mode. Powell headed straight for the scarecrow, who had stopped screaming but still muttered.

"Oh no, this is bad," the scarecrow mumbled. "This is real bad. Real bad. I'm in trouble, big trouble. They're not going to be happy with me. This is bad. I'm sorry, Jimmy. I'm so sorry."

"Shut up!" the private snarled at the scarecrow as he moved toward him. "Just shut the fuck up!"

"This is bad," the man continued to mutter. "I'm sorry, Jimmy. I tried, I really did. Oh, they're going to be pissed at me, really pissed. I'm sorry, Jimmy. I'm sorry. I'm sorry. I'm sorry."

"SHUT UP!" Powell screamed and raised his flashlight as if to beat the scarecrow with it.

The man flinched defensively and cowered back a step or two but didn't bring his arms up to protect himself.

"Aw, fuck," Rossington growled from the other side of the large room.

"Oh shit." That was Arnett somewhat sheepishly.

The private turned to where the other troopers had begun to congregate in the back of the room. Illuminated by flashlights between the silhouettes of his comrades, he saw four or five emaciated humans on filthy cots and hooked to IVs. "You useless piece of shit," Powell snarled at him. "I ought to . . ."

"I didn't have a choice. They made me do it," the scarecrow said. "They *made* me. Do you understand? They made me. I didn't want to, but they made me."

It was at that moment that the trooper realized the barefoot man was shackled by the ankle to a heavy-link logging chain, which was long enough for him to reach the cots but not much beyond that. The scarecrow's skin had been rubbed raw and was festered with sores where half of a handcuff had been snapped shut just above his foot. "Aw, shit," he muttered under his breath.

"They made me do it," the scarecrow pleaded to Powell. "They said they would hurt Jimmy if I didn't do what they told me to do. I didn't have a choice. I couldn't let them hurt Jimmy. Oh no, now they're going to hurt him because I didn't warn them fast enough. Now they're dead, and the others are gonna hurt Jimmy. No, no, no, no."

Powell tore himself away from the man's hazel eyes. There wasn't a shred of sanity left in them. "Hey, Major, you need to see this guy."

Deacon whispered something to Rossington, who frowned but nodded in response, and then he and Terazo walked over to the private.

"You gotta understand, I didn't have a choice," the scarecrow said to the major and the captain as they approached. "I didn't. They made me do it."

"The Kindred must have his kid or something," Powell said to the officers. "He keeps saying that they were going to hurt Jimmy if he didn't do what they told him to do."

"They made me do it," the scarecrow pleaded. "They said they would hurt Jimmy. I couldn't let them do that. But now I fucked up, and they're going to hurt Jimmy."

"Who's going to hurt Jimmy?" Deacon asked the man.

"Them," he answered. His eyes darted back and forth between the three soldiers.

"Who?"

"The bad ones."

"The Kindred?"

The man shivered at the word. "The bad ones."

"When did they get you and Jimmy?" Terazo asked.

The scarecrow thought for a moment. "I don't remember." He shook his head and let out a sob. "They came one night. They attacked the farmhouse. We weren't ready for them, they caught us by surprise and took everyone. They fuckin' took everyone."

"When was that?" Deacon asked.

"I don't know."

"Is Jimmy your son?" Terazo asked.

The scarecrow nodded his head.

"How long have you been down here?" the captain asked.

The scarecrow shook his head. "I don't know. They come every night to check on me, to make sure I'm doing my job, keepin' them alive." He nodded in the direction of the cots. "But now they're going to be pissed because I failed. I didn't warn them soon enough, and now they're going to hurt Jimmy."

"Where is Jimmy? Do you know where the Kindred took him?"

"No." The man shook his head again and hiccupped a sob. "But I have to warn them. I have to let them know what you've done. I have to warn them."

"We can help you find Jimmy, if you help us out," the captain said. "If you let us know where Jimmy might be, we can find him for you."

"No, no, no. I have to warn them."

"We can find Jimmy for you," Deacon said.

"I have to warn them!" The scarecrow began to raise his voice as the level of his excitement rose. "Maybe if I warn them, they won't hurt Jimmy. I have to warn them!"

"You don't want to do that," Terazo said.

"Yes! Yes, I do! I have to warn them!"

"No, you don't," the major said.

"Yes, I do!" The scarecrow's eyes sparkled with insanity, and his slobbering grin displayed ill-kept brown teeth. "I do!" He chuckled. *"Hey! They're here!"*

The three soldiers involuntarily stepped back in wide-eyed surprise.

"*They're down here!*" With chain in tow, the scarecrow danced away from them with unexpected agility and quickness. "*They're here! Come and get them!*" He laughed out loud. "*They're heeeere!*"

Deacon frowned in disgust. "End this shit."

"*They're down here!*"

Terazo raised his assault rifle to his shoulder and squeezed the trigger for a second.

"*Heeey! Th—*"

The burst of gunfire drowned out the scarecrow's screaming an instant before the short burst of full metal jackets tore into the torso of his paper-thin body. The bullets ripped through him and propelled him forward for a couple of yards, ultimately dropping him to the dirty concrete floor and silencing him forever.

Rossington stormed over to the major and stopped directly in front of him. "What, we're shooting survivors now?" It was a question, but not really a question.

Deacon stared at her but said nothing.

"Not a survivor," Terazo said, acrid smoke curling from the barrel of his M16. "He was a traitor. He was—"

"Bullshit!" Rossington turned her glare to the captain, held it for a moment before directing it back at Deacon. "And *you* know it."

"Lieutenant Rossington, you will check with Mr. Traynor to see if he has been able to contact Medical yet," the major said to her after he unclenched his jaw. "If he has, you will have him contact them again and let Ms. Valesquez know that she should gather up medical supplies sufficient to treat and maybe transport five survivors back to the mansion. You will take one trooper and go to the mansion, pick up Ms. Valesquez and Private Baumann, and bring them back here immediately. If he has not been able to make contact with Medical, you will take two troopers and return to the mansion and let Ms. Valesquez know that her services are needed here. You will assist her in gathering the necessary medical supplies, enough to treat and possibly transport those five survivors. You will leave one trooper with Private Baumann back at Medical and proceed back to this location without delay. Do you understand me, Lieutenant Rossington?"

She scowled at him, dark anger clouding her face and filling her eyes.

"Do you understand me, *Lieu*tenant Rossington?"

"Yes, sir." The lieutenant snapped off a crisp salute, pivoted on her heel, and headed toward the doorway and the stairs that led up to the ground floor.

Only the intensity of the heated exchange between Rossington and Deacon had enabled Vann to pry his eyes and shocked sensibilities from the emaciated and naked bodies of the survivors, who were hooked to dirty IV lifelines and covered in their own filth. The stench was unimaginable, and the images were unbearable. But he had been unable to turn away. The only time he had ever come close to experiencing anything remotely like this horror and revulsion was when he had watched grainy, black-and-white video footage of World War II concentration camps.

He didn't recognize any of the apparitions shackled to the cots and tethered to the IVs. There was nothing familiar in their sunken cheeks and haunted eyes. They were all strangers—only vaguely human but strangers nonetheless. Vann was troubled by unwanted thoughts that asked disturbing questions: *Is this what happened to Sylvie and Hal? Are they strapped to makeshift beds and bound to IVs in some other basement? Is this their fate?*

And worst of all: *Do I really want to know?*

Rossington was in a nasty-ass foul mood when she drove the Humvee up to the gates of Wolveshaven. She was seething at a roiling boil and didn't even notice that she drove through three tiers of wideopen gates without stopping. Wade, who had sat stoically in the front passenger seat, saw that they were open and cleared his throat. Even Stroud, who had managed to keep his mouth shut in the backseat during the entire trip, caught on that something was amiss.

"What?" the lieutenant snapped at the corporal in the seat next to her.

"Lieutenant, you just drove through three open gates."

"So?" Then it hit her like a slap in the face. She hadn't used the automatic opener on the key ring that Arnett had given her before she left. She had just driven right through them because they were already open. "Aw, fuck!"

"This is not good," Stroud said from the backseat.

"Stroud, that's probably the most intelligent thing I have ever heard come out of your mouth," Rossington said. "No, this is not good."

She stopped the Humvee near the rear of the medical RV but had already seen that the side door of the vehicle was wide open. The lieutenant tossed the key ring to Wade, who caught it easily, and said, "You and Stroud check inside the mansion. If the outside door is still locked, I think we can assume they didn't get in, but I still want you to take a good look around. Let's not take anything for granted."

"All right," the corporal said.

The three of them exited the armored vehicle. The two troopers headed toward the front of the mansion, while the officer walked to the open door of the RV.

Rossington flicked off the safety of her M16 as she approached the door. She took a deep breath, held it for a moment, then climbed up the metal stairs. The inside of the RV was not as bad as she expected, but there were obvious signs of a struggle: the novel that Valesquez had been reading was on the floor with the dust jacket half off, there were papers scattered about the top of the dinner table and the floor, the doors to both small refrigerators were wide open, and Baumann's assault rifle was snagged on the back of the passenger-side captain's chair with the barrel pointed at the floor.

She snapped on her flashlight and examined both fridges. Some vials of medicine that needed to be refrigerated had been toppled over but otherwise left alone, while the two dozen or so units of blood that were stored in them were gone.

"Aw, shit," the lieutenant muttered when she turned away from the refrigerators. She stopped in her tracks when the flashlight's beam revealed Tran's unnaturally pale mutilated corpse on the makeshift medical bed. She moved forward on unsteady legs for a closer examination. The trembling flashlight beam revealed that his throat had been completely torn out, the undersides of his wrists had been shredded, and the insides of both thighs had been ripped open. Flaps of pale and lifeless flesh hung from the gaping wounds that appeared ghastly in the harsh light. Only a small amount of blood had spilled on the sheets underneath the body, while the wounds appeared to have been licked clean. "Shit, shit, shit!" Rossington turned away in disgust and staggered out of the RV.

She leaned against the Humvee in the sunshine for less than fifteen minutes before Wade and Stroud came out of the mansion. The corporal dutifully locked the front doors behind them.

"It was locked up tight," Wade said as he stopped in front of her and reached out with the key chain. "We didn't find anything out of place or any surprises waiting for us."

Rossington took the key chain. "Okay."

"How about Medical?" the corporal asked.

The lieutenant sighed. "Valesquez and Baumann are both missing, and Tran is dead. They drained him—his throat, wrists, and inner thighs were torn open."

"Inner thighs?" Stroud said. "That's kinda . . . kinky, isn't it?"

"Not really," Rossington said. "That's where your femoral arteries are located."

"Lots of blood flows through them . . ." Wade added.

"Oh."

". . . so they're a blood-gushing treat for vampires," the corporal continued. "In fact, probably a real sweet spot for the fangs. They probably fight over them like my brothers and me used to fight over the turkey drumsticks at Thanksgiving."

Ignoring the mental image that conjured up, Rossington grabbed the Motorola radio off the hood of the armored vehicle. "Come in, Traynor. This is Rossington."

"Hey, Rossy, this is Traynor," the speaker crackled clearly. "Are you en route? You're coming in clear as a bell."

"No, we're still at the mansion."

"What?"

"Yeah, we're out front. I'm probably fifteen feet from the rear of the RV."

"Shit," came from the speaker. "What do you mean? We couldn't get a signal worth shit from that location either last night or this morning."

"Yeah, well, there was a good reason for that."

"And what would that be?"

"The grounds of the mansion were compromised at some point during the evening."

"What do you mean, 'compromised'?" came Deacon's voice from the speaker.

"All three gates were wide open when we got here," Rossington said. "The fangs had gotten into Medical. Valesquez and Baumann are missing, and Tran is dead."

"How did they get in, Rossington?" the major asked.

"The gates were apparently left unlocked. There was no evidence they had been forced open. I would say the last person out didn't lock them."

Deacon started to say something, but what came over the speaker was Arnett's voice: "What kind of cluster fuck are you operating?"

Rossington couldn't help but grin, while Stroud cackled out a laugh, and even Wade turned away to hide a smile.

"I'm gonna tell you once, back off!" came from Terazo.

The response was muffled but it sounded like, *go fuck yourself.*

"Tell me again what happened," the major asked.

The lieutenant sighed. "When we arrived, the gates—all three of them, as I said before—were unlocked and wide open. It looked like the vampires just waltzed down the driveway. The doors to the mansion were locked, and there were no signs of entry or even any attempt to get in. We checked it out but found nothing. The RV, however, was a different story. There were signs of a struggle but not really much of a fight. Valesquez and Baumann are missing, all units of blood were taken from the refrigerators, and Tran had been killed. His neck, wrists, and inner thighs had been ripped open, and I suspect he'd been drained of most of his blood because he's as white as the fuckin' ghost he now is."

"Fuck!" Deacon said. There were similar responses in the background.

"They didn't leave a calling card staked to the front door, but you don't really have to think too hard who did this," the lieutenant said.

"Yeah, I know," the major said. "Rossy, I want you to secure the gates and stay right there for now. I'll get back to you in a bit to let you know what our plans are."

"Yes, sir," she said and set the radio back on the hood. Rossington leaned back against the armored vehicle and rubbed her eyes. *We should just cut our losses and get the hell out of here right now,* she thought, but she didn't like it one bit.

"We've got big trouble," Deacon said to the remaining troopers who had gathered in the street near the two Humvees.

"That's an understatement," Vann said sarcastically.

Terazo made a menacing move in his direction, but the major stopped him with a shake of his head.

"Mr. Arnett, I understand how you feel—" Deacon started.

"You don't have a clue how I feel," he interrupted. "Not a fuckin' clue. You come rolling in here like you're Delta-fuckin' Force, all badass and ready to kick some vampire ass, but you're a fuckin' joke, nothing but a fuckin' joke. Everything you have done so far has gone wrong—not just a little wrong, but major fuck-up wrong. I have no idea—not one fuckin' clue—how you clowns have managed to survive this long. It must be a miracle, some kind of divine intervention, because it certainly isn't skill and talent. And the worst part is, now you're fuckin' with *my* life, you've put *my* neck on the line."

"Mr. Arnett," Traynor said quietly, "you're right, we don't know how you feel right now, but I do know that things have gone to hell very quickly and very unexpectedly. You have every reason and right to be pissed at us, but that's not going to change what has happened or what still needs to be done." He paused to let his words sink in. "The bottom line is that we still need your help."

Vann scowled at him for a moment. "Fuck you."

"Does that mean you will no longer help us?" the black man asked, not exactly certain as to what the two-word comment meant.

"Fuck you." He glared hard and long at the former infantry non-com. "I don't fuckin' believe this. I do not *believe* this."

Traynor smiled at him. "Thank you."

"Whatever." Arnett shook his head as if he really couldn't believe what he was doing. "If you get me killed, I swear to Christ that I will fuckin' come back and haunt your worthless, one-legged ass."

The black man laughed. "I would expect nothing less from you, Mr. Arnett."

Deacon smiled in spite of himself. "We are going to fall back to the mansion and regroup. We need to get our shit back together and fast. We need to take stock of what we've got and decide what we're going to do."

"What about them?" Petrovic asked with a nod of his head in the direction of the basement blood farm.

The major frowned. "Given our current situation, there's nothing we can do for them. They would require more attention than we can give them. I don't like it, but we can't help them."

"Yeah, we can," Powell said softly as he turned away from the group.

"Powell, where are you going?" Deacon asked.

The private kept walking as if he hadn't heard the major.

"Powell!" Terazo snarled. "Where the fuck are you going?"

He stopped and turned back to the soldiers. "I'm gonna do what none of you got the sack to do. I'm gonna help them." Powell began to walk toward the doorway of the building but raised his M16 into the air and squeezed off one round.

His intent was unmistakable. But no one moved a muscle to stop him.

The first handful of them showed up within thirty minutes of sundown while the western fringes of the sky still blazed burnt orange. Over the next half hour the group doubled in size and then doubled again. The catcalls and insults began shortly after Shari Landry arrived with her entourage. The Kindred's twisted carnival had come to town to pay a visit on Wolveshaven.

The vampires not only catcalled Arnett but hurled insults at the troopers, as well. The taunts and jeers had the desired effect on some soldiers, pissing them off and making them want to blindly strike out, but Deacon would not let them respond. He knew what the fangs were up to and refused to fall for their ploy.

"It's just not right, Major," Petrovic complained as he looked out one of the third-floor windows. "We could drop a handful of 'em just like that." He snapped his fingers. "They wouldn't even know what fuckin' hit 'em."

"And what would that accomplish?" Deacon asked, a question that precipitated a disgusted scowl from Terazo, who sat at the security monitors.

"It would show 'em . . ." the private said.

"Show them what, Petrovic?"

"It would . . . it would . . ." the soldier stammered, trying to find the right words to get his point across.

"They would scatter like cockroaches caught in the kitchen light after the first shot," Vann said.

All eyes turned to him.

"You think this is the first time they've been here?" Arnett asked but continued without waiting for an answer. "It's not. This is nothing new. And, yes, I have taken shots at them. At first, I would drop one or two and then the rest of them would scurry for cover. It was easy to hit them—hell, just about anybody with a decent rifle and night-vision scope could do it—but the only thing that did was make their ring leaders a lot more skittish and cautious about standing out in the open. But you know what? They still kept coming back. So I stopped shooting them and went for near misses. As my marksmanship improved, I found that it was much more enjoyable to see their reactions to a well-placed missed shot. Of course, they didn't know I was deliberately missing."

"You are one sick bastard," Terazo said with just a begrudging hint of respect in the five words.

"Maybe if you shot enough of them, they wouldn't bother you anymore," Stroud said in stupid innocence.

"Maybe if I shot enough of them, they would get pissed enough to launch a four-sided assault on Wolveshaven," Arnett said. "I'm only one person, and even with machine guns in the widow's walk, I couldn't get them all before some breached the perimeter. Once that happened, I would have a big fuckin' problem. So, instead, I kind of prefer my own little version of détente. It's not perfect, but if standing down there and insulting me is all they want to do, well, that's fine with me."

A couple hours into the evening, the X-rated floor show began outside. Inside of thirty minutes, everyone but Stroud had gotten bored with the hard-core antics and wandered away from the windows to do other things. The teenaged private, gawking through night-vision binoculars, kept his eyes glued to the window and muttered under his breath about how he couldn't believe what they were doing. Every few minutes he would try to convince someone else to come and look at what the vampires were up to but none took the offer.

Arnett was drying the last of the evening meal's pots and pans when Rossington walked into the kitchen, which was illuminated by several flickering candles. She reached down and scratched Rusty's ears as she passed where the dog sat guarding the doorway.

"Hey," she said as she lithely hopped up to sit on the marble countertop near the sink.

"Hey, yourself."

"I don't know if anyone said this or not, but thank you," the lieutenant said with a slight smile. "And I'm sorry that we fucked up your life."

Holding a large and heavy stainless-steel Emerilware saucepan in his hands, Vann chuckled mostly to himself. "Well, you're welcome, and you really didn't fuck up my life, well, not too bad anyway. Besides, it has been kind of boring around here, so . . ."

"Boring, huh?"

As if on cue, from outside came the call: *AR-nett! Come out, come out, wherever you are!*

"Sometimes, they're not terribly original," he said, almost apologetic.

"Original or not, they are . . . well, downright pornographic."

"Yeah, I will give them that." Vann passed the heavy pan from one hand to the other.

"AR-nett! Hey, ARRRR-nett! Doncha wanna watch?"

"SOLD-jahs, SOLD-jahs, come out a play!"

"How do you put up with that night after night?"

"Put up with what?"

Rossington smiled at his attempted joke.

"They only come here—I don't know—on average, maybe once a week, but they try to be clever about it and come . . . say . . . three times in four days and then not at all for a couple of weeks."

"Trying to catch you off guard." She had considered saying "with your pants down," but she mentally shook that one from her head.

"Yeah, something like that, I guess."

"Has it ever worked?"

"No, not really." Vann thought for a moment, then nodded his head. "And I have done some pretty dumb things since I've been here, but fortunately, they haven't come back to bite me in the ass. I have been lucky."

"ARRRRR-net!"

"They are also annoying," Rossington said.

"Yeah, they are."

"How do you sleep when they're out there like that? Calling out your name and taunting you? And . . . well, you know."

"I don't sleep when they show up."

"Really?"

"Yeah." He nodded. "I stay awake until they get bored and leave. Well, actually I stay up until about an hour after they have left, just to make sure they don't have any surprises for me."

"SOLD-jah boys! SOOOLLLD-jahs!"

"How long do they stay out there?"

Vann shrugged. "They usually run out of steam after midnight . . ."

"Shoot their wad and then can't keep it up any longer?" Rossington mentally chastised herself for seemingly having one thing on her mind, even at a time like this.

He couldn't help but smile at her lascivious remark, forcing himself to turn away from her lest his mind drift too far down that particular road. Vann shifted the heavy pot again and looked at her. "Yeah, something like that, I suppose. They will mill around for an hour or two before they start wandering away. The leaders and most of the warriors are usually the first to go and then the others follow shortly after that. Since I've got . . . got company tonight, I suspect they will be here for the long haul and probably leave an hour or so before dawn."

"Great." She stifled a yawn.

"*SOOOLLLD-jah boys! Come out and play, SOOOLLLD-jahs!*"

"Okay, so this is going to be a long night," Rossington said.

"Yeah, I am afraid so."

After midnight, with several of the troopers softly snoring through restless dreams and the others silently enduring the torments of their fractured slumber, Terazo shrugged the down sleeping bag from his body, rolled off the couch, and quietly padded into the dark kitchen. Less than a minute later, Powell meandered into the room and leaned against the counter with a yawn and a shake of his shaven head.

"So, can you get out of this place without setting off any alarms?" the captain asked in a whisper.

The private, the stubble on his usually clean-shaven head as long as the whiskers on his chin, scowled in the dark. "Not a problem."

"It's a pretty good surveillance system."

"*Not* a problem."

"Can you get past those fences without giving yourself away to the vampires or blowing yourself up? There're spotlights connected to motion detectors and claymores hooked to tripwires."

"I know what there is out there and where they are, and I also know how I'm gonna avoid them. Each and every one of them."

"Well, it's just that this whole thing would be over pretty quickly if you set off one of those claymores and blew yourself to pieces."

Powell snorted out an almost-silent laugh. "I ain't some clumsy dumbass, tripping-over-my-own-feet cracker from Buttfuck, Arkansas, ya know. I can get outta this place like I'm a fuckin' ghost, a black-skinned phantom." He made a sound like the haunting wind and wiggled his hand. "I'm here and then I'm gone. Just like that. See, I scoped out this place during the past couple of days and know how I'm gonna do it. Once I get outside of the mansion, I got my *escape route* planned. I'm gonna—"

Terazo silenced him with a wave of his hand. "I don't need to know what you're going to do or how you're going to do it."

Powell scowled at him again but bit his tongue instead of responding with two words.

"I just need to know that you can do it."

"I said I can, didn't I?"

"Yes, you did."

"Awright then, you got nothin' to worry about," the private said. "I'm gonna sneak outta here all nice and quiet, follow the fuckin' fangs to see where they go, and then report back to you when I get the goodies. Just have your radio turned down real quiet and set it to lucky channel seven and everything will be copasetic. *Capisce?*"

Terazo chuckled softly and said, "Word."

In the early morning umbra of the backside of Wolveshaven, well out of sight from where the mass of Kindred had congregated beyond the fence for the evening's theatrics, Powell silently slipped out the back door. Earlier in the day, he had removed the three two-by-sixes that had been spiked down across the peep-holed security door in advance preparation for this little mission.

Powell, who had ventured out without full battle rattle, leapt off the porch and crouched low as he quickly scurried to the first fence line. In seconds he found the natural dip in the terrain that had created a four-inch gap that was a little less than a yard long under the chain-link. The private was prone in a heartbeat and wriggled under the fence without so much as a scratch. Less than a minute later, he was on his feet and headed toward a similar breach in the second line.

In about ten minutes, Powell had escaped from the mansion and slipped through the triple fence line without being detected by anyone inside Wolveshaven—other than Terazo, that is—or the fangs outside of it. Nor did he blow himself up. *So much for it being impenetrable or inescapable*, the private thought sarcastically as he sprinted toward the cover of the nearest structure.

Eighteen

"Are they still out there?" Deacon asked in a hushed tone so as not to wake the sleeping soldiers sprawled throughout the great room.

"Yeah, still hanging around," Arnett responded as he turned away from the window and lowered the night-vision binoculars. "Only about two dozen or so. Most of them began to wander away about half an hour ago. There's still more than a few warriors hanging around, and that's a little unusual."

"Maybe they wanna put on a show of force for us," the major said as he stopped at the window. "Show us how big and bad they are."

"Could be." Vann offered him the binoculars. "Wanna take a look?"

"No, not really," he answered with a shake of his head. "I've seen enough of them to last a lifetime, a couple of lifetimes, actually."

"I know what you mean."

Deacon took a quick visual search of the darkened room and smiled when he found what he was looking for. The Irish setter, with head on forepaws but eyes open, rested on the hardwood floor beside the recliner where Rossington slept.

"Looks like your dog has a new best friend."

Arnett smiled when he saw Rusty beside the sleeping lieutenant. "Yeah. He does have a thing for women. When the . . . when the three of us were here, Rusty almost always slept in Sylvie's room. She thought he must have been owned by a woman before The Collapse and that's why he was so attached to her."

"Why wasn't he with her when she . . . when . . ." Deacon couldn't get the words out to finish the question.

"If we weren't all together, we always traveled or worked in pairs. Sylvie and Hal were working together out of the city, so the dog was with me. Rusty can't shoot a gun, but he sure as hell can let you know if there's any vam . . . any of them around. I don't know how many times he's saved my ass."

"Well, it seems like the only dogs we've seen now are more wolf than dog. Or at least they're wild dogs."

"And they run in packs, right?"

"Yeah." Growing up, his family had always had a couple of dogs running around and Deacon had expected it to be that way when he was an adult, but when the military became his career there was no practical way for him to have one. It was one of the few regrets he had about his chosen profession. He didn't really want to think about it, so he changed the subject. "Did you get any sleep?"

"Couple hours, I guess. How about you?"

Deacon frowned. "Probably about the same. I haven't had a decent night's sleep in months. I'm not sure I could sleep for more than four or five hours at a time anymore." His face darkened in disappointment. "And that's probably just as well because I don't necessarily like the things I see in my sleep."

Vann could only nod in agreement. He knew what the major was talking about.

"How long before sunrise?"

Arnett turned to the window and scanned the horizon for the telltale signs of dawn. "An hour, maybe an hour and fifteen," he said without looking back at Deacon. "It will start to get brighter out there in about forty-five minutes or so. I suspect the last of our guests will be leaving shortly."

"You can really tell that by studying the horizon for a couple of seconds? I have to admit, I am impressed."

Vann faced the officer. "Hey, it's nothing, just a matter of life or death."

From his vantage point on the second floor of a dilapidated Victorian about a block away with the first hints of dawn smudging the distant horizon, Powell watched through binoculars as the vampires prepared to leave. Four of the fangs carried long blades, but the one with the crossbow slung over his shoulder and the centurion sword in his hand was clearly in charge. He used the blade to punctuate the orders he issued to direct his charges.

Confident the fangs were leaving, the private quickly but carefully hurried down the steps to the first floor and out the back door. He flicked off the safety of his M16 as he crept around the corner of the house. Through the binoculars he watched as the centurion led the vampires—some of whom were still bare-ass naked, having just gathered up their clothes without bothering to put them back on—away from the area, while two warriors fell in at the rear of the group. They moved down a street that had decrepit houses on one side and ravaged multi-level commercial structures on the other.

Powell doubled back around the Victorian and trotted through the thick, knee-high grass of the backyard. He cruised through three lots before coming to a potholed surface street. He was just in time to lose sight of the last warrior as she moved down the street. The private did a mental five-count and dashed across the street to the backyard of the first house on the next block, stopping to control his breathing while leaning against a rusty swing set. He could hear the vampires as they noisily walked down the street in the front of the house.

They don't have a fuckin' clue, Powell thought as he listened to them chitchatting away. *Not a fuckin' clue. They're just strolling along the street as if it's just another night of fun and games. They've got no order, no military discipline. Dumbass fangs.*

He scooted along the side of a re-muddled, two-story Victorian that had no true discernible architectural style, to the edge of its front side. Peeking around the corner with the binoculars raised to his eyes, he watched the vampires amble farther down the broken pavement. Their column stretched almost the entire length of the block. They appeared to be headed in the direction of a multi-level brick warehouse two blocks ahead. The crumbling structure, which looked like it had been bombed out, had at one time served as the demarcation line that proclaimed the absolute end of the residential neighborhood and the actual start of the commercial district.

The private bolted around the house and cautiously dashed through backyards that held countless memories but refused to give up the ghost. He narrowly avoided tripping over the remains of a plastic Big Wheel, cursed under his breath, but kept running to the end of the block.

Using an overgrown blue spruce at the corner of the lot as cover, he scrambled underneath the lowest branches to get a better view. Through the binoculars Powell saw the centurion stop in front of the run-down warehouse and turn back to the column. He could see the vampire's lips move but could only imagine the warrior urging the fangs under his charge to move faster.

It was still dark enough outside to make seeing difficult, but the sky revealed that the arrival of dawn was inevitable.

He plucked the radio from his utility belt and brought it to his mouth. "The last of the fangs are entering a large, blasted-out warehouse five blocks west of the mansion," the private whispered in the microphone.

"Ten-four," came the soft response from the speaker.

Powell shook his head and thought derisively, *Once Five-O, always Five-O.*

He checked the vampires' progress again. About half the column had entered the building through a gaping hole in the side.

"Do you want me to proceed to the warehouse?" he asked into the Motorola.

"Ten-four."

Powell shook his head and muttered, "Fuckin' idiot." He put the radio back on his belt and raised the binoculars. He was just in time to see the female warrior stride over the threshold of the hole and disappear into the darkness.

The private crawled to the edge of his tree cover and surveyed the area in front of him. It was not good. He had run out of recessed residences on his side of the street. Decaying brick structures fronted both sides of the avenue, removed from the asphalt only by the width of a narrow terrace with an odd-out skeletal tree and a cracked concrete sidewalk with some sections shifted by as much as a half foot.

"Fuck," he muttered under his breath and repeated the curse. "I must be fuckin' crazy. No other explanation, just plain fuckin' crazy."

Powell crawled out from under the fragrant pine boughs, popped to his feet, and darted across the street to the structure there, pressing his body tight to remnants of a recessed door to some unknown business. He cautiously stuck his head out but saw nothing. He raised the binoculars to his eyes and saw the same thing. The sidewalk and street were still deserted.

He took a deep breath and held it, wishing he had taken some NVGs instead of just the binoculars. *Can't do anything about it now*, the private thought.

Powell exhaled quietly and ran down the sidewalk, staying tight to the buildings while being careful not to stumble over debris that had fallen onto the concrete. He rushed past one structure and then the next, leaping over a barely visible jumble of bricks that had fallen. Without so much as glancing either way, the private dashed through the intersection before he scurried to a stop about ten feet from the hole in the wall.

With the binoculars in his left hand and his assault rifle clutched in the right, the private concentrated on slowing his breathing down as he leaned against the dry bricks. As he rhythmically inhaled and exhaled, the air smelled faintly of mortar dust and ash. In under a minute, he was breathing normally.

He carefully but quickly stepped over to the hole, raising the binoculars at the same time. From the sidewalk, the private peered into the darkness of the warehouse's interior but saw no movement, much less any signs of the vampires. Then he heard the giggle of a teenaged girl followed by the rutting grunts of another fang.

Powell's heart leapt into his throat and his pulse jumped two-fold as he wheeled away from the hole and slammed his back against the brick wall. Panic-laced adrenaline flooded his system as he fought not to hyperventilate, but the giggling and grunting continued from inside the building. It took him a few seconds before he realized what the noises were, and he let out a silent laugh.

With the binoculars against his eyes, the private slowly stuck his head into the hole and scanned the blackened interior of the warehouse. He found them in less than ten seconds: a teenaged female vampire leaned against the shoulder of a thirty-something male fang. They both smiled at him in the gloom.

"Oh shit," Powell said out loud as he peeled away from the hole in the wall. He stopped dead in his tracks as the centurion leveled the razor-sharp point of his short broad sword at his throat.

"Oh shit, indeed," the centurion said with a toothy smile.

"Come in, Powell," Terazo whispered into the radio microphone as he paced the floor in one of Wolveshaven's bathrooms. "Powell, do you read me? Come in, Powell."

It had been almost forty-five minutes since his last—albeit brief—contact with the private, and the captain feared it was not a good sign. Terazo hadn't expected him to chitchat all the way back to the mansion, but he had assumed the private would at least report that he was heading back. Radio silence was not a positive development.

"Come in, Powell. Do you read me, Powell? Respond, Powell."

Terazo leaned against the sink and sighed loudly. *This is bad*, he thought. *Real bad.*

"Come in, Powell. Answer me, damnit!"

The silence from the speaker of his Motorola mocked him.

The sun had crested the horizon less than ten minutes earlier and spilled its weak but building light through the windows. Arnett and Deacon quietly sat in the main room, while the other troopers restlessly slept around them.

"Looks like we survived another night," Vann said.

"I guess we did," Deacon responded. "And none the worse for the wear, it would appear."

"I'll take that any time."

"I agree."

Looking like he hadn't slept in weeks and the radio in his hand, Terazo slowly stepped into the main room. He moved like a feeble senior citizen without his walker.

"Hey, Zo, you—" The major stopped when the captain practically staggered into the light. "Are you feeling all right? You look like shit."

Terazo frowned but didn't respond.

"Zo?"

"Powell's gone."

"What? Where?"

"He's gone."

"What do you mean, gone?"

Now awake, Rossington sat up in her recliner, while Traynor roused in the chair he had been sleeping in.

"Answer me, Captain," Deacon said.

"Powell's gone."

"What do you mean? Talk to me, Zo."

"Where could he go?" Vann asked.

"What happened, Zo?"

"I . . . I . . . I . . ."

Rossington put the leg rest of the recliner down and threw off her sleeping bag. "What the fuck is going on now?"

"What happened, Zo?"

"I sent him out . . . on a mission."

"Mission?" Rossington asked. "What mission?"

"What did you do, Captain?" Deacon asked.

"I sent him out on a mission," Terazo said slowly. "I wanted him to find out where the vampires went after they left here."

"You did what?" Rossington asked, but it really wasn't a question.

Deacon turned to her. "Give it a rest, Rossy."

"But—"

"Not now!"

"Okay, okay."

"Tell me what happened, Zo."

"I had Powell sneak out of here . . ."

"No way," Arnett said. "No fuckin' way."

Deacon faced him. "Vann, please . . ."

"Sorry."

"I had Powell sneak out of here and he got out of the compound without anyone detecting him," Terazo said. "He followed the vampires as they headed away from here. He said they went into a large, blasted-out warehouse about five blocks from here. I had Powell follow them there, and I haven't heard from him since."

"Fuck," Rossington snarled.

The other troopers slowly began to wake up in the commotion.

"Goddamn it," Traynor muttered mostly under his breath.

"When did you last hear from him?" Deacon asked.

"I don't know," Terazo said, shaking his head. "An hour, maybe a little more."

"Fuck," Rossington repeated.

"Shit," Traynor grumbled.

"What's goin' on?" Stroud asked sleepily.

"Okay, so we haven't heard from him in about an hour," Deacon said, trying to get a handle on things. "And that's all we know."

"Yeah," Terazo said.

"What's goin' on?" Stroud asked again.

Petrovic reached over and slapped him upside the head. "Shut the fuck up."

"What?"

"Shut. Up."

"Did you tell him to go inside the warehouse?" the major asked.

The captain shook his head slowly. "No, but he was on his own and freelancing out there. You know Powell, he will do whatever he thinks is necessary to get the job done."

None of them could argue with that assessment of the private.

"If he thought he could get more intel by going into the warehouse, you know damn well he was going to go into the warehouse," Traynor said.

"Yeah," Deacon agreed, nodding his head slowly. "Yeah, he would."

"Hey, soldiers," a male's voice crackled over the speaker of the radio in Terazo's hand, "did you lose someone?'

Everyone in the room jumped in startled surprise at the voice.

The captain brought the radio to his mouth. "Who is this? Powell, is that you?

"Did you misplace Powell?" the voice asked.

"Who the fuck is this?" Terazo asked.

"It sure ain't Powell," the voice answered.

"What have you done with him?" the captain asked. "Where the hell is he?"

The questions were answered by a laugh.

"*Where the hell is he?*"

"You can see him if you look out the window," the voice answered.

Almost at once and in nearly complete unison, everyone scrambled to a window that would give them a view from the front of the mansion. In the distance, hanging like an upside-down scarecrow on the gate of the wrought-iron fence, was a dark figure.

"Fuck," Rossington snarled.

"What is it?" Stroud asked, and Petrovic slapped him upside the head.

"Let's go," Deacon said, but Terazo was already halfway to the door.

Less than two minutes later, they all stood at the main gate to Wolveshaven and stared at the body in the warming morning sun. The vampires had strung Powell's nude corpse over the gate and left it for his comrades to find. His throat, wrists, and inner thighs had been sliced open, and he had been bled dry and his wounds licked clean. His once deep black skin had taken on an ashen hue in death.

"You're a fuckin' idiot," Rossington said to Terazo and began to walk back to the mansion.

Shaking his head and still holding the keys to the gates, Arnett followed her. The only thing rivaling the insanity of the situation was the stupidity.

"I didn't mean for this to happen," the captain said softly to no one in particular. "I . . . I just thought if we could find out where the vampires went after they left here, we would have a better chance of finding our people. I . . . I . . . I didn't mean for . . . for this to happen."

"Yeah, but it did," Deacon snapped at him. "It did."

"I . . . I know."

"Petrovic, I want you and Wade to cut him down," the major said.

The two troopers nodded solemnly.

"Stroud, I want you to get a shovel and dig his grave in the vacant lot across the street."

"Why me?" the private complained.

Petrovic slapped him upside the head. "Shut the fuck up and do what you're told."

"I'll do it," Terazo said. "I'll dig the grave."

"I don't care who the fuck does it, but we're rolling out through these gates in one hour," Deacon said. "We're gonna go straight to that warehouse and see if we can find something out. Hell, maybe we can make it so that Powell didn't die in vain."

Nineteen

Led by Petrovic and Wade atop ATVs, the other troopers in two Humvees drove away from Wolveshaven after Vann locked the gates. In a matter of minutes the small convoy stopped in front of the devastated warehouse where Powell had reported seeing the vampires enter.

"I'm telling you, I have thoroughly searched this area and there are no Kindred in this building," Arnett said as he climbed out of the armored vehicle. "Or any others in this immediate area, for that matter."

"And I'm telling you, Vann, I don't care," Deacon said to him as he stepped around the front of the Humvee. "This is the last reported position of my soldier, so I want to check it out for myself."

The other troopers, geared up in BDUs and full battle rattle, exited or dismounted their vehicles. Petrovic and Wade wandered toward the opening in the wall.

"It's just that—"

"Vann, I'll be happy to drive you back to the mansion, if you like," the major said, "but I am not going to debate every decision I make with you. I don't tolerate that from my men, even my officers, and I will not tolerate it from you. If you're part of this mission—and, yes, we do need your help—you're going to be under my command, and that means you follow my orders without debating them or questioning their merit. Is that okay with you?"

"Aye aye, Cap'n," Arnett answered in a pirate's voice and followed with a less-than-regulation salute.

"Wrong branch of the service, but I get your point."

"Hey, Major, we found something," Wade called out from the hole in the wall.

The troopers hurried over toward where he and Petrovic stood.

"What did you find?" Deacon asked.

"This." Wade held up the Motorola radio, complete with a slash of blood, still tacky and dark, across the face of it.

"Fuck," Rossington sneered.

"Where'd you find it?" the major asked.

"Sitting on top of the bricks in the opening," the private said.

"It was just sitting there?" Traynor asked.

"Yup, sitting there just like somebody placed it on the bricks," Wade said. "Placed it there for us to find."

"What channel is it on?" Terazo asked.

The private checked the radio and said, "Seven."

"Well?" the major asked the captain.

Terazo frowned and then nodded. "We were operating on seven."

"Still think there's nothing to this?" Deacon asked Vann.

"I never said there was nothing to it," he answered. "What I said was there are no Kindred inside of this building. And I still think that. Just because they may have passed through the warehouse doesn't mean they are actually still inside of it. And let me ask you this. If they were inside this building, if there was a nest of them in there somewhere, would they leave the radio sitting out here for us to find?"

"Stick it up your ass, Professor," Terazo said. "We need to search this building from top to bottom."

"We are going to search it, Vann," the major said.

"Okay, let's do it."

"Petrovic, you got point, and everybody form up on him," Deacon said. "Rossy, you're the rear guard, so make sure nothing sneaks up on our six. Watch your spacing. I want everyone two yards apart, and I don't want any bunching up and no ass grabbing. Understood? We need to stay rock hard and ready, I don't want to go waltzing into a trap. Dave, you and the dog are gonna sit tight out here and monitor radio traffic. We're operating open mics on channel one, so let's keep the chitchat to a minimum. Everybody better be geared up and sharp. Petrovic, you're going through that hole in one minute."

Sixty seconds later, a helmetless Petrovic led the troopers through the hole and into the warehouse. In less than a minute they were all inside the structure. Some forty-five seconds after that, the private made their first discovery.

"Aw, shit," Petrovic muttered when he found it.

"What is it, Petrovic?" Deacon asked from the middle of the pack.

"Clothes, sir."

"Clothes?"

"Yeah, it looks like Powell's clothes, and I think it's his gear."

The troopers formed a rough semicircle around what Petrovic had found. All of Powell's clothes had been neatly folded and carefully laid out on a dirt- and dust-covered counter as if he would be putting them on in a little while. His gear, on the other hand, had been smashed nearly beyond recognition and heaped into one pile on the floor.

"This is just fuckin' weird," Stroud said. "I mean . . . just fuckin' weird."

"I hate to admit this, Stroud, but I agree with you," Rossington said, which caused the teen to grin and Petrovic to chuckle.

"You know what's missing?" Wade asked.

"What?" the major asked.

"His bling," Wade said.

"His what?" Terazo asked.

"His bling, man," Wade said. "He had that goddamn gold dollar sign hanging around his neck on a fat gold chain. He had a couple of other gold chains around his neck, and he had that fuckin' gold Rolex on his wrist."

"That's right," Petrovic said.

"Maybe he left it behind," Traynor said.

"No, he wore it everywhere, all the time," Petrovic said. "Everywhere, man."

"It ain't here, none of it," Wade said. "It wasn't on his body, and it's not here with his stuff. And like Petrovic said, he never left home without it."

"Great," Rossington said, "so some vampire's got sticky fingers, but that doesn't really help us out now, does it?"

"Maybe, maybe not," Wade said. "But if I see a fuckin' vampire with a big gold dollar sign hanging around his neck, I'm gonna shoot the muthafucker dead on sight."

"I hear ya, bro," Petrovic said, and the two of them tapped the knuckles of closed fists together.

"That's enough," Deacon said. "Wade, you got first dibs on the fang who swiped Powell's bling . . ."

"Thanks, Major."

". . . but after that, it's open season on Kindred."

Rossington sighed loudly and started to say something but stopped. The lieutenant knew this wasn't a battle she was going to win, especially right now, so she opted to keep her mouth shut.

"All right, re-form on Petrovic and let's finish this sweep," the major said. "Stay sharp. I don't want any surprises."

There were no surprises. In fact, there really wasn't much of anything discovered during the rest of the warehouse search.

The soldiers had found some additional evidence that the Kindred had been in the structure recently, but nothing of any real consequence, nor did it shine any light on what had happened to their comrades. The warehouse certainly wasn't a nest or even a staging ground. It appeared to be little more than something they had used as a trap to spring on an unsuspecting trooper. To that end, it had been extremely successful.

"So are you going to say it?" the major asked Arnett as they walked out into the street and morning sunlight.

"Say what?"

"'I told you so.' You could, you know. Hell, you probably should. I would."

Vann shook his head. "No, you wouldn't, and I won't, either. It won't solve anything, and it won't help us at all."

"Thanks." Deacon slapped him on the shoulder and headed toward Traynor.

Rossington, who had been cooling her heels a couple of yards away, sidled up alongside Arnett. "You're all right, Vann."

He faced her. "I have my moments every now and then."

She smiled at him. "Probably more of them than you realized." And with that she left him to join the other officers.

It was midafternoon when Petrovic stumbled upon them partially hidden in a darkened basement storage room. In reality, the only reason he even went into the room beyond the threshold was because he thought he heard a sneeze from a pile of cardboard boxes as he did a cursory flashlight search. He found them when he kicked the boxes out of the way. Even though he anticipated finding *something*, the private still cried out in startled surprise with his discovery of five dozing vampires.

In an instant, the other troopers poured into the room with rifles leveled for business, flashlights searching for targets. They damn near pushed each other out of the way to get in first.

"Don't move!" Petrovic screamed at the vampires—a male, two females, and two children—who were lying on air mattresses and covered with blankets. "Don't fuckin' move!"

The vampires attempted to scramble to more defensive positions, the children cowering behind the women and the man moving in front of the long-haired females.

"I said, don't fuckin' move!"

The male held his hands out in front of him. "Easy! Easy! Eeeaaasy! Don't do anything stupid."

"Fuck you," Stroud sneered and stepped forward, but Rossington pulled him back by the collar of his body armor.

"I think he was talking directly to you," the lieutenant said as she stepped in front of the teen.

"Easy," the male said, ratcheting down his intensity level and lowering his hands in equal increments. "Easy. Easy. We don't have any weapons on us. They're . . . they're on the floor beside me, but I'm not going to try anything."

"Wade, get rid of his weapons," Deacon ordered.

The private moved forward. His high-intensity light found a Winchester Super X2 12-gauge shotgun and Colt .45 automatic pistol on the concrete within easy reach of the male, and, without taking his eyes off the vampires, he carefully slid them along the floor away from the owner. Wade then posted himself between the guns and the male, keeping both his flashlight and the SAW leveled on him.

"Do you have any other weapons?" the captain asked.

"Knives, but they're in our jeans or jacket pockets," the male said calmly. "They're all over there on the chairs."

Twin beams rapidly found a pair of folding chairs with clothes draped over the backs and on the seats.

Deacon stared hard into the male's eyes. They had been brown at one time but were now little more than faded tan. "You better not be lying to me."

"I'm not," the male said shaking his head slowly. His dark hair was long and his beard was full but not shaggy. He was shirtless but wore dark sweatpants. "Besides, you're the one with all the guns pointed at us. I'm not lying, and it would be suicide for us to try anything." He looked over his shoulder at the sobbing children behind the women, both of whom were in their thirties and also in sweats and T-shirts. "Shhhh. Steve and Beth, it's okay. I promise." The male turned back to the troopers. "My name is Daniel. The women are Alice and Tara, and, of course, the kids are Steve and Beth."

"Who the fuck cares?" Terazo snarled. "You're nothing but animals to us."

The male only smiled in return but gave him a flash of fangs.

"Are you Kindred?" Deacon asked.

"No," Daniel said, shaking his head. He held out his bare arms to show there were no Kindred markings on them. "The mark of the beast is not on me or anyone else here."

"Then they're of no use to us, Major, so I say we waste them," the captain said. "Right now."

"Yeah," Stroud eagerly agreed. "Waste 'em now!"

The children, who were about five or six, sobbed even louder in terror, and the women, despite their own fear, tried to comfort and shield them.

"Shut up, Stroud," Rossington said. "Just shut the fuck up!"

"Let's do it now." Terazo even moved forward a menacing step or two.

"No," Deacon said softly.

"What?" the captain asked in disbelief.

"I said, no."

"What the fuck?"

The major pulled Terazo aside. "Zo, we need to find out if they know anything."

"He just fuckin' said they're not Kindred. They don't know anything. What could they possibly tell us?"

"That doesn't mean they don't know anything, you fuckin' idiot," Rossington shot in as she tried to join the conversation.

"Rossy," Deacon said with annoyance.

"Shut the fuck up, bitch!" Terazo sneered at her.

Vann grabbed the lieutenant by the back of her body armor in a horse collar tackle but gently pulled her back. "Come on back here," he almost whispered to her. "We need to keep a close eye on Stroud to make sure he doesn't do anything . . . stupid."

She was pissed but knew what he meant. The flint hardness in her dark eyes softened a bit. "Okay."

"We're wasting time here," Terazo said to the major. "We should just kill these fuckin' animals and move on. Kill them right now."

"We need to find out what they know," Deacon said

"They don't know anything . . ."

"We don't know that."

". . . and if we don't kill them, they're going to be racing out of here and screaming like banshees for help. We'll end up with the whole fuckin' coven or nest or whatever the fuck it is crashing down on us."

The major shook his head. "They may know something that will help us, and I intend to find out."

"But . . ."

Deacon silenced the junior officer with a wave of his hand. "I am going to find out if they know anything, and you will not do anything. Understood?"

The captain glared in silence.

"Understood?"

"Yes, sir."

"And that is an order. Understood?"

"Yes, sir." Terazo clenched the grip on his M16 tighter and tighter as his rage burned inside of him.

"My name is Deacon. Major Deacon."

"Daniel." The male vampire offered his hand up to the major, who shook his head.

"That's pretty much the extent of the pleasantries, I'm afraid."

"A major in the *U.S.* Army?"

Deacon smiled. "I'll ask the questions, if that's okay with you?"

"Sorry." Daniel, who appeared to be in his late twenties and was rail thin, sat with his legs stretched out from the end of the air mattress. Behind him, the two females had quieted down the children, but they still stared at the soldiers with wide, nearly colorless eyes. "Ask away."

"First things first. Now here's the deal, I'm going to ask you some questions that I need answers to and you're going to answer them. If you answer them in a forthright manner, we'll walk out of here and leave you alone, untouched and unharmed, but if you don't answer them or lie to me—and I will know if you're lying—well . . ."

"I'll give you any information that I have," Daniel said.

"Okay. You're not part of the Kindred, right?"

"That's right." Daniel nodded. "They're nothing but a bunch of religious nut jobs, blindly following their *prophet* and his gloom-

and-doom preaching straight from the Book of Revelation. They hunt the rest of us—those who aren't part of the Kindred—they hunt us down like animals, and if they catch you, you get a choice: join them or die. Not much of a choice, really. I know a couple of people who were captured, joined them, but managed to escape when the opportunity presented itself. Two of them left the city, while another one stayed. I later found his head on a stake. I hate the Kindred. They're even worse than the other one, the Sun Demon. At least he only comes during the day."

The female child whimpered at the mention of the boogeyman's name.

"Okay, so you don't like the Kindred . . ."

"We hate them."

". . . why don't you fight them?"

"We're vastly outnumbered," Daniel said, shaking his head slowly, "and the truth is, most of us are worried about surviving pretty much from one day to the next. When you spend all of your time trying to find something to eat, and trying to avoid the Kindred, it's damn difficult to think about getting organized, much less do anything about it.

"The Kindred are organized," he continued, "but their leaders use fear and brutality to keep the others in line. The Prophet preaches end-of-the-world stuff, and he claims that his followers are the chosen ones, that if you listen to him and do what he says, you will have eternal salvation. But if you cross him, you're going to die. If you don't do what the Prophet says, you're going to die. If you pick a fight with them, you better be damn sure you're going to win, because if you don't, you're going to die. And so far, nobody has been willing to, much less able to, pick that fight."

"I understand. Where do they live?"

The male vampire smiled thinly and laughed to himself.

"Something funny?"

"No," Daniel said shaking his head. "Not funny, just ironic. The Prophet, the evil and cruel and small-minded bastard that he is, along with his henchmen and their minions live on what had been a place of enlightenment . . ."

Aw, fuck, Vann thought, as the answer became crystal-clear to him.

"... they live at the university. Well, more accurately, they live *under* it. There is an entire city of underground tunnels and passageways and rooms beneath the campus that most people don't know about. If you can gain access to the primary storm drains—the ones that are big enough for a man to stand up in—you can travel from one end of the city to the other without ever going aboveground. That's where they all live, in that underground city."

"Fuck," Rossington muttered under her breath.

"God*damn*," Wade said.

"Where's the best place to find them in this . . . this underground city?"

"The tunnels are under every university building and property, connecting one basement to another," Daniel said, "but the hub was the basement of the administration building. It was a huge campus, but that place was the nerve center for the entire university campus. Everything in both academics and infrastructure was operated and monitored from that building. If it involved the university, either aboveground or underground, it came from that building."

"Why should we believe you about the tunnels? How do you know this?"

"You don't *have* to believe me." Daniel smiled again, this time showing some teeth. "My dad used to work there, and he told me about them. He even showed me the doorways that led to the various tunnels away from the basement. I never actually went into them or walked down them, but I know those tunnels exist, and I know that's where the Kindred live."

"How do you know that?"

"That's where my friends who were captured by the Kindred were taken. That's where they were given their ultimatum. That's where their indoctrination into the Kindred took place after they agreed to join. And that's where the Prophet preached to them about the end of the world and eternal salvation. And they had no reason to lie to me."

"Okay." Deacon grinned at him. "Very good, Daniel. Thank you. You've kept your part of the arrangement, and now I will keep mine. We'll leave you . . ."

"No!" Terazo yelled. "We can't just leave and let them live."

"I made a deal with them, Captain," the major said point-blank in his junior officer's face. "They kept their part of the arrangement, and now we will keep ours. Understood?"

"Fuck that!" Terazo raised his M16, while the vampires on the air mattresses cowered back.

"No! No! No!" Daniel said. "Don't do this!"

As the captain stepped forward and shouldered the assault rifle he heard a loud *click* by his left ear. He knew exactly what the sound was. It was an automatic pistol being cocked and readied to fire.

"Take one more step, and I'll turn what little brains you have into tapioca," Vann said barely above a whisper. The barrel of his Glock 9mm was less than an inch away from Terazo's ear. "Just give me a reason to pull the trigger. Please."

"You don't wanna do this," the captain said.

"No. *You* don't want to do this."

In the din, the troopers stared in openmouthed, stunned surprise at the two men and the standoff that had erupted.

"The choice is yours, Captain. What's it going to be?"

Stroud took one step forward with the intent to aid Terazo, but stopped with an involuntary grunt when Rossington jammed the barrel of her M16 into his crotch. The color rushed from his face as he fought the urge to clutch his groin and double over. Puking up his breakfast was still an option, however.

She smiled condescendingly at the teen. "I'm firing on semi-auto, and it would hurt like hell if I pulled the trigger. You probably wouldn't die right away, but I am willing to bet that you would wish that you had."

"What's it going to be, Terazo?"

"You're making a big mistake, Arnett."

"Maybe so, but you've got a decision to make. I'm giving you until the count of three to lower your weapon and stand down. One."

The captain attempted to turn his head toward Vann, but he just pressed the barrel of the handgun harder into his ear.

"Two."

"Fuck!" Terazo growled as he lowered the assault rifle. He spun to face Arnett, the gun now pointed between his eyes. "You have just made the single biggest mistake of your fuckin' life, you useless piece of shit."

Vann only smiled and tapped him in the forehead with the pistol. "Try to remember that you're the one with the gun in your face."

"Fuck you!"

"Zo, stand down and get your ass out in the street," Deacon said. "And that's an order!"

"Yes, sir." The captain pushed Vann out of the way and stormed out of the room.

"Dave, Terazo will be coming outside in a minute or so with a burr sideways up his ass," the major said. "Keep an eye on him, will ya?"

"Right," Traynor's voice crackled through the speaker.

"Let me know if he doesn't surface in a couple of minutes."

"Can do."

The major turned to Arnett. "Are you trying to get yourself killed?"

"Nope. But I am not going to just stand by and let him kill . . . them for no reason."

Daniel intently watched the two of them, while behind him the other vampires relaxed just a bit. He sensed that the man who had intervened was not a soldier and certainly not part of this group. In that case, who was he? Daniel thought with a slight grin. He wore body armor, but it was different from the troopers, who also had uniforms with U.S. Army rank insignias. The man had none of that. So just who in the hell was he and where was he from? He couldn't be . . . no, that wasn't possible. Or was it?

"You just drew down on one of my officers and threatened to shoot him," the captain said.

"He's a useless piece of shit, nothing more than a bully with an assault rifle," Vann said.

"He's still one of my officers . . ."

"I don't fuckin' care," Arnett said with a slight shake of his head. "If he tries anything like that again, I will shoot him down like a rabid dog—without warning and certainly without remorse."

"I understand," the major said softly with a slight nod. "And agree with you." Deacon frowned and turned to face Stroud and Rossington, her weapon still in position to give him a 5.56mm vasectomy. "Stroud, if you ever do anything stupid like that again, I will let Lieutenant Rossington shoot your balls off. One at a time! Do you understand me?"

"Yup," the teen mumbled while still hunched over.

"What?"

Yes, sir."

"Terazo just came through the hole," Traynor's voice announced with a burst of static.

"Rossy, get my troopers out of here."

"Yes, sir," she said, snapping to attention. "Petrovic, lead the way. Stroud, stop being such a pussy and cowboy up."

Petrovic began to walk toward the door, and the other soldiers fell in behind him.

"Thank you for the information," Deacon said to the male vampire. "And good luck."

Daniel shook his head. "Save your good luck for you and your men." He smiled. "If you're going where I think you're going, you will need it more than me."

TWENTY

The century-and-half-old limestone administrative building sat atop a steep hill like the crown jewel and presented a fantastic view of the campus, which itself melded into the arboreal surroundings as much as possible. To the east, university lecture halls merged seamlessly into the fringes of the central commercial district of the city. To the south and west, research facilities and educational buildings dotted the arboreal cityscape as far as the eye could see. And due north, a narrow band of historic university buildings fronted the northernmost lake of the city before yielding to a marsh that offered a myriad of educational and recreational opportunities.

The Gothic architectural style of the building had landed it on the National Register of Historic Places and roles in a handful of feature films. Not to mention that it had served as the backdrop for hundreds of thousands of photographs, everything from professional art to parental snapshots.

A year and a half of neglect had taken its toll on the grounds—long grass and weeds had overwhelmed the once-manicured lawn, concrete sidewalks had cracked and heaved themselves askew, while fallen tree limbs of varying size had been haphazardly tossed about here and there—but the abandoned four-story structure itself, blemished by only the odd-out broken window, hanging rain gutter, faded paint, and artistic efforts of the Kindred taggers, had endured the indignity of abandonment and yet maintained its stately and elegant beauty like an aged but refined actress.

All of the classic and sophisticated elements of that architectural style from a more cultured age were lost on the troopers when they unceremoniously parked their Humvees in the lot on the north side of the building.

"This is it?" Deacon asked as he exited the lead armored vehicle.

"Yeah, this is it," Vann answered.

"Spend much time here?" the major asked as he surveyed the building.

"As little as possible. This is where all the academic royalty—the chancellor, the provost, the dean of students—held court. It was full of highly paid administrators and their highly paid staff, but not *real* educators."

"Oops, sounds like a topic I don't really want to get involved in."

Arnett snorted out a laugh at the battle between teachers who worked face-to-face with students and administrators who didn't. He had been an all-too-willing participant back then, but now it was irrelevant. "Some old habits die harder than others, I guess."

The rest of the small band of soldiers piled out of the vehicles. Some stretched their muscles while others scanned their surroundings.

"How long have we got?" Deacon asked.

Vann tilted his head to the sky and searched the expanse as best he could from his vantage point. He frowned and faced the officer. "We've got to be rolling out of here in two hours, tops."

"Shit," the major muttered mostly to himself. He had been hoping for more time to get familiar with the place. "Okay, listen up. We don't have much time today, so we're going to do a ninety-minute recon of what's underneath this facility. We'll get a sense of what's here and then we're out of here."

Terazo sighed loudly, obviously annoyed. This was not how he would play it out.

"I really wish we had more time, but we've got to be rolling out of here in two hours . . ."

"Two hours," Stroud said, whining. "That's not very long."

"No, it isn't, but two hours is what we've got, that is if you want to get back to the mansion before sunset," Deacon said, directing his words at the private.

"Yeah, I would kinda like that," Stroud admitted.

Petrovic slapped him upside his Kevlar helmet and mumbled, "Fuckin' dumbass."

"I don't know what we're going to run into down there, so everyone pack as much ammo as you can carry . . ." the major said.

"Can never have too many bullets," Wade said to Petrovic.

"True that," the other SAW gunner answered.

"Everybody needs to gear up and right now," Deacon said, "because, ready or not, we're going into the belly of the beast in five minutes."

With Wade once again walking point, the troopers—armed to the teeth and hauling enough gear for a three-day battle—headed single file directly to the main doors of the building. Traynor and Rusty restlessly cooled their heels in the parking lot.

"Thy gun is my shepherd, I shall not want," Petrovic said as he approached the doors, the heavy glass panes in both of them long ago broken out. "It takes me through desolate pastures. It leads me beside dead waters. It restores my soul. It guides me in my paths of righteousness. Even though I walk through the valley of nightmares, I will fear no fangs, for it is with me. My SAW gun comforts me."

"Amen," Rossington said as she followed him over the threshold and stepped into the lobby of the historic building.

A perfunctory five-minute, flashlight-illuminated search of the wrecked and debris-strewn ground floor was unsatisfying.

"We got nothing on the ground floor, Traynor," Terazo said softly into the hands-free mic in front of his mouth. "There is some evidence of Kindred activity here, the usual and standard assortment of vampire crap, but we didn't actually find any of the bastards."

"Look at this shit," Petrovic said as he shined his light on the wall, revealing what had been spray painted in bright red on its surface.

Repent or else I come to thee quickly, and I will make war against thee with my sword.

"It's from the Book of Revelation," Rossington said. "I don't think it's the actual verse, but it's close enough to give you an idea of what they're all about."

"Who cares?" Stroud said.

"Well, you better fuckin' care," Terazo snapped at him. "You're not just dealing with vampires. You're dealing with vampires who believe in the Apocalypse, the final battle between good and evil. And just who do you think the bad guys are in this one?"

The private thought for a moment and then it dawned on him. "Us?" He spoke the word in surprised disbelief.

"Yeah, us, dumbass," Petrovic said. He would have slapped him upside the head but his hands were full.

"But . . ."

"Shut up, Stroud," Rossington shot in.

"We've got to go downstairs, into the basement," Deacon said. "We're not going to find them up here. And we won't find those tunnels up here, either."

"Find us a way to the basement, Corporal Wade," Terazo ordered. "Traynor, we're looking for a way downstairs. I will let you know when we find one."

"Roger that," Traynor's voice crackled over the radio.

"At the end of that corridor is a stairwell that will take us to the basement," Arnett said, with a nod in the direction of the wing that he and Rossington had searched.

Wade turned to the major, looking for some kind of instructions.

"You heard him, Corporal," Deacon said. "The way down to the basement is that way. Lead on."

"Yes, sir." Wade took a deep breath and headed toward the corridor.

"I don't like this," Petrovic said from the number-three spot in the seven-man, single-file column as the troopers carefully stepped down the flashlight-lit stairs that led to the basement. "I don't like this at all. It doesn't feel . . . right. I don't know. I got a bad feeling about this."

"Put a sock in it, Petrovic," Deacon said from right behind him.

"Traynor, do you still hear me, copy?" Terazo asked from the second position.

Silence greeted his question.

"Traynor, do you hear me, copy?"

Silence again.

"Major, I think it's safe to say we have lost radio contact with the surface," the captain said to the commanding officer.

"Thanks, Zo," Deacon said. "We pretty much knew that was going to be the case, so this isn't a big surprise. Stay sharp up there, Wade."

"I really don't like this," Petrovic said.

"Knock it off, Petrovic," Rossington said from the back of the column. "Keep your mouth shut and your eyes wide open."

"Yes, *sir*," the private said sarcastically. Petrovic wanted to say something about her having the biggest balls in the group, but he was sandwiched between Terazo in front and Deacon behind, so he kept his comment to himself.

"Keep an eye out for booby traps, Wade," Deacon said in little more than a whisper.

"Yes, sir," the corporal said but resisted adding something about this not being the first time he had done this.

The walls were littered with Kindred-inspired graffiti, their ubiquitous sword-and-snake symbols, propaganda-like slogans such as Repent or endure my wrath, and Are you worthy to open the book, and paraphrased Bible verses along the lines of I saw a pale horse and his name is Death, and He cast his sickle upon the earth and the earth was reaped. With each step downward, the scent of the air changed from stale and lifeless to sour and unclean. It was a subtle but distinctly noticeable transformation. The troopers had encountered similar odors in the past, and it was never a good thing.

"I think we're on to something," Terazo said as he reached the end of the stairs and put into words what all the troopers had been thinking. "There are vampires somewhere down here, and I would say there are a lot of them. I can smell 'em."

"I agree, but *somewhere* is the operative word," Deacon said as he slowly followed Petrovic down the hallway the steps had led into. "We don't know where they are, so we really need to be sharp. Wade, I don't want any surprises, and Rossy, I need you to make sure nothing comes up from behind us and pinches our ass, got it?"

"I got it covered," Rossington said.

"I hear ya, Major," Wade added, his voice barely above a whisper but loud enough to cover the sounds of their footsteps.

Kindred symbols and artwork, illuminated by flashlight in the darkness, lined both walls of the corridor.

"We've got open doorways on both sides," Wade said as he halted his progress.

"Okay, we're going to go left-right, odd-even," Deacon said and added over his shoulder to Vann. "You go in the opposite direction of me."

Arnett took a deep breath and nodded silently.

"Do not go more than a few steps into the room," the major said. "I want a thirty-second scan of the room from three sets of eyes, but make it thorough. If you see any signs of trouble—and you know what I mean by that—get the hell out of the room and into the hall immediately, and we're all hauling ass to the surface in an orderly manner. Rossy, you're the anchor in the middle of the corridor, you've got to be our eyes front and back, and you're also the timekeeper.

"Any questions?" he added. Deacon didn't expect any and wasn't disappointed by the silence. "Okay, let's do it."

With surprising discipline and alacrity, the five troopers and their guest executed the search flawlessly, while the lieutenant counted out loudly to thirty. Seconds after she finished, the troopers reassembled in the hallway.

"Nothin' in there but shit," Wade said shaking his head.

"Same for us," Deacon said. "Line it up, and Stroud, I want you in front of me."

The teenaged private gave him a look in the gloom.

"I want an officer in each group," the major said, "and by you going in front of me, we get that. Understood?"

Stroud nodded and moved to his new spot in the formation.

"Let's do it," Deacon said.

"I really hate this part of it," Traynor said to Rusty, who sat upright near the driver's-side door of the Humvee that he had ridden in. "I really hate it."

The Irish setter just stared at the man as he limped and paced back and forth.

"I mean, I know why we can't communicat—there's too many obstructions, too much shit between me and the—but that doesn't mean I have to like it, right?"

The black man leaned against the Humvee, his shadow stretched out long in the receding sunlight of late afternoon.

"Come in, Terazo," he said to the mic of his handheld Motorola. "Come in, Captain."

Silence came from the speaker.

"Shit." Traynor pushed himself away from the side of the armored vehicle and limped into the parking lot. "I hate this, I really do. I hate not being able to hear what's going on, not being able to communicate with them. I hate not knowing what's going on." He faced the dog. "You're not very talkative, are you?"

Rusty, with ears cocked attentively, looked at the limping man.

"I guess more than anything, I hate not knowing what's going on down there," he repeated. "It's frustrating as hell and more than a little annoying, even though there's not a goddamn thing I can do about it." Traynor kicked a rock off the asphalt.

The setter watched it roll into the long grass, then turned his attention back to the man.

"Come in, Terazo," he said into the mic again.

Still there was no answer.

"Shit." Traynor leaned against the Humvee and checked the sun's position on the western horizon. It was a smidge lower than the last time he had looked. "I hate this. I really do, you know."

They had reached the proverbial fork in the road.

The troopers' search of the basement level under the administrative building had yielded little of any value. They had found rudimentary evidence that the Kindred had been there—crushed or folded cardboard boxes lay on the concrete floor, trash and other discarded refuse in corners, a couple of makeshift chamber pots that appeared not to have been used in months—but none of it indicated recent occupation. They had also failed to find anything that could have been construed as personal effects, trinkets and reminders of their previous lives. It appeared as though the various rooms had served as a temporary refuge for the Kindred or other vampires from the immediate fallout of The Collapse, but those inhabitants had now either moved deeper into the bowels of the tunnel system or suffered a different fate. The rooms were home to skittish rats and creepy-crawly insects.

Wade had led his comrades to the heavy and thick metal door with a one-word sign, Tunnels, attached at about eye level. The corporal had opened the door, with hinges bone-dry and rusty creaking in protest, dropped the catch to hold it open, and went down a cinder block–lined tunnel that at the end of a thirty-foot walkway spilled into an open area—too big to be termed a foyer but too small to be considered an actual room. On either side were open thresholds that led to the passageways, while straight ahead was a closed-door elevator. The seven of them filed into the darkened and tight space, weapons and flashlights either pointed at the ceiling or the floor.

"Left or right, Major?" Wade asked.

Stroud went straight to the elevator and stabbed the Down button several times with his index finger. Petrovic cuffed him upside the helmet and muttered something that sounded like *fuckin' dumbass* under his breath.

"Any ideas, Vann?" Deacon asked.

Arnett shrugged. "I suspect it's pretty much like a maze down here, so it won't really matter which way we go."

Terazo rolled his eyes in disgust and annoyance. He knew no one could see him do it but the gesture made him feel better, as if he had actually voiced his sentiments.

"Okay," the major said. "Any suggestions?"

His question was met with little more than shaking heads and frowns.

"Okay, since everyone just screamed out answers on that one," Deacon said, "Corporal Wade, let's try the right side tunnel."

"Yes, sir."

"Zo, what's our elapsed mission time?" the major asked.

Terazo checked his watch. "Forty-two minutes and counting, Deke."

"Shit," the major muttered and wondered to himself why time was moving so fast down there. "We've got about twenty, maybe twenty-five minutes at most, to search this tunnel. Zo, let me know when we hit an hour . . ."

"I will."

". . . okay, we're staying in same lineup as before, and let's keep things nice, tight, and orderly," Deacon continued. "Rossy, leave some bread crumbs behind so we can find our way out of here."

"I'm on it," she answered. The lieutenant grabbed a handful of glow sticks from one of the bellowed pockets of her combat pants, cracked one open, and dropped the luminous plastic stick on the threshold. It cast an eerie and disquieting glow on the floor.

"Take us down that tunnel, Corporal."

Twenty-One

With high-intensity flashlight beams disjointedly dancing off the walls, the ceiling, and the floor, Wade led the troopers down the dark tunnel, cobwebs clinging to the multiple conduits of wiring on top and debris lining the bottom. With each step, the foul odor of vampires—a noxious tang of unwashed bodies, untreated human waste, and rotting trash—became more pronounced as they proceeded deeper and deeper into the belly of the beast.

They were moving down the seemingly endless tunnel when Deacon asked in nearly a whisper, "How long is this thing?"

"We're going between buildings, so I would say a couple hundred yards," Vann answered in a hushed voice. "Could even be longer."

"Shit," Petrovic muttered.

"How far are we?" the captain asked.

"I see an open doorway up ahead," Wade responded, his anxiety ratcheting up a couple of notches. "We're maybe thirty yards from it."

"Steady, Corporal," Terazo said. "I need you to stay sharp."

"Yeah, yeah, yeah." Wade refrained from adding a smart-ass comment, but it didn't stop him from thinking it as he pushed forward.

"This place fuckin' reeks," Stroud grumbled. "I mean, its baaad."

"Stow it, Stroud," Rossington said from the back of the line.

"But it fuckin' stinks."

"Knock off the chitchat," Terazo said. "This isn't fuckin' playtime. We've got a job to do, so let's just do it and keep the commentary to a minimum."

Wade slowed as he neared the doorway, hesitated, and took a deep breath at the threshold and then darted into the room, cutting to his left. The other six soldiers followed his practiced lead and scuttled into the lightless chamber.

Less than a minute later, their light beams searched out the confines of the room from their positions along the wall. In the distant past, it had been an open reception area for the departmental offices that had been located through the doors along the walls.

"What is this place, Vann?" the captain asked.

"Offices for some of the professors and teaching assistants who taught in the building above us," he answered. "It would have been mostly new professors without status or tenure at the university and, well, TAs are considered educational chattel."

"Nice," Rossington muttered.

"Just the way it was." Arnett shrugged. "It doesn't mean I liked it or even agreed with it."

"What's our mission time, Zo?"

The captain glanced at his watch. "We're at forty-nine minutes. Oh, make that fifty minutes."

"Time's gettin' short, Deke," Rossington said.

"I know, Rossy, I know." The major frowned. "Shit, we're here right now, but we really don't have enough time to do a thorough search of all these rooms."

"We've got forty minutes max before you want us topside," Terazo said. "Going straight out that door and back to the administration building isn't going to take us very long. We can probably do it in ten, maybe twelve minutes."

Deacon pondered the captain's words. He knew it wouldn't take them as long to get out as it did to get where they stood, but the major also thought twelve minutes was an overly optimistic estimate.

"Time's wastin', Major," Terazo said, while thinking, *Make a fuckin' decision, will you?*

"I know, Zo, I know." The major sighed out loud, not a good sign. He never liked to waste an opportunity when it presented itself. Still, he wasn't comfortable with this situation. Deacon sighed again. "Okay, we're here right now, so let's get this done. We're going to do this fast but by the book. Three into one room, while the other three are getting ready to hit the next room when they come out. You all know how to do this, left, right, and center. Rossy, you're the timekeeper again. Give us a solid thirty, no more or no less, when the last man enters the room. If we do this right, we can search this whole place and still get the hell out of here on time. Any questions? No. Let's do it."

Traynor anxiously stared at the western horizon for a long moment before he turned his attention to his wristwatch.

"Shit, shit, shit, *shit*," he grumbled, not liking what the displays on the Tag Heuer told him. "Time is getting away from us, guys. Time is getting away, and you need to wrap this shit up and get back here."

He glanced up at the sky and back at his watch.

"Shit."

Traynor faced the red dog, which still sat at attention.

"I got a sick feeling about this one, dog, right down in the pit of my stomach," he said. "Nope, I don't like this at all." Traynor turned his attention to the door of the administrative building. "Come on, come on." He started toward the door and then stopped after three paces. "Just settle down, soldier. It's not like it's the first time that you have done this. This is nothing new."

The dog's eyes followed the limping black man. His thoughts were unknown and his eyes were inexpressive.

Traynor took two more steps toward the building and stopped. "You don't even have your weapon," he scolded himself with a derisive chuckle. His M16 leaned against the armor plating of the Humvee, near the open driver's-side door. "What were you going to do if you ran into some vampires, Dave? Give them a stern lecture? Holler at them? Scold them? Oh Traynor, you are a piece of work, a real piece of work.

"Now just walk back to the Humvee and wait like a good soldier," he chastised himself, turning around and walking toward the vehicle. "Pick up your weapon, put it over your shoulder, and follow orders."

Rusty never took his brown eyes off the man, marking each step of the way.

"Don't worry, dog, I'm all right," Traynor said with a grin. "I have not completely lost my mind. Well, not yet, anyway."

And then he broke out laughing.

"Twenty-nine," Rossington counted out loudly. "Thirty."

An instant later, Arnett backed out of the room, followed by Stroud and Terazo.

"Same shit," the captain said to no one in particular.

"I don't get it. Where are the vampires?" Wade asked as he started toward the next room. "There should be some around here. Where *are* they?"

"What did you say?" Deacon asked.

The corporal stopped in his tracks, causing Petrovic to step off to the side so he didn't collide with him.

"Come again, Wade," the major said.

"Where the hell are the vampires, Major?" the corporal said, facing the officer. "In that last room, there were signs of them *living* in there. Shit, there were a couple of mattresses on the floor, blankets and sleeping bags. There were some knickknacks and other shit—water and candy bars—in there. For fuck's sake, Major, there was a teddy bear on one of the beds. It's pretty obvious there are vampires living in that room. So where the fuck are they?"

Deacon took a moment to digest the corporal's words, but he couldn't argue with what he had said. And the major didn't like the implication of it.

"We're at sixty-two minutes, Deke," Terazo said.

"Thanks, Zo," the major said almost absentmindedly. "Wade, I think you hit the nail on the head. Where are they?"

"Uh-oh, I don't like the sound of this," Petrovic said. "I don't like it at all."

"If they're not in that room, where are they, Major?" Wade asked.

Deacon's stomach fell sickly, like an elevator with the cables cut. "It really doesn't matter where they are. The most important question is, why aren't they in there? If that's where they live and sleep, why aren't they in there right now?"

"Oh fuck," Rossington said. She knew what it meant.

"What?" Stroud asked dumbly.

"This is not good," Deacon said. "Not good at all. I think we should get the hell out of here. And right now."

"See, I told you this wasn't a good idea," Petrovic said. "I knew this was a bad fuckin' idea. I just knew it."

"Shut up, Petrovic," Rossington said sternly.

"Deacon's right, I think we should get out of here right now," Arnett said.

"Okay, so they're not where they should be," Terazo said, "so big fuckin' . . ." And then it hit him. "Oh shit."

"What?" Stroud asked again.

"We should leave now," Vann said.

"I agree," Rossington added.

"Why?" Stroud asked.

"You dumb fuck," Petrovic snarled at him. "The vampires aren't in that room because they are expecting us!"

"Oh fuck," the private moaned.

Eyes keenly attuned to vision in low-light or no-light environments, the five Kindred—a warrior with a nicked sword, two archers with compound hunting bows and a half-dozen arrows each, and two pawns with eight-inch kitchen knives—crept down the tunnel that the troopers had walked less than twenty minutes earlier.

Their mission was to push the troopers forward and deeper into the tunnels, where more warriors and pawns waited in ambush. They were also to slow down the soldiers if they attempted to backtrack out of the passageway, slow them down just enough so that more warriors and pawns could slip in behind them.

It was an ambitious plan that the Prophet and General Abaddon had devised. The two of them knew the soldiers would eventually find out where they lived, so they planned to use that against them. The general had posted sentries throughout the campus, so when the soldiers came looking, he and the Prophet would know about it as soon as the runner arrived at the command post. Minutes later, they would set the plan in motion to lure the troopers into the tunnels and then spring any number of traps on them. The key was to get them in the tunnels and keep them there.

And that's where his squad came in.

The warrior knew the overall success of the master plan depended on his small group doing its job, which also meant that in all likelihood they were going to die. The warrior had accepted that fate for the greater glory of the Prophet. The archers, a male and a female, probably knew the mission was a one-way ticket but had gone along out of fear of retribution, while the two pawns—who were only a couple of rungs up the ladder from animals—probably had no clue as to what was going to happen.

The warrior held up his free hand and halted the other four. He cocked his head to listen, but he wasn't sure if he heard something or not.

"Take your positions," he whispered.

The two archers moved to the sides of the tunnel and knelt. Almost in unison they notched arrows but didn't draw their bowstrings back. The two pawns moved inside the archers, while the warrior took up his position behind them.

He strained to hear anything in the gloom, but the only sound he picked up was his own blood coursing through his veins.

"Steady," the warrior whispered. "We'll wait here and see what happens."

"We could be in a world of hurt here, Deke," Terazo said, standing in the middle of the reception area where the troopers had gathered.

"No shit," Vann said.

"Could be?" Wade said.

"What's our mission time?" the captain asked.

"Sixty-six minutes," the captain answered after a quick check of his watch.

"Sunset is still . . . what? . . . forty, forty-five minutes away, right?" Petrovic asked.

"Doesn't matter," Arnett said.

"What do you mean, it doesn't matter?" Terazo asked.

"They can come out during the day," Vann said.

"Bullshit," the captain said. "Fuckin' bullshit."

"No, I have seen them outside during the day," Arnett said with a slight smile and a nod. "They're pretty much covered from head to toe, but they will go out during the day."

"Oh, we're really fucked," Petrovic said.

"I think you're full of shit, Professor," Terazo said, stabbing a finger in his direction. "Full of shit."

"I. Don't. Care." Vann enunciated each word slowly and carefully.

"Why are we fuckin' discussing this?" Rossington asked.

"She's right. Why *are* we fuckin' discussing it?" Petrovic asked. "We should be haulin' ass out of here."

"Petrovic is right," the lieutenant said. "We should be haulin' ass out of here."

"I agree with them," Stroud said somewhat sheepishly.

"Okay," Deacon said quietly. "Okay."

"This guy is full of shit," the captain said, pointing at Vann. "He's nothin' but a fuckin' liar, and I don't trust him. I haven't trusted him from the first minute I set eyes on him, and I still don't trust him. For all we know, he's fuckin' workin' with the fangs, settin' us up."

"That's enough," the major said. "Enough!"

"You really should see someone about these paranoid delusions of yours," Vann said. "You need help."

"Fuck you!"

"You wish."

"Enough!" Deacon yelled.

"Deke, we need to get out of here now," Rossington said.

"I know, Rossy," the major responded. "I know." He sighed loudly again and scratched the long whiskers on his chin. "Wade, take point and get us the hell out of here. I want you to follow the bread crumbs and backtrack us straight out. We're going to move quietly but quickly. Is that understood?"

There were murmurs of acknowledgment.

"I want single file, same order as when we hit this room," Deacon said. "We need to watch our spacing, so we don't spread ourselves too thin or trip over one another. Corporal Wade, let's go."

Wade sighed wearily, knowing he would be the first one to run into trouble if they encountered any Kindred, warriors or otherwise. "Okay, Major." He took a deep breath and headed toward the doorway back to the tunnel that had brought them in.

Leaving the onetime departmental office area in darkness and disarray behind them, the troopers quickstepped down the passageway, flashlight beams bouncing up and down and jostling from side to side like the headlights of trucks traveling on a rough road.

As he advanced down the tunnel, Wade focused on the fringe of his light, and his eyes strained to pick up something, anything, that shouldn't be there, while his brain worked overtime to process the information. The corporal was concentrating so hard that he didn't see them until he was practically on top of them. He almost didn't believe that his flashlight beam fell on a small group of vampires waiting in the tunnel about twenty-five feet ahead of him. Wade stopped in stunned surprise as his mind finally registered what was right in front of him.

"What the fuck?" Terazo snarled as he nearly stumbled into the back of the suddenly stopped corporal, and then he saw the vampires.

A heartbeat later—about the same instant as the loud *thwang* sound—an arrow slammed into Wade but splintered on his body armor, knocking him backward into the captain.

"Fuck," the corporal sneered as he stumbled off balance.

"*Fangs!*" Terazo screamed as he prevented Wade from tumbling to the concrete.

A second arrow sliced through the air, but whistled harmlessly passed all the soldiers, who started to scramble into action.

Petrovic slipped out of formation and stepped forward as the two knife-wielding vampires, screaming like banshees at the top of their lungs, charged toward the troopers. Deacon and Arnett pushed past Stroud at the same instant Petrovic opened fire. The barrage of hot lead viciously chopped down both pawns before they had closed half the distance. The major and Vann squeezed off measured bursts in the direction of the three remaining vampires. Terazo and Wade did the same after they separated themselves from one another. Rossington shouldered past Stroud, who stared in wide-eyed horror at the sight before him, and managed to snap off a couple of short, measured bursts down the corridor.

"Cease fire!" Deacon yelled. "Cease fire! Cease fire."

An instant or two later, the bristling automatic rifle chatter stopped, the echoes of gunfire rattling in the cinder-block corridor and acrid smoke curling from the barrels of six automatic weapons.

"Shit," Wade said, desperately searching his body armor for where the arrow had struck him. "Shit, shit, shit."

"Are you okay, Corporal?" Deacon asked.

"Yeah, I think so," Wade answered.

"Rossy, check him out, okay," the major said.

The lieutenant grabbed the corporal by his body armor, turned him into her flashlight, and began examining for a wound.

Vann, Terazo, and Petrovic crept forward cautiously and stopped to inspect the two dead pawns splayed out before them. Both of them had been hit by somewhere between fifteen and twenty rounds from the waist up to their heads.

"Nice work, Petrovic," the captain said as he used his boot to reposition the bodies for a better look. "At least you made your waste of ammo somewhat worthwhile."

"Fuck you," the private said in response. "They're dead, aren't they?"

"That they are," Vann said. "That they are."

The trio tiptoed around the two corpses and moved toward the other three vampires sprawled out in slowly pooling blood on the concrete floor ahead. The flashlight beams showed the harsh and brutal reality of what had transpired: the male archer had been hit about twenty times, including a headshot almost centered between his eyes, and had dropped where he had knelt, while the female archer had more than thirty bullet holes in her body and her right hand clutched the second arrow she had intended to shoot, and the warrior had been battered by more than two dozen bullets, including one that had snapped his sword blade in two pieces. Their wounds were savage and bloody, standing out in stark contrast to their pale skin.

"Son of a bitch," Petrovic said as he studied the dead and their battered bodies.

"Dumb fucks, didn't stand a chance," Terazo said, shaking his head.

"They didn't stand a chance, but they stood here anyway," Vann said. "They fired two shots at us and that was it, but she was trying to shoot again. They had to know they were going to get killed—they had to know—but they stood here anyway."

"Stop trying to make 'em human, Professor," the captain sneered. "They're fuckin' rodents that need to be exterminated."

"And you're the Orkin Man, right?"

"You got it, Professor." Terazo pushed past him but didn't venture ahead too far before he stopped.

The other four troopers reached Vann and Petrovic.

"You okay, Wade?" the private asked.

"Not a scratch," the corporal answered and held out a closed fist. Petrovic tapped it with his own fist. "I'm not only fuckin' bulletproof, I am arrow-proof."

"I didn't fire a fuckin' shot," Stroud said dejectedly. "Not a fuckin' shot. I don't fuckin' believe it."

"Don't beat yourself up, killer," Vann said. "I think you'll get your chance before the night is over."

"Really?" The teenaged private seemed almost happy about it. "You think so?"

"Yeah."

"Is that what you really think?" Rossington asked.

"Well, I don't think we're sneaking out of here," Vann answered.

"You're right about that, unfortunately," Deacon said. "We're burning daylight, so we've got to get moving. Let's re-form the line. Petrovic, I want you and Wade to flip-flop positions. You're walking point, Private."

"*Outstanding*," he answered but with no enthusiasm at all.

Twenty-Two

With Petrovic now on point, the troopers slipped past the corpses of the vampires and scurried down the darkened passageway, staying close to the wall. He moved at a little faster clip than Wade had paced them, not because he was gung-ho about it. Instead he was motivated solely by self-preservation and the desire to get the hell out of the tunnels as quickly as possible. At that very moment, the private wanted nothing more than to simply get aboveground, gaze upon the open sky, and smell untainted air again.

"Hey, Rossy, make sure nothing sneaks up from behind us," Deacon said over his shoulder.

"I'm on it, Deke," the lieutenant answered. As if to prove her point, she spun a one-eighty and walked backward for several strides, shining her flashlight all over the corridor they had just walked. It was empty except for the corpses of the five vampires they had just killed and the detritus that had been there previously. She completed the three-sixty and walked normal. "It's all clear."

"Okay," the major said, stifling a smile at her antics. "Let me know if that status changes."

"You'll be the *second* person to know if it does."

Something in the distance caught Petrovic's attention, while his fingers and hand involuntarily tightened on the trigger and the pistol grip of his assault weapon. His heart rate quickened, his palms and armpits moistened while his mouth dried, and he consciously worked to level off his breathing. Even though the beam of his flashlight didn't quite reach that far ahead, he squinted to make out what the distant object was. The private was just about to warn the others when the realization hit him.

Fighting the urge to laugh out loud, he said, "I can see the glow stick that Lieutenant Rossington dropped in the doorway. It's about seventy, seventy-five feet up ahead."

"Stay sharp, Petrovic," Deacon said, "and everyone else, too. We're not out of the woods yet."

Traynor limped around the Humvee, going clockwise first and then reversing it to go counterclockwise. He was not very good at waiting, especially when he didn't know what was going on. He hated being deaf, dumb, and blind. It made him feel helpless, impotent. Suddenly the man stopped and jerked his head to the side, much like a bird hunting for worms after a rainfall.

"What was that?" Traynor asked himself. He turned to the dog. "Did you hear that? Aw, c'mon, dog, you had to have heard that. Didn't you?"

Rusty just eyed him curiously.

He put a finger to his lips and shushed the dog. "We have to be quiet if we're going to hear it." Traynor strained to listen, silently praying for his ears to pick the sound up again.

A gentle breeze rustled leaves that were either dead or dying on their branches.

"You heard it, didn't you?" he asked Rusty, who was unresponsive. "C'mon, you heard it. Didn't you? It sounded like . . . I don't know, it . . . it sounded like . . . Aw, shit, I don't know what it sounded like."

He kicked the ground and pushed himself away from the armored vehicle.

"Shit."

Traynor turned his eyes to the sky and was disappointed—not to mention more than a little concerned—to see that the sun had slipped even closer to the western cityscape and that the shadows had stretched out even longer on the ground.

"This ain't good, dog," he said as he faced Rusty with a frown. "Nope, it ain't good at all."

He checked his watch, and the results were even more worrisome than the last time.

"Aw, shit, the time has really gotten away from us, boys," Traynor muttered, mostly under his breath. "C'mon, guys, you need to get outta there, you need to get back here right now. C'mon, c'mon, c'mon! Goddamn it!" He smacked his palm down on the hood of the Humvee with a dull *thump*. "Goddamn it all!"

Petrovic never thought he would be so happy to see an illuminated glow stick as he was when he stopped by the plastic tube on the concrete floor of the tunnel. He fought the urge to laugh out loud but couldn't help but smile. After all, it was little more than a military application of something that had been sold by the billions at carnivals, county fairs, and festivals throughout the country before The Collapse. But there it was, glowing a creepy pale lime color on the dirty cement of the T-bone intersection.

"Almost there now, Petrovic," Terazo said quietly and slapped him on the shoulder. "A few more minutes and we will be topside."

"Yes, sir."

"Stay sharp, Petrovic," Deacon said from the middle of the column. "No surprises."

"Yes, sir."

Petrovic hung a left into the corridor that would lead them to the basement of the administrative building, when something like a long, angry hornet buzzed past him a split second before he felt a dull ache numbing his shoulder. He cursed out loud and felt himself being pulled backward. The private didn't get a chance to see what his light had illuminated ahead of him.

Terazo hauled Petrovic by the back of his bulletproof vest past the intersection as arrows and crossbow bolts zipped around him and broke on the concrete wall.

"What the fuck?" the private said as he stared at the quarrel buried solidly in the muscle of his left shoulder, blood seeping from around the wound an inch or so from the edge of his body armor. "What the fuck is this?"

"Petrovic's been hit," Terazo called out across the opening of the intersection to the five on the other side.

"How bad?" Deacon asked.

"Can't tell," the captain answered.

"Fuck!" the major snarled. "Any idea how many down there?"

The other four were crowded around him, but all were careful not to expose themselves in the firing line.

"I didn't get a look," Terazo said. "I just grabbed Petrovic and pulled him over here. I . . . I . . ."

"I know, Zo, I know." He took a deep breath and exhaled raggedly. "Petrovic, you okay?"

"Yeah, I'm fine," the private said. "It's getting kinda numb right now, but I'm more pissed off about it than anything."

"Good," Deacon said. He faced the other four. "We need to know how many vampires are waiting for us down the tunnel. If it's just a handful like back there, we can overpower them, but if it's not . . ."

"I got it," Wade said.

Without waiting for an answer, the corporal stepped into the opening and clutched the trigger of his SAW at the same time. In the beam of his flashlight and the muzzle flashes of his machine gun, Wade could see more than a dozen archers about fifty feet down the tunnel. In slow motion, he saw the surprised expressions on their pale faces before some of them reacted by letting loose with another volley, while others grimaced in agony as bullets slammed into their bodies.

A heartbeat later he let go of the trigger and spun away, diving headfirst in the direction of Terazo and Petrovic. The arrows and crossbow bolts harmlessly slammed into the concrete wall and skittered to the floor.

"Wade, are you trying to get yourself killed?" Rossington screamed at him, not quite believing what she had just seen but impressed that he had pulled it off.

"No, ma'am," the corporal said from the other side as he got to his feet.

"Well . . ." She was at a loss for words. "Well . . . don't do it again."

"Yes, ma'am."

"What are we looking at, Wade?" Deacon asked.

"A lot of them, Major," the corporal said across the opening. "I'm fairly certain I saw at least a dozen, but there are more behind them. How many, I don't know."

"Shit," the major muttered, realizing just how lucky they had been. He knew if the vampires had been able to hold off firing for another five seconds or so, the entire column would have been in the tunnel, and they all might very well be dead—or at least severely wounded.

"We have to go down that tunnel, Deke," Terazo said. "It's our way out."

"Not a chance," Vann said, trying not to raise his voice. "Didn't you hear what Wade said?"

"That's our way out," the captain responded.

"It would be suicide, Zo," Deacon said. "And you know it."

"That's the way we came in."

"We'll have to find *another* way out," the major said.

"We can overpower them," Terazo said. "They've only got bows and arrows. We've got guns. We've got the advantage in firepower, so let's use it."

"They've got the advantage in numbers," Rossington countered. "And we have no fuckin' idea how many of them there are down the tunnel. Chances are, we won't even get all the way down the tunnel."

As if to emphasize the point, a crossbow bolt slammed into the cinder-block wall, embedding itself an inch or so into the concrete.

"Shee-it," Stroud said.

"We can't stay here," Arnett said. "We gotta keep moving."

"I know," Deacon said. "I know."

"We have to get down that tunnel," Terazo said again.

"We can't do it," Rossington said.

"We're going to have to find another way out of here," Deacon said.

"But . . ." the captain started to say.

"It's not open for debate, Zo!" the major snarled. "We can't get out that way, so we've got to find another way out."

"No."

"Afraid so," Vann said.

Deacon faced him. "Any idea where that tunnel leads?"

Arnett shrugged. "I'm not exactly sure where we are. I kind of lost my bearings when we went underground."

"Way to go, Professor," Terazo shot in across the opening.

"We've got to get over there," Rossington said with a nod in the direction of where Terazo, Petrovic, and Wade stood. "We get over there, we just keep moving until we find someplace where we can go up."

"Sounds like a plan to me," Arnett said quickly.

"Yup," Stroud added, "me, too."

"We still have to get over there," Deacon pointed out.

"I've got an idea," the lieutenant said. "Follow my lead."

Rossington crouched down near the opening and took out several glow sticks. She cracked them open and tossed them into the opening. A volley of arrows and quarrels responded.

"NOW!" she yelled and scurried across the opening. The three men followed quickly on her backside and scrambled behind the cover of the wall. Another round of bolts and arrows answered the move a spilt second after Stroud cleared the opening, his helmet tumbling back into the intersection.

"Hey, they're not going to stand down there with the puds in their hands forever," Rossington said. "It's time to haul ass." And with that she took off on a jog down the corridor, not even bothering to hesitate to find out if anyone followed her.

In the bowels of a onetime glorious, glass-shrouded sports arena where basketball players battled on the hardwood and hockey players dueled on the ice, the Prophet conducted his war council. He met with his top advisers—General Abaddon, Shari Landry, the Centurion, and several other warriors, along with all of their closest confidants—surrounded by well-armed bodyguards in a large, heavily fortified conference room that at one time had served as the location where members of the media conducted interviews with coaches and players.

The Prophet, whose real name was Andrew Gilchrist, sat at the head of an ornate walnut table. He was tall—about six-four—and thin. His long, dark hair was pulled back and tied off in a pony-tail, while his goatee was neatly trimmed. He wore a black, leather military-style duster over a maroon flannel shirt with black Under Armour beneath it, Wrangler blue jeans, and leather Danner work boots. A regal samurai sword inside an equally elegant sheath hung from a wide leather belt around his narrow waist.

In the flickering candlelight, the Prophet sat for several min-utes, then rose and paced anxiously for several more before he took his seat once again. The advisers, however, remained quietly at the table, while their seconds leaned against the walls behind their re-spective masters. They knew the soldiers had been moving about the campus area, but they waited confirmation that the troopers had actually entered one of the university buildings and engaged the skirmish squads in the tunnels. When that word arrived, the Prophet would spring his trap.

There was a knock on the reinforced wooden door, and a wind-ed runner entered with head bowed after one of the guards opened it.

"You have information?" the Prophet asked.

"Y . . . yes, my lord."

"What is it?"

"Th . . . the soldiers entered the ad . . . ad . . . administrative building," the runner said.

"And . . ."

"They . . . they were engaged in the tunnels."

"Very good," the Prophet said with a malicious grin. "General Abaddon, have your warriors execute the second phase of our plan."

Rossington quickstepped down the dank tunnel, moving at a pace that was faster than an easy trot but not as vigorous as an all-out run. The lieutenant worked to even out and control her breathing, but she knew that in a short time she would be panting heavily and her lungs would begin to ache. She didn't even want to think about how her legs were starting to fill with lead. Trying to ignore it, she pushed forward with one foot in front of the other. The beam of a Surefire flashlight attached to the side of her M16 tracked left and right through the darkness and then back again, searching for potential targets.

Arnett easily kept pace with her, a half stride off her left shoulder. His workout regiment, which he considered irregular at best, was still far more than what the troopers had put in during their long months on the road. Vann could move at this clip for hours on end, which was a long, long way from where he had been a year and a half ago when he couldn't have done it for ten minutes. If he thought it was possible, he would have tried to get the lieutenant to go even faster.

Terazo chugged along a couple of steps behind them. His breathing was labored, his lungs burned, and his legs weighed a ton. Several yards behind the captain, Wade and Stroud loped on either side of Petrovic, the broken shaft of the arrow bobbing back and forth with each stride like a solitary porcupine quill. The wounded private struggled to keep the pace, but his comrades verbally encouraged and physically helped him when he faltered. Five yards farther back, Deacon trotted along through his building pain. Not used to this type of exertion, he suffered like the other troopers but he also eased up every few minutes to let loose a spray of hot lead down the passageway behind them, occasionally drawing a howl of pain when a random bullet found its mark.

Very much aware of the poorly lit surroundings of the tunnels and the rising physical fatigue from their frantic escape, Rossington continued to drive them forward. She knew their very survival might depend upon it.

Twenty-Three

Rossington eased up her pace as she approached another T-bone intersection and stopped before she actually entered the open space. Chest heaving from the effort and sucking air into her aching lungs, she closed her eyes and tilted her head back. She listened to the fast rhythm of her heart as it thumped behind her rib cage and wiped sweat from her eyes.

"How you doing?" Vann, hardly out of breath, asked her.

The lieutenant gave him a look and shot back at him, "Oh, just running for my life. How the fuck am I supposed to be doing?"

"Hey, I was just wondering how—"

"Sorry."

Terazo huffed and puffed to a stop by them. "Fuck," he said as he labored to suck in air, "this is . . . this is crazy." The captain continued to breathe like a faltering steam engine. "Why'd . . . we stop?"

"Intersection," Rossington said and followed with a swig from her canteen.

"So?"

"We have to make sure we're not running into an ambush and then decide which way to go," the lieutenant said as if it should have been obvious.

With the flashlight on his M4 lighting the way and his finger millimeters away from squeezing the trigger, Vann stepped into the intersection. It was only when the light revealed an empty corridor in both directions did he realize that he had been holding his breath. He exhaled with a noisy and ragged sigh of relief.

"Arnett, what the fuck are you doing?" Rossington yelled at him as Wade, Petrovic, and Stroud joined them breathing heavily.

"It's all clear," Vann said.

"You could have gotten killed," the lieutenant scolded.

"Somebody had to do it."

"Yeah, well, let somebody know next time," she said. "That way *somebody* can have your back if there's a problem."

"Sorry."

As the troopers sucked in stale air and swilled water, Deacon trotted up to the group, drawing air greedily. "Why . . . did . . . we . . . stop?"

"We need to decide which way we are going to go," Rossington said. "Left or right."

"Oh," the major said, still working to get his breathing under control while grabbing his own metallic water bottle. "How you doing, Petrovic?"

"Hanging in there, Major," the private said through almost clenched teeth. A sheen of perspiration glistened on his exposed skin.

"We gotta get movin'," Terazo said.

"Which way?" Rossington asked.

"How the fuck should I know?" the captain sneered. "Ask the professor here, he used to teach at this university."

"Hey, I taught aboveground, not down here in the tunnels," Vann said defensively.

"Fuckin' lot of help you are," Terazo said with a smirk.

"We gotta get aboveground, up to the first floor," Wade said.

"No shit," Terazo said. "Tell us something we don't know, okay?"

The corporal's face darkened with anger, but he said nothing.

"Go left," Petrovic said.

"Why left?" Deacon asked.

"Yeah, why left?" Rossington echoed.

"'Cause going right in the first place put us in the middle of all this shit," the private said. "So I say we go left."

Nobody argued with his line of thinking.

"Everybody drink up and then check your ammo," Deacon said. "And then we're going left."

All six took their last gulps of water and stowed their canteens or bottles, checked their clips and replaced them if necessary, and then they were on the move through the dark in less than thirty seconds.

The sun kissed the western cityscape and continued its slow descent. Shadows entombed the parking lot and surrounding grounds, leaving long slivers of daylight that had snuck in between the buildings to slash across the long grass like wounds.

Favoring his left leg, Traynor limped from one end of the Humvee to the other and then repeated his steps in the opposite direction. He glanced skyward but couldn't see the sun because it had slipped behind the buildings, obscuring everything and its fading light.

Rusty lazily strolled beside the man. His pace was slow—actually too slow for the hunting dog bred to run for hours on end —but the dog matched his strides. The Irish setter knew something wasn't right. He didn't sense the presence of the *others* in their vicinity, but that didn't mean they weren't hiding underground in the nearby buildings because they were sneaky like that. The dog was aware that the man who was his master had not come out from the building he had gone into with the soldiers. Rusty also knew that the sun had almost set and that it would be dark outside very soon. And he knew that was a bad thing.

"C'mon, c'mon, c'mon," Traynor growled but not at the dog, who just stared at him as though he were crazy. The soldier had never had a pet himself, but he could certainly see how someone could get attached to a dog. "Time is getting away from us, boys and girls. It's already too late, way too late. We gotta go, and we gotta go now. Time's up, boys and girls, time is up. We gotta get out of here. We gotta get the fuck out of here now."

The parking lot was entirely shrouded in gray shadows that deepened with each passing second.

Traynor looked at his watch and grimaced. Seventy-seven minutes had passed since the troopers had entered the building. It was still within the window but just barely. If they weren't practically climbing the stairs out of the basement, it was going to get bad, and it was going to get bad really fast.

"Fuck," he snarled. "This isn't good, dog. Not good at all."

He checked his assault rifle for the umpteenth time in the past ten minutes. The safety was still disengaged and it was still set for full auto. *Ready to rock 'n' roll*, he thought derisively. The man spit noisily and sighed even louder.

The only thing changing were the hands on his Tag Heuer. And all they indicated was that it was getting later and later, even though the expensive watch that he had plucked from the debris of a ransacked jewelry store like a common looter during The Collapse said nothing about it getting darker and darker.

Traynor stopped his pacing and faced the dog, sighing loudly again. "We're going to have to do something pretty quick here, dog," he said as he shifted the M16 in his hands. "I don't know what it is just yet, but it will have to be soon—very soon. You got any ideas percolating in that head of yours?"

Rusty just stared at him with dark brown eyes.

Spread out over roughly twenty feet, the troopers quickstepped in defensive crouches down the darkened and debris-strewn tunnel. They kept their backs close to the walls but were careful to avoid stumbling over trash and other rubble on the floor while ignoring the handful of irritated rats that scuttled on ahead of them. They had separated into three small groups: Vann, Rossington, and Terazo were the lead trio, Wade and Stroud helped Petrovic in the middle about a dozen paces behind, while Deacon covered their six a couple of yards in the rear.

The major slowed to a walk and then stopped. He cocked his head and strained to hear something other than his own pounding heart and laboring breath along with the flight of his troopers. The darkness of the passageway enveloped him as he stood with his

Surefire flashlight pointed straight at the floor, its beam ending in a tight circle on the concrete. Deacon wasn't certain, but he thought he could hear something—something like the sound of a lot of feet hustling along the cement floor of the tunnel—but it wasn't easy to tell with his own blood throbbing loudly through his ears. He concentrated on picking up the sounds for several long seconds, but it was like trying to hear the ocean surf from several miles away. You knew those sounds should be there, but you weren't sure if you actually heard them or just imagined the distant noise. The major knew he couldn't take a chance.

"Hey," he called out.

Ahead of him in the din, the troopers slowed and then stopped.

"What is it?" Rossington shouted as she turned back.

"They're . . . coming," the major said between breaths.

"No shit," Vann said, almost as a laugh.

"We know that, man," Wade said very quickly before he sucked in more wind.

"Yeah," Stroud added.

"No, they *are* coming, a lot of them," Deacon said, attempting to clarify things while he regained his breath. "They are coming up hard behind us. It sounds like a lot of them."

"Then let's move," Rossington said.

"I agree," Terazo said, blurting out the words with his chest heaving. "Let's pick up the pace."

Deacon moved forward to join the middle group. "How are you doing, Petrovic?"

"Hanging in there, sir."

The major shined the light beam on the private's wounded shoulder—it looked painful—and wondered how the shaft had managed to miss the body armor. The blood had pooled around the broken arrow shaft and coagulated with the consistency of tomato paste.

"Can you pick up the pace?" Deacon asked him.

"If I must . . ."

"I think you're going to have to."

"Can do, sir."

"What's the road ahead look like, Rossy?"

"Like we're not getting down it fast enough," Terazo muttered mostly under his huffing and puffing breath.

Vann and the lieutenant shined their lights down the passageway. It was empty except for trash, a couple of annoyed rodents, and the odd-out sagging conduit.

"Looks like it's clear," Rossington said as she and Arnett turned back to the others. "Can't see anything from here, anyway."

"Okay." Deacon held his breath and listened. He was now certain he could hear them. "Let's move out, and pick up the pace, Rossy."

The major punctuated the order by cutting loose a short burst down the tunnel. The echoes of gunfire covered the metallic clinking of the brass casings showering down on the concrete. There were, however, no distant cries of agony as the bullets dropped harmlessly and silently in the dark distance.

"Let's go, Rossy," Deacon ordered.

The lieutenant took off at an accelerated clip, flashlight beam probing the thick gloom ahead of them.

Vann had no idea how long—much less how far—they had run in the disjointed beams of the flashlights. It could have been forty-five seconds or four minutes, a hundred yards or a half mile. He just didn't know. He had lost all perception of time and distance down in the tunnels, so he focused on placing one foot in front of the other and avoiding obstacles that could trip him up.

And then they were on the troopers.

The first half-dozen vampires materialized out of the umbra right behind them. One instant there was nothing but blackness trailing them, and then there were crazy-eyed, pallid apparitions in tattered rags. Their appearance had elicited a round of startled profanities, which was followed almost instantly by an excessive staccato of automatic weapons fire.

The initial six vampires had hardly fallen dead or mortally wounded to the dirty floor when nearly twice that number—armed with kitchen knives, hatchets and axes, baseball bats, wrenches, tire irons, metal pipes with threaded ends, or any object that could be used as a battering weapon—emerged from the murkiness a few strides behind the troopers. Their fang-accented mouths growled and snarled, while their pale but dirty faces loomed in the din like malevolent full moons. Additional waves of similarly armed vampires joined the ranks at the back of the mob.

The troopers scurried forward, slowed for an instant or two to unleash a barrage of hot lead, then took off sprinting again.

"SHIT!" Deacon screamed as he fired without really looking back.

As her pace slowed dramatically, Rossington kept her eyes and weapon mostly forward but occasionally snapped off a short, controlled burst after making sure none of her comrades were in the line of fire. Vann and Terazo spent less time moving forward and more time firing their weapons at the snarling pack of vampires hot on their heels. Wade and Stroud practically pushed Petrovic forward, but that didn't stop them from cutting loose with hot lead when the opportunity presented itself. Deacon slowly brought up the rear but shuffled backward and squeezed the trigger of his M16, blasting away at the nearly shapeless mass of bodies falling back from him.

"Fuck this," Terazo growled as he stopped, squared up, and leveled his assault rifle in the direction of the approaching vampires.

Wade and Stroud pushed Petrovic past the captain and assumed similar positions, the corporal taking a knee. Deacon scooted to Terazo's side, while Arnett shoved Petrovic forward toward Rossington, who grabbed him by his body armor and sidled up to Stroud. Without orders, they opened fire.

It was no well-aimed and careful burst of gunfire conducted with the objective of maximum effectiveness with the minimum expenditure of ammunition. Instead, it was a savage and merciless torrent of bullets with the single-minded purpose of stopping the vampires in their tracks, *dead* in their tracks, preferably. The soldiers released their death grips on the triggers only long enough to replace depleted clips with full ones. They ignored the occasional long knife or lead pipe hurled blindly in their direction, and gunfire deafened their ears to the horrific screams of the wounded and dying piling up in front of them. Vann swore he heard Wade scream, *"Taste the rainbow, motherfuckers!"* over the cacophony of automatic weapons.

There had been no order to cease fire. They had just stopped several seconds after there were no more upright vampires rushing them. Those that weren't dead or dying in front of them had turned tail and fled in terror, leaving a trail of crimson in their wakes.

Blood spiked with adrenaline roared through their ears and combined with the gunfire's concussive assault on their eardrums to make hearing practically impossible. The smothering silence was deafening, while acrid smoke curled from rifle barrels too hot to touch, and the odor of cordite assaulted their nostrils. For several long minutes the soldiers communicated by speaking too loudly and using hand gestures to actually get their message across to one another. It took longer than it should have, but Deacon eventually got his troopers moving forward down the tunnel again.

The major took one last look through the lazy wafts of gun smoke at the carnage and devastation they had left behind. In the flashlight's harsh and unrelenting beam, he saw dozens—perhaps as many as a hundred—of shredded and torn vampires sprawled out dead across the floor as bright red blood dripped from their fatal wounds and pooled about the mass on the concrete. Brutal close-action wounds were visible on the bodies of both male and female fangs. Every so often an arm or a leg of a wounded and dying creature twitched or a hand feebly clutched at stale air that was now rich with the copper scent of fresh blood. As Deacon's hearing slowly returned to normal, he ignored the moans or cries or pleas of those few still alive in the scrum. He knew couldn't afford to waste bullets on such highbrow concepts as mercy and compassion.

"Shit," he said softly with a frown before he turned and followed his soldiers into the darkness.

Twenty-Four

Just a few minutes after he left the pile of dead and dying vampires, Deacon caught up to Wade. The corporal had been repeatedly and impatiently looking back over his shoulder for the officer.

"How you doing, Corporal?"

"We need to do more conditioning as part of our training," he said, breathing in deeply and exhaling raggedly. "I ain't used to this type of effort, Major."

"I'll make a note of it and let Command know when we get back to The Base," the major said with a labored chuckle.

They trotted on in silence for a moment, somewhere between fifteen and twenty feet behind Stroud and Petrovic, who was now moving better.

"Are they still back there?" Wade asked, not certain he wanted an answer.

"Yeah," Deacon said after thinking about it and breathing deeply for a moment or two. "I think we pounded them pretty good, but I also don't think they're going to give up, especially since they know that we're down here. This is their turf."

As if to emphasize the point, the major squeezed off a burst down the tunnel, but there were no howls of pain at the other end of it.

"Nothin'," the corporal said.

"Doesn't mean they're not back there," Deacon responded.

Wade frowned in the darkness. "I know, I know."

Right on cue, a metal-tipped crossbow quarrel clattered to the concrete and skidded to a stop about five feet short of them.

"Don't say nothin', Major," the corporal said with a shake of his head.

"They've got archers down here now. We'd better get moving," Deacon said, stifling a smile despite the situation.

"I hear ya, Major. I hear ya."

Petrovic was not going to rely on Stroud to help him along. He would be damned if he would stoop that low, to let that snot-nosed dumbass give him a shoulder to lean on. There were a lot of things he would do, but that was not one of them, so mostly out of spite he trotted on and ignored his wound. His shoulder and upper arm had gone numb. On the bright side, the dull ache that had been deep in the meaty muscles of his shoulder had dissolved in the numbness, too. The private still had some feeling in his fingers. Admittedly, it was just a faint tingling, but at least there was some sensation in the digits.

"How ya doin'?" Stroud asked.

"Fuck you."

"Hey, I was just wonderin'," the teenager said, "'cause you seem to be movin' better, a lot better. So you don't have to get all pissy about it."

"Fuck you, Stroud." Petrovic grimaced as a spike of pain shot down his arm, but he chased it away with much better thoughts.

It seemed like years ago—not just a couple of months—that he had stumbled upon Butler bathing in a shallow river. With her long, auburn hair glowing like fire in the late afternoon sun, she stood bare-ass naked in the thigh-deep water of some ice-cold trout stream in Ohio as she washed up. With a wagging finger, she brazenly told him to stay where he had bumbled to a stop, but she didn't tell him to leave—or even turn around—as she proceeded to finish bathing. Butler had taken her time and used a lot of extra care with certain areas of her body. He had been unable to stand it, watching her do what she did, and he took matters into his own hands.

"Wha'chu smilin' about?" Stroud asked him as they jogged in the dark.

"Fuck you, Stroud." He knew that Butler had been sneaking peeks at him, and she had caught him gawking at her about a thousand times, but he had never approached her after that encounter, in part, because he couldn't believe what he had done in front of her. He regretted not making an attempt to really talk with her when he had had the chance. Now, he didn't even know if the red-haired beauty he had lusted after was alive or dead. Or worse. "Just be quiet, okay, Stroud?"

Vann and Rossington ran on ahead of the rest of the troopers. He knew she was laboring but she wouldn't budge an inch from the pace they were trotting at. Arnett had only known her a couple of days, but he tagged her as a scrappy fighter who wouldn't back down from any challenge, anywhere or any time, even if she was getting her ass kicked.

The lieutenant glanced back over her shoulder, did a double take, and said, "Aw, shit."

"What?"

"We've got to slow down."

"What do you mean? We've got to keep moving."

"They can't keep up."

Arnett looked back and saw that Terazo was struggling about thirty feet behind them and fading like a long-distance runner who had not only hit the wall but crashed into it, while Petrovic and Stroud were another fifteen feet behind him, moving steadily but losing ground with each leaden stride, and he could only see the dancing flashlight beams of Deacon and Wade as they trotted even farther behind the others. "Aw, shit."

"We've got to slow down," Rossington said again but very quickly in between gasps of air.

"But . . ."

"We've got to slow down," she said for a third time, but they kept jogging at the same clip.

"Shit."

"We *have* to, Vann."

"Shit." Arnett knew they couldn't leave the others behind. Well, he might be able to, but Rossington wouldn't do it. She wouldn't run ahead to her own possible salvation while letting her comrades fend for themselves.

"Vann . . ."

"Shit!" Quite reluctantly and against his better judgment, not to mention the strong desire for his own self-preservation, he eased back on his pace, shortening his stride and decelerating his leg turnover, and Rossington matched his slowing tempo.

Terazo was on the verge of panicked hyperventilation.

His lungs burned as he greedily attempted to suck stale air into them, but he just couldn't seem to draw enough in to satisfy the tortured void. His heart, fueled by uncut fear and pure adrenaline, thundered at an unhealthy pace. It felt like someone had poured wet cement into his combat boots and replaced his leg muscles with molten lead as he labored with each aching stride. He was also certain the tunnel was getting narrower and the walls were closing in on him. While his body pushed past its physiological red line and threatened to melt down, his brain operated on a single-minded mantra.

I gotta get outta here! I gotta get outta here!

The unspoken words pulsed through his terror-stricken thoughts, throbbing like the pain from a broken tooth. The captain was hardly aware that those five words were even in his consciousness, but they pushed him forward in the darkness.

I gotta get outta here! I gotta get outta here!

Terazo had been an efficient and effective detective, with a solid clearance rate and no credible mention of impropriety in his jacket, but none of his law enforcement training or his years of experience in the thin blue line had prepared him for this. On the streets, the captain had been in charge. He had demanded respect and dealt severely with those who questioned whether he had been entitled to it. Terazo had operated in a world of black and white, with no gray area in between, but he—and only he—was the arbiter of what was black and what was white in that world. But this . . . this was chaotic insanity in hell. Not a single thing from his past life or his current one, not even his previous life-or-death encounters with the fangs, had prepared him for this, and he wanted nothing to do with it.

I gotta get outta here! I gotta get outta here!

It had all become very simple as the captain willed his body forward, desperately trying to ignore the flaming agony that erupted like solar flares in his chest and legs. His only objective was to make it to the surface, to survive.

I gotta get outta here! I gotta get outta here!

"We must get more warriors down into the tunnels, my Lord," Abaddon whispered into the Prophet's ear as he stood beside him, "and we must do it now. We need real soldiers down there, not just cannon fodder. Now is our chance to trap them down there. We may never get another opportunity like this again, so we cannot let them—*him*—slip through our fingers. We must act now."

The Prophet stared ahead as he pondered the words from his most trusted adviser, who had turned away from his master. He knew the truth of what he had been told, but he still needed to make sense of it, to put it into context.

All eyes in the room focused on the tall and thin onetime divinity student at the head of the table. From their locations, Shari Landry and the Centurion watched the Prophet intently, unconsciously sliding forward to the edge of their seats. Each hoped to hear the words that would enable them to lead their cadre of elite fighters and expendable pawns into battle.

"My Lord . . ." General Abaddon said softly as he turned back to his master.

"'And it was given unto him to make war with the saints and to overcome them'," the Prophet said strongly but without actually looking at any of them. "'And it was given unto him authority over every tribe and people and tongue and nation. He said with a great voice: Fear God and give him glory, for the hour of his judgment has come.'" He closed his eyes and smiled. "'The hour of his judgment has come.'"

The Prophet turned to his military commander. "As you wish, General. 'Send forth thy sickle and reap for the hour to reap has come. The harvest of the earth is ripe. He cast his sickle upon the earth, and the earth was reaped.'"

Deacon thought he could hear them coming up from behind, the sounds of shuffling feet and the clatter of weapons, but he couldn't be certain. His heart pounded behind his ribs like a panicked bird trying to escape its cage, and he breathed so heavily and loudly that he couldn't trust his own ears. The major had no idea whether he was actually hearing them or if his mind was just playing tricks on him.

He and Wade relentlessly but slowly pushed on, moving forward through the din but falling farther and farther behind the dancing beams of Petrovic and Stroud's flashlights with each arduous stride of their weary legs. It was a losing proposition, but Deacon knew they had to buy some more time. He eased his pace and turned sideways, swinging his assault rifle around behind them.

Before the major could squeeze the trigger and let loose another salvo, an arrow streaked out of the darkness and unexpectedly hit its mark.

Without even knowing it, Deacon stumbled and went down hard on his backside. It was an instant later that he suspected something might be wrong and another second before he actually knew that he had been hit.

"Fuck!" Deacon croaked out. Only then did he realize that an arrow had struck him. He dropped his flashlight and his free hand found the shaft of the arrow. The tip was buried in the soft flesh of his neck, just above his clavicle, in a one-in-a-billion shot that had hit the mark. His fingers immediately were slick with blood. "Fuck!"

Wade instantly stopped and knelt by the officer. "What the . . ."

"Fuck!"

The corporal's flashlight beam found the wound. "Oh, damn! It's . . . it's . . ." He couldn't finish the sentence.

"I know, I know."

"Shit," Wade growled. "You're bleedin', Major. Bleedin' bad."

"I know. Fuck!"

Another arrow sluiced over their heads. If either of them had been standing upright, it might have been lethal.

"C'mon, Major," the corporal said, resecuring the M249 SAW machine gun and reaching to help the officer up. "We can do this together."

"No."

"But, Major . . ."

"No." Deacon shook his head. "You can still get out of here, but not by dragging me along."

"No, Major, I can't do that." The corporal shook his head as an arrow zinged overhead, quickly followed by another. He let loose a barrage of hot lead down the tunnel. "I can't leave you behind, Major. I won't."

"Yes, you can," Deacon said with a grimace. "You can and you will."

"No, not that, Major. Not that."

"Yes!"

"Major."

"Go, Jim. You have to."

Wade frowned in the din.

"Just go."

The corporal rose to a crouch. "It was an honor to serve with you, Major."

Deacon coughed. "The honor was all mine. Now go!"

An arrow skidded off the concrete wall.

"Let me give you some more ammo, Major. I think I've got a couple of clips here somewhere."

"No." The major shook his head. "You're going to need it more than me. Now go."

"It doesn't seem right, Major. Not right at all."

"Doesn't matter. Now get the fuck outta here."

"Damn it!" Wade hesitated and then saluted.

Deacon lowered his weapon and returned the gesture. "Now go!"

The corporal took off running low and hard.

A moment or two later, Wade caught up to Petrovic and Stroud, who were scurrying along but losing ground on the troopers ahead of them.

"Where's Major Deacon?" Petrovic asked.

The corporal shook his head and frowned. "He took an arrow in the throat. He's bleedin' real bad and . . . and not gonna make it."

"Fuck," Petrovic muttered.

"And you left him?" Stroud said. "We gotta—"

"Shut the fuck up, Stroud," Petrovic interrupted with a snarl. "Just shut the fuck up, you moron!"

"But—"

"Shut the fuck up!"

"But—"

"Don't make me shoot you," Petrovic said.

"The major's gonna try and buy us some time, so let's pick up the pace," Wade said, then stared at the teenager. "And that is a fuckin' order, *Private*. His fuckin' order."

Twenty-Five

Deacon thought the wound would hurt more than it did. He knew it was there—hell, he could see the feathered end of the shaft sticking out from his body—but there really wasn't much pain, just kind of a throbbing, dull ache by his right collarbone. Nothing he really couldn't handle. However, the major knew he was losing blood, probably a lot of it, and that wasn't good.

Right now, he was just too tired to care, too tired and too weak. All he wanted to do was close his eyes and go to sleep, but he suspected that if he did nod off—actually closed his eyes and welcomed the sandman's comforting embrace—he probably would never wake up.

Would that be so bad? Would it really be all that bad?

The major thought about it for a minute. No, it probably wouldn't be that bad, not really. *So just close your eyes and go to sleep, it's as simple as that.*

You can't do that, Deacon silently scolded himself. *You've got a mission to take care of, soldier. You've got a job to do. And you will do it!*

He picked up the flashlight—it felt so damn heavy, but not as heavy as his assault rifle in his right hand—and shined it down the tunnel. The major was surprised when the beam illuminated a group of lightly armed vampires cautiously approaching him. The fangs, who were about thirty feet away when the light unexpectedly fell on them, stopped in their tracks with open mouths and wide-eyed shock.

Deacon smiled. "Come and get it," he croaked out hoarsely.

He leveled the M16 and held the trigger down.

Running as silently and quickly as possible down the darkened tunnel, Wade thought he heard something behind them. The corporal wasn't sure, but he thought he knew what it was. "Stop!" he barked out and slowed to a halt. "Stop, goddamn it."

"What?" Stroud asked as he literally skidded to a standstill.

Petrovic staggered on a couple more paces before stopping.

Wade knew what it was. They all did.

In the distance, maybe a hundred yards or so behind their position, an assault rifle chattered on with a long, continuous clatter, like the dull roar of a waterfall crashing into a faraway pool. And then it fell silent.

"Aw, fuck!" Wade snarled and grimaced in frustration.

"Shit," Petrovic muttered. He knew what the silenced M16 meant.

"Keep moving," the corporal said.

The trio trotted on in silence, but Petrovic grew weary and slowed a little more with each stride.

"I'm slowin' you guys down," the private said around heaving breaths but thought, *The SAW gun and its ammo is so damned heavy, I should just put it all down.*

"So pick up the pace," Wade said.

"Can't." Petrovic slowed to a stop with a heaving sigh. "I can't keep this up."

"Yes, you can," Stroud said as he turned back after a handful of strides. "You can do it, Petrovic."

"Fuck you, Stroud," the private snarled at him. "You ain't no Nike commercial, so fuck you."

The teenaged private started to say something.

"Save it, Stroud," interrupted Wade, who had stopped about halfway between the two privates.

"I can't keep running at this pace, so I'm slowing you down," Petrovic said.

"So?" the corporal asked.

"So get fuckin' moving," Petrovic said.

"Fuck that," Wade snapped.

"But I'm slowing you down. If you stay with me, none of us are going to get out of here. *None* of us."

"Hey, I ain't doing that again," the corporal said. "Not again. Major Deacon had an arrow in his neck. He knew he was a goner and was going to buy us some time. I ain't throwing away the time he bought us and paid for with his life."

"You stay with me and you are."

"Fuck you, Petrovic," Wade said, walking up to him. "I am not leaving you behind."

"But—"

"Not a fuckin' option, man."

The private frowned, but he wasn't going to argue the point.

Wade faced the teenaged private. "Stroud, haul ass and catch up to the others."

"That's okay. I'll stay with you guys."

"That's not an option, either, Private," Wade said. "Get moving. Now!"

"Hey, don't make me come up there and smack you in the head, you dumb fuck," Petrovic said. "If you hustle, you can catch up to them. Find Captain Terazo . . . no, find Lieutenant Rossington. She'll get you out of this."

"Fuck," the teenaged private grumbled. He was confused. "Fuck."

"Go!" Wade ordered. "Now!"

"Don't seem right," Stroud said.

"I'm not asking you what's right," said the corporal. "I'm tellin' you —no, make that orderin' you—to get moving."

Reluctantly, Stroud took off running into the darkened tunnel.

"Come on, Petrovic. Let's go, and you set the pace."

"You're a fuckin' asshole, you know that?"

"Yeah, so I've heard. Let's go."

The private took off at a labored jog, while the corporal followed him a step or two behind.

Blocking out his internal agony and using the cadence of his own mantra—*I gotta get outta here! I gotta get outta here!*—Terazo had made a concerted effort to run harder and had closed to within a couple of yards of Vann and Rossington. They eased their pace as the captain joined them and fell into the rhythm of their strides.

"Where are the others?" Rossington asked, breathing heavily.

"I don't know," Terazo said, huffing and puffing. "They fell behind."

"What do you mean, 'They fell behind'?" Arnett, hardly out of breath at all, asked sarcastically.

"They fell behind, that's what I fuckin' mean." His tone was indignant.

"Asshole," Vann muttered out loud.

"What about you two?" Terazo asked. "Sprinting ahead of everybody, leaving us to fend for ourselves. What's up with that?"

"We're trying to save your goddamn ass," Arnett snapped. "If you had managed to keep pace with us, we wouldn't be spread out all over God knows what down here." He glanced over his shoulder but saw nothing in the gloom. "Who the fuck knows where the rest of them are? All they had to do was keep pace with us."

"Keep pace, fuck, we're not marathon runners," Terazo snarled, sucking in air heavily and loudly. "How about you slow the fuck down and run at a pace that we *can* keep up with?"

"And *let* the fuckin' vampires catch us."

"Where are the others?" the lieutenant asked again. She was getting pissed.

"*They fell behind!*" Terazo screamed, his chest heaving and spittle flying. He didn't like the implication of her question, even though she had pretty much hit that particular nail squarely on the head. "That's all there is to it. They couldn't keep up and fuckin' fell behind."

"You are a fuckin' coward," Rossington said with disgust and, worse yet, contempt.

"That's not how it is," the captain responded.

"A fuckin' coward." She said each word slowly.

"I am not going to die down here!" Terazo yelled at her while his brain chanted: *I gotta get outta here! I gotta get outta here!* "Do you understand that? Do you? I am getting out of here! I *am* getting out of here, do you fuckin' hear me?"

"Yeah, I hear you, you useless piece of shit," she snarled. "You . . . you . . ."

"Save your breath, Rossington," Arnett said, glaring at the captain while fighting the urge to smash in his smug face. "He's not worth it, and you're going to need it."

"Fuckin' coward." She spit in his direction and jogged on even harder.

Deacon sat on the dirty and dingy floor of the tunnel, resigned to his fate. The major knew in his heart of hearts that it would all be over soon, one way or another. He had never felt so tired or weak, and he wanted nothing more than to lie back and go to sleep. He knew it was a combination of blood loss and shock, but he couldn't muster the energy to care which one would actually lay claim to him. He breathed in raggedly, ignoring the odor of decay and mold that assaulted his nostrils.

The major didn't fear the snarling and growling mass of nearly invisible vampires that had surrounded him in the gloom. *What are they going to do? Kill me? Big deal, I'm already dead but just haven't stopped breathing yet. Are they going to chain me to a cot and tap me as a source of food? No way, I have already lost too much blood for that. Are they going to torture me for information? Go ahead, do your worst. I have nothing of value to tell you.*

Death was the only end result. It was irrefutable. The sole question that remained was how that result would be attained.

But Deacon didn't care. He had made his peace long ago with those who had gone on before him. He longed for death's icy and loveless embrace. He sought the release it would give his trapped soul. Death would make all his physical pain and mental anguish disappear. It would be a blessing, a final recompense. The major chuckled out loud at that prospect.

The vampires hushed and fell silent.

Just for an instant, Deacon thought his laughing had silenced them, but then he realized it was something else, something more . . . sinister. He felt the strange presence—like hitting a pocket of damp, cool air on a humid summer night—before he actually saw the indistinct mob of fangs part like pocket doors and a half-dozen vampires approach him through the opening. They arrived like plumes of smoke in the haze. Fear tingled down his spine like a drop of frigid sweat. The major squinted as a tall, thin vampire in a long, military-style duster over body armor—flanked by an even taller shave-headed black vampire—racked into sharp focus and stopped in front of him.

"This is the leader of the soldiers?" the tall vampire asked.

"Y . . . yes, m-m-my Lord, we believe so," one of the ragtag fangs answered and then shrank back even farther into the darkness.

"I am the Prophet," the vampire said as he crouched down before the officer, scrutinizing his appearance and assessing him as an adversary. "And you are?"

Deacon studied the vampire's narrow face, his colorless but soulless eyes, porcelain-like skin, thin lips that hid sharp fangs, and neatly trimmed beard. It was like going eye-to-eye with a statue. He couldn't help but think derisively, *This geeky dork in a makeshift BDU is what all the fuss is all about?*

"What is your name, soldier?" the Prophet asked.

"Fuck you," the major answered.

The Prophet reached out and tweaked the arrow shaft, and a flare of pain shot through Deacon's shoulder and upper torso.

"'I know thy works, and thy toil and patience'," the Prophet said, "'and thou cannot bear evil men and did try them that call themselves apostles. But they are not, and I did find them false. Repent or I come to thee quickly, and I will make war against them with my sword.'"

"Repent?" Deacon chuckled and shook his head with a slight grin, struggling to maintain his composure against a wave of nausea that roiled through his body. He damn sure wasn't going to tremble in fear or terror to this apocalyptic, Book of Revelation–spouting asshole. "Arnett was right. You're nothing but a religious whack job."

The Prophet visibly flinched at the mention of Arnett's name. General Abaddon stepped forward menacingly, putting his hand on the hilt of his sword, but the vampire leader halted him by raising his hand with an open palm and a slight shake of his head. He smiled condescendingly at the man.

"I was expecting more," the major said and coughed. "I really was. You know, I have to admit that I am disappointed."

The Prophet's grin evaporated. "'And the angels were loosed that had been prepared for the hour and day and month and year, that they should kill the third part of men.'"

"Reeeeaaaally disappointed."

The Prophet rose to his feet and turned as if to walk away. In a blur of motion and flying coattails, he withdrew his ornate samurai sword, spun on his heel, and slashed the blade toward the man's head.

Deacon knew he had touched a nerve and pissed the Prophet off, but he was surprised as the vampire stood and turned away. He was just about to say something else when the leader of the fangs pivoted faster than his eyes could see in the din or his brain could comprehend. The major didn't see the brief flash of the highly polished Japanese steel, nor did he feel the cold sting of the blade slice clean through his neck. He was confused for a nanosecond before his vision went inexplicably blank. Synapses misfiring, Deacon felt nothing as his head sloped off his neck and rolled down his slumping and twitching body to the concrete.

"'And there was given unto them authority over the fourth part of the earth, to kill with sword'," the Prophet said, standing over the major's body with a thin line of blood sluicing off the blade. "You cannot hide 'from the wrath of the Lamb for the great day of my wrath has come'.

"Oh, and fuck you!"

Twenty-Six

"Where the fuck are we?" Terazo managed to gasp out in between greedy gulps of rank air as he caught up to Vann and Rossington, who had stopped at a darkened crossroads intersection.

"I'm not sure," Arnett said as he shined his flashlight down each of the three options before them.

"You did work here, right?" the captain asked, wiping sweat from his forehead, chest still heaving beneath his body armor. "I mean, this is part of the university, right?"

"As I said before, I worked aboveground, not down here in the tunnels. I've never been down here before."

"You're really not much help then," Terazo said.

"Which way?" Vann asked, ignoring his sarcasm and the urge to punch him squarely in the face.

"Left," the captain said and sucked in a deep breath.

"I say we keep going straight," Rossington said, shining her own flashlight down the tunnels and frowning. If nothing else, she figured straight would allow them to put more distance between their backsides and the pursuing vampires.

"I'm going left," Terazo said, adamantly. "I don't give a fuck which way you go."

"Terazo, you know our best chance to get out of here"—Rossington was going to say *alive* but skipped over the word—"our best chance is to stay together. Strength in numbers."

"Maybe so, but I'm going left." His cocksure attitude seemed to return with his breath.

"Terazo . . ."

"Do what you want, Rossington, I don't really fuckin' care," Terazo said. "I really don't, and you know that. I'm going left, because Professor Fuck-nuts here has no idea where he is or where he's going, much less what he's actually doing, and I am not going to blindly follow him—or you, for that matter—down here with my dick in my hand. I'm going left, and I *am* getting the fuck out of here."

"Terazo . . ."

"Let him go, Rossington," Vann said, the four words almost a growl. "Just let him go. Besides, he can't keep up and will only slow us down."

"Fuck you," Terazo sneered before smiling at him, "but thanks."

"Asshole," Vann muttered.

The captain flipped him off. He then checked the clip of his assault rifle and slapped it back into the weapon, satisfied there was sufficient firepower left in it. He started down the left side tunnel in an easy trot, but stopped after a couple of strides and turned back to the two of them with a chuckle. "Good luck, and don't let the vampires bite."

Arnett and Rossington watched him jog down the tunnel, marking his progress by the dancing beam of his flashlight. Terazo's silhouette disappeared in less than a minute and his light followed shortly after that.

"We gotta get moving," the lieutenant said with a sigh.

"Straight?"

"Yeah, straight."

"Why."

"I don't have a fuckin' clue why," she said, smiling and shaking her head. "Not a fuckin' clue."

"Sounds like a plan to me."

She reached into one of the bellowed pockets of her combat pants and pulled out a pair of glow sticks, cracking them both open. The sticks' iridescent greenish glow cast an unhealthy pall on them. Rossington dropped one at their feet and tossed the other one in the tunnel straight ahead of them.

"Let's go, Hansel," she said.

"I'm with you, Gretel," he countered.

The two of them took off at an easy jog, trotting down the tunnel as their lights illuminated the passageway ahead of them.

Traynor and Rusty sat in the Humvee with the engine idling and the doors locked but with the parking lights on. Even with his limited mobility, he could drive the armored vehicle when push came to shove. Push had come to shove. The man was distressed about how things were going, while the dog continued to sit in stoic silence.

The sun had set countless minutes ago, and the ever-increasing darkness spun its web around the administration building, the parking lot, and other nearby university facilities. A rising sense of dread flooded the man's psyche as dusk gave way to night.

"This is really bad, dog," Traynor said, tapping the palm of his hand on the steering wheel. "Really bad. I mean, not even remotely close to good. Hell, we're not even in the same state as good. We'd have to drive for hours just to get close to good."

He looked at his watch but didn't truly see the dials, much less comprehend what they indicated.

"I gotta admit it, dog," Traynor said, shaking his head. "I don't like just sitting here doing nothing. I don't like it at all. I feel like we've got a target on our back, like there's a damn big sign saying: *here we are, come and get us.*"

He sighed and slapped the steering wheel.

"Goddamn it! We gotta do something, dog, we can't just sit here and do *nothing.*" He sighed heavily and noisily. "But if we leave and they get out of there, that won't do them any good. Hell, they can't all fit in one Humvee. Well, they could, but they would be packed in tighter than sardines. And it would probably be nothing but a huge cluster fuck to get everyone in it at the same time. Shit!"

Traynor scanned the area from the driver's seat, checking the windows and the mirrors. He saw only dark shadows against an almost equally dark night shroud.

Part of him—just a small part, but a part nonetheless—wanted to flee, to race back to the relative safety of the mansion, but a larger part couldn't do that. Discretion may have been the better part of valor, but Traynor was, after all, a soldier, and he had a job to do, a duty to uphold. Like a good soldier, he pushed aside his fears, his desire to run and save his own neck, and held firm.

"We'll probably regret this, dog," Traynor said, facing the Irish setter, "but we're gonna stay put. We're not going anywhere."

Terazo raggedly plodded forward, the beam of his flashlight jumpily slicing through the gloom. His body emphatically protested the ongoing effort. Leaden legs threatened to cease functioning with each stride, while every breath seemed to be edged with cut glass. He knew he was in big trouble and had to find a way out of the tunnel very quickly. The captain suspected he would be shuffling along in a matter of minutes and staggering just a short time after that.

Panic and fear seeped into his core when his light weakly illuminated a dead end at the far end of its range. Claustrophobia smothered him. Terazo coughed out a sob as his heart sank in defeat, but, unable to make his feet stop, he stumbled forward mindlessly. He fought to hold back tears of frustration and anger, but then the beam fell on something in contrast to the din.

What? He faltered but wobbled forward, trying to steady the light on what he had seen. *What the fuck?*

Terazo chuckled and tears of joy slipped down his cheeks when he determined what it actually was. He teetered to a stop in front of what he had thought was a dead end and laughed out loud.

His high-powered light illuminated six white letters against the black background of a sign. The single word on the sign was STAIRS.

Terazo shook his head in disbelief as he reached out to touch the dark plate on the steel door, smiling as his fingers rested on the recessed letters. He tried to temper his reaction, but relief washed over him like cool water, sending a burst of energy through his soul and reinvigorating his body. The captain felt a burst of optimism.

I am going to get out of here.

He lowered his hand and grasped the heavy brass knob, turning it without thought or hesitation. It twisted smoothly in his grip, and the door swung open easily and almost noiselessly on well-oiled hinges. An ever-expanding chasm of darkness filled the void behind the steel slab as it opened wider and wider.

The captain shined his light into the opening, and he laughed when the beam lit an empty landing and stairs that went up.

"YES!" he said. "Yes! Yes, yes, yesyesyesyes!"

Terazo took a deep breath and exhaled slowly. He held the door and hesitated for an instant, wondering if he should drop a glow stick at the end of the corridor. It would be easy enough to do—he had about a half dozen of the sticks in one of his pockets—and it might help the others escape the tunnels. It was standard operating procedure among the troopers. It would be the proper thing to do, it would be the ethical thing to do, it would be the moral thing to do, and it would be the *right* thing to do.

Fuck 'em, he thought bitterly. *Fuck 'em all!* Terazo stepped over the threshold, letting the heavy steel door swing shut with an audible and very solid click behind him.

With sword drawn and ready for business, General Abaddon stepped in front of the Prophet as the dark shape hurried toward the group of about a dozen vampires the two of them led. He relaxed just a bit when he realized it was a runner with news from one of the pursuing groups, but he didn't lower the sword.

The pixie-thin teenaged girl with dirty blond hair and ragged clothes stopped before her leader and his entourage, bowing her head nervously. "My lord . . ."

"What is it, my child?" the Prophet said.

"The . . . the . . . the soldiers are se . . . sep . . . separating," she stammered softly, raising her head only slightly but not looking at the tall man. The teen had never been this close to *him*. She was so nervous she couldn't think straight. "They . . . they're breaking into . . . into sm . . . smaller groups. Some can't keep up and are falling behind."

"Do you know which direction they're going in?"

"We . . . we think . . . we think they're ju . . . just going straight."

"My lord, we need to get more troops into the tunnels ahead of them," the general said. "We need to keep them down here. We cannot let them slip through."

"I know that." the Prophet stroked the dark whiskers on his chin and thought for a moment. He knew the moment was almost at hand, and they had to act decisively to take full advantage of it. "Get runners to Shari and the other commanders. Tell them to split their forces so we can get more fighters into the tunnels ahead of where the soldiers seem to be going, as well as some of the side tunnels where they might try to go. We also need some warriors aboveground, just in case they manage to find or shoot their way out."

"Yes, my Lord." Abaddon quickly spun on his heel and pointed at two eager vampires—both males—in the group behind them. "You and you, come here."

The Prophet stepped forward to the trembling teenaged runner. "You did well, my child. Very, very well." He bent down and kissed her on top of the head.

Stroud was lost.

A few minutes after leaving Wade and Petrovic, he had been unable to find any trace of Lieutenant Rossington or the others and where they had gone. He had pushed forward and frantically searched for a glow stick on the concrete floor of the tunnel, something that indicated the direction they had gone, but the private had found nothing in the din. He contemplated backtracking, going so far as to even taking a handful of steps in that direction, but stopped. He convinced himself that he could find the lieutenant if he just pushed forward. In the darkness and stale air, he panicked and ran blindly. As terror overwhelmed him, his thoughts were jumbled and incoherent. He was uncertain if he had gone straight or made any turns along the way.

And now, Stroud had no idea where he was.

His M16 clutched in both hands, the private made spastic, herky-jerky turns, the flashlight taped to the barrel of his assault rifle slashing through the darkness like a blind swordsman in search of an unseen target. No one and *nothing* showed itself in the beam, but that afforded him no comfort.

Stroud was tempted to call out. He suspected that if Wade and Petrovic heard him yelling, they would be pissed at him and probably pound on him, and he had no clue if Lieutenant Rossington and the others were even within earshot. He also didn't know if there were any fangs in the immediate vicinity to hear him calling out, and he just didn't want to risk drawing their attention to him.

He sighed loudly, and it sounded more like a sob.

"Fuck," the private muttered. He checked the clip in his M16, and it was almost completely full. Stroud sighed and slammed it back into the weapon, cocking it so it was ready for business. He wiped his sweaty palms on his combat pants, but it didn't really help.

The private took a deep breath and exhaled raggedly as if the dank air was catching on the uneven edges of his fear-constricted throat. "Fuck, fuck, fuck," he said, trying to clear the passageway. "Aw, fuck."

He took another deep breath.

"Okay, think, man, think," Stroud told himself as he paced in a small circle. "Okay, okay, think. What would Wade do? What would Rossington do if she were here? Hell, she'd never be in this situation. C'mon, man, think!

"Aw, fuck, I can't think. I can't think!" The private shook his head as if to clear the clutter and mental flotsam of confusion. "C'mon, man, think! You gotta do something, you just can't stay here. Think! Think!"

The harder he tried, the worse it got. There was nothing.

"C'mon, man, you gotta do something! But what? I don't know, anything. You can't stay here. C'mon, man, think! Think!"

But there was nothing. His mind was a blank.

"Aw, shit." Stroud sobbed and continued to circle. "Aw, fuck."

Twenty-Seven

The two soldiers ran as fast as they could. A group of twenty or so lightly armed but lethal fangs was hot on their heels with the single-minded goal of catching them.

Petrovic knew he couldn't keep going much longer. The pain in his shoulder was a throbbing ache that radiated through his upper torso, his weak legs felt like sacks of wet cement, and his lungs burned hotly as if each breath were acid fumes. The barrel of the SAW was just barely inches above the concrete. The private attempted to function on autopilot, blocking everything out and concentrating on just placing one foot in front of the other and repeating the process. It worked to some degree, but he wasn't even aware that Wade had clutched the shoulder of his body armor and pulled him shuffling along.

Petrovic heard the pit bull–like snarls and growls behind them as the vampires narrowed the gap with each faltering stride, but he was helpless to do anything about it. Even the occasional over-the-shoulder bursts that Wade cut loose from his weapon didn't dissuade them for more than a couple of seconds.

"We gotta move, Petrovic, we gotta move," the corporal yelled.

"Can't go . . ." The private was too winded to finish his response.

On the flickering edge of the light's beam, some thirty feet away, Wade glimpsed something that might get them out of this nasty predicament, or at least a chance to escape it: a side door beckoned like salvation in the flickering light. He pushed on harder, dragging Petrovic along, and covered the distance in seconds. The corporal whipped open the door, pushed the private over the threshold, turned back on their pursuers, and squeezed the trigger.

The roar of gunfire was deafening, and he didn't even hear the belt run dry or his own savage scream. Only when the SAW stopped bucking in his hands did he realize that the belt was empty, and the gun was out of ammo. Wade scurried through the doorway and slammed the door shut behind him. He frantically searched for the lock and literally sighed and closed his eyes when he found it, engaging the dead bolt with a quick twist of his wrist.

"Oh man," Wade sighed but stifled a relieved laugh as he turned to see where he had pitched Petrovic into the room, hoping he hadn't hurt his friend too badly.

His relief lasted only a heartbeat or two before his light illuminated the pale-skinned vampires in the room—mostly women and children along with a couple of warriors for protection. Then they swarmed over him.

Arnett and Rossington arrived at the end of the line, stopping in front of a steel security door with no sign on it while they tried to catch their breath, ignoring the stink of rot.

"It's got to go somewhere," he said, lungs heaving under his body armor. He wiped away beads of sweat that rolled down his face.

"Yeah, but where?" the lieutenant asked, squeezing the words around quick breaths. She brushed a rogue strand of dark hair from the spot along her cheek where it had stuck in her perspiration. The lieutenant closed her eyes and sucked in dank air through her wide-open mouth, forgetting all about the exercise routine of *breathe through your nose and exhale through your mouth.*

"That's the million-dollar question, Rossington," Vann said, shining his light up and down the jamb. "Where does the door lead? Remember that old TV show? I'll take what's behind Door Number One, Monty."

She shook her head slowly, sucking in air through her open mouth. "I don't know what's behind Door Number One, Arnett, but it's not like we can stand here and debate it all night. Either we go through or we turn back." The lieutenant passed her light down the corridor behind them, and the beam revealed an empty tunnel, but its path didn't cut very far in the din. "Nothing. But I don't think going back is really an option."

"I think you're right," he agreed with a nod of his head. "Well, here goes."

Vann took a deep breath and pulled the heavy door open. It creaked as dry hinges protested against the unwanted movement. Through the stale gloom their flashlights revealed an open landing, tall metal storage cabinets adorned with cobwebs along the walls, and a stairwell that went up.

"Jackpot," he said with a smile, while Rossington actually let out a quick chuckle at his enthusiastic optimism. "Well, what do you think?"

"Let's go, but we gotta be careful," she said. "Who knows where we're going to come out and what the hell is waiting for us up there."

Arnett could only shrug in response.

Rossington took a quick step toward him, kissed him on a whiskered cheek, and slipped past him. "C'mon."

Arnett, blushing in the darkness, could only stare at her silhouette as she walked confidently toward the stairs, flashlight illuminating the way. He silently laughed and then followed her.

Stroud had sagged down to the floor, resting against the dirty concrete wall. The private was lost, confused, and terrified. At least he had stopped sobbing, but he still sniffed back the tears every now and then.

He leaned his head back against the cement and tapped the back of his skull on the wall. He resisted the urge to slam his head against it when he realized he had lost his Kevlar helmet somewhere during all this.

"Oh man, the sarge is gonna be pissed," he muttered, almost childlike. "He hates it when we lose stuff, especially when we lose our gear. 'It's not like we can just go out and replace this stuff, ya know. We ain't got an unlimited supply of it, ya know.' He's gonna be pissed at me. He's gonna be *righteously* pissed at me."

Stroud snorted out a pathetic laugh. He was so lost in his own little world that he didn't even hear them approach.

"Well, what do we have here?" the warrior with a huge battle-ax in one hand and a serrated Ka-Bar combat knife in the other asked. "Are you lost, little boy?"

The private jolted back to reality as the vampires—a mixture of lightly armed males and females—laughed derisively at the warrior's remarks. He spastically shined the flashlight in the direction of the sounds and huffed audibly as he lost his breath. Fear and panic spurred on by adrenaline flooded his body, while his bladder vacated its contents.

"Fucker's pissin' himself," a shirtless male vampire with long hair and a scruffy beard snickered. "The pansy-ass is pissin' himself."

The Surefire's beam found the tormenting fang. A gold dollar sign on a heavy gold-link chain hung around his neck and glinted in the light. Something clicked inside of Stroud's brain and he smiled. He knew what he was going to do.

"Nothin' but a fuckin' pansy-ass—" The vampire stopped in midsentence when the private grinned.

Without hesitation, much less an inkling of thought, the private raised his assault rifle and clutched the trigger. The tormenting vampire's mouth dropped into a stunned *O* an instant before bullets tore up his chest with tiny explosions of blood and tissue that propelled him backward, out of the flashlight's beam.

Snarling like a cornered animal, Stroud clenched the trigger but wasn't aware that the weapon had stopped kicking in his hands. He never saw the caught-off-guard Captain Axeman regain his composure and step forward with the axe raised one-handed over his head. The private didn't hear the whisper of the descending heavy blade nor feel the razor-edged steel bite deep into his skull. He was only aware that the final synapses that fired without interruptions were: *That's for Powell!*

And then there was nothing.

"Thirty more minutes, that's all we're going to give them," Traynor said to the Irish setter in the seat next to him. "Thirty more minutes, and then we're outta here."

In the faint dashboard-illuminated darkness, Rusty just stared back at the black man, sensing his confusion, frustration, and fear, but unable to do anything about it.

"Christ, who am I kidding?" the man said. "It's already too late—way, way too late. Shit, it's nighttime. The sun's gone down. Do you see that, dog? The sun has gone down, and it's already nighttime."

The setter didn't know what the man was saying, but he knew that the sun had set. He also knew *what* came out after the sun set.

"Aw, fuck," Traynor growled as he fidgeted in the seat. "I wanna get outta here now, but . . . but I gotta stay. I won't leave a man behind, I won't do it." He faced the dog. "I won't do it, you hear me? I won't do it, dog. I won't do it!"

"Aw, shit." He smacked the steering wheel again. "This is crazy. This is stupid, really stupid."

Twenty-Eight

Terazo slowly exited the stairwell and stepped into a ground-floor hallway, with long, vacant classrooms, most with their doors open, lining either side of it. Unable to suppress a smile, he snapped off the flashlight and waited a moment for his eyes to adjust to the darkness. Peering through an open door at the grime-covered classroom windows, he could see that it was dark outside. Even though the sun had slipped behind the horizon and day had passed into night, the captain was no longer wandering around in the tunnels, and that, he believed, gave him at least a fighting chance to get out of this cluster fuck alive.

"Okay, okay, you gotta be smart now," he said, checking the assault rifle for the umpteenth time since he had separated from the bitch and the idiot professor. "Use your head, and you can get out of this."

He crept down the hall in the direction of what he thought would be a doorway out of the building. The captain was right. Terazo quietly pushed one of the double doors open and slipped into the atrium, which was at the corner of the building. He cautiously crossed the open area, wishing he could switch on the flashlight to get a better look at his surroundings, but he knew that he couldn't risk it. Less than a minute later, he stepped out of the building but hugged the exterior wall.

Terazo greedily sucked the cool night air into his lungs as if he had just broken the surface of a lake. Each breath seemed to cleanse and refresh him from the inside out.

He tried to get his bearings, but without any success. The captain was outside, but he had no clue where. His surroundings were unfamiliar, and in the darkness he couldn't really distinguish any of the lightless structures. He cursed under his breath and wished he had paid closer attention to the route they had taken to the administration building instead of merely following the vehicle ahead of him. Still, aboveground and out in the open was better than the close confines of the underground passageways.

"Well, I can't just stand here all night with my dick out," Terazo whispered. "If nothing else, I've got to find a good place to hide until sunrise."

The captain slowly and carefully crept along the wall of the building, his M16 leveled waist-high and his finger resting on the trigger. He had made the decision to proceed uphill because he remembered the building they had entered sat atop a long hill and, with any luck at all, if he could find it, at least one of the Humvees should still be parked there.

Terazo practically kept his back pressed to the wall as he made his way. It seemed to take him ten minutes to sneak along the edge of the building to the far corner. He peered around the edge of the building's dry masonry, and the first thing he saw was a wide-open expanse, with an odd-out stately oak here and there and a concrete walking path curving through the long grass and weeds.

"Shit," he muttered. The captain had been hoping to see an unobstructed view of the tall administration building perched atop the hill, but whatever was up there was hidden behind the handful of towering trees that had been strategically placed by a landscape architect to provide shade for the walkers on the pathway. "Shit."

He scanned the immediate area and saw nothing lurking in the din, but that didn't reassure him that there was nothing actually hiding out there. The captain took a deep breath, held it for a several seconds, released it quietly through his mouth, and stepped away from the building.

Terazo was three steps away from the building when he saw it and actually smiled. Around the tree trunks and through the mostly leafless low branches, the lieutenant saw a pair of lights—not headlights, mind you, but the twin beams from the parking lights of a vehicle—on the rise in the distance. He was probably a hundred to a hundred and twenty yards away.

"I'll be a son of a bitch," he whispered with a chuckle. "Traynor is still sitting there waiting for us. Once a soldier, always a soldier."

He realized that he was far behind enemy lines and moving about when they were most active, but time was of the essence. The sooner he got to the vehicle, the sooner he would be sitting in it, and the sooner he would be getting the hell out of this mess. The captain had a little more spring in his step and strode with more cocksure confidence as he walked toward the lights, although he kept his eyes peeled and the M16 ready for any fast-approaching trouble.

Vann and Rossington cautiously exited the stairwell into the middle of a long hallway that was almost identical to the one that Terazo had stepped into minutes earlier. In eerie unison and without a single word, they both snapped off their lights, pitching the hall into darkness.

"Shit," the lieutenant muttered. "I can't see a damn thing."

"No shit," Arnett said in the darkness. "Give it a minute, let your eyes adjust."

"I know that. I just don't like not being able to see."

"Listen."

"What? I don't hear anything."

"Exactly."

"What?"

"No sound," Vann said as the shapes in the darkened hallway became more distinct.

"You're right."

"But we still have to be careful."

"You're right again."

He could see reasonably well in the gloom. Vann knew they were on the ground floor of a building filled with classrooms along the outer walls and lecture halls with theater seating toward the center. Without hesitating, he went into the nearest classroom and walked to the dirty window, scanning the surroundings outside the panes of glass. Rossington stopped alongside him.

"We're still on campus," he said.

"Where on campus?" she asked. "Where are the Humvees?"

He moved to another window at the far end of the classroom with Rossington in tow at his hip.

"Where are we?"

Arnett frowned in the darkness. "I think about a half mile from where we left the vehicles."

"You think?"

"Yeah . . . I think."

"Did you actually teach at this university?"

"Yeah."

"Sure it wasn't Bob's garage college?"

"No, it was"—Vann pressed his nose to the window and searched the grounds—"it is . . . was a god*damn* big campus and spread out over something like a thousand acres in the city. I didn't teach in this building, but I'm trying to get a fix on where it is in relation to the ones I taught in or where my office is . . . was."

"Okay, okay. I get the picture."

He turned away from the window and faced her. "We're still pretty much in the middle of the campus," Vann said, "but we're closer to the east end than the west end."

"You sure?"

"Yeah, pretty much."

"Pretty much?"

"Hey, if you've got a better idea . . ."

"No," Rossington said, shaking her head. "No, I don't. I just don't want to wander around out there without a clue as to where we are going."

"We have to go west, about a half mile west," he said. "That way." Arnett pointed to his right, the direction they would have to walk.

"You sure?"

Vann nodded and softly said, "Yeah. I'm sure."

"Okay. Let's go."

The two of them headed toward the door of the classroom.

Terazo dashed out of cover as he cleared the last big oak tree, leaving only a long and weedy expanse of grass between him and the Humvee. He hoped it was Traynor in the idling vehicle, but he wasn't going to take any chances. The captain turned on his flashlight and then snapped it off.

The response from the vehicle was identical: headlights on, headlights off.

The captain chuckled to himself as he trotted toward the armor-plated military transport. *Traynor, you are* so *predictable.* He had closed half the distance when the door opened. Still not taking any chances, he hooked his finger through the trigger guard of his assault rifle.

"Goddamn, Terazo, it's good to see you," Traynor called out as he limped from the Humvee and stepped into the parking lot. The dog followed him out the door and scooted discreetly off into the shadows.

"Good to see you, too," the captain said as he stopped fifteen feet from the man.

Traynor scanned the area behind the officer. "Where's everyone else?" he asked.

Terazo shook his head. "They didn't make it."

"Shit." The black man literally kicked the asphalt. "What happened?"

"We were ambushed," the captain said. "They let us go down a tunnel and attacked us from front and back. Fuck, they were *everywhere.* All we could do was blast away at just about anything and everything that was moving. They fuckin' overwhelmed us. We got . . . we got separated. It . . . it became every man for himself."

"Sure." Traynor eyed him suspiciously. "How'd you get out?"

The captain sighed exaggeratedly and shook his head slightly. "Pretty much just dumb luck."

"Dumb luck, huh?"

"Yeah, dumb luck."

"Sounds kind of . . . suspicious to me," Traynor said. "How did you manage to get out with just dumb luck?"

Terazo had suspected something like this might happen and had worked a plan out in his head, just in case. "Well, it went pretty much like this." He raised the M16 and squeezed the trigger, stitching a dozen shots across the army veteran's chest. About half the bullets thudded into the open flaps of his unsecured body armor, while the remainder slammed into his unprotected chest.

Traynor stumbled backward and dropped to the pavement of the parking lot, fumbling unsuccessfully in an attempt to secure his weapon into a firing position. "Fucker," he growled at the officer.

Knowing that this situation had gone bad—real bad—Rusty scurried away into the darkness of the night.

Terazo shuffled over to the black man and kicked his assault rifle away. "I may be a fucker, but I am the only one who is going to survive this little misadventure. *The only one.* There is a heavily fortified mansion not too far from here with more supplies than I can use in a lifetime. Shit, I've got it made, Traynor. I have got it made."

"Fuckin' coward." The black man spit and coughed blood. "You probably ran away on first contact."

"Not quite," Terazo said, with a grin, "but I am still alive, and they're not. And neither are you." He leveled the assault rifle and squeezed off another burst, killing Traynor instantly with several head shots.

The captain let out an emotion-filled sigh that sounded like a sobbing hiccup. He wiped his face and took a quick scan for the dog. It was nowhere to be seen, having disappeared into the dark. He really didn't care—he didn't need a pet. "I'm gonna get outta here," he muttered, walking toward the idling Humvee. "I *am* gonna get outta here."

The Prophet, with General Abaddon at his side, led his entourage of vampires down a darkened tunnel, when a scrawny female runner approached from the front. With head bowed, the young teen cowered in front of them.

"What is it?" the Prophet demanded.

"I was told to tell you that the soldiers have split up," she said barely above a mumbled whisper. "I was told to tell you that they're moving in small groups, but they're going in different directions. I was . . ."

"Shit," Abaddon sneered.

The runner cringed and slouched down.

"It's okay, my child," the Prophet said, soothingly. "Did your sergeant—who is he?"

"Tabitha," the teen aged runner whispered. "Sergeant Tabitha."

"Did Tabitha give you any other information to tell me?"

"No, my Lord, I was told to . . . to ask you . . . to ask you . . . she wanted to know what she should do next."

Sometimes they could be so trying, he thought. If they could only show a little initiative, but then he didn't want them showing *too much* initiative. The Prophet faced the general. "I need you to take direct charge of this operation," he said.

"Yes, my Lord," General Abaddon answered with a slight bow of his head.

"I need you to take some of our group and get to Tabitha as quickly as possible. We need to find out what she knows," the Prophet said. "We need to know where the soldiers are going, what direction they're running."

"Yes, my Lord." The general hesitated.

"What is it?"

"My concern is for your safety, my Lord."

The Prophet waved him off and shook his head. "Leave me several of your most trusted warriors and take the rest. We will follow after you at a respectable pace, but I need you to get to Tabitha immediately. General Abaddon, we can't let this opportunity slip past. Send a runner back to us if you diverge from this tunnel."

"Yes, my Lord." Abaddon turned to the group arrayed behind him and pointed at three warriors—two males and a female—who were front and center. "You, you, and you, stay with the Prophet. Guard him with your lives. If anything happens to him, you three will suffer the consequences. Do you understand?"

The three heavily armed warriors nodded and muttered in solemn unison.

"Very good." He turned to the runner. "Take me to Tabitha."

"Yes, General." The teenaged girl turned on her heels and scurried off into the darkness from which she had come.

Abaddon took off after her. He was followed by a couple of warriors and the remaining pawns.

Twenty-Nine

Arnett and Rossington ducked in and out of the dark shadows, moving cautiously but quickly along the exterior of a multi-story concrete lecture hall.

"We're headed in the right direction," Vann whispered.

Are you sure, boy?

"How do you know?" she asked.

"We're going uphill," he answered her question and ignored the taunting voice in his head. "The admin building sits atop a long hill. We're headed in the right direction."

"You'd better be right about this."

"I am." He grabbed Rossington by the arm, stopped her, and stared directly into her eyes. "I *am*."

"Okay." She nodded slightly. "I . . . I trust you."

Ooh, I am impressed, boy, but her judgment is suspect.

Vann thought, *Not today, you bitter old man, not today*, and smiled at her. "Then let's keep moving, but keep your eyes open. We are behind enemy lines."

Rossington chuckled as they started to scurry forward. "You know, you're starting to sound like me."

"Oh Christ, we're in trouble now."

"Hey!" She swatted him on the shoulder.

In his head, he thought he heard a derisive and disgusted snort.

General Abaddon led a ragtag band of vampires, a handful of warriors mixed in with a large number of pawns, down a lightless tunnel. The teenaged female runner and Tabitha trotted alongside him, both of them beaming with pride in the darkness.

"Stop," he commanded with a raised fist.

The group shuffled to a clattering halt behind him.

He drew his sword and cautiously stepped toward the intersection, approaching what had caught his eye. The general chuckled when he saw what it was. They were relics from his past life.

Two glow sticks faintly illuminated the darkness along the dirty floor, one in the intersection and the other a few strides down the tunnel straight ahead.

"This way," he commanded with a wave of his sword and took off down the passageway.

Terazo was lost.

Illuminated only by the headlights of the Humvee, the one location in the darkened campus pretty much looked like another. They all appeared pretty much the same in his eyes. Once dignified educational buildings that had declined to various states of neglect and disrepair, surface streets that had cracked and heaved, the myriad of identification signs that had faded to illegibility—there was no difference among any of it.

The captain felt he was driving around in circles, but he knew that wasn't the case because he hadn't gone past the other Humvee or Traynor's corpse cooling in the night chill. Terazo fought against the creeping edges of panic as his frustration grew. He hadn't seen any vampires, but he knew that didn't mean they weren't out there, and he was fearful he would inadvertently cross their path.

He stopped the armored vehicle and scoured his surroundings through the front windshield and side windows, searching for anything that would give him a clue for a way out of the campus. None of it appeared different from what he had already seen.

"Damn it," the captain snarled mostly under his breath and slapped the steering wheel out of frustration in a gesture that was eerily similar to that of Traynor's. "Damn it, damn it, damn it!"

He sat back in the seat and checked his assault rifle yet one more time.

"Maybe I should just find a nice, safe place to park this thing until sunrise and then drive the fuck outta here," he muttered, pondering what he had just said and kind of liking it. "That's not a half-bad idea, not too bad at all. It beats the hell out of wandering around in the dark without a clue as to where I'm going."

The captain weighed the plan in his head. It wasn't, perhaps, the ideal course of action, but it seemed like the best one—or at least the most prudent one—he could come up with at this point in time.

"Fuck it," Terazo said in defiance and determination. "Now all I have to do is find a place to hole up for the night."

He put the Humvee in gear and eased the big vehicle forward in the night.

Arnett and Rossington stopped in startled surprise with muffled curses when headlights rounded a corner about two blocks in front of them. The two of them couldn't help but grin when they realized that the lights belonged to a Humvee.

"No shit," she said, her spirits lifting. "I don't fuckin' believe this."

"No way," Vann said with a grin of disbelief.

"I do *not* believe this."

"It's right there in front of us, so you'd better believe it."

They quickly moved from the shadows along the building to the dark of the empty street. Rossington turned her flashlight on and then off as they quickly walked.

The vehicle's lights went out and then back on.

"C'mon," Rossington said as she started to run toward the Humvee. "Let's go!"

Arnett quickly caught her, and they jogged stride for stride.

Even though it wasn't traveling very fast, the vehicle skidded to a stop with a whine of rubber on the pavement and gravel. The driver's-side door swung open, and a dark shape slowly exited the Humvee.

Thirty

Vann and Rossington literally skidded to a stop on the pavement about twenty feet from the front bumper when they realized who had just gotten out of the Humvee: Terazo.

Taking advantage of the headlights blinding them, the captain smiled as he sauntered toward the professor and the lieutenant, leveling his M16 in their direction. He enjoyed the identical stunned looks of surprise on their faces.

"Well, well, well," Terazo said, "look who we have here."

"Terazo, what the fuck are you doing?" Rossington sneered at him.

"I was just about to ask you the same thing, Rossington. I really was. I have to admit, I didn't think I would ever see you again. Quite frankly, I am surprised, because I really didn't think Professor Numb-Nuts here would be able to find his way out. In fact, I didn't think he'd be able to find his ass with both hands and a flashlight."

"Where's Traynor?" Vann asked, ignoring the remarks directed at him.

"Yeah, where's Traynor?" the lieutenant echoed.

"He . . . he had a little accident."

"What did you do, Terazo?" she snarled at him.

"Me?" the captain said with feigned innocence. "Nothing. He had an accident. You know how he was, always getting into accidents with that bum leg and all. It made him clumsy. Really clumsy. You know, I think he was the single most accident-prone person I have ever met."

"Bullshit!" Rossington sneered.

"What did you do?" Arnett asked.

"Shut the fuck up, Professor," Terrazzo growled. "I'm running the show now. Me! And if you're lucky—and I mean very, very fuckin' lucky—I'll let you back into the citadel . . . what's it called? Wolf-something-or-other."

"*Let* me back in," Vann repeated in disbelief.

The captain eased the barrel of the assault rifle over so that it was pointed directly at Arnett's midsection. "That's what I said, Professor, *if* I let you back into the citadel."

Vann snuck a quick peek at their surroundings and realized that Terazo didn't know where he was and had no clue how to get off of the campus. He was headed away from Wolveshaven. "So tell me, how are you going to get there if you shoot me?" he asked.

The smug smile on Terazo's face flickered but didn't disappear. "Maybe I'll just wound you, shoot you in the leg or something." He took a couple of steps beyond the front bumper. The former detective wasn't someone to back down from a confrontation, especially when he had the advantage.

"I don't think so." Heart pounding, Arnett shook his head. "Right now, a gunshot wound is a death sentence, so why would I tell you anything if you shoot me?"

From the depthless umbra of black velvet behind the Humvee, a four-legged shadow ambled like a dark phantasm in India ink toward the vehicle. It moved with the easy and silent grace of a hunter on the prowl, a hunter that had found its prey.

Both Arnett and Rossington saw the canine shape glide through the din and fought to hold their emotions. Glancing at it from the corner of his eyes, Vann, who recognized the shape, knew he had to stall Terazo and keep him from doing anything rash.

"So I'll shoot Rossington instead," the captain said and shifted the barrel in her direction.

The lieutenant flinched, but Arnett put his hand on her arm.

"Not gonna happen, Terazo," Vann said, shaking his head. "Not gonna happen. If you shoot her, you don't get anything from me."

"I can make it painful for her, very, very painful."

"I don't doubt that, but if you shoot her, you get nothing from me. If you hurt her in any way, you get nothing from me. Nothing."

The captain, backlit by the headlights, frowned visibly.

The long, four-legged shape passed through the halo of the tail-lights. It wasn't what Vann had expected, but he hid his surprise with a laugh and a shake of his head.

"Looks like you've got a decision to make," Arnett said, subtly moving to his left and forcing Terazo to turn toward him and away from Rossington, whose eyes had fluttered wide open before stifling her surprise with a cough. "So, *Cap'n*, if you shoot either one of us, you're stuck right here, but if you deal with us, you just might make it back to Wolveshaven alive tonight."

"Fuck," the captain muttered after mulling it over for a couple of seconds. This had not gone anywhere near how he had thought it would, and now he had to figure out how to get control of the situation.

"So what's it going to be, Terazo?" Vann asked, ever the gambler. Against his agent's advice, he had turned down the publisher's first offer for his manuscript, but that gambit paid dividends when two weeks later they doubled it. "It looks like you've got a decision to make."

"Don't fuckin' rush me!"

"We don't have all night to discuss it, Zo," Rossington said.

"C'mon, Terazo, what's it going to be?"

"I said, don't fuckin' rush me!"

The shapeless shadow became distinct when it rounded the front of the Humvee and stopped in the corona of the headlights. The emaciated tiger crouched as it prepared to pounce. Its tail twitched once, twice, and then the animal leapt with a growling roar.

"Terazo, behind you!" Rossington yelled, but it was too late. She had waited just long enough.

The captain turned as the Siberian tiger took flight at him. He saw a streak of orange launched in his direction. His first thought was: *That goddamn dog snuck up on me!* His last truly rational thought was: *That's not a dog!*

The tiger raked a large paw across the captain's head and face, slapping him to the ground like a rag doll. Terazo screamed as the beast lunged toward him, a high-pitched shrill sound.

"C'mon," Arnett said, grabbing Rossington by the arm. "We gotta get out of here!"

"That's a fuckin' tiger!"

"I know," Vann said as he pulled her in the other direction.

"A fuckin' tiger, Vann!"

"I know." He had managed to get her to run alongside him.

"What's a fuckin' tiger doing here, Vann?"

"Savin' our asses right now."

"It's a fuckin' tiger!"

The two of them sprinted away from Terazo's mauling, flashlights they had snapped on showing the way. Vann and Rossington ran in the direction they had just come from, but after a block and a half cut between two tall classroom buildings before they emerged onto another street. They eased their pace and realized they could no longer hear the captain's piercing screams. Neither of them knew— much less cared—if they were out of earshot or if the screams had stopped.

"Vann, that was a fuckin' tiger!" Rossington said in disbelief as she sucked in air.

"I know."

"What's it doing here?"

Arnett shrugged. "I can only assume he escaped from the zoo during The Collapse, but I don't know for sure. There were a handful of adult tigers in the zoo at that . . . at that time. I guess this one managed to find a way out."

"A tiger, Vann, a fuckin' tiger."

"I know, I know." He checked their surroundings. "We can't stay here. We gotta keep moving. We know the Kindred will eventually realize we have managed to get out of the tunnels, and they will come looking for us."

Rossington sighed loudly, almost a sob. "I know, I know."

"C'mon, we gotta get movin.'"

"Where are we going?"

"Anywhere but here."

They had jogged a half block when the first of the vampires spilled out of the lecture hall about two blocks in the distance. Vann and Rossington stopped dead in their tracks as more and more of the fangs exited the building.

"Shit," Arnett snarled, barely above a whisper.

Behind them a loud whistle cut loose.

The two of them spun on their heels and saw a man-sized shape emerge from the shadows of a building. The figure waved an arm, indicating for them to head in its direction.

"Who the fuck is that?" Rossington whispered. "Who else got out?"

"I have no idea," Vann answered and glanced over his shoulder. The vampires had still not seen them. "Let's go." He grabbed her arm and ran toward the vaguely human figure, which ducked back into the shadows of the building.

Thirty-One

"This way!" a male voice called out from the din. "Hurry, hur-ry!"

Vann and Rossington veered off the surface street and into the heavy shadows of the adjacent building, shutting off their lights. They scurried in the direction of the voice, unsure of what they would find.

"Over here! Hurry!"

They both gaped in surprise at the source of the voice.

"You?" the lieutenant said in disbelief. She was so stunned that she didn't even think to raise her weapon.

"Yeah, me," Daniel answered her.

"But . . . but why?" she asked.

"We don't have time to talk right now," the vampire said, shaking his head slowly. "Follow me."

He ducked back farther into the deep shadows and led them along the side of the building, eventually taking them down an alley. They sprinted across a street and into another alley.

Rossington grabbed Daniel by the sleeve of his jacket, stopping and turning him to face her. "Why are you helping us?"

The vampire stared directly into her eyes. "Because not to would be wrong." He glanced at Arnett and then back to Rossington. "You and *he* didn't let the others kill us when they could have. You stood up for us and saved us. I felt that I owed you, and this is the least I can do."

Daniel turned away from her and stared at Vann.

"What?" he asked.

The vampire smiled and shook his head. "Nothing."

"What?"

"We have to get moving," Daniel said. "We must be very, very quiet. The Kindred will be all over this area very soon. Let's go."

He led them down the alley in silence, moving quickly but with confidence. It was as if he had done this many times before.

The Prophet and his small cadre of warriors exited a building. He surveyed the area as a teenaged male vampire sprinted toward him.

"My Lord . . ." the teen said breathlessly.

"You have news?"

"Yeah."

"What is it?"

"General Abaddon thinks some of the soldiers have gotten out of the tunnels," the young male vampire said as he caught his breath. "We have killed several of them and one was killed by the tiger . . ."

"The tiger?" the Prophet said with an unexpected smile.

"Yeah . . . yes, my Lord."

"We will have to be careful if he's roaming about."

The teen dropped his head, smiled, and looked back up. "My Lord, he . . . he was eating when we saw him."

The Prophet chuckled at the remark. "What else?"

"We killed some of them in the tunnels, but not all of them," the teen said, gaining some confidence in front of his leader. "We haven't found any of the others, my Lord, so General Abaddon thinks they must have gotten out of the tunnels, especially since the one killed by the tiger was outside."

"Does General Abaddon have any idea how many of the soldiers may have escaped the tunnels?"

"No, my Lord."

The teen started to say something else but hesitated.

"Yes?"

"My Lord, the general said to tell you that Ar . . . Ar . . . Arnett was not among the soldiers that we have killed."

The Prophet smiled broadly, fangs glistening in the faint light. "Very good."

Daniel led Arnett and Rossington into a dilapidated four-story building and immediately down a back hallway. The soldiers snapped on their lights as they trotted behind the vampire, who suddenly stopped.

"We can rest for a couple of minutes," he said, leaning against the wall as he worked to control his breathing.

Both Vann and the lieutenant lowered the weapons and lights.

"Shouldn't we keep moving?" Rossington asked as she huffed and puffed.

"Catch your breath," Daniel said. "When we get moving, we won't be stopping until we're out of Kindred territory. If things go right, it will only be a couple minutes of hard running."

"And if things don't go right?" she asked.

"It might be a lot more hard running." He smiled, giving her a brief glimpse of his fangs. "Or it might not be much running at all, and it will be a very, very short escape attempt."

Vann snorted out a laugh. He couldn't help it.

"I'm not sure I like the sound—" Rossington stopped in mid-sentence after hearing a loud clunk and muffled voices down the hall.

Daniel brought a finger to his lips in the universal sign for silence.

As the voice drew nearer, Vann realized their flashlights were still lit. "Shit," he muttered under his breath. "Turn off your light."

Before they could shut them off, a group of four vampires stepped into the hallway. All seven let out surprised curses.

In a matter of heartbeats, Arnett and Rossington raised their assault rifles and let loose with a barrage of hot lead as the startled fangs drew their weapons. It was over in less than five seconds.

"Break time is over," Daniel said, his hand on the grip of his Colt .45 in the back waistband of his blue jeans.

Rossington swung the barrel of her assault rifle in his direction.

"Whoa, Rossington," Vann said.

"He's armed," she said.

"Yeah, I'm armed, all right," Daniel said. "The Kindred have an aversion to guns, but I don't."

"Rossington . . . Ross . . . Rossy, if he was going to hurt us, he wouldn't have rescued us," Vann said to her.

"Let me see it," she said to Daniel. "Slowly."

He pulled the pistol from the back of his jeans and held it out for her to examine.

"You got anything else on you?"

"Yeah," he answered her. "A Swiss Army knife."

"Really?"

"Yes." Daniel nodded. "It's in my back pocket. Would you like to see that, too?"

"No." Rossington shook her head. "No, I wouldn't."

"Let's get out of here, okay?" Vann said.

"Yeah, that's a good idea," she said.

"Follow me." Daniel led them down the hall.

The Prophet's bodyguards protectively drew their swords and flanked out around him when they heard the distant pops. From defensive postures, they visually searched the surrounding area.

"Shit," the Prophet muttered under his breath. He was surprised to find that he had actually crouched down and placed a hand on the hilt of his sword at the sound of distant gunfire. "Where'd that come from?"

"A couple of blocks in that direction, I think," a tall, ashen-gray vampire said.

"Are you certain?"

"Yeah." The warrior nodded. "That way."

"Let's go."

"My Lord . . ."

"What is it?"

"They have . . . guns."

"And it might be Arnett," the Prophet said, looking from warrior to warrior. "We cannot let this opportunity pass by."

"My Lord . . ."

"Let's go—NOW!"

The Prophet brushed past the warrior-bodyguards and quickly headed in the direction the tall vampire had indicated.

The trio emerged from the back of the building, and Daniel led them in a dash across the street into a multi-story parking garage. The vampire jogged purposefully toward the stairs in the far corner of the lower level, weaving around the odd-out, flat-tired vehicles still parked in the facility. Arnett and Rossington hesitantly followed in the dark, exchanging concerned looks with each stride. Daniel reached the door to the stairwell, pulled it open, and was surprised to find the two soldiers were lagging back.

"There is an underground passage out of this garage," he said as Vann and the lieutenant stopped in front of him, "but we have to go down to the lowest level in this garage. It's two stories underground. Is that going to be a problem for you two?"

After a moment's hesitation, Rossington said, "I've recently had a bad experience in a parking garage."

"I know," Daniel said matter-of-factly.

She stared at him in surprise.

"I know that the Kindred attacked your . . . your group in a parking garage near the square," he said. "News still travels fast in the city."

"Is there another way?" Vann asked.

"The underground passageway will takes us several blocks from here," the vampire said. "It should be relatively safe, and once we get to the building at the other end, we'll almost be out of Kindred territory. That won't stop them from coming after us, of course, but we can put a lot of distance between them and us. We can do it aboveground, but we'll be out in the open, and they will be able to see us pretty easily."

"Rossington . . ." Vann said to her.

"We don't have a lot of time," Daniel said. "They may be here very soon."

"Let's go," the lieutenant said. "Let's do it right now before I think about it and change my mind."

"Okay," Vann said softly. "Lead on, Daniel."

Daniel stepped into the stairwell and went down the stairs. Rossington followed him, while Arnett brought up the rear.

THIRTY-TWO

Daniel led them out of the stairwell and into the lowest level of the garage, trotting in the pitch black toward the far side of the bottom floor. Rossington ran a couple of steps behind him, while Arnett was several more behind her.

"Be careful," Daniel called out. "There are more vehicles down here than on any other level, so don't run into them."

Vann concentrated on following Rossington, who was practically keeping pace in the footsteps of the vampire. Something in the corner of his eye caught his attention, and he slowed his run. Arnett shone his flashlight in the direction of what had snagged him and stopped dead in his tracks when he realized what it was.

"Oh no," he muttered and moved almost drunkenly toward it. "No, no, no. It can't be. No."

Rossington slowed and then faced him, while it took Daniel a couple of seconds to realize something was amiss.

"Vann, what is it?" she called out to him. "Vann?"

Arnett kept the beam centered on it as he staggered forward, unwilling or unable to accept what he saw in the light. "No, no, no, nonononono."

The lieutenant turned her light to what Vann's illuminated. It was a dust-covered SUV, a Ford Explorer that had been modified with jury-rigged armor plating on the sides, wire mesh over the windows, and a rack of halogen lights across the front of the roof. Then it hit her. "Aw, shit," she muttered.

Vann stopped alongside the SUV and put his hand on the dusty surface. "No, no. It can't be. No, it just can't be."

He gently tugged on the handle and the passenger door opened with a creak, dust falling through the beam of his light. The interior of the vehicle was empty, but there was a smeared and dried brown substance on both front seats. His heart sank, and his knees went weak, while sour acid churned in his stomach. He put his hand on the door frame to prevent himself from falling face-first into the cabin. Arnett knew all too well what it was.

Rossington reached him and placed her hand on his back. "Vann . . ."

He didn't answer. It was as if he hadn't even heard her.

"Vann . . ." she repeated.

Arnett lowered the beam of his light to the floorboards of the passenger seat. On the rubber mat were the smashed remains of a small remote control unit. It was the device that locked and unlocked the gates of Wolveshaven. It had been destroyed beyond repair.

"Vann, I am so, so sorry," Rossington said.

"They're gone," he said softly, resisting the urge to reach out and touch the interior of the Explorer. "Gone."

"I know."

He turned to face her. "I guess I always knew it, but I just didn't want to believe it. And as long as I didn't have any evidence . . . of it, you know, I guess I kind of considered them still alive. Know what I mean?"

"Yes, I do."

"Crazy, huh?"

"No, not at all." She leaned against him and whispered in his ear. "Vann, we gotta go, we gotta keep moving."

"It's very dangerous here," Daniel said from behind her.

"We gotta go, Vann."

He smiled at her.

The five warriors had been in hot pursuit of them, tracking the two humans and another vampire from the shootout in the abandoned building to the parking garage and down to the lowest level. The leader, a skinny and short male with his hair pulled back into a ponytail and a full beard, knew their quarry was close, but he mentally debated whether he should wait for more bodies to throw at them. As his feet clipped down the stairs, he decided they couldn't wait. He wanted the glory for himself.

The Kindred rushed through the doorway and into the open area of the garage. With weapons drawn and battle cries screamed, four of the warriors charged straight for the unsuspecting trio that milled about the big vehicle, while the leader slipped into the darkness.

"What the . . ." Rossington didn't finish the sentence. She raised her assault rifle and lit up the group of Kindred warriors charging at them. "Shit!"

"Damn it," Daniel muttered as he reached for his pistol.

The lieutenant cut loose with a controlled burst. The gunfire helped knock Vann back to reality. He stepped away from the SUV, lowered his M4, aimed at the staggering vampires, and squeezed the trigger. The last warrior, a female with blood flowing from multiple wounds, fell to the concrete about fifteen feet from them.

"We must go now," Daniel said.

"I'm really sorry, Vann, I really am, but we have to go."

Arnett frowned and softly said, "I know, I know."

As the three of them slowly stepped away from the Explorer, the fifth warrior—with his sword drawn and ready—burst from the darkness with a scream. He lunged at Rossington and stabbed the long blade at her abdomen, sending her stumbling backward and to the concrete floor.

In an instant, Arnett spun, sighted his target, and clenched the trigger down as tightly as he could manage. His scream was lost in the roar of the gunfire from his assault rifle. The bullets shredded the warrior, driving him backward and dropping him to the floor, while his sword tumbled from his grip. The M4 stopped bucking in his hands when the clip emptied. It seemed an eternity.

Rossington scrambled to her feet and struggled to catch her breath while cursing. "Shit, shit, shit, shit, shitshitshitshit!" With panicked and palsied hands she clutched at her body armor, feverishly trying to undo the Velcro straps and zipper that secured it.

"Rossington!" Vann called out as he scrambled to her side. "Rossington!"

She managed to get her armor open and lifted her T-shirt to an immodest height, while at the same time tugged down the waistband of her combat pants. "Shitshitshit!"

"Rossington, where'd he get you?" Arnett asked as he grabbed her shirt and lifted it even higher. "Where is it?"

"Shit!" She examined her stomach, above and below her belly button. There was no wound, not even a red mark or a bruise. The lieutenant pulled the top of her pants even farther away from her body for a better look down there.

"Where is it?" Vann asked, panicked, frantically staring down the front of her BDU trousers, not even conscious of what he saw. "Where'd he get you?"

Rossington chuckled hollowly, letting go of her pants an instant before he reached out to pull them open more, if not down.

"What?"

"He didn't get me." She laughed and then sobbed. "He didn't get me, Vann." The lieutenant still held up her T-shirt. "Look."

Vann stared closely at the smooth skin of her stomach. It was unmarked. He snorted out a laugh.

"He didn't get me, Vann," Rossington said, letting the shirt drop. "He hit my body armor. He hit my fuckin' body armor." She displayed the flap. The material had been cut about two inches above the bottom hem, but the Kevlar and ceramic plates had not been penetrated.

"No shit." He laughed again and pulled her tight, breathing in her scent, her life.

"We have to go now," Daniel said. "There may be more of them coming, so we should go now."

Arnett released her from his embrace. "He's right."

"I know, I know. I've got to do one thing first." Rossington strode over to the dead vampire and kicked him. "Fuck you!" She picked up his sword, feeling the weight and assessing its balance. "Let's go, Daniel."

The Prophet, now joined by General Abaddon, Shari Landry, and the Centurion and their charges, entered the lowest level of the parking garage, the stinging smell of cordite still hanging in the air. The already assembled mass of vampires, both warriors and pawns, moved aside as the group marched in like royalty.

Captain Axeman reluctantly approached the group.

"Yes, Captain," the general said.

"My Lord, General, we believe they have escaped into the passageway. Should we follow them?" Captain Axeman asked. "We believe they are being helped by a non-Kindred."

The Prophet surveyed the scene, taking in his five dead warriors. "What are our losses like?"

"My Lord . . ."

"How many have we lost?"

"We have killed most of the soldiers," the captain said, reluctant to answer the question posed to him. "There aren't very many left alive, and we believe they fled into the passageway."

"That's not what I asked. How many have *we* lost?"

"I've been told that casualties have been high, my Lord, very high."

"How high?"

Captain Axeman glanced at General Abaddon and then at the Prophet. He and the other warriors had been assessing casualties when they unwittingly stumbled upon Stroud. "At least fifty percent. Maybe even as high as two out of three."

"My Lord, we should get warriors out to the mansion. We can cut off their escape routes or at least deny them access to the fortress," Abaddon said. "We need to get warriors out there. We—"

"We have paid a terrible price tonight," the Prophet interrupted him.

"Yes, my Lord . . ."

"I know, General Abaddon, I know. We have lost far too many this evening, and we know where Arnett will be."

"My Lord . . ."

"We have killed most, if not all, of the soldiers who came here," the Prophet said. "It is a great victory"—he looked down at the dead warrior nearest his feet—"but it has come at a terrible price."

"Yes, my Lord."

"'Worthy is the Lamb that hath been slain to receive the power, and riches and wisdom, and might and honor, and glory and blessing'," the Prophet said. "'They shall hunger no more, neither thirst any more, neither shall the sun strike upon them nor any heat.'"

Abaddon frowned. "Yes, my Lord."

Thirty-Three

A little before midnight, Daniel slowly led Vann and Rossington along a sidewalk in the downtown commercial district of the city, moving quickly and surely through the dark. They were almost a mile from the eastern edge of the campus, out of what was Kindred territory and traveling on his familiar turf. Plus, the trio had not encountered anyone since killing the five warriors in the lowest level of the underground parking garage.

The vampire stopped and turned back to the two following him.

"What is it?" Vann asked, a hint of concern edging into his voice, while the lieutenant tightened her grip on the M16 in one hand and the sword in the other.

"We're going into that building up ahead," Daniel said, "the theater." He nodded in the direction of the listing overhead marquee, all of the red letters announcing the current attraction missing. The decayed two-story structure had its ground-floor windows boarded up.

"Okay," Arnett said.

"There's probably twenty-five to thirty of . . . of my kind inside the theater, but you will be safe with us," Daniel said.

Rossington sighed loudly as the two of them stared at the vampire.

"Trust me, you won't be harmed."

"Okay," Vann said.

"If anything, they will all be terrified of you," Daniel said, nodding at Arnett.

"Me?"

"Yes, you."

"W . . . why?"

"*You* are the monster of their nightmares," the vampire said bluntly. "You are the one who comes in the daylight and kills our brothers and sisters. You . . . you are what they call the Sun Demon."

"I . . . I . . . I don't know what to say," Vann said softly and apologetically. "I . . ."

"There is nothing to say," the vampire said.

"I . . . I . . ."

Daniel shook his head.

"Are you their leader?" Rossington asked after what seemed like an endless silence.

The vampire shrugged. "They listen to what I say and do what I ask them to do, but I don't know if I'm their leader or not."

"Sounds like a leader to me," Arnett said.

"Me, too." The lieutenant smiled at him.

Daniel blushed in the darkness and turned away from them for a moment. "Follow me," he said, with a wave of his hand, and walked toward the theater.

Daniel used the well-worn brass handle to pull open the door about a foot and slipped inside, disappearing into the darkness of the lobby. Arnett and Rossington shared a look, readied their weapons, and followed.

The aroma of buttered popcorn and boxed candy a distant memory, they emerged into the lightless but carpeted foyer of the movie theater as two male vampires, both armed with hunting rifles, came forward.

"No," Daniel said, moving in front of them. "No."

"What are you doing, Daniel?" the taller of the two asked, disbelief in his voice. "Do . . . do you know who . . . who that is?"

"Yes, I do. I also know these two saved my life earlier today when some of the soldiers wanted to kill us. They put their own lives on the line to save my life and the others. I know Alice and Tara told you."

"But Daniel—"

"I don't want to hear it, Joe!"

"But—"

Daniel shook his head. "No, Joseph."

Vampires—males, females, and children of various ages—crowded into the two doorways that led down to the large screen, spilling tentatively into the lobby. The group included two infants held protectively in the arms of their mothers. They were all frightened but curious. They wanted to catch a glimpse of the two humans, including the Sun Demon.

A teenaged female vampire brazenly pushed her way through the crowd and approached them. Long, dark hair hung well past her shoulders and framed her pretty, youthful face of porcelain. Pale, colorless eyes were sharp and intelligent. Dark, baggy clothes hid her undernourished body. She defiantly strode past the two armed vampires without hesitation.

Vann recognized her instantly, although she was younger than he had expected.

The teenager stopped in front of Daniel, but some of her burgeoning confidence waned as she stared at Arnett.

"D-d-do . . . do you remember me?" she asked shyly.

"Yes," Vann answered and smiled. "Yes, I remember you. I . . . I . . . I have dreamed of you." His words were barely louder than a whisper.

"Me, too. I dreamed of you," the teen said, some of her poise returning. "My name is Virginia, but everyone calls me Gina."

"Hello, Gina. My name is Vann."

"Hi, Vann."

Rossington watched the two of them with open-mouthed amazement. Her perception of vampires had changed dramatically in the past few hours. It was going to take her some time to get used to the adjustment.

"I told everyone about meeting you, about your kindness toward me," Gina said with a smile. "At first, they didn't believe me.

They didn't think it was possible for you to show mercy and . . . kindness. A few thought I was making things up, telling stories, but I convinced some of them. Some of them believed me, including Daniel. And now here you are."

"Yes," Vann said with a smile. "Here I am."

Rossington couldn't help but grin and shake her head. She had a difficult time believing it, and she was witnessing it.

"All we want is to live our lives in peace and without fear," Daniel said softly. "We just want to live."

"That's what I"—he turned to Rossington and back to the vampire—"what *we* want, too."

"Then we have something in common."

"Yes, we do. And if we have one thing in common, we probably have a lot more things in common."

"We are not your enemies," Daniel said to them.

"I know that . . . I know that now," Vann answered. "From now on, you and your people"—he glanced at Gina—"will have nothing to fear from me . . . us."

"Nor you from us."

Rossington saw one of the mothers with her infant. "You have babies?"

Daniel glanced back at the group of vampires in the doorway before he turned his eyes to the two of them. "Yes, we have babies. There have been about a dozen or so births in the past year, but it is difficult. Not all of them have survived. There is so much we don't know about our . . . our condition."

"Are they like . . . like you?" Rossington asked.

"Yes, the babies are like us in every aspect."

"Then you and your people will have a future," Vann said.

"If we can survive the Kindred," Gina said.

"Yes, if we can survive the Kindred, we will have a future," Daniel said. "You will be welcome in our future. You can be part of it."

"That's very kind of you," Arnett said, "but I can only imagine if our ki . . . those of us uninfected will even have a future. We can't seem to rise above our nature and desire to kill one another."

"It's a terrible world out there, Daniel," Rossington said. "It's a terrible world for anyone still alive."

"But we are still alive," Daniel said.

"We are, but it's difficult to stay that way," Vann said.

"Well, you will have nothing to fear from us," the vampire said again.

"And you have nothing to worry about from us," Arnett said, looking at Gina and then back at Daniel.

"Nothing at all," Rossington added.

"And we will do whatever we can to help you," Vann said. "To protect you from the Kindred."

The male vampire smiled and nodded slowly.

Vann held out his hand to Daniel. "Thank you."

The vampire stared at the proffered hand, then took it, shaking it slowly. "You're welcome," Daniel said with a grin. "You're very welcome."

THIRTY-FOUR

The sun was an ever-brightening crimson smear on the horizon as Vann and Rossington, still in their body armor with weapons hung over shoulders, emerged from the theater through the door they had entered. Dirty, grimy, and splattered with slashes of dried blood, the two of them stood on the sidewalk outside the building and turned their faces skyward as if sunning themselves.

"Feels good, like a brand-new day," Arnett said.

"Maybe it is," she said, smiling at him. "Maybe it is."

Half a block down the street, Rusty crept out of the alley and cautiously stepped onto the debris-strewn pavement.

"Rusty, where have you been?" Arnett called out.

With tail wagging, the dog trotted toward the two of them. For the first time, he headed straight to Vann, who crouched down and rubbed the dog's ears.

"Where have you been?" he asked.

Without answering, the setter sidled over to Rossington's legs. She dropped to one knee and took the dog's face in her hands.

"That's a good boy," the lieutenant said, just barely managing to avoid his flicking tongue. "That's a real good boy."

The Irish setter responded with enthusiastic wagging that wiggled his entire back quarters.

Vann laughed. "I've never seen him do that before, not even with Sylvie. He really likes you."

She shrugged. "I'm not sure why, but dogs have always liked me."

Vann watched her with the dog. "Hey, Rossin . . . Rossy . . . what is your first name, anyway?"

She chuckled. "Deborah. My name is Deborah."

"Hey, Deborah, let's go home."

Rossington stood up. "Yeah. Home."

Arnett glanced up to a second-story window in the theater.

Looking through the dirt- and grime-streaked glass, Gina, her body wrapped in the same protective clothing she had worn when she had encountered him in the mall, her face covered behind a bandana with dark Speedo goggles over her eyes, watched the three of them in the street.

In the growing light of morning, Vann smiled and waved to her.

The teenaged vampire hesitated for a moment, as if pondering her response, then shyly waved back at him.

Thirty-Five

That evening, as the sun rushed to complete its diurnal cycle, Vann sat in the main room at Wolveshaven with his laptop on the table in front of him. He leaned back in the chair and stared at Deborah as she sat on the sofa with Rusty on the floor at her feet. She intently read the galleys of his second novel on the coffee table in front of her.

Earlier in the day she had spent more than two hours in the master bathroom of the mansion after he had hauled in hot water and filled the huge, ornate claw-foot tub. She had just wanted to soak and clean up, and he had been happy to oblige her and respect her privacy. Rossington had emerged with damp hair and rosy-pink cheeks, wearing an oversized maroon, terry-cloth bathrobe that had been Sylvie's and laughing that she felt like she had scrubbed several months' worth of crusty dirt and crud from her body. Arnett thought she was stunning, but he could only dumbly smile at her.

Vann watched her read the words that he had written more than two years earlier. The sentences had seemed so important and significant back then. Despite his tendency for self-deprecation, his debut novel had garnered solid reviews and strong sales, but both his agent and publisher were confident that this second effort was going to be the breakthrough that launched his career onto the bestseller lists.

All that promise didn't really matter now.

Enduring what they had, not only in the past couple of days, but in the lifetime that had led up to it, he was amazed they were still alive and in one piece. At this moment, there was only one thing Vann could do, and that was to stare at her. He found he couldn't take his eyes off her. He couldn't help but notice how her lips moved subtly and she occasionally bit her lower lip as she read. He couldn't help but notice that she had crept her butt toward the front edge of the sofa as her eyes scanned the pages. He couldn't help but notice how the front of the bulky robe drooped open to expose the titillating fact that she wasn't wearing a T-shirt—or anything else, for that matter—underneath it.

Arnett literally shook his head to clear the enticing thoughts that had forced their way into his mind, turning his attention to the laptop monitor and the empty page it revealed. A moment later, he began to type.

Man is a resilient and adaptable creature. It's one of our greatest strengths, but it's also one of our most notable faults.

Even in the midst of facing our species' greatest calamity, the one that may finally shove us over the edge of extinction, we demonstrate the full range of our humanity, the good and, unfortunately, the bad. Even when it's against our best interest, we can't help but be human. And maybe that will be our ultimate downfall.

Have we doomed ourselves? Perhaps, but I can't really say. I know it doesn't look good right now, and all too often we are our own worst enemy in this life-or-death battle for survival. It seems we just can't stop being human. But it's not in our nature to give up, to surrender without a fight. Our history is littered with stories and legends of humanity being at its best when times were at their worst. I hope that's the case now—I really do—but part of me fears that I'm merely chronicling the final chapter of man's history, of our history.

Even if that's how it will be, I will continue to do what I am doing. I will continue with my struggle for survival, to scratch and claw out an existence each and every day. Despite everything that has happened and probably against some pretty long odds, I am still alive. Alive. So I will keep on living day-to-day, week-to-week, but I won't go it alone in this kingdom of perdition.

Grey Gecko Press

Thank you for purchasing this book from Grey Gecko Press, an independent publishing company that focuses on new and emerging authors, bringing readers the best in fiction and non-fiction at reasonable prices in all formats.

With books in nearly every genre of fiction and non-fiction, there's something for everyone, and you can be sure that buying books from us leads directly to the support of independent authors like Michael Wentela. Grey Gecko pays our authors some of the highest royalty rates in the business and strives to produce only high-quality books.

Visit our website to purchase our titles, pre-order upcoming books at a discount, sign up for our free monthly newsletter, and find out about two great ways to get free books, the Slushpile Reader Program and the Advance Reader Program.

And don't forget: all our print editions come with the ebook free!

Authors First!

www.greygeckopress.com

store.greygeckopress.com

About the Author

Michael Wentela is a writer of science fiction, horror, thriller, crime fiction, mystery, and numerous other genre stories. He has been a writer most of his life, working professionally in a number of writing-related positions.

Michael's writing ranges from novels to short stories in science fiction, horror, crime fiction, mystery, thriller, or whatever idea sparks his creativity. The desire to write blossomed in junior high school with hand-written short stories in school notebooks and continues to this day. *Fallen is Babylon* is his debut novel.

Connect With Michael

Email: michaelwentela@gmail.com

Facebook: www.facebook.com/MichaelWentela

Web: www.michaelwentela.com